TOOLS of the TRADE

TOOLS of the TRADE

Philip B Persinger

TOOLS OF THE TRADE

This is a work of fiction. Names, characters, businesses, places, events and incidents are either the products of the author's imagination or used in a fictitious manner. Any resemblance to actual persons, living or dead, or actual events is purely coincidental.

ISBN-13: 978-1530197361
ISBN-10: 1530197368

Book cover design by Glen M. Edelstein
Book design by Glen M. Edelstein

To Absent Friends

TOOLS of the TRADE

1.
GURLS

IT IS SECOND BREAKFAST and the maids can scarcely contain themselves. Young Miss Victoria has returned from the States. She was away for weeks and Mistress missed her so very much. The house is giddy on her return. Yet the maids are also aware that it is important to pay special attention to the tasks at hand. Despite the relaxed atmosphere in the lounge, Miss Lavinia remains very strict, and any slip or stumble—even on a happy day like this—will be a costly one. They do so want to please Mistress. They are proud to be in her service, as they are thrilled to be allowed to sweep, mop, and clean this posh townhouse just four blocks from Harrods in Knightsbridge.

Janice is senior. She is wearing a high-necked, satin, parlour maid's uniform. It is turquoise. She wears black full-fashioned stockings on her legs and court shoes on her feet. Sarah is the under-parlour maid. Her uniform is similar but lavender in color. Sally is the new girl, which is why her uniform is pink and why she wears shackles on her ankles with just eight inches of steel links between them.

While Miss Lavinia stirs her coffee, the gurls standing at the sideboard know that under the proper protocol they should be directing their gazes to the floor. But they can't help themselves. Mistress is so elegant and stylish that it is impossible to keep from peeking. Today she is wearing a stunning satin blouse with large puffy sleeves and a dramatic matching bow. A proper black pencil skirt flatters her trim waist. She has lovely shoulder-length blonde hair and bangs that frame her high chiseled cheekbones and those dramatic piercing blue eyes, brought out and enhanced by the rich royal blue of the blouse.

Miss Victoria is a bland poor relation in comparison. But in her defense, coming straight from Heathrow, she hasn't had time to change into something more appropriate. She is wearing what she traveled in—a charcoal gray Burberry suit, along with a white oxford shirt and an Etonian tie, appropriately arranged in a loose Windsor knot.

"That must be some sort of trophy," Janice whispers to the other gurls as they struggle to stifle their giggles.

Lucky for them, Miss Lavinia is too caught up in the small screen to notice this bad behavior. Miss Victoria announces each location as she swipes from one to the next on her tablet, "Vestibule. Gallery. Their version of a lounge—no need for a door—everything is overheated. Dining room. Kitchen. Pantry. Bedroom. Bedroom. Bedroom. Library. Torture chamber."

The two ladies scroll through the images anew as the maids struggle from a distance to spy over their shoulders. When Miss Lavinia gestures vaguely, Janice knows exactly what she desires and rushes off to fetch her reading glasses. While she waits, Miss Lavinia absentmindedly puts her palm to the coffeepot. Her disappointment is immediate and profound. With the senior parlour maid out of the room, it is up to Sarah to nudge the new gurl to hot it up. Ever anxious when under the critical gaze of her Mistress, Sally minces toward the breakfast table—poor silly gurl. At the worst possible moment, she misjudges the scope of the chain between her ankles and takes a tumble.

Returning with Miss Lavinia's spectacles, Janice sees a dire tableau. There is no sound but the sobbing of the ashen-faced, soon-to-be scullery maid, Sally. At the sideboard, Sarah stands straight and stone-faced. Miss Victoria is at the disrupted table dabbing at her iPad with a linen napkin, as Miss Lavinia sits icily still without expression.

Janice has no idea what has transpired during her short absence, but she does know where the responsibility for the whole sorry affair rests—with her, the senior parlour maid. She doesn't wait to hear the recrimination. Nor does she look at her Mistress. She cannot bear seeing the censure in those eyes. She goes straight to the leather "horse" in the corner of the room and leans over it, tightly grasping the handgrips near her knees. She can sense Sarah behind her, lifting the skirt of her uniform and her petticoats—and then the waiting begins.

This is the part that all the maids who attend Miss Lavinia dread the most—the waiting. Mistress does like to stretch it out. They all agree that the waiting is worse than the ultimate punishment. Janice tries to think of something to distract her from the torture of the extended moment, and, just as she is about to succeed, the searing hot stripe of the cane crosses her backside. She squeezes tighter at the grips and at least this time avoids crying out.

"One," she counts with forced calmness. "Thank you, Mistress."

Janice figures that it will be around seven or eight when the welts start to appear.

"Actually, it was six," Sarah, a.k.a. Reggie, says a few hours later in the maids' quarters as they change out of their uniforms and into Savile Row bespoke suits.

"She's brilliant," Sally, or Hugo, comments.

"I was right, wasn't I, chaps? Definitely worth the preposterous fees she charges," Janice points out as the trio climbs into a waiting company car to take them to The City. It is almost two o'clock, and Wall Street will soon begin the day's trading. They have to get to work.

2. WOODY

NO ONE IS CERTAIN WHETHER Woody Steele's nickname came from his early days in the lumber business or from a particularly impressive physical attribute, but everyone, whether friend or foe, calls him Woody. Grinning at Big Red, who is standing next to him with a sixteen-pound sledgehammer, he jerks the starter cord and the massive chainsaw in his hands comes to life with a pop and then a roar. It is professional grade with a long, forty-eight-inch guide bar—the only thing that can fell the massive trees surrounding him. Even though Big Red's hair is now gray, he is still a powerful presence. Woody has known him for over twenty years and shows him the same deference that he did on that first day he worked for him. The fact that Big Red saved Woody from cutting off his foot when he was a stupid, careless teenager only makes the bond tighter. But that was years and many billions of dollars ago.

Woody doesn't need to cut down trees to earn a living anymore. In fact, his board of directors hates that he often risks life and limb in this manner. But it has become a tradition—a signature part of his brand. Whenever his lawyers triumph against the eco-terrorists and win one of his companies the right to clear-cut another old-growth forest, it is always Woody who drops the first majestic, ancient monument standing in the way of progress—as well as the company's greater profits. Yet it isn't just about the money. It is also a great stress reducer.

While his $50 million loft in Tribeca has been featured in almost every style magazine, to Woody, there is nothing more welcoming than the camp's double-wide bunkhouse with its fridge full of beer. His current position of running one of the world's largest conglomerates is just fine, but he loved his first job even more. Waking up to a hot cup of bad coffee and walking out into the cold morning is best.

He pulls the trigger five or six times—gunning the two-stroke engine—hamming it up for the crew. Then he gets serious, leaning into the tree with determination, relishing first contact as the chain bites into the wood. At that moment, he is lost in the zone. Despite the heavy weight that he is lifting, he can feel his shoulder muscles relax. A calm washes through his body. He is laser beam focused on the cutting edge. His hands guide the powerful saw with a virtuoso's subtlety. There are years of practice behind every nuanced shift of the voracious blade.

Life is good, Woody thinks, as the freshly sharpened teeth of the chain slice into the trunk and a plume of sawdust jets past him. Gone are the petty cares that had plagued him just yesterday. There is no attempted hostile takeover of his casino in Macao now. The EPA is not riding his ass over some blind two-year-old boy who just happens to live next to one of his smelters in West Virginia. There is no subpoena lying on his desk from the House Committee on Homeland Security that wants to know about the private army for hire that he is training at his 3,000-acre *summer getaway* in the Ozarks. There are none of those annoyances here. It is just a man, a chainsaw, and a tree—gravity is on his side.

Moments before Woody senses that the weight of the tree will begin to bind the chainsaw, he can hear the metallic ring of steel on steel as Big Red starts driving wedges into the cut, opening it up to keep the blade running freely. Woody is grinning again as his crusty old friend wields the hammer in a way that would make John Henry envious. The morning sun clears the canopy and sends a beam down to spotlight their work. The warmth feels good against his face, and his experienced hands can sense through the growling chainsaw that the tree is ready to fall. All that is good in his world keeps getting better—at least until a perfect morning turns to crap.

The shrill warning of an air horn suddenly shuts down the site. Because of his training, and even though he knows it might destroy a perfectly good chainsaw, Woody lets go of the dead man's switch and walks away from the tree. Pulling off his work gloves, he looks quizzically at the safety officer blasting the alert; the other man shrugs and points directly into the tree's drop zone. Woody can feel his blood begin to boil as he turns his gaze downfield. He is almost tempted to fire up the chainsaw to finish the deed—felling the timber on the heads of the goddamn tree huggers. He doesn't have to say anything. He holds out a hand and Big Red quickly passes the boss a pair of binoculars.

"You're going blind," Woody mutters as he adjusts the spyglasses.

As they come into view, he resents each and every one of the trespassers. How dare they invade his forest? He makes a slow sweep. There is a television crew—camera, sound, reporter, and producer. There are fifteen or so paparazzi. Woody can't tell who the rest are, but he guesses that they are PR lackeys, publicists, and the rest of the camp followers that celebrity attracts. Their clothes give them away—stupid outfits. This walk in the mud will cost them thousands in Louis Vuitton frequent-flyer miles.

"Must be a biggie," he says to no one in particular.

Woody is correct. His team soon recognizes a pretty-boy movie star, who they all know but can't name, wearing a generic, manly safari jacket, trudging up the slope. They lose interest in him quickly, but then *she* pops up over the rise. Wearing a safety-orange, neoprene hunting vest and a Rodeo Drive camouflage miniskirt, she is tall, stacked, and beyond gorgeous. Her Gucci boots are totally inappropriate for the terrain.

Mouth agape, Big Red muses, “If only I were twenty years younger.”

Nodding in agreement, Woody thinks, *If only I still had my prostate.*

3.
SVETLANA

THE BEAUTIFUL INTERNATIONAL movie star is slogging up a rain-soaked gulley. She knows that she must be in Siberia in springtime. Her grandfather had been sent to Siberia by Stalin. He told her all about what Siberia feels like as he bounced her on his knee when she was a child. It feels like the end of the world. It feels like you have died and gone to Siberia, and that is where she is now. The gulley is a raw scar ripped up by heavy machinery. It has been raining steadily for over a week.

The scheme made sense on Thursday, when her publicist first explained it to her. The need for damage control was clear to everyone on her team. Two months ago, she was the toast of the town. She had just starred in the newest, most expensive movie ever made. She was Catherine the Great—and the critics agreed that she was. So was opening weekend. The film broke records. *Variety* said it would TORPEDO *TITANIC*. But less than one week later her career was in the toilet. Someone had hacked into the studio's digital asset management system and downloaded some raw green screen footage. Forty-eight hours and one virtual stallion later, *The*

Secret Sex Tapes of Catherine the Great and Mister Ed went viral on the Internet.

"Fuck him," she curses under her breath as she drags her feet through the muck, cursing the asshole who digitally put her *in flagrante delicto* with America's favorite talking horse.

To make matters worse, after the movie went south and she was sent north, she was photographed wearing her grandmother's sable hat, which was totally reasonable because it's goddamned cold in Siberia. But her team was too slow to patch things up with the animal rights people. They landed on her like a ton of bricks.

"Fuck them," she curses under her breath at her management team, which is staying high and dry, chowing down at the modest field catering services table across the ravine.

"Fuck him," she curses under her breath at the sissy scampering up the hill in his Timberlands. He is currently starring in *Roto-Robber VII 3-D,* now in general release. Its gross flew past *Catherine the Great* on opening weekend. The tabloids have them patching up a stormy relationship that is held together only through their environmental activism. In reality, the beautiful international movie star is his beard.

"Fuck them all," she curses under her breath as she slogs up the steep trail of liquidity. She doesn't even try to look glamorous for the swarming photographers at the top of the rise. It won't be the first time some papa-RAT-zi captured her world-famous scowl in frame.

According to the press kit, her name is Svetlana Petracova, the orphaned daughter of a warlord who was murdered before her very eyes by an overly aggressive suitor. But by dying slowly Papa bought just enough time for her to escape over the Carpathian Mountains while being pursued by horsemen in a blizzard. She is a classic blonde Ukrainian beauty. The flash of those sapphire blue eyes overlooking her scornful sneer inspires crazed men to do stupid things just to be rewarded with the briefest moment of her dismissive contempt. There's a long line of them waiting for this pleasure.

Many in the industry think that it was her blue-flamed temper that launched her career when she dumped a large bowl of paella into the lap of an Oscar-winning director at some after-party. Others insist that it was a bouillabaisse.

Struggling as the terrain grows steeper and more waterlogged, she puts an Italian boot in the wrong place and, with dismay, feels a thousand bucks get sucked off and swallowed up by the hungry mud. She knows that it is long gone when she comes up with a naked foot.

"Fuck me!" she curses.

When she looks back up again to the top of the rise, she sees that all the lumberjacks are grinning eagerly and nodding, *You betcha.*

"Grrrr," she growls, and they back off—but only for a moment. Before she knows what's happening next, they start to run.

Don't even know my own strength, she gloats to herself as the photogs flee after them in full flight.

Her instincts tell her to follow suit, but her feet are getting sucked deeper and deeper into the mud with each step. As the mob dashes up the hill, she panics. Then she looks in amazement as the massed exodus parts like the Red Sea and a lone lumberjack charges through the divide, racing against the current, straight toward her. Just before he hits the impassable part of the trail, he leaps from the brow of the hill and flies toward her with open arms that lock around her on impact. Before she has time to think, she too is airborne.

They land with a thud in the brown slurry. Her neoprene vest is wet from the fog and rain. It creates a frictionless system. They toboggan down the mountain faster and faster. As trees and stumps begin to threaten their descent, the lumberjack, facedown on her, begins to steer her like a Flexible Flyer. He's a good driver. She feels only a few bumps and crashes at the start, and, just as the discomfort starts to offset the thrill of the ride, he takes a radical turn to the left and they are airborne again, flying high and long until they land unceremoniously in a freezing mountain lake.

The intense cold makes him release her, but it does nothing to cool her red-hot temper. She claws her way to the surface, ready to do the same to his eyes. As she shakes her head to clear her vision, she looks up and sees a massive tree crash down beside them, just feet away from where she is treading water.

Then his head pops up out of the lake. His long hair is wet and stringy. The cold water has given his weathered face an unattractive hue.

Thank God he's underwater, she thinks. *He must have toxic body odor.*

To make matters worse, he has the unmitigated nerve to look the beautiful international movie star straight in the eyes and say, "You're welcome." It's too much to bear. She rolls over and with a measured and consistent stroke swims away from him, showing off the form that won her the silver medal at the Junior Nationals when she was in high school.

4. MACKENZIE

THE YOUNG TROPHY WIFE is about to meet the "other woman," the one who has been stealing her husband's attention and affection. Since she is the fourth Mrs. Ivan Greenbriar, she is throwing some back into the effort. It goes better than she could ever hope for. While the interloper might be much younger, she is a zillion dress sizes larger. The encounter takes place in a large airplane hangar at Floyd Bennett Field, in Brooklyn. Mackenzie is a size four. Her rival is seventy-four feet at the water line. Mackenzie is wearing a vintage Diane von Furstenberg wrap dress. The catamaran is naked except for a pair of modesty skirts that cover the four top-secret under-hull wings that allow her to fly out of the water and hydroplane

So that's what twenty million dollars of sailboat looks like, Mackenzie thinks.

Her husband is at the far end of the hangar, staring at the three ubiquitous screens that are always anywhere he is—even in the bathrooms of his many houses. Mackenzie is not at the point where she would refer to them as *our houses*. She doubts that she ever will be. The first golden parachute mentioned in the prenup is only five years away. No! Make that four and a half—*has it been six months already*? No way is she going for a child support battle. *Size four, thank you very much*. But the math isn't dispiriting. Even if she has to maintain the current average of 2.65 sexual interludes a week—which must certainly diminish over time—at the end of the contract that works out to $13,986.03 for each faked orgasm—and that's just pin money.

She had set her sights on him the minute it was announced that he was to be a guest lecturer. Thanks to her own due diligence, Mackenzie was the only one in the class who knew that his stint that semester was in lieu of a longer one in federal prison—pleas and thank you of the rich and powerful. Through court-mandated community service at the Wharton School, he would share helpful hints to train the white collar criminals of tomorrow.

The perennial good student, Mackenzie sat in the first row. Always running late, damned if she didn't sometimes forget her panties—well, most times—that's a point spread you should bet on. Although he was lecturing on long-term corporate planning, she quickly had him by the shorts. She rejected him so convincingly that he knew he had to have her. Then there was that special night when he plied her with a second glass of Zinfandel and she lost control of herself. Being from a quaint generation that shared a precious tenet that "going all the way" deserved some kind of compensation, he financed her Internet start-up the next morning. *Who am I to marginalize ancient rites and traditions?* Mackenzie acknowledged to herself piously.

It would be disingenuous for her to pretend that it was all her craft and guile and that she was immune to the irresistible power of wealth and charm that he controlled. Or that she wasn't flattered by his focused and orchestrated hunt to capture her once she revealed an ankle—not to mention the omnipresent testosterone tsunami that crashed over her head every time he came within ten feet of her personal space. He was, after all, an alpha male among and above most alphas. The Third Richest Man in

America, according to *Fortune*. The most eligible three-time loser in the world, according to *New York Magazine*.

Even though it seemed like a cliché from a bad movie, she had to admit that jet skiing to Capri for Italian food or flying down to Belize for an afternoon swim in February was pretty cool. Which was only just so much dating fun until she sealed the deal naked in a hot tub on Corfu, stroking his dick with the soles of the same feet that won her that soccer scholarship. "Of course I'll marry you, darling," she said as he squirted something nasty into roiling spa waters, confident that, since she had just given him a blow job, it was an oral contract that would hold up in any court of any land.

As they curled up in bed later that night in the sumptuous stateroom of his yacht, anchored off Mykonos, and after yet one more misguided penetration—*what is it with assholes and assholes?*—she got him to repeat his proposal of marriage and her acceptance and his eagerness to sponsor the IPO of her start-up, which she dutifully—so that there could be no misunderstanding in the stark light of day—recorded on her iPhone. The last line of the court transcript of this conversation will be her saying, "Can I get you another tumbler of vodka, darling? Or can I just go to the bathroom? I really need to go to the bathroom."

She can see his profile as he tracks the graphs and charts on his screens. *There's not a moment to lose when the market is your heartbeat.* She convinces herself that he is as handsome now as when she first met him. "He looks like Machiavelli," she whispered to her girlfriend when he walked up to the podium in the lecture hall at Wharton.

"Five hundred years dead?" Vix replied.

Mackenzie laughed that off. At that moment he was handsome, manly, and winnable. He was in fact so handsome that he remained attractive almost up to the honeymoon. Today, however, his eyes are beadier, his near beard more scraggly, and his critical pursed lips look more prissy hissy fitty. In a word, less Machiavelli, more Vincent Price—or Vincent Price's less attractive brother.

In the Olde Tyme parlance of Wall Street in the 1980s, he is a *big swinging dick,* and, indeed, it is formidable. But it ends up being more of a siege weapon than a purveyor of pleasure, and over recent weeks—especially as the America's Cup trials grow nearer—that tiger is rarely at her gate. She walks over to the catamaran. She caresses then kisses the glowing port hull with its new car showroom sheen. "Thank you, sweetie," she purrs. "He loves you."

5.
VICTORIA

VICTORIA IS BACK IN NEW YORK CITY. The journey across The Pond is turning into a commute. While she should be wallowing in jet lag and sore feet—she is her mother's daughter when it comes to shoes—with wheels down, she has hit the ground running, albeit in stilettos. She has had two teleconferences in the car on the way from JFK and one face-to-face with a member of the co-op board. Interesting factoid: the penthouse above is an independent city/state, outside of all the rules and regulations that govern the other tenants. Nobody knows why. Some old foreign guy has lived there forever. He rarely comes out.

When she experiences a little dip as she drops off her bag in the private apartment, she scarfs an energy bar and takes a quick restorative shower. Drying herself off, she can't bear the idea of putting on any of the tired business clothes she travels with, so she slips into her favorite kaftan, that's hanging on a hook—old, worn, torn, and beloved. She throws herself into the only chair in the empty apartment and pours herself a Scotch.

Then another.

Ahh.

She swirls the third around the two ice cubes in the glass—one of the few things that Americans get right—and lets the warmth in her belly dance with the satisfaction in her head. It is finally coming together. The business plan is ironclad. Professor Chalmers would be so proud. The timing couldn't be better: moving the family business to the States on the wave of the Second British Invasion, riding the red coattails of the BBC, bringing class to a classless society and a land of anglophiles—make that anglophonies—where a tradesman in the suburbs is saying *cheers* when he makes change and his wife invites you in for a *cuppa*, and anyone with an English accent can walk off a plane from Heathrow straight into an executive job, even though his resume is shite and his university brick.

"God bless America," she says out loud as she finishes off the whisky.

She opens up her laptop and writes to her mother. She always enjoys writing to her mother. If she is writing to her mother it means that her mother is nowhere nearby. *Distance* makes the heart grow fonder. It's a mother-daughter thing. A daughter spends a lot more than nine months joined at the uterus. There was a lifetime of maternal embarrassment in just one year when she hit twelve. And now, despite the veneer of sophistication, the Knightsbridge townhouse, the Bentley, and the shopping sprees at Harvey Nichols, Victoria knows her mother only too well and sees through the cracks to the coarse yet insecure girl from the East End—especially when it comes to money. At first, Victoria was shocked that her mother bankrolled the MBA—but upon reflection—not so much. Which is why she is so motivated to pay it all back as fast as she can. She wants to keep that balance sheet clean. The most you'd ever want to owe Lavinia is an apology for leaving the kettle on.

When she pours the next whisky—number five, but who's counting, it was a long flight—Victoria knows she should eat something—as soon as she writes her mother. She is feeling so warm and cozy now, and it is so easy to be lovey-dovey and upbeat about this new scheme. The words fly from her fingertips until she wraps it all up with a big red bow.

Done.

She hits the Send button.

Nothing.

Just a rude message telling her that she's got no Internet connection.

Bollocks.

Now she is lost in the basement looking for the building superintendent. Not quite sure how she got here. Stairs or elevator? Lights are very bright for this time of night. There's an ethereal hum permeating the glossy, sickly green painted corridors.

She wanders. It is a crazy subterranean maze. There are growing piles of computer bits and pieces: piles of cable, abandoned printer guts, a stash of damaged keyboards with no vowels left on them. As she goes deeper into the catacombs the air becomes very warm. She hears a growing growl—angry metal fighting a solid foe. She can feel beads of sweat forming on her forehead. She walks to the source. The screaming whirl of a machine at war deafens within the confined space. Turning left into a dark corridor, she can see a sliver of light at the end—a door is ajar. Just past the boiler room, which is spitting out BTUs and even more jungle-grade humidity, she peeks through the crack in the door and—oh my God—it's Adonis. Wearing Ninja Turtle pajama bottoms and flip-flops—nothing else—barechested and sweating like a Turk, he is leaning into a massive drill, white knuckles clutching two large handles, throwing his weight against the concrete wall. The sound is deafening. Dust and grit fly up in a cloud around him.

"Motherfucker," he swears when the mason bit binds in the wall and the jammed-up drill spins him counterclockwise.

He is upside down for a moment with a look of surprise on his face that is so comical that Victoria covers her mouth so that he won't hear her laughing at him. He lands without ceremony on the hard floor, the drill still stuck in the wall. She can hear the breath leave him. She rushes up with concern.

"Are you all right?" she asks, looking down at him.

"Am I dead?" he asks. "Are you an angel?"

"No," she says. "But I don't think you should be allowed to play with power tools."

He thinks about that a moment. He looks into her eyes as if for the first time. His face melts. He goes artless.

"You are beautiful," he says.

"Have you not looked in a mirror?" she asks with a serious squint.

Victoria scans his young body from toes to nose. He's probably in his mid-twenties, so slight of frame and practically hairless that he looks like a classical sculpture—third-century Greco-Roman kiddie porn. She decides that his bra size would be 34-B. That's just out of habit. Thanks, Mom.

6. IVAN

IN THE CAVERNOUS HANGAR, the Third Richest Man in America is multitasking, despite the many distractions. His buttoned-up wife has gone strangely ditzy—baby talking to a sailboat—and this week's skipper, an expensive New Zealander, is stomping around looking sour. Let him wait. This deal can't. Ivan's eyes dart across the screens like the sticks in a hot drum solo as his fingers dance over the keys. He could always type faster than every secretary he ever had, but who's surprised? Throughout his life he has always done everything better than everyone else—except for two people—the Second Richest Man in America, and the first.

He hits the Send button and folds his hands on the table in brief meditation. Two minutes later, he's five million dollars richer. But it's a pipsqueak deal—not worth celebrating. Deals like this are more to pass the time than anything else—like sitting next to a bowl of cashews. He texts the Kiwi and gets back to his screens. On one screen he is following a live feed of the annual meeting for USYS Integrated, in Cupertino. Right on schedule, a nasty proxy fight has broken out. In the upper corner of the opposite screen he is streaming a promotional video feed from SteeleX International—*Today in Woody*—he's Number Two in the Richest Man in America department and number one on Ivan's Hate Parade. Today he's hanging out of a helicopter over Machu Picchu in a wing suit. As Ivan focuses his bitter gaze on that window, in the reflection he can see the sailor pull out his mobile and read it.

"We would have lost the mast," the skipper protests, staring at the back of his boss's head.

Ivan is half listening as he watches USYS CEO Tom Hasbrook go red-faced at the microphone. "How do u know that?" he texts.

"It was kicking up to thirty knots," Kiwi says defensively. "It could have happened."

"But u don't know for certain," Ivan texts. Then he sends an IM to his man on the ground at the shareholders' meeting. "Release the dogs," he types.

"It's your boat," Kiwi says bitterly.

"Yes it is," Ivan texts.

Shoving has broken out in the question line in Cupertino. Hasbrook is shouting for order. He is clearly losing control of the meeting. The board is visibly distressed. But Ivan is distracted as Woody Steele casually lets go of the helicopter and tosses himself earthward in free fall.

"I'm responsible for the safety of my crew," the skipper sniffs.

"They signed waivers," Ivan texts as he recovers the moment and reinserts himself back into Silicon Valley, smiling with glee as enraged shareholders storm the dais.

"I used my best judgment," the Kiwi says to Ivan's disgust. It sounds like he's whining now. "You pay me for my experience and instincts."

"Not anymore. Pack your things," Ivan texts, then actually cheers, "Whoo-hoo," as his man on the ground takes over the microphone and harangues Hasbrook to universal cheers.

The winner of two OSTAR races and one Whitbread, the yachtsman storms out without another word.

"Leave your badge and body armor with Randall after you clean out your locker," Ivan calls over his shoulder, gleeful as he watches fists flying in Cupertino.

But the man in the flying suit has distracted him again. Anyone would be gripped watching the small image of Woody drop down into a tight canyon and soar down, down, and down at impossible speed with the rock walls just inches from his extended arms as he maneuvers the wing suit. Ivan only snaps out of it when bile fills his mouth with jealousy. Back in the moment, his fingertips are a blur as he shorts USYS, USYS Holdings, usys.com, and USYS Taiwan LTD through a dozen different trading accounts. This is just gravy. He will buy the company tomorrow for a song. He puts his hands behind his head and leans back and relaxes as he watches the trades execute, feeling good that the day has turned around. The New Zealander was a pussy. How can you know what a boat can do until you know what a boat can't do? Sure he pushes the limits. But as of today he's got no crew members in the hospital. The Kevlar they got from the Seals is certainly helping—yes, definitely a good day. He looks over at his wife French kissing the catamaran.

Hell, he thinks. *I feel so good I might even fuck Blondie this afternoon.*

He picks up the *Fortune* magazine lying under his screens. He feels the same tingle he used to feel when he was a teenager staring at the cover of a *Playboy*. There he is—Tom Hasbrook—cover girl. Ivan takes the top off a felt marker and draws a big X through the soon-to-be ex-CEO and smiles.

One more down, he delights.

No one else knows about this guilty pleasure that he enjoys so much. Within the rarified atmosphere of the 500 it is a mystery, like the *Sports Illustrated* curse, where any athlete who is depicted on the cover one week suffers a bone-crunching loss the next. In this manifestation, any CEO who is featured on the cover of *Fortune* loses his company the following week. This is perhaps

Ivan's most satisfying hobby—perhaps his only true hobby. All his other hobbies aren't really something to do to relax. They are not fun. They end up being work—like now. Sailing is work. Because once there is the chance of competition any chance of fun evaporates. It is only about winning. Perhaps that is what has earned Ivan his nickname. Among the big swinging dicks on Wall Street he is known as the *Raging Hard-On*.

7.
TIM

THE YOUNG MAN LYING HALF NAKED in a junkyard of broken or obsolete technology—flat on his back, desperately trying to catch his breath—is Tim. If you are making a Hollywood movie and you call central casting and say, "Send over a nerd," or, "We need geeks," they come in two flavors—pizza-colored, fat, gross, slobby baby men with a smear of chin hair, or guys like Tim—slight, bony, with a wan prison pallor and sunken, searching eyes.

Once he has gulped enough air back into his lungs and tries to stand up, Victoria plants a stiletto heel into his sternum, pinning him to the floor. "No need to rush, Poindexter. Take a moment. Count your ribs. Deep breathing."

Tim takes a moment, then says, "I'm okay."

"Sure?"

"Sure."

The dangerous high heel is removed from his chest. Dangerous because it has an incredibly sexy red sole and Tim is having enough of a hard time keeping his eyes off Victoria's inner thighs to avoid a visible erection. The kaftan has a long slit up the leg that one would not notice standing up in polite society. Gazing up at her bending over, however, he's got great sight lines that leave little to the imagination. Being a computer jock he has a limited artistic vocabulary, but he is pretty sure that her panties are teal. And while he isn't technically a virgin—unless the clock doesn't start until you have sex that's good—he is certainly subject to titillation. He desperately keeps his eyes from wandering farther north.

Tim is only too aware of how flimsy his PJ bottoms are and is desperate to avoid the embarrassment of erection detection when he pulls himself up. Fortunately he long ago anticipated such a moment and has developed techniques to counter it. He closes his eyes and relaxes his body. As Victoria watches from above, he slips into a meditative state, cycling through a mental slide show that he has prepared over time. It is a horrific voyage starting with Holocaust snapshots of corpses stacked up at a concentration camp, segueing into forensic photos of burn victims, then cancerous lungs of chain-smokers, images of backstreet abortions gone wrong, the killing fields of the Khmer Rouge, a desiccated eyeball. The routine culminates with a series of gross, disgusting atrocities that would thrill a nine-year-old sociopath who revels in pulling the wings off of flies. By now he is in a Zen state of flaccidity—success. He leaps to his feet and asks confidently, "How may I help you?"

"I can't email," Victoria says.

Tim sheepishly holds up a severed tangle of fiber optics. "Oops."

"How long?" she asks.

"Not long," he answers.

"Is that in IT years or dog years?"

Tim holds up a finger. "Don't move."

Like Tarzan in an old movie, he dives into a Gordian knot of wires and wrestles it like river snakes, disappearing for a few minutes before he claws his way back out with a blue Cat 5 Ethernet cable clamped in his teeth.

"Apartment number?" he asks.

"6A," she replies.

"I'll need your hands," he says.

She follows him as he wanders around the cluttered room studying the many pipes overhead. They all have hubs and switches and junction boxes duct-taped to them.

"That one," he says, pointing. "Third port."

"Port?"

"Third hole from the left," he says, handing her a cable. "Stick it in."

"Aye-aye." She salutes.

Although he looks like the ninety-seven pound weakling in the *before* picture of a Charles Atlas body-building ad in the back of a comic book, he lifts her up like he is totally, awesomely *after*. Before she knows what has happened, her head is in the pipes and she is fumbling with the cable.

"Your other left," Tim says from below, the exasperation evident.

"Right," she says. "Port."

When he hears the satisfying click of a network connection, he says, "It's a Band-Aid, but that should do it."

As he brings her back to earth, her breasts slide down across his bare chest, defying the kaftan.

"Oops," he says.

"They won't kill you," she says.

But it's too late. Tim has gone crimson and is on his way back to Auschwitz.

8.
SVETLANA

THE BEAUTIFUL INTERNATIONAL MOVIE star wants to flee the Left Coast. Hollywood is a company town whose company she can't part with fast enough. Everywhere she goes, she is trailing the bad toilet smell of a career waiting for the final flush. Just the night before, while trying to cheer her up on the lowest of her bad days, her agent landed a table at the newest, hottest eatery—*Les Tables*. It was a total disaster. Before they were even seated, but once identified, the entire restaurant broke out in song.

A horse is a horse, of course, of course, And no one can talk to a horse of course . . .

It was the whinnying at the end that was most upsetting.

Svetlana spends the next day with her life coach working through the many issues that polluted her the night before. It is a good session. She feels re-empowered until afterward, when the jerk in the coffee bar stomps his hoof while counting out her change. She wants to die. She dumps the mocha half-caf on his fetlock—to his dismay—and drives straight to LAX, where she hops a red-eye to LGA. It is a horrible flight. She is surrounded by a trifecta of howling babies. She hasn't slept for days as it is.

Now she suffers from infantile paralysis. Each scream morphs into an auditory root canal, mining wormholes into her skull. By the time she staggers off the plane, she's gone feral. When she spots an unhappy and unhealthy pasty and pudgy toddler way too old to be sitting in—no stuffed into—a stroller in front of an ice cream stand away from his mom—not hollering, but shrieking—she just barely resists the urge to pull the huge display spoon off the wall, crack his fat baby head wide open, scoop his brains out, and eat them like a three-minute egg.

She knows she is in a bad way. *Stop thinking*, she thinks. She gets in a taxi and sets off to Uncle Dmitri's—a safe place with comfort food—and vodka. He runs a humble tea room on Central Park South—as loud to the ear as it is to the eye—Rasputin & Co.—but it's the closest thing to home in New York since her parents died and her grandfather slipped back behind the Iron Curtain for the last time, which was no small feat since he's still living on the Upper West Side.

The cab drops her off at the top of Seventh Avenue on the near side, where two mounted policemen are waiting for the light to change. As she climbs out of the car and stands up, one of the horses looks her straight in the eye. The other horse turns his head. He clearly recognizes her. He bobs his head up and down, laughs out loud, and then releases a profound fart. The splat of the proceeds hits the pavement audibly a moment later.

"Move along, miss. Nothing to see here," his rider says.

As she bristles, the other mounted cop warns with a smirk, "We know who you are. Stay away from our boys."

The light turns green and the pair trots across the street into the park without looking back. Svetlana is steamed. She turns on her heels and stomps into her uncle's tearoom. As usual, the place is mad crowded, mad loud, and mad crazy—loud mad Russian crazy. She waves off the maître d' and stands alone seething—a maelstrom within a whirlpool. She looks about belligerently, daring anyone to slight her.

Got a problem with that?

Neigh.

World War III.

At a near table, an unsuspecting diner bends over to pick up a napkin that has dropped to the floor. The poor innocent soul is in the wrong place at the wrong time. When he looks up and catches her eye, after a brief pause his face reflects recognition. Then he turns his eyes away politely as Svetlana's are darting back and forth, trying to decide whether to dump the tureen or the samovar into the now guilty party's lap. She goes for the borscht. But doesn't make it halfway to the soup bowl when she feels strong hands clamp onto her elbows and lift her off her feet. She kicks her legs and squirms, enraged with the frustration of the powerless—then weightless as she is tossed without effort into the air and spun around.

When she opens her eyes again, she is looking into the bright smile of her uncle Dmitri, who is showering kisses onto alternate cheeks. "Lanie, you are so beautiful. Why didn't you call?"

"Grrrr," his niece replies.

"Be nice and I'll give you a treat," he coos.

She tries to knee him in the balls, but he anticipates her every move.

"Svetlana Ilyanovitch Petracova," Uncle Dmitri chastises sternly.

This has an immediate effect. Her head drops. Her shoulders droop. She stops kicking. She is deflated. He lowers her gently to her feet, and she throws herself desperately into his inviting arms. In his warm embrace, her eyes well up and she can feel the floodgates ready to breach when he whispers in her ear, "Don't cry, Lanie. Come with me. The fun's about to start. You'll laugh so hard you'll wet your pants."

He leads her by the hand to his office, a rolltop desk in the corner of the kitchen, which is even louder and crazier than the dining room. He sits her down and starts piling little dishes and saucers in front of her—dark bread, caviar, smoked salmon, and a dozen other yummy treats—along with peppered vodka. Svetlana breaks her fast with relish and pickled eggs. By the time she has almost forgotten why she is in a bad mood, Uncle Dmitri lights up even brighter.

"Here she comes," he gushes with delight as he plops down on a stool beside his niece. His eyes shine with excitement as he scoops up caviar in his fingers and tosses back a glass of vodka.

She is a very pretty and a very young girl. She is dressed in a white chef's uniform. Blonde hair cascades out from under her toque, which is way too tall and so big that it's practically resting on her ears.

"She's the sous-chef," Uncle Dmitri explains. "From Odessa."

Svetlana throws him a questioning look.

"Just watch her work," he replies.

It starts out slowly, with only minor accidents, a dropped spoon here, a broken plate there. But as she gets up to speed, the tiny Ukrainian displays a level of gross incompetence that rivals famous Veebo the Clown Prince of the Prague Circus. The other cooks are clearly familiar with her work habits and duck on cue as lost knives come sailing through the air or burning oil is sent cascading across the floor. It is all well choreographed. No blood is spilled, no bones broken, only the crockery.

By the time the pretty young cook sets off the smoke alarms due to an overzealous flambé, Uncle Dmitri is laughing so hard he has to wipe his eyes.

"It could happen to anyone," he says defensively.

"Uncle," Svetlana asks, "why do you put up with her?"

His eyes are dancing—clearly a satisfied man, happy in all aspects of his life—eyes full of love for that and for her.

"I own the restaurant," he explains. "And she lets me fuck her."

"I understand," she replies.

And she does. Later that night, she sits up in bed reading *Fortune* magazine. She thumbs through it like it is a mail-order catalog—shopping for someone to buy her a major Hollywood movie studio.

9.
MARY MARGARET

IN A CORNER OFFICE on the seventieth floor of the Steele Building, on Water Street in New York City, a chief operating officer steps out of a pair of charcoal gray Paul Stuart wool trousers and kicks them onto a black leather Italian couch in front of floor-to-ceiling windows. The view of the lower harbor is breathtaking. Sitting on the block of polished granite that acts as a coffee table—and certainly a bitch to vacuum under—the COO admires a fresh pedicure as a sheer stocking unrolls up a silky smooth leg. After the garters are clipped and running true, she steps into a matching short pleated skirt. She studies her reflection in the window. *Yes*, she thinks. *This will do.*

She should know. The secret to sleeping your way to the top—which she did brilliantly, thank you very much—is the trappings. As Einstein said, "Genius is one percent inspiration and ninety-nine percent really hot lingerie." Clichéd but true, the head is the sex organ you're aiming for. Presentation is everything. Be a pastry chef. Make yourself a yummy piece of eye candy. Don't let Daddy get all mellow and boozy. You want him fucking you with his eyes open so he remembers which one you are.

"I should be a mentor," she says out loud as she pulls on her suit jacket.

Her name is Mary Margaret Zielinksi. She is in charge of all daily operations for The Steele Group, an umbrella holding company of seventy-one wholly owned subsidiaries, four of which are Fortune 500 companies in their own right. She answers to no man. But she pretends to listen to Woody Steele, because he signs her check, and it's huge.

The phone on her desk warbles. She picks up the handset. "Yes," she says.

"I know," she says.

"On my way," she says.

Whenever she leaves her corner office, she prefers to walk out into chaos. She likes the bullpen when it is loud and crazy—mass hysteria. Hubbub is good. The quiet of a crypt is bad. That means two things: Number one, Woody is on-site. Number two, Woody is in a bad mood. As she hits her stride, the mood in the air is toxic.

We need to fix this, she thinks as she clicks along the marble floor corridor. The carpeting was the first thing to go when she bought this building. *High heels and carpets?* Broken ankles, nothing more. *Did Gypsy Rose Lee ever strip on a shag rug?* I don't think so. That thought alone puts a little more swivel in her hips as she struts through Mergers & Acquisitions. On both sides of the aisle she sees glum faces begging her to make it fun again. That inspires her to take her attitude to altitude. She's Rocky Balboa in Christian Louboutins. *I know it's your company, Big Boy,* she thinks. *But that doesn't give you permission to break it.*

As she gets closer to the inner *Sanctum Sanctorum,* she sees clusters of EVPs, VPs, and simple folk—mere MBAs—helping each other stagger away from the big corner office. It reminds her of a documentary she saw about Dunkirk. Outside Woody's door, an intern is holding the shoulders of a CFO, whom Mary Margaret recognizes but cannot name, as he pukes into a potted palm. *This better be good*, she thinks as her knuckle raps the door a nanosecond before she turns the knob.

"What's wrong with you?" she accuses as she thrusts herself into the middle of his office.

Woody's face betrays a look of confused innocence. *Moi?*

Mary Margaret starts pacing around the room. "I hate when you do this," she says.

"What did I do?" Woody goes defensive.

Mary Margaret stops short. "Who's the finance guy in Shenzhen?" she asks.

"Willoughby," Woody replies.

"Why is Willoughby fertilizing the pygmy date tree with his breakfast?" she asks.

Woody simply shrugs his shoulders and looks at something on his computer.

"What's going on? Are you on the rag?" She resists screaming at Woody. She'd pull at her hair for effect, but she had it done yesterday. "You're making everybody miserable."

Woody puts on his serious I'm-not-a-doctor-but-I-play-one-on-TV voice. "Am I wrong in expecting everyone to do his or her job?" he asks.

Mary Margaret can't bear it any longer. In a remarkable vault—well, why should it be that remarkable, she was a varsity gymnast at Villanova—she straddles his lap and begins to beat against his chest like he is two kettledrums in Handel's "Hallelujah Chorus."

"What is wrong with you?" she pleads, tears welling up in her eyes.

She is so vehement that she tires quickly. She slumps against him, throws an arm over his shoulder, and not so much sobs as breathes through her unhappiness.

As she recovers from her emotional moment, he rubs her shoulders. Their breathing is synchronous in a way that can only come from shared years.

Finally, she sits up in his lap and studies his face. It is a familiar face. She can read him like a book. But it is a complicated mystery with twists and turns and weapons hidden up sleeves.

She raises an eyebrow.

He cocks one.

She puts a hand against his cheek and looks deeply into his eyes and asks, "Well?"

Woody smiles wistfully. It is a smile that fades quickly as he goes away again.

But he comes back.

He takes her hand in his. Kisses it. Then looks up at her.

"I miss my dick," he says.

She sighs deeply. Takes his face in both her hands and kisses him on the lips.

"Don't we all," she replies.

10. TIM

HE IS STANDING IN FRONT of apartment 6A. As he waits, he wipes his sweaty palms against his jeans. He can't get the girl out of his mind. He had been looking for an excuse to ring her bell. He could never do that. He hasn't the nerve. When he saw the note in his box he was giddy—then terrified. This is the girl of his dreams, but not of the real world. In his universe he gets crushes on avatars. If only he can remember what she looks like. First impressions matter, and at that special moment all he saw was the gusset of her panties. That makes him believe that her eyes are teal, but he can't be sure of anything. What did she think of him? What *could* she think of him? He was wearing cartoon pajama bottoms and nothing else. He wants to die—but he wants to see her one more time before that finality.

His heart skips a beat when he sees the knob turn. He wipes his hands against his flannel shirt. That should be more absorbent than denim. The maid opens the door. He had no idea that she has a maid. It's a small building—staff knows staff—but such a maid. How could they all have missed her? He is overwhelmed. He has to take a half step back. She's got a tiny waist and endless legs. She's a knockout. She must be six feet tall in those heels. She fills the doorway. She is wearing the full-blown French maid uniform that you'd see at a Halloween party—or in a wet dream: the little lacy cap, the plunging bodice, the starched apron, the flouncy petticoats, the garters, and, oh my God, fishnet stockings.

"Yes?" the maid asks in a throaty, sultry voice.

"I'm the super," Tim chokes out once he finds his voice.

"Follow me," she says. Turning on her stilettos, she does a catwalk strut down the hall.

As he follows, her hips fill his field of vision as her firm cheeks roll from side to side in time with the cadence of her heels. Tim reconsiders his fantasy life. *After all, if the lady of the house is clearly out of my league . . .*

The maid opens a door at the end of the corridor. "The Teenage Mutant Ninja Turtle, Madam," she announces to her Mistress.

"Thank you, Fifi," the girl replies inside the room.

Tim has to contain himself. Fifi? He is instantly giggly at the ludicrosity of the situation, but he wants to maintain his professional demeanor. He takes a quick trip back to Auschwitz so that he can enter the room with a straight face.

"Thank you for popping in," she says. "I know this is above and beyond the call, but I am desperate."

She is looking up at him from a large overstuffed leather club chair. The wide arms are stacked with legal paperwork and blueprints. She is again wearing the kaftan. Her legs are tucked up beneath, so there will be no panty sightings today. But this is all secondary information. He sees none of the aforementioned at first. For him there is no kaftan, no easy chair, no Persian rug, no window, no street outside, no sky, no planet Earth, no solar system. In the moment there are only her teal eyes.

Time stops.

He is not exactly sure when the clock starts again. But once it's ticking away he feels like he's coming out of a dream—albeit a productive one. She is standing beside him watching with interest as he finishes reconfiguring the email on her laptop.

"Would it be too much to set up Mummy's?" her huge eyes ask.

"No biggie," Tim replies.

She turns the key and opens up the antique mahogany secretary in the corner of the office.

"What's her password?" he asks as he sits down.

Her brown eyes look perplexed. "I have no idea," she says.

Tim shrugs his shoulders and starts typing.

"Hmmph," he says as he pauses to think for a minute.

Then he's typing again.

"You call this secure?" he mumbles under his breath.

He swipes something with the mouse. Then pastes something. Then hits the Enter key. He stares at the screen. Half a minute later he leaps to his feet and does a kind of hula.

"Victory dance," he explains.

"It works?" she asks.

"See for yourself," he replies.

She sits down and logs into her mother's mailbox. Tim watches over her shoulder. A computer screen is the only thing that will distract him from stealing glances of her. A list of email builds steadily. One of them has a red exclamation point in a yellow triangle next to it. She double clicks on that one. She barely starts reading when her face falls. "Oh, Mummy." She sighs.

The girl closes the laptop quickly and calls for the maid. "Fifi."

The door opens instantly.

Victoria turns to him. "Thank you, Mr.—?"

"Just Tim."

"You've been a lifesaver," she says.

"Are you sure?" he asks. "You don't look so good."

She laughs darkly. "Just the thing to win a girl's heart," she says. "Share that with the guys in the tech department, Casanova."

Tim is gut punched. "Sorry," he says. Victoria shakes her

head and collapses into her leather chair and curls up as Fifi holds the door.

"Just Tim is leaving," she tells the maid.

As they walk side by side down the long corridor to the front door, Tim is disciplined. He doesn't gawk at her breasts, her ass, or her legs. When he does look at Fifi at all, it is tastefully above her shoulders. This close he notices a little more about her than before. Her hair seems a bit stiff. She seems to wear an unusually heavy mask of makeup. Most unexpected is the biggest Adam's apple he's ever seen on a woman.

11. IVAN

THE BUGATTI IS IN THE SHOP. The Third Richest Man in America spins the wheel, guiding the canary yellow Lamborghini up the circular ramp from the underground garage beneath his 6,500 square-foot country cabin in the woods. It is a lovely day in Bedford Hills. The singing birds are only periodically drowned out by the throbbing rotors of helicopters as his neighbors pop in and out of their third, fourth, or seventh homes. He feels like going for a drive. *My appointment calendar says, 2:00-4:00: Do something spontaneous,* he often quips. Also, he wants to talk to his wife, and that is always done best in a car. When he is driving he is so intense that it actually appears that he is listening to her.

Waiting for a light to change, he tosses a mental bitcoin to determine the route—parkway or interstate—rolling vistas and windy turns or red meat? His thoughts are interrupted by the jarring grumble of a badly tuned motor. He looks to his left and sees an asshole in a NY Jets jersey grinning at him and gunning the engine of a candy-green Trans Am. *Pulleeze,* Ivan thinks wearily, resting his head on the steering wheel. He hasn't seen a muscle car with the screaming chicken on its hood for years. He can't believe they're still making them.

Again with the revving? Ivan lifts his head and half nods at the trailer trash across the lane. They both intently watch the traffic light.

When it turns green, the Pontiac takes off in a fit of screeching belts and burning rubber. Ivan gives him a head start to be sporting, then pops the clutch and effortlessly passes him in seconds. He looks in the rearview mirror, not so much to relish the victory as to savor the humiliation on the gavone's face. Right on cue, the blue and red bubblegum lights of a police cruiser kick on to join the chase. Ivan doesn't slow down, but he doesn't speed up. Once the patrol car pulls alongside they turn and acknowledge each other. The cop salutes. Ivan gives a thumbs-up. Then the cop drops back and pulls over the Pontiac. Ivan takes the turn for I-684—red meat.

The trip is uneventful until a multicar pileup on the Cross-Westchester Expressway, but weaving in and out of traffic, he leaves it well behind. He is a superior driver. He can't help it if the others on the road have such bad reaction times.

He pulls up in front of his wife's lawyer's building on Forty-Ninth Street. Springing open the glove box, he pulls out an official looking NYPD placard. *Medical Emergency,* it reads. He tosses it on the dash and clicks the car key to arm the security system.

On his way to the elevator, he stops by the lobby newsstand. "*FT,*" he says.

The owner of the concession doesn't even look up. He is talking in Spanish to a short, swarthy woman. *Probably a guat,* Ivan thinks. He has never seen either one of them before, but he decides they're both from Guatemala. They are looking down at a subway map.

"*Financial Times,*" Ivan repeats.

"One moment, please," the other man replies, then slides back into Spanish, tracing a route on the map with his finger.

"*The Financial Times of London, por favor*," Ivan says loudly.

The newsstand guy turns defiantly and faces him. "I heard you, sir. Please be patient. I am helping this young lady." By now, Ivan is texting on his phone.

As the woman folds up her subway map and walks away, the newsstand guy addresses Ivan. "Now, sir, how may I help you?" he asks.

"Too late for that, Pedro," Ivan replies as he hits Send with his thumb. Stepping onto the elevator, he says, "*Vaya con Dios*," as the doors close.

Her lawyer's office is on the forty-seventh floor. He is recognized the moment he steps into the reception area. An obsequious junior partner appears as if by magic and shows him to the nicest waiting area. They've got levels, like the airlines. If you're on the A-list you get a selection of current magazines. The new *Fortune* isn't out yet. The one on the coffee table has Tom Hasbrook on the cover. He's the guy that Ivan corporately emasculated recently. So that's old news. Truth to tell, Ivan wishes now that he had been a little more patient and waited to drop the hammer on Pedro until after he had gotten his *Financial Times*, but that's just effluence under the bridge. He picks up a *People* magazine and spends the next ten minutes seething through a puff piece profile on Woody Steele, the Second Richest Man in America.

By the time Mackenzie gets out of her meeting, he has his own personal black cloud hovering over his head.

"Where's Thomas?" she asks in surprise.

"I gave him the afternoon off," he says. "I felt like a drive."

"Right," she replies. "Note to self, be spontaneous from two to four."

"What's wrong with a man wanting to be in a car with his bride?" Ivan says, covering a sharp pang of irritation by cobbling together the best bonhomie he can manage on the fly.

"How delightful," his wife says. She walks up to him and kisses him on the lips, lifting her right leg behind her to the specified Junior League angle.

They link arms and exit the law offices like the loving newlyweds that they are. As they walk through the lobby, workers from the building are sliding the boards in place to close up the newsstand.

"It's a little early in the day," Mackenzie wonders. "What's that all about?"

"A learning experience," Ivan replies.

"Who learned what?" she asks.

"A guat learned who owns this building," he answers.

12.
WOODY

"I HATE THAT SLUTTY THING you do with your CV," he complains.

"*Pardonnez-moi*," she replies, batting her eyelashes and sipping Champagne.

"You got to the top on your own merit," he says. "You only slept with me because the sex was good."

"*Peut-être*," she says.

"What's with the French?" he inquires.

"I'm trying to be seductive," she explains.

He laughs, grabbing the bottle. "We need more wine," he says and gets out of the hot tub.

"Did you take your pill?" she asks.

"Yes," he answers, looking around the room, blinking his eyes. "Everything's gone bluish."

"Why not?" she says. "It's a blue pill."

He turns and ponders her for a moment. "Looking good, Mugsey," he says. "Still perky."

"Thank you, kind sir," she replies.

"No *merci*?" he asks.

"Mercy is reserved for the weak," she says. "You told me that at the beginning."

"So I did." He smiles. "What happened to your bikini top?"

"He finally noticed." She sighs extravagantly.

"What part of perky did you not understand?" he replies as he walks off, pleased to feel the thong land on his shoulder. "Good throw."

Woody Steele and his COO are curled up in the grotto beneath his hilltop villa on Virgin Gorda. Ever since he was a young millionaire, he has enjoyed having sex on Virgin Gorda—and it looks like it might happen again—despite the rude things that those surgeons did to his special friend. Mugs—that's Mary Margaret—came up with the idea. He owes her more than he can say—or is this the wine talking?

He stops at the top of the stone steps and looks down into the pool. She's leaning against the side, floating with her legs spread slightly. He grins again when he notices that she has trimmed her pubies into a downward pointing arrow. He timidly presses through his trunks and is delighted with the pushback. He looks at her again. She must know that she's got his attention because she is touching herself in a different way. If she were wearing a G-string, it would be stuffed with dollars by now.

Their eyes lock as her other hand begins to massage her breasts. She throws him a smoky look, questioning, *Well?*

Woody grins like a schoolboy. Feeling cocky for the first time in months, he pulls out his waistband to revel in the return of the prodigal. But when he looks down into his bathing suit, the blood drains from his face. There will be no fatted calf today.

"Oh my God," he wails, staggering around with his trunks held open as if it were a ritualistic dance.

A naked, dripping Mary Margaret races up the stairs. "What's wrong?" she asks. "Are you having a heart attack?"

Woody shakes his head no, but looks at her with a desperate expression.

"What?" she asks. "Is it a freakishly huge erection? Are you afraid of hurting me?"

In total defeat, Woody pulls down his bathing trunks to expose the problem.

"Whoa," she says, taking a step back.

All in all, it is a perfectly respectable erection—except for one thing. While it is firm and rigid, practically parallel to the ground, the last two inches at the tip are skewed in a radical thirty-degree twist. He looks down at this new freakish disfigurement in horror.

"The Sunday talk shows are going to be on about your new liberal turn," Mugs says.

When Woody looks questioningly at her, she adds, "To the left," and laughs so hard that Champagne streams from her nose.

"That's not helpful," he snorts and stomps into the pool house.

"Come back, Little Sheba," she entreats as she follows him inside.

He despondently tosses his body down onto a sofa. She perches next to him.

"I don't know what to say," she says.

They are surrounded by the detritus of an aphrodisiac battlefield. Piles of oyster shells, composting artichokes, avocados, pomegranates—everything but powdered rhino horn, because that would be wrong.

They sit quietly for about ten minutes until Mugs, nibbling on a chocolate-covered chili, says, "I'm really sorry about your recent setback."

"Thank you," he says.

"But what about me?" she asks.

"What about you?"

"Well for starters," she explains, "you've spent the last four hours getting me into a state of intense sexual arousal."

"You see how it is." Woody sighs. "What can I do about that now?"

"How about let's have a big hand for the little lady?" She smiles and spreads her legs.

13.

MARY MARGARET

MARY MARGARET LOOKS UP at her boss and friend of over fifteen years. Her heart goes out to him. He is so sad and frustrated. They haven't done it in over a year—if not far longer. But when they used to be a gossip item around the water cooler—bring on that hostile work environment any time—they were brilliant in bed—or wherever they happened to be at the time. He had a magical penis. Her attempt to bring back Lazarus tonight almost worked. But now they are sitting shiva in the last act of a depressing foreplay. She's naked—but to little effect—he only has eyes for the new sharp turn in his road of life. She shakes her head to clear the cobwebs. She has to fix this. She kicks him in the nuts—in a loving way.

"Hey," she barks. "Snap out of it."

He looks at her like a lost puppy.

"Don't be so negative," she exhorts. "Look at the upside."

"Like what?" he asks.

"You can piss around corners," she says.

Nothing.

They both stare at it for a moment longer.

She asks, "Do you mind if I . . . ?"

"Not at—" he replies.

She flicks it. It bounces up and down but stays bent.

"Trauma," she concludes.

"You bet it's traumatic," he agrees. "Look at it."

"It's the result of trauma," she clarifies. "Something happened to it."

"Like what?" he asks.

"Like cancer?" she points out the obvious.

"Oh, right," he replies. "That."

She flicks it again and it bounces again.

"It certainly is hard enough," she says.

"But it won't win any prizes now." He sighs.

"You won prizes before?" she asks. "Why wasn't I at the award ceremony? And who was she, the bitch? I'll kill her."

He smiles for the first time in a long time. "Too late for that," he flirts. "It was Margaret Thatcher."

She aims for another penalty shot, but he blocks the kick.

"But it works, right?" she asks.

"If you call that working," he answers.

"And you're not dying?"

"No, I'm not dying."

"I think you can't complain then," she says.

"I know that intellectually," he says.

"But?" she asks.

"I want my old dick back." He sighs again.

"I know," she commiserates.

She wraps her hand around the shaft and kisses the tip.

"Owie," she flirts. "I almost threw my neck out."

"I hate you," he grumbles.

Suddenly she is inspired. "Hey," she says. "You should go to Australia. With a dick shaped like a boomerang, you'll always cum back to where you first took her bra off."

She's laughing at him with her eyes. His expression softens.

"I can't complain," he admits.

"No, you can't," she agrees. "Do you leak?"

"No."

"Then you really really can't complain," she says.

"I did my exercises religiously," he replies. "I can break a pencil."

With a full-throated gleefulness, she laughs from the gut and from the heart. She throws herself at him and entangles him with her arms, legs, and breasts.

"I've missed this," she says before they launch into an extended kiss.

While they are catching their breath, they lean back in the sofa. Nuzzling her face in his neck, she takes it in hand and slowly strokes.

"See how my wrist turns as I come up the shaft?" she lectures. "That's the proper way to hook a bowling ball. I read that on a plastic beer cup at the Starlight Lanes in Omaha."

He laughs out loud. "You are a bad person."

Mary Margaret leans up on her elbows and looks down into his face.

"Do you want to try?" she asks.

He thinks a minute, but concludes, "I don't think so."

"Okay," she says and kisses him sweetly on the lips. "Then it's my turn." She squirms and gyrates, making a snow angel in the white sofa. Once comfy, she parts her legs and declares, "Time to pay the piper."

Above her, she can see him smile affectionately. He kisses her on the lips—the neck—the breasts. His hands touch every part of her body. Her shoulders relax. She settles deeper into the soft leather. But then she feels him slip a finger up inside her.

"Hey," she calls out. "What are you doing down there? Are we making a porno?"

He looks sheepish, but she lets him off the hook. Clutching his wrist firmly like the grip of a tennis racket, over time and with proper guidance, she helps him get the job done.

14.
MACKENZIE

STUFFED INTO THE PASSENGER SEAT of the low Italian sports car, the young trophy wife is looking between her knees at oncoming traffic. She is so close to the road that she is looking up at hubcaps. She has always hated this car—as she hates the way he drives it. The way he rockets when he can—and slams on the brakes when he has to—not unlike his lovemaking. *I'm a bad wifey,* she thinks, just before she grips the armrest in terror as they are almost run over by a pedicab. She knows better than to say anything. She hasn't said what was on her mind since the rehearsal dinner, and that seems to be the way to go.

To distract herself and postpone a full-blown panic attack, Mackenzie reviews what the lawyers talked about in the IPO meeting. There has been an ongoing debate on which financial banker should handle the stock offering. Goldman Sachs has been kicked around a lot. There is a consensus that her husband should stay out of it. The company line is that as a CEO of a new brand she should stand on her own feet. This isn't a vanity project for the *little woman* and should not be perceived that way. Mackenzie had cobbled together the start-up's DNA before she even met Ivan. It's her show. That's the narrative, but in reality it's simpler. Pretty much everyone involved doesn't want to work with Ivan because he's either a prick or a putz, depending on your ethnicity.

There is also the question of the initial offering share price. While this is solely at the discretion of the offering bankers, the lawyers are really interested in the subject because a lot of their fees are going to be paid in stock—but not all. That was the awkward final discussion: accrued accounts payable to date. That's the challenge, isn't it? While that magic moment off Mykonos was a special act of intimacy for Ivan at the time, the loss of her second virginity is proving hard to monetize in the here and now.

Mackenzie turns to look at her husband. He is so focused on the traffic that she can't tell if he remembers she's there. There is one advantage to driving with him; it's like sleeping in twin beds.

When they stop at a red light he speaks for the first time. "How was the meeting?" he asks, eyes straight ahead.

"Fine," she replies and then rolls the dice. "They want some money?"

Her heart is pounding as she waits for his answer, but it will be a long wait. The light turns green and there is no traffic ahead of them. As her husband puts the hammer down, Mackenzie is pressed back into her seat. She fights the g-forces of acceleration to turn her head. His expression shocks her. His eyes are steely and dead. His mouth is set. She is aware that her husband loves driving his exotics and always adopts best practices to protect his huge investment in his expensive automobiles. If she didn't know that, from his demeanor she would think he was angry. But it must be just from fighting Midtown traffic, right?

They screech to a stop so suddenly that she is surprised that the airbags don't deploy. She knows that she will have a bruise from the shoulder belt. There's street work or something with a lot of flashing lights up ahead.

He tosses the *People* magazine that he stole from reception into her lap. It's folded open to an article entitled, "The Eye of the Needle."

"It's war," Ivan snorts, drumming his fingers on the steering wheel.

While waiting for her husband to calm down, she tries to read the article, but her eyes don't seem to work. Ivan has no patience, so he fills in the blanks.

"The old man in Peoria has called us all out," Ivan gripes. "It's going to be one hell of a pricey dance marathon."

Mackenzie has found her glasses and she's catching up. That *old man in Peoria* is the Richest Man in America, and the *call to arms* is a challenge to the current crop of robber barons to put crowbars to their wallets and do the right thing for charities and the commonweal.

She puts down the magazine and says, "So write a check."

Ivan turns and gives her a look like she's rude or stupid. "My money's not good enough," he sneers. "Great White Father wants us to bundle, and he who rakes in the biggest pile of cash for the purest lily-whitest goodest deed doers will be declared *Bestest Rich Person on Earth*."

Mackenzie pauses a moment. As his seething seems to subside, she asks, "Who cares what the old guy wants?"

The look she gets from that comment starts out as disbelief, but it turns so ugly that she averts her eyes and tries to forget what she saw. But she knows that, whatever he says, it's really about his competitive streak. After another interval when it feels safe, without looking up she asks, "What can I do?"

She is surprised and relieved that his voice is back to normal and it's all business.

"You are the wife of an important captain of industry," Ivan says. "It's time you assume a leading position in society. People should look up to you. You need to chair committees and host benefits. The world should see why you are worthy to be married to me."

Mackenzie hides behind her boardroom face. *It's official,* she thinks. *The honeymoon is over. Note to self: reread the prenup.*

When traffic starts moving again, his wife says, "I know what to do and it's a lot. I think I should stay in the city tonight."

"Good idea," Ivan agrees. "Sutton Place?"

"No," she says. "My old apartment, I think."

When he drops her off on West End Avenue, he actually gets out of the car to kiss her. That surprises her.

15.
SVETLANA

THE BEAUTIFUL INTERNATIONAL movie star is sitting cross-legged on a bed in an extra large UCLA sweatshirt and nothing else, working on a tablet while Gerard or Jared, the owner of the sweatshirt and bed as well as the apartment that they are both in, sits across from her in a chair. He is nursing a beer. They were roommates a few years ago—not exactly roommates—she just lived with him near Echo Park for a short period while she was between jobs. She can't remember if he thought that she had been his girlfriend, but she is pretty sure that she wasn't. She grins at Gerard or Jared coquettishly.

"If you were in a position to buy a major motion picture studio, it would make everything so much easier," she says. "Good night, Gracie. We turn out the light and cuddle. Can you do that little thing for me?"

Gerard or Jared glowers at her and takes a sip of beer.

She sighs dramatically. "Then I suppose it's back to the Google," she resigns herself. "Is there a dating site for billionaires?"

Gerard or Jared seethes silently as her fingers tap and swipe across the screen. She pauses and reads intently, finally proclaiming,

"Well, he's out."

There is a crash as Gerard or Jared tosses the empty beer bottle into a trashcan. He gets up and walks into the kitchen.

"Why is the Richest Man in America out?" she asks. "For one thing, he is the grandfather of four—and a deacon in his church—and where is that church?"

Gerard or Jared walks back in with a new beer. Svetlana looks him in the eye and says, "You know how on every project, management is always asking, *Will it play in Peoria*?"

He pops the bottle cap off with his teeth and spits it into the can. Svetlana ignores this and goes back to the tablet.

"I have no interest in actually being in Peoria," she sniffs. "Let's check out the next one on the list."

It would take an upgrade to elevate the mood in the room to an awkward silence. But finally the enthusiasm of discovery unleashes Svetlana again.

"Number Two looks very promising," she burbles. "Especially in a tuxedo. He's fit and natty in all the downloadables. He's never been married—but I can tell by looking at him that he is no *confirmed bachelor*." She titters.

She spins the tablet around to show off her find. Number Two is immediately recognizable. She has seen him on so many magazine covers and gossip shows that she feels like she's met him in person. He has boyish good looks along with a strawberry blond complexion and hair that makes his mustache and goatee look cute and sexy and not like something on a greasy saxophone player in a dingy supper club. He is dapper and gorgeous and, as the Wiki search reveals, he is not just a philanthropist—he is a brave philanthropist. In 1995, following a devastating earthquake, he parachuted into Osaka, bringing violin strings to isolated Suzuki students. He climbed Mount Everest just to bring down the garbage. He played right wing for Manchester United wearing a disguise.

But there's more. He has another reputation—a physical distinction so impressive that cafés and restaurants in Paris are about to rename their pepper mills. Svetlana's jaw drops at the sheer scope of his romantic conquests. It's every starlet, superstar, and has-been she's ever heard of. Who isn't on this list?

"Why am I not on this list?" she complains.

"Too much horsing around," Gerard or Jared mumbles under his breath.

"I can't believe you said that," Svetlana says, her face betraying genuine shock as if he had blasphemed while standing on the Bernini altarpiece in St. Peter's Basilica.

"Sorry," Gerard or Jared says awkwardly.

"I had nowhere else to go," the diva launches into an aria. "Grandfather is impossible, and all of Midtown Manhattan is nothing but humiliation traps. You do know the Royal Lipizzaners are playing Madison Square Garden, don't you?"

Tears are flowing freely as she sobs. "I thought this was my last safe haven."

Gerard or Jared goes to her, opening his arms to offer her the comfort that she cries out for. She throws her body into the warm embrace, but just before contact her eyes light up in recognition.

"I know you!" she erupts, pointing at him. "You're Gerhardt!"

He steps out of her way and she crashes to the floor.

"That hurt," she moans.

Gerhardt stands over her and looks down.

"You are a horrible human," he says.

16. VICTORIA

SHE IS DOING SOMETHING that she hates when other people do it. If she were sitting in the backseat of a taxicab, watching another person doing as she is now, she would tell the driver to, "Speed up and put the zombie out of her misery." But at this moment Victoria is way beyond Zombie Town because she is lost to the world—wandering through traffic, talking on her mobile.

She gets across Columbus and Amsterdam Avenues surprisingly unscathed. But Broadway is a different matter—perhaps because she comes to a full, screeching stop in the middle of the uptown lane.

"Mummy, what are you thinking?" she cautions into the phone.

Fortunately for Victoria the Jeep that's speeding straight at her is driven by a man with incredible reflexes. It lurches to a halt and stalls just inches from her long, shapely legs. The guy in the Lexus behind him isn't so swift. He rear-ends the Jeep and then makes with the horn. That's what gets Victoria to look up as both drivers jump out of their vehicles. The first one is noticeably upset that he almost hit her. The second one, after a brief inspection, is furious that she got Jeep on his Lexus.

Victoria quickly takes in the situation. There's nothing for her here. She offers the mobile to the two men. "Do you think you can do better?" she asks crossly.

They look dumbfounded at her reaction.

"I didn't think so," she says dismissively and continues on her way, deaf to the cacophony of horns from the nascent traffic jam that she has inspired.

"Uncle Sid—the Cutty Sark?" she says incredulously into her mobile.

But that bit of cockney rhyming slang—Cutty Sark: Loan Shark—is the last concession to her mother's old neighborhood. Now the gloves come off.

"Ma," Victoria brays into the phone, reverting to the Philly accent that she picked up in business school. "Are you out of your fuckin' mind?"

By now she has reached West End Avenue. While waiting for the light to change—the first one she's noticed so far—she holds the mobile away from her ear. She's heard this lecture from her mother before. A mélange about language befitting a proper young lady along with shockingly out of place Bible references about honoring one's parents. That presentation always has Victoria wondering exactly how many *uncles* she does have. It must make for one hell of a large family.

By the time she's past the doorman, she can tell that her mother is winding down. While she knows that it is yet one more exercise in futility, in the elevator Victoria once again tries to educate her mother about the sustainable enterprise model. But this time she goes a little farther and points out that, "Any business plan that includes paying vigorish to a shylock in its core SOP is probably a bad one."

Standing in front of Apartment 6A, she can't get her key to work. Whether it's from nerves or anger she can't tell because her head is swimming. It's as if time were going backward. The trap opens and falls and she flies up onto the gallows. The noose is tightened around her neck and she walks down the thirteen steps, tread by tread, as the coarse rope slowly squeezes the breath out of her.

"How much was that?" she asks.

The connection on her mobile goes dodgy for a minute.

"You're breaking up." Victoria laughs. "I thought you said two hundred thousand quid."

The blood drains out of her face when she hears the response.

"Ma," she pleads. "Don't tell me you signed with Sid."

"Of course not, lovey," her mother replies. "You did. I signed for you. You're the businessman in the family. I should know. I paid for it."

"I don't believe it," Victoria stammers. "I don't know what to say."

"*Thanks, Mummy* would be a start," her mother replies. "Few girls get an opportunity like this."

"What you did is illegal," Victoria squeaks as her throat tightens to the choking point.

"Nonsense," Lavinia tosses off. "It's as natural as teaching a chick how to fly. Must dash. Sid says the vig's due Tuesday next. Love you, sweetie."

Click.

Victoria snaps out of it when the apartment door opens by itself. No. It is Fifi. "Madam," she says.

Victoria knows that she needs to collect herself before dealing with the help. She goes to her bedroom and takes off her jewelry and washes her hands, holding a moistened cloth against her forehead and temples.

Slightly revived, she heads back into the inner workings of the apartment. She finds Fifi and today's other maid, Giselle, in the utility room next to the kitchen. They are in matching maid uniforms working at matching ironing boards. The matching sour looks on their kissers actually revives Victoria a little. She dips into her mother's playbook that she grew up with.

"Out with it," she barks.

That immediately deflates the maids.

"I'm waiting," she says.

Giselle looks to her sister.

Fifi gets up the nerve. She arranges her apron and steps away from the ironing board.

"Well, Miss . . ." she begins but falters.

"I'm listening," Victoria says.

Fifi braces herself. "Madam," she blurts out. "We don't know how it is in the UK, but we paid a lot of money to be here, and so far all we have done is your laundry."

She runs out of steam. The two maids stand awkwardly, not knowing where to look for the moment that Victoria intentionally stretches out.

"That's it?" she asks finally.

The two maids nod with growing trepidation.

Victoria walks over to one of the many canes wall-mounted throughout the facility. She takes it in hand and flicks the thick switch two then three times in the air.

"Then this is your lucky day," she says with a sinister smile.

17.
SCANLON

4teen4U: im wearing the white panties you asked for daddy

spanker472: good girl that makes daddy very happy

4teen4U: ooh daddy i m soo xcited about today

spanker472: so am i sweetie

4teen4U: im wearing the training bra mommy got me 2

spanker472: you are my angel

4teen4U: how long daddy? i cant wait much loonger i'm so excited

spanker472: i'm parking the car hunnie

4teen4U: you WILL kiss me like you promised to kiss me like a naughty girl

spanker472: you can count on it sweetie

4teen4U: o daddy i hope my white panties are still fresh when you get here

spanker472: lol an angel and a little devil

4teen4U: hurry daddy my little heart is pounding

spanker472: you left the door open sweetie?

4teen4U: yes i'm upstairs lying on my bed with all my favorite animals

4teen4U:	wearing only my panties and training bra
4teen4U:	and white anklets
spanker472:	ready or not here i come

In a dark corner of an NYPD squad room, Sergeant Scanlon leans back from a desktop computer and cracks his knuckles. He thinks for a moment, then types in, *o daddy i hear you on the stairs*. Perhaps that is gratuitous. He deletes it. Just nerves. He unwraps a stick of sugarless gum, folds it in half twice and stuffs it in his mouth and waits.

The clock seems to be frozen.

A few minutes later his radio squawks. "Honey Trap calling Tiffany. Come in lil' darlin'."

Scanlon grabs the handheld and squeezes the button. "That's Sergeant Tiffany to you," he barks into it.

"Caught the bastard with his pants down," a different voice he recognizes as Cooley reports. "Good work, Sarge."

Scanlon cracks his neck from side to side.

"Making the world safe for the scourge of all humanity," he replies.

"Who would that be, Sarge?"

"Fourteen-year-old girls."

"Say it ain't so."

"You haven't met my stepdaughter," Scanlon explains as he signs off.

After putting the computer to sleep, he stands up and stretches gingerly.

"Time to run the gauntlet." He sighs as he heads into the locker room.

He knows that they've been waiting for this moment. The teasing taunts start before he's even close.

"Incoming."

"Hide your junk, boys. It's jailbait running wild."

"If I'm going to prison for this, at least show me your thong."

"Lo-li-ta!"

"What you got? What you got?"

"Give us a peak."

"Want to suck a lollipop, sweetie pie?"

This is water off a duck's back to Scanlon. He is used to it by this point. It's been a daily ritual since he was reassigned. At first he parried, trying to match them with repartee. Then he ignored them. Tonight he barely notices. His wounds are pinching in a very uncomfortable way. He sits down on a bench between lockers and peels off his shirt to check the dressings.

You can hear a pin drop. The locker room is suddenly a crypt as he awkwardly touches the bandages on his back to make sure they are still in place. He then stands up and lowers his trousers, pulling down his briefs to inspect the exit wound next to his balls.

He looks up to the stunned faces around him and says, "That one really hurt."

Silently and solemnly they clear the room, touching him on the shoulder as they file past. He is left alone to change his clothes and tie his shoes.

18.
MACKENZIE

I COULD GET USED TO THIS, Mackenzie thinks as she soaks in the tub in her old apartment. The place isn't nearly as grand as any one of Ivan's temples to excess and conspicuous consumption, but it is definitely more homey. Yes, there are cracked tiles on the wall, and the floor is worn through in places. Some of the Persian rugs are a bit threadbare, and a sconce in the front hall is hanging out of the wall by its wiring. But it sure is nice to be in her own place for a change. As she feels her muscles relax and her spirit refresh and her eyes get leaden, the trophy wife and nascent CEO in her own right mentally slaps herself across the face and says, "Don't get too comfortable."

She pulls her body out of the steaming hot nurturing tub and dries it off, slipping into a cherished, fraying chenille robe. In the same pink fluffy slippers that she wore through all-nighters in B-school, she shuffles off to the kitchen. She opens the narrow door to a broom closet and pulls out one of her guilty pleasures—a jug of red California wine. She would be totally humiliated if any of her Silicon Valley gourmandising colleagues—or her husband—ever caught wind of her pedestrian palate. She takes a cherished

Fred Flintstone jelly glass from the cupboard—instinctively looks inside to make sure there's nothing gross—and tops it up. After a quick chug, she grabs a Lean Cuisine at random from the freezer and tosses it into the microwave. She kills the glass, tops it up, then walks into her office and groans as she turns on the computer. At this point in her life she hates computers. But they are a necessary evil. Using computers, she hopes to get rich enough that she won't have to have a computer—or even an email address—that's rich.

She creates a new empty database that she saves as *$4good.db*. First she downloads an online archive of all the not-for-profits in the region, filtering out anything associated with a political organization or a disease, condition, syndrome, or disability. Next she imports the Social Register. By the time the microwave dings, she has no appetite and the wine jug is hanging out by her feet. In an epiphany, she realizes that she has been so caught up in her work at the start-up that she has forgotten how much she enjoys working. The next few hours fly by as she data mines the current state of philanthropy in the state of New York.

One thing quickly becomes crystal clear. Trying to get on the board of one of the more venerated pillars of the New York cultural pantheon is for chumps. The Mets (both Opera and Museum), MOMA, the Ballet, even the Bronx Zoo are grandfathered with bitter feuds and rivalries going back generations of filthy rich and powerfully connected families. Her darling husband could write a check large enough to fill Madison Square Garden and it wouldn't get her into a management position in the bulb shop at the Botanical Garden.

Mackenzie drinks a glass of wine and thinks. She sets down the jelly glass and broadens the query, typing in, "syndromes or conditions affecting pretty young white girls."

"That should do it," she says out loud and hits Enter.

The search result is huge. She filters out "anorexia." The return is still significant, but workable. She idly scrolls through the list, looking for inspiration.

Gross, she groans as she skids into thumbnails of girl babies with operatic cleft palates.

Oh my God! She goes wobbly in shock as she clicks on one with an upside-down nose—nostrils pointing to the sky—perched over an especially profound rictus. *The poor dear will drown the next time it rains.*

It's too much to bear. She tweaks her search engine. What part of *pretty young white girls* did we not understand? Pretty means pretty, as in good-looking. Not pretty as in pretty amazing that they're still alive.

The next query has a better result—oops, got to strip out the anorexics again. While we're at it we can lose the obese girls—eat a salad, Bertha.

"Oh, I like this one." Mackenzie giggles as she reads from the screen. "Chronically Ginger."

After that there's more and more of the same: spazzes, autistic spazzes, spazzes that are really smart despite their spazziness—and the retards—OMG.

Then it gets worse. A series of pubescent girls each more odious than the last. Sunken sullen eyes volcanoing contempt. Mackenzie doesn't even bother to read what their problem is. She wants to bitch-slap each and every one of them—a new premium in fundraising—better than a tote bag.

Her energy starts to wane as the wine runs out. She's got that catatonic point-and-click, past-your-bedtime, propeller-head thing going. Not much is registering. Except of course for elephantiasis. That's always a crowd-pleaser. But this year the benefit dinner is somewhere in Chad, so that is off the list.

An hour later and it's time to prop up her eyelids with toothpicks. She is really going to bed now. Just a few more web sites.

Then there he is. Looking straight into her eyes. He immediately understands everything about her—more than any human being has ever understood or bothered to delve—and more important—he doesn't give a shit. Mackenzie is transfixed. Who is he?

She is totally awake and focused now. She studies the face on the screen that is dissecting her very soul. She looks again, shocked to discover that he's a baby. Around eighteen months, she guesses. But she hasn't been around a lot of babies.

Why is he so wise?

19.
TIM

HE IS MOONLIGHTING. He would have done it for free, but he doesn't want to give his hand away. It's in Apartment 6A, of course. Wiring every inch it seems, except for the private living quarters—sound and web cams all over the place—even in the bathrooms. At first, Tim balks at that.

"Isn't it illegal?" he asks.

Whereupon Victoria shows him the waiver that all the maids must sign if they want to work for Mistress Lavinia. It's a phone book.

"Don't forget the cams on the floor around the toilets," she directs. "For up-skirt shots."

She is gone before Tim has time to process the request. She is everywhere and nowhere, carrying on three conversations on-site and another on the omnipresent cell phone that seems glued to her ear. To his further disappointment he is not the only contractor at the work site. There must be at least a dozen tradesmen finishing up the project—carpenters, tapers, painters, electricians, plumbers—Victoria riding them all hard, checking off the punch lists. Tim is demoralized, until he gets a bounce when she pauses in one of her flybys.

She stares directly at him and says, "What you are doing is the important bit. It's billable." But he can't tell if she's talking to him or into the mobile. Then she is gone again.

He is smitten. He is actually in love with her ratty kaftan as well. Rooting for every failing seam and popping stitch—especially around the spreading sleeves. He has gotten sneak peeks of her breasts four times this afternoon. It's still her eyes that own his soul, but her breasts are mighty fine. What color are her panties today? He does not know that yet. Here's hoping.

The walk-in closet in the changing room proves problematic. He spends twenty minutes with his head in a dropped ceiling. It all goes wrong. It's hot and sweaty. He keeps dropping his tools. When he finally gets the junction box secured and climbs down from the ladder, the cool air is refreshing. He wipes his face with his sweatshirt, and, when he tosses it away, there she is on the mobile.

"Do I want my own web host or a virtual domain?" she asks.

He goes all stupid. She's changed her outfit. No kaftan. Now she's wearing a simple black dress. Tim has no idea that it's Chanel, but he can tell that it's sophisticated. His jaw drops and his heart sinks. She's red carpet good-looking. He knows he doesn't stand a chance.

"Do I want my own web host or a virtual domain?" she repeats.

He stands by patiently, trying to hide his disappointment, until she pulls the phone away from her ear and snaps her fingers right in front of his eyes.

"Oi," she shouts. "Wake up."

Tim is startled.

"I thought you were on the phone," he says.

"On hold," she says, rubbing her ear. "Bollocks, I've lost a dangle." She looks frantically around the room.

"What's it look like?" Tim asks, trying to be involved.

"Like its mate," she says, pointing to a thing hanging from her other ear. "It's Etruscan."

Tim has no idea what she is talking about. All his degrees are in engineering. As far as he is concerned, Etruscan must be the small gold penis hanging from her left earlobe.

"Fifi!" Victoria's cry echoes throughout the apartment.

Tim hears the snap of a lash and then a groan. It repeats. He looks down the hall for the source of a painful punishment as Victoria answers her mobile and the ringtone goes silent.

"Do I want my own web host or a virtual domain?" she asks.

"It depends on what you want to do," Tim replies.

Victoria looks cross. "I'm on the phone," she mouths.

Fifi hurries into the room. Tim is surprised that she can stand let alone mince in the heels she is wearing. Once she sees that her Mistress is occupied on her mobile, she stands perfectly still, demurely staring at the floor.

"You must know what you're talking about," she says to Tim. "He's asking the same questions you did, and he's really expensive."

Fifi throws Tim a scathing look.

Why is she so mad at me? he wonders.

"What do we want to do?" Victoria asks into phone as she wanders away in concentration. "We want to make money—a lot of money. We want to print money."

When she is out of earshot, Tim is convinced that the maid is hissing at him.

Victoria looks at her watch and winds down the call. "I have to go. I want a quote tomorrow morning." She thumbs off her mobile. Then she walks across the room to the now servile maid.

"Head up," she commands.

When Fifi raises her face, Victoria slaps it—not too hard—but hard enough.

"I don't know what you're up to, but I don't like it." She cocks her arm again, enough to get a flinch from Fifi—and Tim—but pulls back.

She takes a cane off its mount and hands it to Tim. "Behave yourself," she says to the maid. "While I'm gone, he's in charge."

"What?" they blurt out in unison.

"Do us this little favor," she says to Tim as she checks the contents of her handbag. "Mind the store while I'm gone."

Tim looks at Fifi with trepidation. In her heels she seems to be a head taller than he is. She has broad shoulders, like a halfback.

"And make sure the bitch finds my earring," Victoria tosses over her shoulder on the way out.

Alone in the room together, Tim can't tell whether her heels walking down the hall or his pounding heart is making more noise. He doesn't have the courage to look at Fifi. Her presence in the room is debilitating. He feels that the cane in his hand is an insult to her, as he also knows that he should not show any fear. But of course that's academic by this point. She can smell his fear. They both know that. The room is stinking with it.

He finally works up the nerve to raise his head. Her look is scalding. But he resists the urge to look away. He does not know how long he looks into the furnace of her fury, but he will never forget when she smiles and sticks out her tongue—flicking it back and forth so that the Etruscan bauble hanging on a stud dances in the light—challenging him.

20.
IVAN

THE THIRD RICHEST MAN in America is hovering over Dead Horse Bay in his second favorite helicopter. His preferred ride is in the shop getting an upgrade—a new interior of endangered Brazilian rosewood with marble accents. As he watches the laborious boat launch on this part of the Brooklyn waterfront, he realizes once again that it would be so much easier if he had staged the campaign in San Francisco Bay. But he doesn't like that neighborhood very much. He's been dissed too often and way too much by the Silicon Valley set. He is much more comfortable with the WASPs on West Forty-Fourth Street. Despite the fact that the New York Yacht Club is old money, he speaks their language. Their money is so old that it is running out, and they need more.

The catamaran is finally in the water and slowly wending its way out through the inlet, surrounded by an armada of gawkers on every sort of float—Jet Skis, runabouts, sport fishing boats, and daysailers. Moving this racing machine slowly is one of its greater challenges. That's the proper terminology for it. It's a racing machine, not a sailboat. From high above, surrounded by its smaller, almost tiny, nautical cousins, it looks more like a massive black origami spider than a ship.

Ivan doesn't need to be here. He could watch the afternoon's events unfold on one of his computer screens. But the markets are closed today, so he can be anywhere. More important, he wants to show his support to the new skipper and his team. Leadership 101. Nothing like a flyover to show how much you care. It's an inspiration thing.

"Get inspired or get off the pot," Ivan mumbles as he fusses with his phone.

As the boat gets away from traffic and finds some leeway east of Sea Gate, it shakes off whatever cramps it got overnight in the damp hangar, comes about across the wind, and gracefully lifts up out of the water on its under-hull wings and begins to fly.

"Shit," Ivan curses as he reads a post on his phone that the Dutch have dropped out of contention.

"Sorry," the chairman of Philips Nederland texts him. "Your toys are too rich for our blood."

While his new crew are knocking themselves out, showing off what the boat can do, 500 feet above their heads Ivan is lost in a vitriolic rant against all things Dutch. What has a tulip ever done to him? Or a wooden shoe? For a brief moment he looks out the window at the technological marvel below and hates it.

His phone chirps. It's a text from Teddy Edwards, an ex-spook who's doing some work for him.

Update: Steele is squeaky clean except for a fucking record.

Ivan is delighted. He texts back.

State or Federal? Jail time?

His phone chirps.

Correction. Should read: he set a world record for fucking.

Anyone I know?

Anyone you don't?

The Third Richest Man in America drums his phone against his thigh in irritation. He's been trying to get dirt on Number Two for months now, and this is worse than worthless. It's deification. How can he emasculate a satyr?

Below him the catamaran is practicing racing turns. Ivan looks out the window for the briefest moment. The taste of bile in his mouth is driving the agenda. He is back on his phone—back on his least-favorite web site—*www.SteeleX.com/todayinwoody*. It's like touching a bad tooth to make sure it still hurts. Ivan is in a private helicopter on a beautiful day flying over one of the most spectacular harbors in the world and all he wants to look at is the tiny screen of his smartphone. He's acting like a teenager. That's what acrimony will do to a grown-up. Hold the phone—the jury is still out on Ivan's maturity.

It quickly gets worse. Clear those bile ducts. More vitriol is on the way. While he may be the Second Richest Man in America, Woody is coincidently Numero Uno when it comes to world-class pollution and has a Herculean toxic footprint. Today he is in Fukushima, Japan, hosting an international conference to make the world green, clean, and safe for babies everywhere. Ivan is so blind with rage that he can only stare with wonder as Woody takes the stage, bookended by two rows of bright orange hazardous material suits. An embarrassingly inappropriate stereotypical Mr. Moto—thick round glasses and buckteeth—walks out carrying a silver tray holding water tumblers. The girls on either side rip off their breakaway hazmat suits. They are all wearing skimpy bikinis. They toast Woody. Woody toasts them. The crowd goes crazy. Ivan is so mad he does something he hasn't done in over a year—including on his wedding night. He turns off his phone.

And seethes.

For the next few minutes Ivan fumes so intensely that he loses track of where he is. What brings him back is the sun crossing his face as the helicopter banks. He looks out the window and refocuses. His mood improves. There is his boat. It is big and fast and beautiful. Woody Steele does not have a boat. Woody Steele will not win the America's Cup this year. Woody Steele will not hold the *Auld Mug* in his hands. Ivan is practically giddy.

"Time for a prank," he says to the pilot through his headset.

"A prank, sir?" the pilot asks.

"You bet," Ivan replies, rubbing his hands gleefully.

"What sort of a prank?" the pilot wonders aloud, unable to hide the concern in his voice.

"Just the flick of a towel in the locker room," Ivan explains, a grin spreading across his face. "Drop down to the deck and fly across the beam—port to starboard."

"Is that a good idea, sir?" the pilot asks.

"Let's think about this." Ivan bristles. "It's my helicopter. My boat. My people. And my idea. Tell me what I'm missing."

The pilot follows orders. He slips into a descent and transits the sailboat amidships. The turbulence from the rotors jibes the boat immediately. The port hull lifts precipitously out of the water. Only thanks to their exceptional skill as well-trained sailors does the crew avoid capsizing. The helmsman deftly kicks the bow across the wind and does a 180.

As Ivan watches from his perch above, he can't help but delight in the antics of the crew as they try to save the boat. It looks like a clown act when three or four are tossed into the drink. He can't contain himself. It's the best laugh he's had in years.

21. SVETLANA

THE RUSSIAN BEAUTY IS IN JAPAN with dear sweet wonderful Gerhardt. Gerhardt is handsome. Gerhardt is witty. But most important, Gerhardt just happens to be a sound engineer for *Today in Woody*. Svetlana has scored a hat trick. They are roommates in a sprawling trailer farm a few miles outside of Fukushima. The neighbors are all global media or folks working the conference—like adorable Gerhardt. Now that she remembers his name, she can't say it often enough. And Gerhardt, in his light, easygoing Teutonic way, seems to have forgiven and forgotten.

They are coconspirators. By hook or something else crooked, Gerhardt has snatched a copy of Woody's itinerary for the entire conference. His life is scheduled to the minute—including downtime.

"Why is that written in pencil?" Svetlana asks.

"Shhh," Gerhardt replies with a finger to his lips. "Top secret."

"Holy moly," she gasps as she leafs through the information packet and discovers that there is even a floor plan to Woody's quarters. He's in the triple-wide, just overlooking what they are calling Half-Life Bay, attached to the huge tent where the event is being held. A plan starts to germinate.

"If only I could get in there." She sighs.

Gerhardt flashes an impish Bavarian grin and holds up a key.

"What?" Svetlana gasps—then exhales *my hero,* hugging him tightly as she grabs the key out of his hand.

She also gives him a kiss—a totally pro forma kiss. Gerhardt is history. He was very useful, but so past his sell-by date at this point. Now it's off to the races.

As she threads her way through the compound to Woody's prefab, the plan coalesces in her head. It's quite simple, actually. It just comes to her when she remembers the art-house film she made at the beginning of her career. Did it just pop into her head now, or has it always been in her thoughts? It was a French-Canadian indie called *L'Etranger et La Douche*. The shower scene put her boobs on the map. They still have over a million views on YouTube—each—but who's counting? Yet at the end of the day, she owes so much to that douche. It launched her career, which was stellar until that fucking horse shat all over it. She frowns at the memory and pushes her way through the growing crowd.

When she reaches her destination, her simple plan collapses from complications. For one thing, there are rent-a-cops all over the place. The triple-wide is cordoned by rings of security. There are spotlights. Fortunately, even in Japan she is recognizable enough that she passes through the first two checkpoints simply by waving her driver's license. The third one proves thorny—TSA-level stuff, with metal detectors and scanners and very serious-looking people giving everyone the hairy eyeball. Worse—everyone passing through the gate has to swipe a badge. Svetlana has a key but not a security badge hanging on a lanyard around her neck. *Fuck you, Gerhardt, if that is your real name.*

She studies the operational zone perimeter looking for a back door—like all of a sudden she is Jason Bourne. She knows she is conspicuous standing still. Everyone else is either in the queue or tending it. She looks to the right and left, relying on her theatrical training to keep a look of panic from creeping across her face. Her *deus ex machina* arrives in the form of a van that pulls in just up the hill from where she is standing. The doors open and disgorge a bevy of tiny Japanese girls in tinier bikinis. The driver gets out and gives them direction. They hover around him in a tight orbit, giggling and bowing and looking like borderline illegal pornography.

By the time they are lined up and prepared to go inside the triple-wide—*yes, there is a back door, thank you, Jason*—Svetlana has stripped off her clothes, down to a matching bra and panty set. Inserted into the center of the group, she is crouched down on bended knees and willing her breasts to be Eastern tiny by way of alternate nostril breathing that a yogi taught her in Bhutan. They march off in step as the guards hold the doors wide open, grinning and bowing as the girls grin and bow and Svetlana hobbles and can't believe her good luck.

But her mood is quickly tempered with feelings of contempt for America's Second Richest Man. He has a harem? Of course her righteous indignation is immediately overshadowed by thoughts of how to separate him from said harem. She stands up straight to reconnoiter. That's sure a heads-up in this diminutive crowd. What to do? What to do? Are tiny Japanese easier or more difficult to herd than cats?

On her right there is an open door to a deep utility room. Leaning against the wall is a wet mop sitting in a bucket. She studies the door handles. They are perfect for the task—but how to lure them inside? She is stumped. That is until one of the girls shows off her new wristwatch to her friend.

"Swag! Swag!" Svetlana shouts, pointing into the janitor's room.

The tiny Japanese girls look at her in questioning confusion.

Svetlana raises the bar. She charges the door, stopping just short. Hopping about she goes mental—chanting high-end brand names, pointing inside the cavernous room.

"Prada. Gucci. Fendi. Cartier. Hermès. Rolex."

There is a deafening silence. All the girls look up at her in disbelief.

Svetlana points at the slop sink and says, "Mikimoto."

That's the last straw. With the bright hunger of avarice in their eyes, all the girls rush through the doors. It is deep enough that they are all well inside before they realize that there is nothing there. Svetlana closes the doors and slides the mop handle through the two door pulls, effectively locking them in.

As she sets off in search of the living quarters, Svetlana rehearses that pivotal scene from *L'Etranger et La Douche* where her character is discovered naked in the shower.

"C'est vous!"

"C'est moi."

"C'est horrible!"

She then wraps her hand around his growing manhood.

"C'est tu."

22.
SCANLON

GoodGod: have u been a good little girl
bobbiSux: i try to be good, but it's so hard
GoodGod: don't make me pull ur panties down and spank u
bobbiSux: oops. i didn't mean to say that GG.
GoodGod: thats ok honey
bobbiSux: well is it?
GoodGod: is it what?
bobbiSux: so hard [blushing]
GoodGod: it is always difficult to behave and do our best, dear
bobbiSux: i always try to do my best even when im asked to do naughty things
GoodGod: why would u ever want to be naughty, little girl?
bobbiSux: for the treats. i luv sucking lollipops
GoodGod: [sighing] i dont have a lollipop for u
bobbiSux: yes you do i can see it bulging in your pants daddy
GoodGod: GET DOWN ON YOUR KNEES
bobbiSux: oh goodie lollipop time

GoodGod: PRAY TO OUR LORD AND SAVIOR JESUS CHRIST
bobbiSux: really?
GoodGod: really. ask for God's Grace to cleanse the evil that lurks inside your panties

"Pervert," Sergeant Scanlon says as he closes the NYPD-issued laptop in disgust.

He's working from home—feeling generally crappy all over, body and soul. These days the department has a very flexible work schedule for officers who get shot up in the middle of an antiterrorism sting gone bad. While the general public wouldn't find it surprising, everyone who works there does. Up until now they haven't been very forward thinking on PTSD—not that the sergeant still freaks out at things that go bump in the night. But he'll never forget those eyes. That's pretty much all there was to remember. The balaclava hid most of the shooter's face. It was just two miles south of Indian Point. Scanlon was parked by the river selling ersatz plutonium out of a Dodge Caravan. He didn't think for a second that the scam would work—until it did—and then he was in a medevac on the way to Bellevue.

He stands up and bends over. His wounds are pinching again. Actually he is pleased to feel any sensation at all down there. When he was in the hospital for so long, he could tell by the happy talk that he shouldn't hope for any radical improvement to his situation. On a brighter side, he won't have to worry about getting an embarrassing hard-on at Jones Beach this summer during the bikini festival. He grabs his coffee mug and starts down to the kitchen. As he passes the door to his stepdaughter's room he pretty much successfully shuts out the squeals of hilarity emanating from within. He loathes and detests teenagers—girls especially. While he still resents the hell out of getting shot by an Islamic crazy, he's got to hand it to those people, they get one thing right. If he could sell fourteen-year-old Bitzi to one of her uncles today—she'd be in the car right now. It could be for a six-pack. Scanlon is not greedy.

He's almost past—safe and away—but the training and behavior kick in. His hand is on the knob. The door is open. He is in the room. He's right. It is weed he smells.

"Excuse me," Bitzi complains loudly. "Don't you know how to knock?"

She pulls a long toke from a Hello Kitty bong. Scanlon is disgusted. He sees four girls lolling around in a pigsty. There's a stack of greasy pizza boxes on a bed that has nothing on the mattress but a stained liner. The floor is strewn with every piece of clothing the girl owns, covered with a layer of skimpy thongs—dozens of thongs. One of the girls is drawing cocks on the wall with a marker. Another is writing rude aphorisms next to them. Scanlon duly notes that the C word is no longer taboo. The other girl is swiping through photos on her phone.

"What are you doing here, anyway?" Bitzi asks with irritation.

"This house has rules," Scanlon says and moves to grab the big pipe.

She is too fast. She is out of reach, hopping up and down on the bed. "You're not my father," she snarls.

He bites his tongue and does not say, "Thank God."

"I am going to have to ask you all to leave right now," he does say.

"Fuck you," the girl on the phone replies.

The girl with the marker draws a large magnifying glass three feet up the wall over the shoe rack.

"What's that?" Bitzi asks.

"That's to help you find your dad's thingie," she replies before she convulses in giggles.

"He's not my dad," Bitzi howls in righteous indignation.

The literary one with the updated vocabulary whispers into her ear. Bitzi grins and nods. She finds her phone in the clutter on the floor and aims it at her stepfather just as the other girl jumps up next to him and whips up her tank top, exposing her pubescent breasts along with a huge smile as Bitzi takes the pic.

Scanlon doesn't waste any time thinking this one through. The next thing anyone knows, Bitzi is facedown on the funky bed with her wrists handcuffed behind and her stepdad is thumbing around, grown-up stupid on her smartphone wondering, "How do you delete?"

"I'm telling Mom," the cuffed girl howls, albeit muffled.

"Where is your mother?" Scanlon asks.

Bitzi turns her head. "Probably looking for a real man," she says before verbally spitting in his eye. "For her sake I hope she finds one."

23.
WOODY

WOODY IS PACING IN THE GREEN ROOM, waiting for his entrance. He's not nervous. He would just rather be somewhere else—like at the meeting in the triple-wide. It's the Due Diligence Working Group for the mergers and acquisitions crowd. He loves crunching the numbers as much as he enjoys watching really smart people juggle hand grenades around a boardroom table. Today Mary Margaret is running that show. Short agenda. Does SteeleX International want to buy Japan? It's a good deal on paper. Even better—it would be a distressed sale.

But at this moment Woody has to be the familiar face of a publicly traded company. This is as much a part of his job as signing the checks or hiring the CIA to overthrow unhelpful regimes—just kidding. He can do these dog and pony shows in his sleep—like rolling off a log—and he doesn't have any lines this time around. It's all canned. He just has to flap his lips and gesture.

A production assistant discreetly knocks at the door. "Five minutes, Mr. Steele," he says as he evaporates.

Woody stands in front of a dressing mirror and grunts sardonically. The wardrobe girl looked surprised when he stepped behind a screen to put on the swim trunks. He had never been so modest in the past. There was that time when he changed into a wet suit during an IRS audit. It was notorious. It made the *Wall Street Journal.*

"Your secret's safe with me," he says, pulling open the waistband and looking down at his little friend—emphasis on *little*.

The rest of his costume for the show is made up of a thick, luxurious terry cloth robe—white—flip-flops and a kamikaze headband with the big red rising sun meatball centered over his face.

Wait a minute. Something is niggling at the back of Woody's head. Something familiar. He never forgets a face. He pulls open the waistband again and looks down, studying intently. Where have I seen him before? Of course the question is academic because he's been looking at his little friend almost every day of his life. But it never looked like this until recently. We are not even going to revisit the Dr. Penis and Mr. Hyde episode. He still shudders when he relives that evening with Mugs when his dick took a radical turn for the worse. But this is the new normal. What is he seeing now? What is so familiar? He pulls down the trunks and looks in the mirror. He squints to focus. He grabs a table lamp to shine a light on the issue. He tries to study it from every angle, until—

He freaks out. He tosses the lamp away and pulls up his swimsuit as the words burn into his brain. *Volvariella volvacea*. He learned that name from one of his childhood treasures: *The Boys Book of Fungus*. Made famous by oriental stir fry, the paddy straw is the teeny peenie of all mushrooms—the teeniest. He grabs one more fast peek down his trunks. His heart is racing. It's smaller than he remembered—not that he's had the courage to go hunting for it these days. If only it could be at least morel sized. Maybe if he shaved down there it would help. Perhaps his bushy pubes make it look even smaller.

He lets the waistband snap back into place just as the door opens and the production assistant calls, "Places."

He grabs his prop, a large back scrub brush, and staggers out onto the stage. The lights are bright. The venue is large—three thousand seats, four TV cameras. One of them flying around overhead on a huge mechanical arm. Woody doesn't notice. He is in a daze, wandering through the set. Putting his feet on the little yellow dots like he knows where he is going and what he's talking about. The voice-over is explaining how SteeleX International has developed the processes to save Japan after the catastrophe. Now Woody is marching on a treadmill in front of a huge projection screen while images of the devastated containment building morph into the new infrastructure and the pipes and catalytic converters and other processes that neutralize the nuclear waste and make the water more than clean—and green. We follow the trail through to the end—from damaged nuclear rods to a locker room—zoom in on the showerhead.

The treadmill stops. Woody barely keeps his footing.

Fanfare.

"Ladies and gentlemen, please give a warm Fukushima welcome to the Japanese Olympic Gymnastics Team."

The screen goes up into the flies, revealing a large shower room—largely empty. There are no teeny Japanese gymnasts in teeny bikinis as expected. Just a voluptuous naked Russian beauty with soap in her eyes. Svetlana had been washing her hair. Woody takes off his terry cloth robe and starts toward her.

"You!" she says when she recognizes the lumberjack.

Woody is a bit of a film buff. He can't resist.

"*C'est moi*," he says.

24.
MACKENZIE

SHE IS RUNNING LATE. There's a heat wave in Iceland—or more like it's just not cold enough outside Husavik where her start-up runs its large server farm. She has been on the phone all morning. When they finally open the windows and doors like she told them to do from the beginning, things cool off pretty quickly. No downtime, but plenty wasted. She shows up on East Fifty-Seventh at the trendy restaurant du jour nearly an hour after wine time. Her group is not only seated but staring at their luncheon.

Why do they all look so miserable? she wonders. Then a waiter hands her a menu and it all becomes clear. This place is hardcore. At *Sans Viande,* fennel isn't an ingredient, it's a category. After a moment of panic—she is hungrier than she thought—she practically has an orgasm when she discovers Welsh rarebit in the fine print under *For Him*.

Sipping from her water glass, she scans the room, assigning names to faces. She comes up empty. She and Ivan don't go out much, and she's certainly a fish out of water here. Walking into a room full of men is more up her alley—getting patronized, hit on, or dismissed—she knows how to handle those situations. This crowd is definitely from Venus—proper society ladies doing good works. *How did this happen? What wrong turn did I take on a dark rainy night in Transylvania?*

It's called The Shiny Penny Foundation, which is a subset of the larger good-worky mother ship. Penny Miller is a real little girl with some horrible disease that no one else has ever had but is just too terrible for words, and she is so brave and cute despite the rash. It's definitely a gateway charity. The names on the letterhead are all A-list trophy wives and a few lifers. Mackenzie ran them all. Many of them own a trophy-wife business. Most of those are licensed interior decorating firms. Two of the others have boutiques with the word *princess* in the name above the door. One runs an award-winning cupcake emporium. It was easy enough to buy a seat at the table. Ivan wrote a check. It will take a little more effort and guile to get to the head of the class.

As she waits for her lunch, Mackenzie finds it a little odd that no one has spoken to her since she sat down. *Do they know that I'm a fraud?* she questions herself. *Can they tell that I don't give a crap if Penny lives or dies*? Maybe she should have introduced herself when she walked in. Or apologized for being tardy. *I'm the rudest woman in New York City. Worse. Arrogant. Hubristic. Trying to insert myself into this cohesive group of ladies who only care for a sickly little girl and not about themselves. And why am I really here? For my own advantage. To self-promote. To please my husband.*

The thought of doing anything to please Ivan makes her forget her hunger momentarily and she is nauseous on a totally different level. She raises her head to focus on the horizon to stop the rolling queasiness in her gut. Looking up at the ladies, she realizes that they are not not talking to her, they're not talking among themselves either—or eating. The only thing they seem to be doing is drinking white wine with a steely determination.

"Hmm," she says audibly, but just.

By the time the waiter places the fancy cheese dish in front of her, Mackenzie has lost her appetite. She pushes it away.

"Are you sure?" the woman facing her asks.

"Excuse me?" Mackenzie says.

"Done with that?" the other woman repeats.

Mackenzie scrunches up her face in recognition. "We've met, haven't we?" she says. "Joanie?"

"Jodie," the other woman replies as she pulls the plate across the table and tucks into it eagerly with knife and fork. "I'm starving. I could eat a radish."

Mackenzie looks around the room, trying to capture any reaction that an actual conversation is taking place—nada. She leans in so close to Jodie that she can hear her jaw working. "What's going on?" she whispers.

"Something tragic," Jodie answers.

"Penny?" Mackenzie asks.

"Yes," Jodie replies.

"Is she . . . ?" Mackenzie chokes. "Is she dead?"

"Worse," Jodie says. She puts down the knife and fork. She chews and swallows and dabs her lips with her napkin. Turning to Mackenzie with a solemn face, she explains, "They found a cure."

There is dead air until a sob at the head table shatters the stillness, which acts like a starter's pistol. Now everyone is talking—to themselves. But since they are all talking at the same time, it creates the impression of conversation.

"All that work for naught."

"Did she even say *thank you*?"

"What will we do now?"

Once they shoot their load they go even more quiet and look distinctly more miserable.

"Which one is the boss lady?" Mackenzie asks.

Jodie points her out.

Mackenzie digs out her phone and swipes through the photo albums until she finds Him.

"There you are," she coos to his image, immediately enraptured as she always is every time he looks into her eyes. The little baby—the wise old man.

Jodie is looking over her shoulder. "Oh my God," she gushes. "He is a miracle baby."

"Isn't he wonderful?" Mackenzie sighs. This must be the hundredth time she has looked at him today.

"What's wrong with him?" Jodie asks.

"It's very bad," Mackenzie answers.

"It couldn't be anything average," Jodie says. "Not with him."

"No," Mackenzie agrees. "Not with him."

They both stop and stare, taking him in.

Finally, Jodie says, "Show them."

Mackenzie hesitates.

"You must."

She takes her phone over to the head table and hands it to the boss lady. At first she waves it off, but Mackenzie is insistent. She is a rock. Finally the other woman takes the phone to end the standoff. She barely glances—then gasps. Now she is all eyes and the entire room is sitting on her shoulders. There are no words—just guttural sounds of admiration.

After a long interval, she looks up at Mackenzie with soft, questioning, sincere eyes. "What's it called?" she asks.

Mackenzie knows that she is beaming, but the truth shall set you free.

She stands in the center of the room and announces to the gathered host, "Ours for the taking." She takes a bow and heads for home. She has a need for red meat.

25. VICTORIA

VICTORIA'S DAY IS ENDING better than it began. On her way back to the flat she buys a bottle of Champagne—a modest thank-you for that unassuming young bloke who babysat Fifi for her. His name is on the tip of her tongue. He is definitely not her type, but she hopes that he will share the bottle with her all the same. She takes the elevator to the basement. It's late. She can't imagine he's still upstairs. She wanders through the green corridors that are familiar in the way that a dream might be remembered. Around the next corner she spots a metal door with a handwritten sign taped to it: *Knock Hard*. So she does and the unlatched door swings open.

"Hello?" she says as she sticks her head in the room. The rest of her body follows soon after.

It is a small apartment crammed with a lot of stuff. Victoria has spent too many years sharing a confined space with her mother to have any tolerance for piles of crap. But curiosity about the boy lures her inside. On the other hand it is definitely three-star crap. Along one wall is a metal workbench stacked high with electronic components from this and the last century—logic boards, transistors, resistors, and a whole bunch of who knows what. On the other wall are books, books, and more books—predominantly physics and engineering (mechanical and electrical)—but a mess of philosophy, too. He seems to like the Enlightenment. Victoria arrives at that conclusion from the plethora of empiricists present: Locke, Barclay, and Hume. But there are phenomenologists represented also.

She approves of the artwork. He has cut up a calendar and taped Edward Hopper pictures on every open space of wall. He has some Turners also, and while the place is cluttered in a way that she finds displeasing, it is not boy disgusting. There are no gross stacks of dishes or prehistoric food mounds. No fermenting laundry. The futon in the corner might be unmade, but the sheets appear to be clean. She smiles when she notices the framed diploma hanging above the bedding—obviously photoshopped—an ABD in nuclear physics from Columbia University.

"Who's the clever boy?" Victoria says aloud as she hits six in the elevator. She holds the Champagne bottle by the cork and away from her body heat to keep it cool. In a few minutes she will share it with him. Too bad he won't be around to enjoy it.

I need to do something about supper, she thinks as she slides the key in the door. She kicks off her heels, her liberated feet delighting in the cool marble of the foyer. She drops her handbag randomly and drifts into the lounge. She grabs a flute from the sideboard and blows off the imagined dust, then popping the cork, she ultimately collapsing into one of the overstuffed club chairs and luxuriating in the power of Champagne on an empty stomach. Well deserved, nonetheless. Victoria sang for her supper all day long. Even though she didn't hit the high notes until the late afternoon.

The morning meetings followed the script and original business plan. She had the PowerPoint presentation and the supporting documentation. It makes for a convincing narrative—a storied and successful, culturally rich family business moving to exploit a growing demand in the United States. She could feel the interest as she could hear her British accent thicken to the point of caricature—but they ate it up. Her pitch evolved throughout the day.

As she pours another glass of bubbly, the mellowing process is momentarily disturbed by the neighbors. She's tempted to bang on the wall, but she curls up with her wine instead, continuing to relive today's glory.

The first meeting was polite enough. There's nothing more polite than a banker who's talking about panties. He did seem genuinely interested in the merits of the scheme. But he wasn't completely sold on her financial projections for a *Lavinia's Maids in the USA* for the Columbus, Ohio, marketplace. The second meeting had a slightly better reception when she Americanized the name to *Sissies R Us* and floated an Internet tie-in.

"Goddamn it," she curses and does bang on the wall this time. "Sex doesn't require groaning."

Victoria is slightly surprised when she pours the last of the Champagne into her glass. They clearly use smaller wine bottles in the States. She curls up and smiles as she relives the last meeting. She had proposed moving the whole shop—lock, stock, and barrel—online at this point. Web-based pornography is something that bankers can easily understand. They have templates and standards. Pornography is easy. It's just about money. The last meeting went so well that Victoria is breathing easier—albeit with the occasional hiccup—it looks like she will be able to pay Uncle Sid his vig this month.

"Again with the groaning," she complains at the disruptive noises coming from next door.

Enraged, she grabs a shoe and stomps to the wall, ready to rail on it. Only then does she realize the moaning is an echo, bouncing off the wall. The unfortunate misery is coming from somewhere inside the apartment. Her grip tightens around her stiletto, now become a defensive weapon, as she sets off to investigate.

Nothing in the kitchen, but she can hear it more clearly here. She tiptoes down the hall to the source. She carefully turns the knob and opens the door to the library as soundlessly as she can. But that silence is quickly shattered as she drops her shoe and it crashes into the fireplace guard with a clang.

"Mummy?" she asks plaintively.

Victoria's heart practically stops. Her mother is sitting in the settee in the center of the room looking out the window. It has to be her. It's her hair, isn't it? But what is she doing here now? She's not due for two weeks.

"Why didn't you tell me you were coming? I would have met your plane."

Victoria walks around to face her mother and gets the second shock of her evening. Tim—that's right, his name is Tim, she remembers—is bound and trussed on the settee. He's heavily made-up, wearing one of her mother's more preposterous wigs. He's still wearing a Columbia University sweatshirt, but down below are fishnet stockings and high heels.

Victoria looks at him sadly. "That ball gag's got to hurt," she says sympathetically, and then, as she starts to untie him. "I guess Fifi has given her notice."

26. TIM

THERE ARE NOT ENOUGH DEAD babies in the world—or desiccated corpses—or gangrenous festering ulcerated limbs—to distract Tim away from the largest erection of his lifetime. Every trick he has successfully utilized in the past has proven to be ineffectual. On the other hand, this is the first time he has attempted to deploy his proven tool set to deflate a situation that's clad in French-cut satin bikini panties—turquoise. Failing that, he at least hopes that he can keep from drooling. She puts a hand on each arm of the chair he is bound to, very close to his restrained wrists, and leans in close. Her eyes bore into his. The neckline of her little black dress beckons. She is so close that he doesn't have to look to experience her cleavage. Her breasts are omnipresent. He can feel the heat emanating from her body.

"You have no idea how badly I feel about this," she says as her gaze drifts down to his rigid embarrassment. "I guess I feel even worse about it than you do." She giggles.

Despite his predicament, Tim thrills at a new coy twinkle he sees in her eyes. She puts her lips just inches from his ear.

"I'm in a quandary," she explains. "I really want to remove

this unpleasant gag from your mouth, but I'm worried that you will scream bloody murder and I will spend the night in jail."

Tim tries to explain that she doesn't have to worry about that, but everything he says is distorted and unintelligible.

"I know," she agrees. "You must be very mad at me."

Victoria steps away into the middle of the room—studying him. One hand is holding her chin, the other arm hugging her body.

"I'm putting on my thinking cap," she says.

Tim is a captive audience in no hurry for liberation. While he has in the past appreciated mental snapshots of her glimpsed in passing, this is his first opportunity to take her all in—all of a piece—of perfection.

A lightbulb goes on over her head. "Eureka," she says.

She looks deeply into his eyes as she pulls her arms down to her sides, pressing her open palms against her hips. "You must be very embarrassed," she begins. "If I meet you halfway, we can be friends again. Does that make sense?"

Tim is confused. It shows.

Victoria's voice drops to sultry as she explains, "You've shown me yours. Now I will show you mine."

Her palms slide down from her hips, and in one fluid motion she pulls the little black dress over her head. She tosses it away and stands in her bra and panties, looking boldly at Tim.

"Sorry, I'm wearing tights," she apologizes. "I know that compromises a major fantasy for you chaps."

Tim's eyes are leaving Earth's orbit as it is. He has no problem with pantyhose.

Standing directly in front of him, she says, "Just to be on the safe side." Then she pulls down her bra cups and mashes Tim's face to muffle any protest that might escape his lips as she unbuckles the ball gag. Once confident that he's docile, she steps back and studies him anew. Tim is opening and rotating his jaw to alleviate the cramping.

"Okay?" she asks.

He nods.

"But how do I know you won't jump me when I untie you?" she asks.

"I won't," Tim squeaks, his voice unused for so long.

She rubs her chin.

"I've got it," she says. "We will do it in stages."

She squats over his legs, sliding from side to side—kissing him with her lips. They are both naked now. His hands are on her breasts. She centers over him and drops suddenly—

Boom!

Tim bolts up. He is alone on the futon. Every light in his basement apartment is on. The physics book he was reading is on the floor. He reaches for a tissue.

27.
IVAN

HE IS AT HIS RETREAT IN BEDFORD HILLS, working the phones—shaking down everybody who owes him a social IOU.

"It's called *early onset infantile ennui,* Lawrence," Ivan starts his spiel. "They're eight—nine—ten months old, good-looking normal babies—then BAM. Suddenly—almost overnight—they look like they're so fucking bored with everything that they just don't give a shit about anything. You should see a photo of this one kid. It'll break your heart."

Then he cajoles or threatens, depending on the historic favor or offense. After a final, "You can do better than that," he directs them to "Make out that check to The Shiny Penny Foundation." He hasn't broken a million today, but it's still early. Silicon Valley hasn't opened for business yet.

While Ivan talks on the phone, he is looking out the window in his office, into the woods. A deer that doesn't look like a deer catches his attention. When he turns back to his screens, one of them is flashing a red Stop sign. Now his cell phone sounds an air raid siren. Without pausing, he speed dials his favorite insider trader.

"You rang?" Ivan says.

The expression on his face goes through stages, starting with a confident happy-go-lucky look—to a mad-at-self grimace—ending up at a furious-at-the-world glower. Ivan has committed the ultimate sin. He didn't follow through. He walked away when a deal was . . . unclosed. As a result, even after that toxic shareholders' meeting and the total repopulation of the board of directors, Tom Hasbrook is still hanging on to USYS. His lawyers have filed a barrage of lawsuits, successfully locking out the new team. Over the same period, a large network of stealth traders bought up huge blocks of USYS, USYS Holdings, usys.com, and USYS Taiwan LTD. This quadrupled the parent company's market value and made the average share price go up 380 percent. Because of a stupid rookie mistake, his five million dollar windfall has turned into a twenty million dollar liability—plus or minus.

He talks to the trader about how to pull this one out of the crapper. There are no good options—no options at all. As Ivan talks business, he is able to calm down a little. By the point one of them says, "You win some, you lose some." They agree, "It's time to pay the casino."

Just before the sign-off, Ivan insists, "You find out whose hand was behind the stealth trades." His face has a look of fierceness. "The second you know who it is, you tell me . . . and hire the guy who wrote the code."

His attention is drawn back into the woods. He absentmindedly hangs up the phone. He spins his chair around and toggles a screen to the security system, then launches an app that displays a schematic view of the property and all the sensors. Different color icons show the status of each. If you click on one, you get the history of what's happened at that motion detector in the last thirty-six hours. A string of orange safety cones across the map shows that the trail hasn't gone cold. Ivan isn't sure whether it was Wife Number Two or Number Three who made him buy all this security crap. He remembered that when it was installed, he couldn't be bothered to read the manual. Today the whole interface seems almost quaint. He launches the camera archives and cycles through the last two hours in quick time. Every now and then something catches his eye. He can double-click and watch that real-time video historically.

She is very lithe. She is very fast. Ivan can tell it's a woman because she shows a lot of leg. There is no screen capture of her face. He turns back to the window. He thinks he sees a flash or a sparkle. He grabs his binoculars and looks into the hot spot of recent activity as informed by the data. He has to focus the glasses for distance. *Damn*. Her head is behind a leafy branch. But he can now confirm that it is a woman. Her curves make anything else unthinkable. It takes him a while to find her because the formfitting, sleeveless sheath she is wearing is made in a *Deep Woods Camouflage* print.

Ivan opens his desk drawer and pulls out a Remington automatic. He checks the clip and slams it back home. He crouches down and slips out the side door and into the woods. The reason why he doesn't call his security guys to do this is because he doesn't have any. He fired them. They were all a bunch of bums. He gave them a chance, but they always came up short. In every aspect of the job—in every skill set—on balance: anything they can do, I can do better. Ivan knows this to be a fact.

He keeps the gun down at his side as he moves low and swiftly. A distance from his goal, Ivan can tell that she got away. He recognizes the location from the security tapes. A flutter of color in the periphery pulls his gaze in that direction. He can make out a scarf caught on thorns in front of a deep thicket. He unhooks it, touching it with two hands, studying it. It is very lovely and very expensive. Ivan should know. He owns half the Champs-Élysées. He turns it over. Another curiosity. Obviously this is a plant. She has ruined the scarf, scrawling a huge question mark in lipstick on the underside. Mysterious—also a little creepy. He decides he would rather look into this situation from inside his fortified country cabin.

It goes faster downhill. He locks the side door. He puts the Remington on the top of the desk. He freezes. Momentarily he steps back and takes it in. Standing tall and proud in an open vodka bottle is a single black—as black as roses can get—rose. Next to that are two shot glasses side by side. One is empty. One is full. They are sitting on a signed cocktail napkin from Rasputin & Co. She has left a big wet one—a huge Revlon *Love that Red* smackeroo. Ivan doesn't bat an eye.

"No Number Five," he says gruffly.

His phone sets off an air raid siren again. Ivan picks up and clicks on his favorite insider trader.

He's got the answer to Ivan's stealth question. Two words.

Woody Steele.

28.
WOODY

ON THEIR WAY BACK FROM JAPAN, they have a stopover in Singapore. Mugs is launching something or breaking ground on something or shutting something down. Woody can't keep track any more. He doesn't contribute that much to the meetings that he can't get out of either. To stay awake in those, he passes the time beating his smartphone at chess. The press conferences, on the other hand, are command performances. Woody is the face of SteeleX International and its biggest marketing tool. His larger-than-life persona is a worldwide phenomenon. Stories of his real-life escapades and derring-do are reported in the popular press almost daily. Tabloid readers particularly savor his antics—and gossip—snarky and scantily clad is best, please. That charming schoolboy grin can cover a host of sins. On a serious note, his calendar is posted on most business outlets. At the same time he is *numero uno* in viral videos on YouTube—beating out even the cutest and most angry kittens. Most telling is that over 15,000 web sites post a *Today in Woody* link.

He doesn't mind press conferences—probably because he's done a gazillion of them—but by this point they all seem to be a continuation of the same one. The first question is always directed to Mary Margaret—a topical question that asks something along the lines of: Why are we here today? This is usually asked by a cub reporter who is young and eager enough to think that both the question and the answer are important. There might be a follow-up. But without fail by the third question—whatever it is—Mugs has passed the baton to Woody and goes to ground until the bitter end when she closes things down lest anyone forget that she's the COO.

After a few technical questions—Woody loves using the words *logistics* and *metrics* at this part of the dog and pony show—there are general questions about strategy.

"Are you making a play for USYS?" someone asks.

That question is rewarded with Woody's big preemptive grin that says—*I didn't break your vase yet, but, when I do, you know you will forgive me.* There are so many follow-ups to that that Woody ultimately has to answer the question.

"It's kind of embarrassing," he explains. "An intern in a training session just happened to get lucky. He shouldn't have been sitting at a live terminal in the first place."

He shrugs his shoulders in a *gosh shucks gee whiz* fashion to make it go away. But it doesn't. That got their attention for sure.

He holds up his hands. "That's off the record," he pleads. "Off the record."

"Why?" more than one demands.

"We don't want to upset my buddy Ivan," Woody replies with a twinkle in his eyes. "He takes this money stuff so seriously."

Just about all the male reporters chuckle at that. Woody can count on those guys—a walk in the park. They throw up one softball after another—about the broad du jour; the picture in the tabloids of naked women on his beach; cracks about pepper mills; joke questions about Porfirio Rubirosa—Woody can't keep track of how many times he has answered the same questions with a smirk and a wink. But it works. These guys are his constituency.

He can glad-hand them in his sleep. They probably all have man crushes on him in the first place.

Not surprisingly, today's focus is on the Russian beauty in the shower.

"Never saw her before," Woody lies transparently. "Especially not in any compromised position of an equestrian nature."

A smirk and a wink as the frat house chuckles around him.

"I think comparisons are silly, and I certainly don't want to make the horse feel inadequate," he concludes to the universal merriment of his lads.

He's not so comfortable with the ladies. It's not that they are less lazy than the men or that they ask more insightful questions or that they are more tenacious. The problem is that while each one is asking her question, the computer in Woody's head is clicking away like crazy, running through a huge database trying to remember whether he's slept with her or not. He's getting on. He's feeling his years. His facial recognition protocol is not working that great.

That bitch from the *Christian Science Monitor* steps up to the microphone. He has no doubts about this one. Even if he didn't remember her, the look in her eye says loud and clear, *You didn't do me, and you never will.* She asks him a detailed question about the next fiscal quarter.

Woody can see her lips flap but he hears nothing. He's got something else on his mind. He doesn't know why it should happen at this particular moment—maybe it was seeing her face again—but, for whatever reason, there is something bad going on in his pants. This has never happened before. Since the surgery, Mr. Pepé has shown a propensity to the diminutive, but, up until now, he has never gone quite so micro. At this moment he has practically disappeared. Even though Woody is circumspect and circumcised, it's as if a foreskin on steroids had swallowed his penis whole, and, although small in stature, Mr. Pepé is still home to millions of nerve endings. The resulting sensations are an excruciating tickling and pinching at the same time—a sweet and sour poke. What he wouldn't give to be standing behind a podium. But the designer went with open concept today. There is no way he can make any adjustments at this time. He is quickly in such discomfort that he can feel tears forming in the corners of his eyes.

The reporter repeats the question.

Woody clicks on the autopilot.

"Despite a flaccid market," he says, "we are confident that future growth and rock-hard fundaments will result—after an intense injection of resources—in a universal release of liquid assets."

There is no follow-up. Miss *Christian Science Monitor* is scribbling in her notepad. Mary Margaret is laughing so hard that she is snorting and she can't stop.

29.
SVETLANA

IN THE *HELL HATH NO FURY* DEPARTMENT, Svetlana is on hold with the Centers for Disease Control and Prevention in Atlanta. She is now staying at a cousin's house in Brighton Beach. She can't go back to where she was before. She blames Gerhardt for that—she blames Gerhardt for everything. She was humiliated before the world. She hasn't yet decided what disgusting apocalyptic superbug she is going to infect Gerhardt with, but she hopes whatever she picks will come with a long quarantine and multiple rough cleanings with brushes on pink, raw skin. She would prefer a flesh-eating bacterium, of course, but those symptoms aren't ambiguous enough to get him locked up.

When you are on hold with the CDC you get so much dire health information from their running commentary that you are soon itching all over. Svetlana grabs her iPad and googles herself to pass the time. She is pleased to note the huge uptick in the result count—until she works through the list—sorted by most popular. *How can she walk?* one blogger wonders. This concern is shared by many others. There are fake sympathy cards along with fake sciencey-looking charts and illustrations showing the difficulty of fitting an Olympian-god penis into a human-woman-sized vagina. There's even an obviously photoshopped classical masterpiece *Svetlana and the Swan,* à la François Boucher, which has been turned into a triptych—swan checking out her girl bits—Mister Ed the talking horse wide-eyed and speechless scoping out the fowl siege weapon. On the right side of the screen there are sponsored links. The top of the list is *DoesItHurtDownThere.com.*

She is so angry that she slams down the phone. She types in: *how do I get even and not get caught?* Her red hot ears are steam geysers. She taps Find. *Ask.com* returns 45,000 suggestions. After she taps on the top of the list—*snarky-revenge.fu*—it takes her a little while to figure out what she's looking at. She taps on the Gallery tab and sees a bunch of thumbnails. She taps on one and downloads a jpeg of a fat bride with her feet up and legs spread wide over her head sitting in a wedding cake. She taps the > symbol, and it's a large guy in a football uniform looking to his left unaware that a black Newfoundland is taking a leak on his right leg. She taps on Categories and pulls down to Brothers-in-Law. There's a guy with a beer belly standing in a swimming pool with an eddy of something brown swirling around his waist. There's an Ichabod Crane look-alike in a top hat with a crow standing on it taking a dump on Ichabod's nose. There's a picture of her ex-faux-boyfriend, the star of *Roto-Robber VII 3-D,* passed out in a Barcelona chair with penises drawn on his cheeks in Sharpie.

"This is a great site," Svetlana says as she taps on the Let's Get Started button.

That launches the Snarky Revenge Wizard.

Hello, I am Medea. I am here to help you get even with that:

O Bastard
O Bitch

Svetlana works through the questionnaire and builds a virtual Tool Kit along with a helpful Suggestion Box:

1) Size does matter
2) It matters a whole bunch
3) It's all that matters
4) It's the alpha and omega
5) Don't make me laugh

Finding the press kit for the SteeleX event in Japan takes no time. She downloads a profile shot of Woody in his trunks holding the bathtub brush against his shoulder like a rifle. Then she scrolls through the royalty-free Snarky Revenge Clip Art Library.

"Perfect," she delights as she drags and drops. "What fun."

All the tools are intuitive. It only takes her a few minutes to build the image. She puts her hands behind her head and admires her handiwork. We are living in the golden age of fraud. The photo looks so real that Svetlana almost believes that she was there when it was taken—and she was there.

Woody is standing on the stage at the Fukushima power plant. A team of scientists in white lab coats is crouching in front of him. They are all holding huge magnifying glasses—obviously trying very hard to find something microscopic in his crotch—excellent. *Vengeance is mine sayeth Svetlana.* She is laughing out loud when she taps the Publish button.

30.
VICTORIA

SHE IS WAITING FOR THE LIGHT to change so that she can cross West End Avenue. She stands idly by as it cycles through four times before she notices the walky man brighten up. She's zoned out. She is stressed out. She is spiraling out of control. It is D-day minus ten. Her mother will be here—right here—on these shores—on this island—on this street—in just ten days. She tries to look on the positive side of things, but there isn't one. The decorators are woefully behind. She doesn't care about the family quarters, but she needs at least a finished dungeon if she hopes to open for business on time. But even if the paint is dry, everything coming from Brooklyn Leather Restraints is on back order. The Iron Maiden has a faulty vacuum pump. None of the latex wear is hypoallergenic, as promised. All the enema bags are from the States, but the tubing is metric, which results in a huge puddle before things even get started. The X-frames are warped and tend to fall over without warning. Half of the floggers are fabricated from some kind of cheap leatherette that has no sting at all and—can you believe it—the *Made in the USA* canes are Teflon-coated to "minimize discomfort and reduce embarrassing *day-after* welts." What a country!

But these little niggling irritants are just gnats on a summer's eve. The omnipresent, onerous dread hanging over her head is the marker that she didn't sign over to Uncle Sid, who possibly is her father, or, if not that, the one who plausibly did her father in. Whatever the relationship, Sid will have no compunction in making her life—or body—very uncomfortable if required to do so to support his business model. Victoria feels like she's going to blow chunks right in front of her own building. How embarrassing would that be?

With a heavy foot, she plods into the lobby. She sees that sweet boy from the basement. Good. She owes him an apology. Sadly, before she can catch up with him, he evaporates into thin air. She goes to the mailboxes. There is a letter from her mother. Like a dope she opens and reads it where she stands. It is four pages long in her tight, cramped, angry hand. It is an itemized critique of everything that her daughter has done wrong to date. Victoria wants to kill herself—but then she sees the boy across the lobby.

She catches his eye. They both freeze. They share an afternoon's conversation in three blinks. When she feels his mortification, she starts to cry. It takes a minute to find her hankie.

"I'm so sorry," she says as she dabs her eyes.

When she looks up again he is gone and she is in the bottom of a deep trench and the sand is starting to begin the burial process. She goes up to the flat. She runs the bath. She takes off her clothes and slips into a bottle of whisky.

Sometime later she puts on her most favorite robe. Kaftans pair well with whisky.

Sometime after that she turns off the tub. She grabs all the towels out of the linen closet and throws them down in the overflow on the tile floor. She does a little peasant dance on them to help them sop up the spill.

Sometime later she goes into the kitchen to cook something. She eats a small jar of peanut butter with a spoon.

Sometime later she wakes up with a stuffy mouth. It's really horrible. She drinks a glass of water. It tastes bad. She opens a bottle of Champagne and has a couple of flutes. That is surprisingly refreshing.

Sometime after that she wakes up and she is very sad—sadder than even before. She slides her bare feet into her rubber Wellies. She drops her house key into the right boot. She goes to the desk and writes a note: "Key in right one." She stuffs the note in her left boot. She closes the door to the flat and tugs on the knob eight or nine times to make sure that it is locked tight. She takes the elevator to the basement.

Victoria doesn't get lost this time. She walks straight—not a stagger in the beeline—to Tim's *pied-à-sous-la-terre*. She knocks on the door and says in her gruffest voice, "Busted pipe."

She doesn't knock a second time. She can hear movement inside the basement apartment. He is pulling on a robe when he opens the door.

Victoria doesn't even wait to see the surprise register on his face. She pushes past him, pulling the kaftan off over her head. She slips into the rumpled sheets of the futon. She spreads her arms and looks up at him and says, "Please."

He looks confused and uncertain.

"Please," she repeats.

Tim's face loses expression. He turns off the light and settles down next to her.

"Please," Victoria says a third time, and this time he takes her in his arms.

They lie still together as their breathing coordinates. It is a process. They settle in—skin finding skin. She sinks lower as some—not nearly all—but some tension leaves her body.

"Thank you," she says as she turns and puts her face into his chest and weeps.

Sometime later she wakes briefly. When she sees that she is now wearing Thomas the Tank Engine pajamas, she squeezes the boy and drifts off into an even happier place.

31.
MARY MARGARET

MARY MARGARET IS IN HER CUPERTINO office putting the annual report to bed. This is her seventh year as COO and her ninth signing off on the yearly corporate version of fantasy football. It's no big deal. This is not what's making her anxious, although it is what she's taking it out on. She has twisted up the dummy markup she was thumbing through into a very tight roll, and she is wringing its neck as she studies her computer screen with dismay.

Next to Woody's, hers is the largest office on the campus—a huge number of square feet that still feels crowded. It's the vibe—the ambient hum of too much thinking going on all around. As a rule, she is not fond of Silicon Valley—overpopulated as it by all those brilliant minds whirring away and spinning out of control—and each and every one is some kind of a jerk. Today she was in a Porsche-only traffic jam. At least for the most part they are all guys. Mary Margaret prefers working with guys. They're good with code, and they think with their dicks, but other than that, they're just stupid. Thank God for stupid. That's why she won't let Woody bump her up to CEO. She would rather eat rat poison than have to sit on one of those panels with clever names like *Valley of the Dolls: Women & Tech*. Yuck.

Speak of the devil. Woody galumphs into her office eating a bagel. Watching him move, Mary Margaret can think of no other descriptive for him at this moment than the *big galoot*.

"Did you know that everything in your cafeteria is free?" he asks as he wipes a smear of cream cheese from his cheek. "How can you afford to keep the doors open?"

Mugs will not be distracted. "Look at this," she says, pointing at her computer screen.

"I've seen it," Woody replies. "I remember that trip to Japan, but I can't say that I recall a bunch of white coats with magnifying glasses. Don't tell me I've started drinking again."

He grins. Mugs looks glum.

"It hasn't *just* gone viral," she explains. "It's pandemic."

"Lucky for me it's my good side," he says, popping the last bagel bit into his mouth.

"There's nothing good about this," she says dourly.

"It's just a joke," he says.

"There's no such thing as just a joke," she says. "Especially down there."

"I'm not so thin-skinned." Woody shakes it off. "It doesn't bother me."

"This is not about *you*," Mugs says with an edge to her voice. "It's about the brand."

She clicks on Woody's Facebook page and scrolls through images of daredevilry and extreme moves—each one more life-threatening than the last—each accompanied by thousands of starry-eyed comments swooning at his manly prowess. Mary Margaret pauses at the post celebrating the day he broke a land speed record. Woody is displayed standing next to a massive mucho macho turbocharged twelve-cylinder stretch motorcycle on the Bonneville Salt Flats. He is in full body armor and a state-of-the-art piece of protective headgear. There are over five million *Likes* on this post.

"How do you think your fans would react if they knew your dick could protect itself with a thimble?" Mary Margaret says flatly.

Woody deflates. He looks tired. Mugs picks up her phone and punches numbers.

"Send him in," she commands into the phone. Then she turns to Woody and explains, "He's our best forensics guy."

He must have been waiting just outside the door because he is in there instantaneously. Definitely from a low pizza orbit in the Geek Galaxy, fat boy lacks the grace to even tuck his shirt in when he walks into the executive suite.

"I'm on lunch," he says blithely.

"Where did that come from?" Mary Margaret says, pointing at the offending jpeg.

"May I?" he says.

She steps away from her computer and the techie drops down into her chair—the pneumatics resigning with a sigh as fat boy sinks down so low that he can rest his chin on her desk. His fingers are rattling the keys before he hits bottom.

Mugs and Woody stand back and watch him work with the same awkwardness as if he were a Martian fixing his flying saucer that broke down in their backyard.

"That's lovely," he says after a few minutes. "Fucking beautiful."

He stops typing and cracks his knuckles. Leaning back in the chair, he puts his hands behind his head.

"I've read about it," he explains. "But I hadn't see it in action."

"What?" Mary Margaret asks.

He spins around in the chair, which groans in protest.

"The picture of our illustrious leader was posted on Snarky Revenge, as we know," he starts. "But how it got there is the interesting bit. It's a start-up called ColdTrail, and as far as I can tell it's every bit as wicked cool as advertised. It's an anonymous proxy site, but the best ever. It's a server farm of host machines with localized variables so that the logging IP address can't be traced, and if it could be, which it can't, the encryption changes between each and every packet."

Mary Margaret wields the rolled up annual report and whacks him on the back of the head. "Eugene. Speak English."

The computer nerd takes a moment to get his breath back.

"As you know," he begins slowly and methodically, "up until now whatever you did on the Internet left a trail. Wherever you went you left Hansel and Gretel breadcrumbs showing where you were going and where you had come from. Got that much?"

"Got it," Mary Margaret replies.

"ColdTrail.com is a new web site that lets you do things without your fingerprints ever touching it," Eugene explains.

"How?" Woody asks.

"Too complicated for mere mortals like you," Eugene says.

"In layman's terms," Mary Margaret demands.

Eugene scrunches up his face and thinks.

"It's like your neighbor is on the Internet, and you are standing outside looking in his open window," he begins. "You whisper what you want him to do, and he does it. At the end of the session—whatever you have done or looked at—you just walk away. Nothing sticks to you. If anyone gets arrested, it's your neighbor."

Woody and Mary Margaret look at each other, unsure what to think.

"If I had the money and connections," Eugene adds, "I would definitely make a play for the IPO."

"Who's taking it public?" Woody asks.

"Don't you know?" Eugene is in shock. "It's the Raging Hard-On's wife."

"Greenbriar?" Mary Margaret asks.

Woody is speechless.

Eugene is back at the computer—lost in his own world.

"If this code had a pussy," he says to himself, "I would marry it."

32. MACKENZIE

MACKENZIE, TROPHY WIFE extraordinaire, is on her best behavior. She is in the belly of the beast. She has made a cut—but not the prime one. Although finally sitting on the board of directors for The Shiny Penny Foundation—that took all of two weeks—she's below low man. In reality, she's the espadrilles on the totem pole. *Thanks for the check. Take a seat in the back, and nod in agreement when we look at you.* The board meets in a conference room in a largely deserted floor that makes up their clubhouse in the Ascii Building—the corporate headquarters of the company owned by Boss Lady's husband. Mackenzie realizes that for this venture to succeed Ivan will have to buy him out or leverage a takeover. There can't be two boss ladies in any successful not-for-profit, which is perhaps the most cutthroat enterprise of them all.

She really did try to put names to faces—she's pored through those tiny gala benefit photos in the *New York Social Diary*—but they all look the same. It's just impossible to tell them apart. Yet she has to do something if she wants to win hearts and minds, so she goes all Linnaeus and classifies them into a system of mnemonics. First of all, she breaks the group down generationally. That's easy. There are the younger trophy wives and then the ladies of a certain age who have passed It (for *It,* read menopause). Those are easy enough to spot by their shiny, tight skin, and while they might not be related by blood, they sure are by plastic surgeon. So there's Epstein One, Epstein Two, Epstein Three, and the Rothman Twins.

The younger ones in the trophy case can be broken down by degree of enthusiasm. There's the perky and the blasé. It's hard to decide which are more irritating. By inclination, Mackenzie generally prefers the blasé because they tend to be so overcome by inertial forces that they won't hound you into doing something that requires any effort. The jolly hockey sticks crowd, on the other hand, is on a perpetual campaign to get you to jump into a freezing Maine lake before you've had your morning cup of coffee. She assigns names to these women, matching their personalities to cherished characters from her youth. In the *turn that frown upside down* group, there's Pippi Longstocking, Pollyanna, and Becky Thatcher—she really looks like Tom Sawyer's Becky—a teacher's pet ready to rat you out in class but a total pussy in caves. On the dark side, Mackenzie registers Camille, White Fang, and Eeyore. When she takes a moment to review her choices, she realizes that the similarities are shocking and the resemblances uncanny. She does not bother classifying Boss Lady—soon to be Boss Lady Emeritus—if things work out.

At the previous meeting, they closed out the Penny Miller file. It was not without bitterness and rancor. Now that she isn't going to die, the consensus is that she has been faking it all along. Eeyore contends that they were misled by the girl's mother. White Fang says that Penny Miller has to be at least thirty years old, and Camille insists there's proof that she used foundation money for a boob job. The Epsteins are mum on that point, but the Rothman Twins are irate—seemingly proud of their natural silhouettes. Mackenzie is unhappy because this new mood of distrust has inspired a rethink of future plans.

"If the next one is in a coma we won't have to worry about another disappointment," Pollyanna says.

"We'll have to focus-group the tubes and ventilator look," Boss Lady points out.

"It will be even cooler if she talks with a robot voice like that brainiac in the wheelchair," Becky Thatcher adds.

Pippi Longstocking stands up and puts her fists against her hips in an aggressive stance. "I want to sponsor a monkey," she demands.

By this point in the meeting, Mackenzie is missing the company of belittling, patronizing, and arrogant men. They at least make sense. She knows how to play that game. This mix of toxic venom laced with treacle is something foreign to her. But she soldiers on.

"The minutes from the last meeting will show," she begins once she has the floor, "that there was unanimous consent to throw the full weight of the foundation behind the effort to find a cure for EOIE."

"E I E I Oh" Pollyanna giggles.

"And on his farm he had some monkeys," Pippi Longstocking chants.

Mackenzie is beside herself. *Who are these people? And where do they come from?*

"The Chair notes Mrs. Greenbriar's reference to the minutes," the Boss Lady says in that officious voice of hers that got her to where she is today. "Early onset infantile ennui is still under discussion."

"Ennui sounds so boring," Eeyore groans.

"It sounds French," Pollyanna notes.

"If it's French, I can't have anything to do with it," Becky Thatcher says. "We're Republican."

"Does anyone move to table the condition, heartbreaking though it may be?" Boss Lady asks.

But before the gavel falls, there is a discreet knock. The receptionist pokes her head in and announces, "Delivery for Mrs. Greenbriar."

A woman carrying a small baby walks into the conference room. Mackenzie goes to meet her.

"Thank you so much," the woman says on the verge of tears. "My husband is on a flight to Reykjavik. God bless you."

"Not here. Not now," Mackenzie whispers as she takes the baby.

The woman nods and leaves, closing the door behind her.

Mackenzie stands beside Boss Lady. She is holding the baby properly—with confidence. She's ready. She has practiced for hours with a Tickle Me Elmo.

"Ladies," she announces. "Please allow me to introduce James."

Holding him under his armpits, she stands Joyless James up on his little baby shoes. At first, he seems interested in his fingers exploring his mouth and nose—but that is fleeting. When he looks up and gazes upon the ladies, it is obvious that he is interested in nothing. The ladies gasp as they take in the powerful depth of his disinterest. But that is just the tip of the iceberg. While his disinterest is profound, it can't hold a candle to the dark cloud of nihilism that the tot exudes like a poisonous mist. The ladies are laid low. He waves a hand at them and they are dismissed, as if by the rudest headwaiter in the most expensive restaurant on the Left Bank. The mood in the room turns on a dime, and it will take millions of dollars to claw their way out.

Mackenzie holds out an open palm. Boss Lady places the gavel onto it.

33.
IVAN

THE THIRD RICHEST MAN in America and his trophy wife are enjoying an intimate evening in their published country hideaway in Bedford Hills. They are swirling the rich amber perfection of a Cognac from his vineyard in Champagne-Vigny in massive snifters that look like they are nine months pregnant. The roaring fire is Ivan's only comfort. It's been a mutual bore fest listening to her try to discuss brandy intelligently, but that was a stoner comedy compared to Mackenzie's litany on early onset infantile ennui. Ivan could kick himself for his newest stupidest idea ever—which one is that again?—getting remarried or trying to make her a proper socialite wife.

Which is not to say that she is not perfect as she is right now. Her start-up is going gangbusters. It might even turn a profit in this fiscal century. The IPO will be great, of course. It has to be. Retail investors are morons—no—they're sheep. BAAA.

The fire pops.

She sighs.

He sighs.

"We should get away," he suggests.

"Yes, we should," she replies.

Is she thinking from each other *at the very same moment as I am?* Ivan wonders.

"We should do something with your children," she says.

"You only want to do that because they like you better than me," he panders.

"Well," she thinks for a moment. "I do get their names right, unlike some."

"There you go," he says.

They smile blandly at each other. Time passes. Brandy swirls. The fire spits. Ivan stands up and puts his snifter down.

"Nature calls," he announces.

He walks down the corridor toward the living quarters, passing the powder room, which is close by. Up three steps and turning to the left he disappears from view. Taking a covert detour, he slips silently into his office in the dark and hits the space bar to wake up the computer, then clicks on the seditious picture. He can't stay away. It pops open, filling half the screen with Woody and none of it with Woody's famous dick. Ivan is gleeful like a five-year-old watching a cherished Disney cartoon over and over again, enjoying it more and more with each viewing. He studies Woody's bullshit ruggedly handsome face, looking for telltale signs of insecurity, but he can't find them—yet. He will. There are no secrets from the Raging Hard-On.

After a sharp click of a wall switch, he is temporarily blinded as the full array of ceiling lights kick on.

"Sorry," Mackenzie says as she dims them down. "I just wanted to make sure you didn't have another woman hidden in here."

"You know that will never happen, my chic shiksa," Ivan mutters, failing entirely in his effort to make it sound flirtatious. "There's that poison pill in the prenup—'til debt do us part."

"So why are you sitting in the dark, sweetest darling?" she asks as she walks around to perch next to her husband. "Kosher porn, or something fun?"

"I'm actually working," Ivan says defensively.

"And so you are," Mackenzie concedes once she takes in what's on the screen. "This must be the notorious download du jour."

Ivan squints up his eyes and reads the small print. "Over thirty-five million views so far today."

"It's obviously a fake," she says.

"Of course it's a fake," he replies, barely concealing his irritation. "But whose fake?"

"Still," his wife says, bending over for a better look. "He's got one heck of a profile."

"It could be an inside job," he muses, right-clicking all over the image, looking for any clue. "There's no meta data."

"Do you want me to find out where it comes from?" Mackenzie asks innocently.

"I will do that," Ivan flashes. "You can count on it."

His wife shudders at that. "So sorry, Sahib," she responds deferentially. "Wife-saab only trying to help her Lord and Master."

Ivan has to fake sincere laughter at this. When they were dating they did this role-playing thingie in Mumbai. It got really hot and heavy. Whatever the mood is in the room tonight, he is required to revere that piece of courtship history with official fondness. Unofficially he also remembers that they had to throw out the sari they ruined at the end, and it was expensive.

"I will get to the bottom of this," he says as he starts to surf with a vengeance.

"I'm sure you will, dear," she says, already ahead of him as she works the problem on her phone.

"They can run but they cannot hide," he clichés. "Ours is a very small fraternity."

"That's the problem in a word." Mackenzie sighs to herself.

"What word?" he asks.

"Fraternity," she replies.

"I'm sure you're right," he says, drifting off into his computer.

Many minutes later, when Ivan has a technical question about

FTP protocols, he realizes that his wife has left the room. He goes to the door and looks down the corridor. The coast is clear. He returns to his desk and opens a bottom drawer. He pulls out an illegally obtained draft version of the annual report for SteeleX International and drops it with a plop onto his In basket. Then he reaches back into the drawer and pulls out a silk scarf. He shakes it open and puts his nose against the question mark in the center of the reverse side. Sniffing deeply, he tries to recognize the perfumer. Does he own it—yet?

34. SVETLANA

SHE IS ABOUT AS FAR NORTH as you can go on Manhattan Island, in Inwood, just south of Washington Heights. This isn't Sutton Place, Central Park West, or even Brooklyn—neighborhoods that she is familiar with. This is unexplored territory for her. The streets are dark and forbidding. She has the feeling that she is being followed. More than once she doubles back, convinced that she spied a tall dark stranger clad all in black—even his face—or was it a shadow in a doorway? Of course she is paranoid. It's in her Russian DNA—Moscow Rules.

She breathes a sigh of relief and slips into her destination, a stuffy meeting room at the YMCA. The Russian beauty can feel a bead of sweat gently slalom down between her shoulder blades. She knows that this is a minor event so she isn't shocked that they didn't send her agent. In reality she hasn't been in contact with her agent since a certain talking horse rudely ended their last phone call. But Svetlana is surprised that they sent anybody at all, even if he's only an intern.

"I loved your last film," he gushes when they meet. "I thought it was great, despite what they said."

"Fawning is even more effective if you can avoid using words like *despite*," she replies.

The boy blushes. Svetlana feels bad and apologizes.

They are sitting on uncomfortable, squeaky folding chairs, trying to keep awake through a tedious presentation about the apocalypse. They have to stay through to the bitter end because Svetlana has lines. She has reunited with her old eco-friends at the Something Something Something Environmental Action Committee for the Something. She has a strong bond with these people and shares their commitment to make everything that's bad, better. She also feels guilty. Understandably, they took a bad hit in the publicity department when Svetlana's *boyfriend* [air quotes] left the organization. It probably didn't help that at the time Svetlana referred to him as a friend who happened to be a *boy* [air quotes]. For that cheap rimshot then, she's making amends now—an act of contrition.

After a series of slides of melting ice caps, Svetlana wants a gin and tonic something chronic. She scans the room to take her mind off her thirst. It's the classic collection of the über-politically correct thinking Upper Upper West Side. You've got your cat ladies, which are kind of like the chicken stock for this sort of meeting. There's the earnest quasi-Bolshie crowd that thrives in argument even when you are on their side, along with assorted cranks and crackpots. Also, like a pod of whales or a parliament of owls, there is a smattering of the press. As far as Svetlana can guess, they are reporters from the local *PennySaver* as well as overachieving students from the local high school. She thinks she recognizes a guy from Channel 12, but, even if it is him, that's immaterial because she sees no camera.

Around the room there is a general shifting and stretching as the speaker changes and a new topic comes in on little cat's feet spreading like a narcoleptic fog. Svetlana knows that she's on next, so to marshal her resources she takes a little phone break—good time to do a little research. This evening's topic—Mackenzie Greenbriar.

Holding her phone discreetly between her knees like most everyone else in the room, including the last two presenters, she scrolls through a long queue of query results. She taps on a thumbnail and looks Mackenzie in the eye. Not bad. Not great. Not stylish. Rather conventional. Not striking, although pretty enough. But Svetlana is uninterested in anything else about her appearance. She moves on quickly. This woman is not a rival. Svetlana has no intention of replacing her. She is no home wrecker—at least not this month. She just wants the woman's husband to buy a major motion picture studio. If it all works out they will probably end up being friends—like sisters.

She is very impressed by Mackenzie's resume as well as by her recent extracurricular activities. Of course she would be—Svetlana has been a feminist in two films—both indies—which means they were sincere and heartfelt. Altruism? Svetlana can play that too.

"Five minutes, Miss Petracova," the intern whispers.

"You're sweet," she says, squeezing his knee.

Then she seems to go catatonic.

But she wakes up right on cue as the current speaker staggers to a conclusion. Svetlana collects her notes, which are blank pieces of paper—she's a notoriously fast study—and walks to the lectern. She stands for a moment—statuesque despite the seedy surroundings—ignoring the quadraphonic sound of mouth breathers. She seems to look in the eyes of each and every one in the room before she declares her subject.

"Ocean acidification," she announces and pauses to allow the collective gasp to wash over the place.

Thank you, Jesus, she gives a silent hallelujah as the guy from Channel 12 pulls out a camcorder and points it her way.

The rest is forgotten as quickly as the words fly out of her mouth and melt like snowflakes in a May shower. She remembers nothing—except that she gets the most enthusiastic applause of the evening—and that during the Q&A she gets all the questions.

Let the parry and thrust begin.

"Svetlana, how's Woody?"

"Woody who?"

"He had a shower in Fukushima."

"Oh, that Woody!"

"Correction: You had a shower in Fukushima—naked."

Gentlemen, put on your protective eyewear. Svetlana is about to release the dental powerhouse. She parts her lips.

"I'll always go clean for green," she says, blinding everyone in the room with her smile.

She pulls open the neck of her loose chemise, revealing a shoulder and rotates it in a vamp. Then she laughs when Channel 12 almost drops his camera.

"Last question?" Svetlana says as she adjusts her clothing.

"I have one," declares an elderly woman in a jumper covered with a dozen appliqués of cats—their names embroidered underneath each one.

"Ask away," Svetlana acknowledges.

"It was a lovely speech, darling," the woman says, "as lovely as you are, dear . . ."

"Thank you," Svetlana responds.

"But do you actually believe a single word of what you are saying," the woman continues, "or are you only here because your career is in the toilet?"

Svetlana switches gears so fast that you can hear ears pop throughout the room. She skids into her serious face, but takes a moment to reset.

"It's not about me," she finally says. "It's about the children."

She takes another moment. She pans from face to face.

"We are not just talking about losing fish," she explains. "We are talking about our babies losing joy."

She looks up at the Channel 12 guy. *Getting this?* He nods.

Svetlana is ready for her close-up, Mr. DeMille.

"This is all about the science." She is talking directly into the camera now. She waves her blank pieces of paper. "The report makes a direct link between ocean acidification and early onset infantile ennui. It's all about the children."

35.
TIM

THE YOUNGEST BUILDING SUPER on West End Avenue and the only one who's been tied up by a transvestite—without paying for it—is standing in an antique claw-foot bathtub studying a leak in the ceiling that's making a mess on the Persian rug beneath it. The source of the leak, which is halfway between a drip and a waterfall, is obvious. The mystery, on the other hand, is—and remember, Tim is not a design junkie, but this one gets even his attention—why would anyone have Persian rugs in the bathroom?

"Where is it coming from?" Mr. 11B asks.

He and the fretting Mrs. 11B are standing clutching hands, looking strained and anxious as if he had just asked his oncologist, "How long do I have, Doc?"

"From above," Tim replies, pointing up and trying to maintain a brave face.

He knows what's up there, and it scares him. But he is also a bad actor. The 11Bs look up to the ceiling, staring at it—trying to see through the floor to the goblins, dragons, and spiders—one floor up.

"Is there anything you can do?" Mrs. 11B asks with a bit of a quiver in her voice.

"I will go upstairs," Tim answers as he climbs out of the tub. "It's just like pulling off a bandage fast or yanking a tooth."

"Excuse me?" she says.

"You haven't met Mr. Pavlenko," Tim observes. "Have you?"

"No, we haven't," her husband replies.

"I have," Tim says. "Wish me luck." He spontaneously shakes hands with the grown-ups and marches off with a resigned look on his face—not of an ironic or cathartic resignation. It's a *next stop the guillotine* look of resignation.

He has to go down before he goes up. The penthouse has its own private elevator. In fact, the penthouse has its own frame of reference—of the building yet not "of the building." His mind drifts to thoughts about ambiguity—then the liar's paradox. Tim's head is getting hot to the touch. Of all the hateful things he has to do on his job—and some of them are quite disgusting—the thing he dreads the most is having to ring the penthouse doorbell. No! No. There is something he fears more than that—having anything to do with Mr. Pavlenko—on any level, real or imagined. Just two nights ago Mr. Pavlenko sneaked his way into one of Tim's dreams. He just popped up in there. It had been a fine night's sleep until that moment, and then—boom—there he was. That was so unfair. Tim woke up screaming, "I'm off the clock. I'm off the clock."

By this point in his life, Tim has ridden this elevator hundreds of times, both up and down, yet he still can't shake the habit of watching the numbers above the door move up or down. It's a moronic exercise, but he can't help it: 9-8-7. Then he experiences a brand-new terror as the elevator stops. The doors open. Then she steps in. Both he and the girl share a spontaneous awkward gulp. The elevator cab is a small space, but Tim and Victoria seem to maximize it as they plant themselves in the most distant corners available.

5-4-3.

"Um," she says.

"Yes?" he asks.

He looks at her. She shakes it off. "Nothing."

Tim cannot bear it any longer. He looks at her and explains, "Busted pipe."

She chews on that a minute. Remembers. Grins. He breaks out a smile. She leans into him and kisses him lightly on the lips just as the elevator doors open.

"You're sweet," Victoria says as she steps out.

That is the last thing he wants to hear. As he pushes the button for the express elevator next door, Tim can feel a new black cloud building over his head. Sweet? That word doesn't stand in for *great* or *cool* or even *fuckable*. Sweet is the death sentence to a guy who wants a girl. Sweet is a gay boy friend remembering your birthday with a pedicure. Sweet is a sugary confection. *Oooh! Cupcakes!* Sweet is kind and considerate. Ultimately, sweet is dancing with really gross old people when they are wearing totally age-inappropriate dresses so that you can't help but touch their skin. Nothing good ever comes of being sweet.

He jabs at the button and looks up. In this elevator there's not much to choose from. There are only two buttons that work: L and PH. The others are there but they are disabled. This is a dedicated elevator. As the cab begins to rise, Tim's spirits continue to descend. He likes this girl very much. He hates that she thinks he is sweet. After he deals with—oh my God, he has reached his destination, the penthouse. The doors open and he is stepping out onto the twelfth floor. It is an older building, so the elevator does not open directly into the apartment. There is a lobby and one more button.

He presses it four or five times, counting thirty seconds between each ring.

"Mr. Pavlenko," he calls through the door after he reverts to knocking with his knuckles. "Mr. Pavlenko, please open the door."

Finally, he hears the familiar squeak of the left wheel of Mr. Pavlenko's wheelchair. As the frequency of the clicking speeds up, Tim steps away from the door as Mr. Pavlenko crashes into it. After the dust settles, Tim demurely raps on the door again.

"Mr. Pavlenko," he says. "It's the building superintendent. Please let me in."

"Go away," a gruff voice on the other side of the door barks.

"Don't be that way," he pleads. "You're leaking again."

"This is international zone. Go away. I have diplomatic immunity."

From past experience, Tim knows that once diplomatic immunity is invoked it's a losing proposition. "As you wish," he says and turns, stomping his feet loudly as he moves away from the door.

He calls the elevator. When it arrives, he sends it back down to the lobby. Then he recalls it. Once he hears the clear-toned ding of its arrival he walks back to the door and hits the buzzer again.

"Mr. Pavlenko," he says, two tones higher than before. "It's me. Tim from downstairs. You promised to tell me all about Stalingrad. Remember?"

Tim steps back as he hears the seven massive locks that secure the door being opened up one at a time.

36. WOODY

WOODY AND MARY MARGARET are riding in a common taxicab—shocking.

"Lighten up," Woody says. "Limos do break down. It happens."

She says nothing and gives him a sour look.

They are in Las Vegas. He's here to sponsor the US Women's Olympic Beach Volleyball Team. Generally he finds girl athletes a little too wholesome for his taste. He prefers ballet dancers, even if they do smoke like chimneys. But he doesn't mind watching beach volleyball—not one little bit.

"Remind me why you are here again?" he asks Mugs as they carry their own luggage up the stairs.

"I have a fiduciary responsibility to protect you from yourself," she replies. You can hear from the irritation in her voice that she's at her breaking point. She drops her bags and speaks directly into a security camera. "Excuse us."

That must have echoed in the bowels of the building. Instantaneously a dozen lackeys appear out of thin air and all of a sudden Woody and Mugs's feet no longer touch the ground. They are spirited up and into The SteeleX Pier—a forty-eight-story casino/

convention center attached to a replica of its 1908 namesake from Atlantic City and which juts out into a body of water that seems to flood The Strip.

"Slow down," Woody calls out once they hit the lobby.

It is clearly high tide and he wants to enjoy it. Eddies of babes and bimbos gather and swirl and pass by Jocks and Jills on a mission—all wearing the standard regulation beach volleyball uniform of a skimpy top and nonexistent bottom. Their tight buns and rippling abs roil the crowd as their chiseled cheeks cut through it—streamlined—and leave a wake.

"Don't make me slap you," Mugs hisses in his ear.

"I don't know what you're talking about," Woody replies.

As they step on the elevator the sycophantic operator says, "Glad to see that you still have it, sir?"

Woody and Mugs jump down his throat in unison. "What do you mean by that? Still have what?" they snarl at the guy who escapes through the closing doors in a panic.

The owner's suite is low-rent compared to the over-the-top fantasy theme parks upstairs where they put the high rollers. Woody likes it this way—modest—but he does still have a well-situated balcony to take in the sights. After they shoo away the worker bees, who are buzzing around obsessing over meaningless details, they open the French doors and look down over the pier.

"It's better than I hoped," Woody says, unable to hide his excitement as he points to a strip of pink, sandy beach alongside the man-made lagoon. "It's from Bermuda."

"Ludicrous," Mugs sniffs with contempt. "And so Vegas. Who else would ship sand to the desert?"

"Gawd," he groans. "I hate it when you go all flat-footed."

He stomps off to his room, and he can tell by the way that her door slams that he is not winning any friends today. But he is a guy. He can't stay angry for long—especially when smack dab in the center of such a high concentration of T&A. By the time he slips out of his street clothes and into swim trunks, he's ready to make a peace offering, and, in Mugs's case, he knows exactly what that is—a bourbon Manhattan with two cherries.

Woody is at the bar humming contentedly when she comes back in. She has on a severe business suit with a skirt and hose.

"Is that what you plan to wear?" she asks with no question intended.

"Did I forget an anniversary?" he replies with a smile as he pours his divine mixture into chilled glasses. "Oh, that's right. We're not married."

"You can't wear that," she says.

"For the first time I will say it a second time," he says as he hands her a drink. "Mugs, lighten up."

She tosses back the cocktail and hands him the empty glass. He bends over and kisses her.

"That's my girl," he says.

"No one can know," she explains in a quiet, hurt voice.

"Know what?" he asks as he dumps more bourbon and ice into the shaker.

She nods her head down toward his trunks.

"You're paranoid," he accuses as he starts mixing the next drink.

"Am I?" she pushes back. "Haven't you noticed that all the paparazzi have attached telephoto lenses to their cameras? And they aren't aiming them at your face."

"If anything, I'm heroic," he says, topping her up. "A cancer survivor."

"Sick and drunk are only attractive when you're young and pretty," she explains. She grabs her drink and starts to fire off bullet points on her fingertips.

"One: You have a reputation, and size does matter.

"Two: You are leveraged up the wazoo to buy Japan. Any weakness is death.

"Three: You've picked a fight with Raging Ivan at the wrong time."

"He started it," Woody interrupts.

"Be that as it may," Mugs replies, "he's ticked. He wants to hurt you."

She tosses the drink down and holds out the glass.

"But it works," Woody says.

"How can that be?" she asks.

"It must be all these girls," he explains. "I'm so horny. They must have jump-started it or something."

Mary Margaret gives him a searching look, then shrugs and reaches for her drink on the bar. "Did you take a pill?" she asks.

"Never again," he says. "But I don't need to." He grabs her wrist and presses her hand into his crotch. "See?"

"See what?"

"It's hard," Woody insists. "I can feel it."

She tries to take her hand away.

"It must be a phantom boner," she explains. "Like after you get your leg cut off and your toes hurt."

"You're wrong," he says. "It's real. Touch it."

Woody slides a hand between her legs.

"Like this," he croons as he applies pressure against her through the gusset of her pantyhose.

He does nothing to violate her clothing or her. He just touches her as she coached him that evening on Virgin Gorda.

"This is crazy," she protests.

He demonstrates the move but it is barely any move at all. His hand is practically stationary. It is she who starts going kinetic. Just a little in the beginning, but the rhythm clearly intensifies.

When her breathing changes, Woody knows that it's showtime. He doesn't change his technique, which is minimalist, but he does follow her lead.

As her body seems to clench and a slight gaspiness enters her breathing pattern, he is encouraged but concerned that his wrist will give out prematurely. But he grits his teeth. He ignores his discomfort and listens to her with everything he's got.

Then she stops breathing.

He studies her with concern.

Her eyes open and she looks into his eyes.

"Prestidigitation," she proclaims.

"It's just sleight of hand," the defeatist says.

"There's nothing slight about that at all," she says. "Take my word for it. You have a gift."

He perks up at that. "I do feel a certain connection these days," he admits. "Like I'm sticking my finger in an electrical outlet."

"I know you do," she says. "What's that all about?"

"I guess it's like how when you go blind you get heightened senses to compensate," he says.

"Like I said," she finally comments when her eyes uncross, "you've got moves."

"I call that one the Cement Mixer." Woody grins.

"Aptly named," she replies.

37. VICTORIA

WITH BARELY A WEEK TO GO before the grand opening, Victoria walks through the work site. The men are gone for the day. The rooms are quiet. The screams are all inside her head. She has never been under such pressure. Her bones ache. It looks like a war zone. The only walls completely painted have fresh holes in them for new switches and junction boxes. The rich, stained paneling and built-ins look cheesy when you can see the fresh, bright plywood that holds them all together. There are wires and cables everywhere—hanging from the ceiling—cascading down the walls—pooling all around the floors. Most of it is Ethernet connecting all the webcams that are omnidirectional. That's the sales pitch. Miss Lavinia's Townhouse will offer *24-Hour No Place to Hide*™ online streaming. That's the money shot. That's what won over the bankers. With cameras running all day long, there will be no secrets at Miss Lavinia's—well, maybe just one—the bankers don't know about Uncle Sid.

Victoria staggers through the maze of construction. Her mind races, reviewing every bad decision she's made in the last month—and her lifetime. They all seemed to be good ideas at the time, but now the only comfort she can cling to is finding new despairs to wallow in. Each room is worse than the last until she staggers into the most important place in the suite. She looks in through the door with trepidation, but then the dark clouds part, and there are bluebirds over the White Cliffs of Dover.

"It's you," she shrieks. "You've finally come."

Spreading her arms wide, she runs forward, hurling herself at the Iron Maiden, which is standing in the middle of the nearly finished torture chamber—only awaiting a floor—then wailing and anguish.

"I knew you wouldn't let me down." She sighs on the verge of tears, pressing her cheek into the large gal's ferrous neck—

Victoria jumps at the unexpected voice behind her.

"Would Madam care to meet the household?" the maid asks.

"Oh, it's you, Feefs," her Mistress acknowledges, turning to face her. "Why is your arm in a sling?"

"Tendonitis, Madam," the maid replies. "Overuse."

"I will meet the staff," Victoria announces. She's asked too much as it is. That's from *Mistressing 101* as taught by her mum. Keep things impersonal. If you show interest in the well-being of your gurls, things can get awkward at the whipping post.

Victoria has forgiven the contractor for disobeying orders. She is relieved that the family quarters are completed first. It affords her a tiny sanctuary in the midst of all this dirt and chaos. He won't be punished.

Fifi opens the door to the residence. The six maids that make up today's household staff are lined up along the wall of the gallery. They are wearing long frumpy dresses with poufy sleeves at the shoulders and long white aprons with wide straps and complicated ties in the back. Because of the huge popularity of a certain BBC soap opera in the States, Victoria has gone with an Edwardian theme. *Follow your market* is how it is taught at Wharton. Of course her mother thought that her idea was shite. Lavinia has done quite well with Belle Époque, thank you very much—but she has never been to the States. They fought on the phone like cats for weeks. The olive branch was a proof-in-the-pudding kind of thing, and Mummy promises to forgive her when the money starts rolling in. This puts Victoria farther out on a limb. By this point she is out on so many limbs that someone will have to chop her up so she can dangle from each one. Is that Uncle Sid's master plan? Victoria collects herself and walks past the maids—reminding herself to critique each of their curtsies.

"Thank you," she says in a practiced pro forma voice. On her way into the lounge she announces that she now will enjoy a refreshing beverage.

She tosses herself into an overstuffed club chair, grabs a pillow and hugs it tightly to herself as she practices deep breathing. It seems to work. Her heart rate slackens. The pounding in her head abates. The muscles in her neck finally ease up. She is actually starting to relax. When the door opens behind her she can smell the whisky—yummy single malt—but then she hears the tinkle of the chain links. She knows that they belong to a novice maid's manacles as surely as she is sitting in a room with a déjà vu. She watches it happen in her mind's eye. The high heel turns the ankle. The gurl goes down. The precious whisky is spilled. Now the ritual begins in front of her. The maids march in to witness. The guilty party bends over. Knickers go down. Cane comes out. Senior Parlour Maid officiates. *Feef's arm does seem tender,* Victoria notes.

After the pantomime has played out, she announces, "I will have my whisky with dinner."

The second Scotch seems to do a lot more to get her back to her previous meditative state than drumming her fingers on the table did. Even better, she actually has an appetite after all. Her eyes light up when one of the smaller gurls enters with a roasted leg of mutton on a platter overloaded with potatoes and carrots along with a cornucopia of other roots. Overloaded being the operative word, the maid is heels up long before she reaches the table.

The crash is louder than the dinner gong. In an instant there is a flock of maids fussing around the crash site. Victoria is tired and hungry. She leans over and stabs the mutton with a serving fork, drops it on her plate, and starts hacking at it. The determination of her chewing eclipses the goings-on around her as the errant maid bends over—pulls her knickers down, et cetera, et cetera.

After the gurls have withdrawn and Victoria is alone enjoying her brandy—a cigar might be good tonight, of all nights—there is a loud arpeggio of shattering glass somewhere nearby.

Fifi sticks her head in the door. "That was your mother's Waterford," she says. "The gurl will be punished."

Victoria is on her feet. "Enough," she roars. "Everyone in here now."

The maids scurry into the dining room, their heels clicking on the hardwood floor.

"All but one," Fifi says.

Victoria doesn't wait. "I get it," she begins. "I know why you're here. But please show a little patience. When you leave tomorrow your arse will be covered with welts. I guarantee it, but—"

She pauses a moment before she pleads, "Stop breaking all my stuff."

Silence. All the gurls look at the floor.

There is a tiny knock. One of the maids opens the door. The tardy one enters carrying the coffee service—a huge tray with all Lavinia's Spode. The gurl stops in the center of the room. Looking directly at Victoria, she releases her grip on the tray. It crashes to the floor.

"Oops," she frets as her palms go to her cheeks and her red lips make a perfect O. "What will you ever do to me now? Oh dear."

38.
IVAN

IT IS A LOVELY DAY IN SAN JOSE. The temperature is a perfect California mid-seventyish. The sun is shining. The sky is blue. Our Raging Ivan is sitting in a box overlooking center court in the USYS Community Tennis Center.

"Enjoy those naming rights while they last," he thinks aloud—no one is listening—he is alone in the box. He didn't have to make a special trip to watch this tennis match. He could have streamed it on his computer, but he wanted to feel, taste, and touch the humiliation firsthand—up close and personal.

He fusses with his phone. He has just downloaded a new app called *SpyGlass*, and it's not working as advertised. Ivan's got a two-track mind. Whenever the right side of his brain is troubleshooting a problem, the left hemisphere is working up a class action suit to nail the bastards that sold this crap to an unsuspecting public. But there will be no litigation today. After Ivan follows the prompt that has been flashing at him for the last couple of minutes, the app starts up fine. It's pretty cool, if he has to say so himself. It turns his phone into a 15-55X pocket telescope. Ignoring the ongoing match below, he methodically scans the spectators across the way, coming to a screeching stop as he spots his prey—Tom Hasbrook, CEO of USYS Integrated—he who dared to be inhospitable to Ivan's hostile takeover attempt.

Ivan zooms in. Even from the other side of the stadium you can see that proud Papa is about to pop his buttons. When he waves to someone, Ivan zips down his sight line and lands on the ground behind the referee. There they are—the famous Hasbrook twins—Patti and Lotti—number-two seed in the Junior National's Girls Doubles—so cute. They are idents wearing nearly matching outfits, except that one has purple stripes and the other's got a pink thing going on. If he weren't a sociopath and had any sense of empathy, Ivan would feel bad that last night he used a proxy Twitter account to rename them the Potti Twins—and even worse—that it went viral and all their classmates spent the entire day tormenting the unfairly bullied sisters.

The current match ends uneventfully. Someone wins and the other guys lose. Nobody seems to care. Ivan certainly doesn't. His phone buzzes. It's a text from an Internet private eye Ivan hired to find out who photoshopped the embarrassing Woody meme. He taps on it.

re steele micro penis jpeg, reverse engring dies at coldtrail.com

Ivan texts back, *dead dead?*

deader than a door nail. best anonymous site on web. ever!!!

Ivan is impressed. This guy is a tough customer. He doesn't bandy about exclamation marks like a schoolgirl. With this stamp of approval, Ivan will have to take his wife's start-up seriously in the future. Maybe pump a little—a lot—more money into it. Obviously her hobby isn't a suburban wife's gluten-free yarn store.

He looks up as the Hasbrook twins take the court. Ivan smiles when the announcer is overly careful pronouncing their names and then continues, "Ladies and gentlemen, we have a substitution. Playing for Javorka Tmiziri and Saloni Chatterji are Janet Jones and Samantha Smith from Palo Alto, California."

There is no more than polite applause from the spectators

because no one knows anything about them—that is, no one except for Ivan. He should know plenty because he paid for their fake passports and flew them in from Albania. They're ringers.

The match begins with the Hasbrook twins serving. Ivan's cell vibrates. It's his favorite insider trader.

"They're moving tons of paper," he reports. "By the truckload."

This is an important call. Ivan scrunches up his eyes and pulls down a cone of silence, shutting out the tennis match and any other distractions around him. He listens to the trader explain a series of financial instruments—each one more complicated than the last.

"I have no idea what you are talking about," Ivan admits.

"Nobody does," the trader says. "But we do know that he's leveraged out the window."

Ivan briefly looks at the scoreboard. It's a rout. Smith and Jones are up 4-0.

"Say again," he requests.

"The boys in the basement have built a computer model to make sense of the damn thing," the trader says.

The continuing explanation is so complicated and arcane that Ivan's attention drifts back to the tennis court where the famous Hasbrook twins are swatting and flailing like a couple of blind girls who just stepped on a beehive.

"I still don't know what the fuck you're talking about," Ivan confesses into the phone.

"The computer boys and girls swear they have found the sweet spot," the trader says.

"On pain of death?" Ivan asks.

"They know Daddy's temper," the trader replies.

"Talk to me," Ivan says.

"There is a tranche in a secret derivative," the trader explains. "He's totally vulnerable."

"Where is the sweet spot?"

"Just behind Woody's family jewels."

"Hold the phone," Ivan says.

Having swept the first set, Smith and Jones are up 3-0. It is 40-Love. Smith serves an ace. It flies right between the Hasbrook twins. Their frustration is manifest. They look at each other with recrimination—shame blame. There are unspoken twin words. It is a special relationship. It is a shorter fuse. Rackets clatter to the court and sister is on sister—pulling hair—gouging eyes—rolling around on the clay. If not for the color coding of their outfits it would be hard to tell who was getting the upper hand or who was the dirtier cat fighter.

Ivan aims his phone at proud Papa across the way and drinks in his shock and dismay. What he sees would be heartbreaking—if he had a heart. He picks up his phone and directs his trader to "go large."

To his dismay, the match is called. As the stands clear out he is on the phone with Mackenzie, chatting her up about the start-up. Strangely enough, all she wants to talk about is The Shiny Penny Foundation. The crowd is merging from both sides of the stadium into a common exit. Ivan notices that the closing bell has just rung, so he calls his Wall Street office. He's waiting to get transferred when the line halts again. He looks up.

Perhaps Shakespeare or Cicero or Demosthenes could use their genius of expression to describe Tom Hasbrook at this moment, but is there anyone with today's limited modern vocabulary who can capture the pure hatred now on that man's face?

Ivan grins at him and says, "Like mother's milk to me."

39.
SCANLON

LIKE A GHOST WHO DOESN'T belong, Sergeant Scanlon is haunting his house—technically it's his house. His name is on the mortgage and the title, even though since the day they moved in, he's felt like the territory was clearly marked and owned by his distant wife and her horrid daughter. On a good day Scanlon feels more like the old guy who's renting the spare room upstairs than the King of his Castle. Tonight he is haunted and pacing. He would give anything to have a drink, but the peritonitis that's married to the bullet still lodged in his gut—the one without an exit wound that they can't dig out—has come back for a visit. The hostess present is a series of antibiotics so potent that Scanlon isn't allowed to put rubbing alcohol on a gnat bite—forget about tossing back a Jameson's or even a Bud Light.

He knows that today was a mistake, just like he understands that the guys were only trying to help. But any way you cut it, it was a bad idea. He was on-site with a NYPD-issue smartphone—texting away—springing the trap. He was with the guys who took the pervert down—texting up until the moment they cuffed and Mirandized him. It was awful. The perp wept like a baby. He collapsed to the floor—writhing—crying out, "Mommy, don't hate me." Scanlon wanted to escape the moment so badly that he almost jumped through a closed window.

It doesn't help that he likes the perp. They had a relationship. He's a funny guy—a decent guy—who just happened to be in the wrong place at the wrong time, and that would be being born to a dehumanizing, castrating bitch of a mother who hated anyone with a dick, especially her only son. Scanlon feels awful that because of his efficient police work this tormented soul will be sleeping on Rikers Island tonight. He tries to convince himself that he's not the bad guy in this one and he shouldn't be feeling so awful about it.

Tonight of all nights he should be feeling just fine. He's got the house to himself. His wife is off at whatever she's off to. She's gotten lazy. She doesn't bother to come up with an alibi these days. And stepdaughter—horrid Bitzi—is simply defiant. When she was leaving the house tonight she stood in the door, lit a cigarette, and said, "Off to Bible school. Don't wait up."

Pacing through the empty house just doesn't do it. Scanlon feels like his brain is about to explode. He goes over to the refrigerator in the kitchen and reaches to the right of it, grabbing the dog's leash off its hook. Once the links in that chain rattle and make a sound, life gets a lot simpler. There is an interested dog involved.

He follows Sparky's lead, only tugging on the leash to keep him from eating a cigarette butt or a condom. He makes a mental note of any burnt-out streetlight—force of habit for an old beat cop. They end up behind the high school. It is all closed up for the night and dark. The sodium-vapor lights bathe the yard in a jaundiced yellow. He hears familiar laughter. Sparky picks up on it too. There are some kids sitting on the bleachers next to the basketball court. No one is playing basketball. He recognizes her about the same time as she spots him. She is sitting off to the side with a boy—a large, older boy. When he's within earshot she starts making out with the boy—heavy stuff. He stands next to them on the bleachers until the boy stops. The girl doesn't.

When the boy pushes her away, Scanlon says, "And you are?"

"Who's asking?" the boy says, standing up. He is big.

Scanlon pulls out his badge and slips the lanyard over his head.

"It's written down here," he says, holding the badge in the light to make it shine.

"Ignore him," Bitzi purrs, holding her arms open wide. "It's just the local schoolyard pervert."

"Nope," the boy says, shaking his head.

"Do you know how old she is?" Scanlon asks, holding back Sparky, who is desperately struggling to get into Bitzi's open arms.

"I'm out of here," the boy says to her. He flips up his hoodie and walks down the bleacher benches with long strides.

"Happy?" the girl says.

"Your mother wants you home," he says.

"You have no idea what my mother wants," she spits. "And if you did, there's not a damn thing you could do about it."

She starts out after the boy. Scanlon follows.

"Or are you a faggot?" she shouts over her shoulder.

She stops dead and turns to face him.

"Oh my God. I can't believe I've missed this for so long," she says as her hands slap to her cheeks in revelation. "What was I thinking? Of course, it all makes sense now. You're a faggot!"

When it's clear that they're not going to go anywhere in a hurry, Sparky takes a seat.

Scanlon says, "Come home, Rebecca."

She makes tight fists and holds them to her sides as she bows at the hips with an upraised head. She brays like a donkey.

"You want it up the ass," she shrieks at him.

Scanlon resists the urge to look around to see what sort of audience they are attracting. He puts on his most rigid cop face.

"My poor mother. Married to a faggot," the girl singsongs. "You want it in the ass."

She drifts too close with her taunt. Scanlon grabs her wrist hard. She is his as long as he maintains his grip.

"We are going home," he says quietly out of the side of his mouth.

"Rape," the horrid stepdaughter screams at the top of her lungs. "Rape!"

Scanlon has turned himself into a robot. He marches her homeward on the quick time.

"We're calling the police," someone shouts from an apartment overhead.

"I am the police," Scanlon replies.

He manages to get the door open with the dog in one hand and the girl in the other. He lets Sparky loose the minute they are in the kitchen. The girl's wrist, on the other hand, is in total lockdown until Scanlon drops her unceremoniously on her bed. He closes the door from the outside. He heads to the den. God, he would love a shot of something right now. He figures he'll go crazy if he just sits and waits for the next salvo that she's cooking up up there. He needs to take his mind off things. He might as well work. Technically he shouldn't. He doesn't have a departmental computer with him. If you go strictly by the book, it's a no-no to use your personal devices. But it's no big deal. He opens his laptop and logs on to the Internet.

lilSue: hi Daddy r u here 2nite

Scanlon goes into the kitchen and makes a cup of instant coffee. By the time he gets back to the den, the conversation is ready to begin.

oldJim: hey darling
lilSue: o i m soooooooooooooooo glad u r here daddy
oldJim: whoa whats up with u suzyQ. r u ok?
lilSue: no i am no ok
oldJim: oh sweetie i m so sorry tell Daddy all about it
lilSue: theres this girl and shes very mean to me

40.
MACKENZIE

MRS. BRIARCLIFF IS CRUISING at 35,000 feet, returning from a meeting at the office in Santa Clara. She didn't have to show up in person, but it's so convenient in Ivan's personal corporate jet—there are others, but he has to share those. More important, she likes keeping her staff on their toes since she caught them green screening a teleconference last month. The giveaway was when she watched Judi Reich making a photocopy in the background as the same Judi Reich was delivering a report into her webcam. Her new regime will make it so they all have to show up at work two times a month at least. On the other hand, she can see it from their perspective. All the processes are so automated at this point they don't have much to do. She's shrunk the company to a bare-bones skeleton crew and there's just not enough for them to do.

But she's leaving all that behind her for now. Everything they discussed today, including the IPO, will have to wait. Mackenzie is on deadline. The Shiny Penny Foundation benefit is only seven days away. They are fast-tracking things just to be on the safe side. In a month or two their poster child can easily grow out of his early onset infantile ennui, and then where will they be? By providing the venue at the last minute, her husband is a lifesaver.

"Thanks for the use of the hangar, darling," she says, glancing briefly at Ivan as her fingers rattle over the keys of her laptop, answering a zillion emails related to the event.

"It's a million bucks of publicity, babe," he replies halfheartedly. He too is lost in his computer to the point of consternation. "This can't be true."

"What, hon?" Mackenzie replies reflexively, keeping the irritation out of her voice as she tries to concentrate.

"It says here that you have only forty-five employees in Santa Clara," he says. "This must be a mistake."

"You are correct," she says. "That is wrong. It should read forty-five employees worldwide."

"That's impossible," he says. "The payroll must be a joke."

"At the moment," she replies, "they are paid in pizza and sushi . . . and stock."

"Buy them out now," Ivan demands.

"Can't," Mackenzie explains. "They know better than to fall for that. I hired them because they are really, really smart."

She holds her fingers above the keyboard for a minute or two. When he stays quiet, she starts another email.

"How can you turn one platform into one hundred and twenty-eight virtual computers?" he asks.

"I told you," she repeats. "They are really, really smart. It will be two hundred and fifty-six each sometime next month."

"That's incredible," he says.

"Why are you so interested all of a sudden?" she asks.

"I've always been interested," he replies. The lie is obvious.

"That's one of our more important patents," she says, unable to contain the pride in her voice.

"Interesting," Ivan mumbles into his computer.

"But that is all up and running," Mackenzie segues. "Now it's time to work on my new, more important job."

She looks at him for a moment.

"Thanks to you," she adds.

If he grunts now or not it is impossible to discern—such an understated grunt—if there is a grunt. Mackenzie contends there was a grunt. But she is also honest in admitting that she was looking for a slight—know thyself.

"We've sold forty-eight of fifty tables," she says to see if he's listening at this point.

He stops and looks up. "That seems exceptional," he says.

"It's for a worthy cause," she replies. "It also seems that we have an anonymous benefactor."

"I'm not terribly fond of anonymity," he says.

"We are." She grins. "In our business plan we're betting the farm on it."

"But how many years will it take before you turn a profit?" he asks.

"That happened last Tuesday night," she responds frostily. "I emailed you the balance sheet."

"I see it now," Ivan says, his eyes glued to the screen. "I see it."

He is quiet for a long moment while Mackenzie can hear the adding machine keys clicking inside his skull.

"We also have science on our side now," she says.

"Hmm." he responds—pro forma.

"We know that this tragic ailment is not being taken seriously by the mainstream medical establishment," she explains. "You can imagine our relief when a peer-reviewed cause and effect was established and published."

She hears it. That is a grunt this time. No doubt about it.

"I'm sure you'll be speaking—or drooling—out of the other side of your mouth when you meet our new spokesperson at the benefit," she scolds.

"Whatever," Ivan says into his screen, channeling his inner twelve-year-old.

Mackenzie has no idea why she is being so defensive—yes she

does—she's angry. Ivan is pissing her off, which he does often, but today she's sick of it and him. She has to impress now to get him back. She drops the name like she's the *Enola Gay*.

"No one less than Hollywood megastar Svetlana Petracova," she crows disingenuously. It's not like Mackenzie had heard of her before last week.

But Ivan must know who she is. He leaps to his feet so suddenly he knocks his laptop to the floor.

"No way," he explodes.

Gotcha, Mackenzie gloats. "Yep," she says, doing a bit of a victory strut.

"I mean it," Ivan commands. "No way. You can't use her."

Mackenzie throws a questioning look.

"She's fucking Woody Steele, for God's sake," Ivan explains as he picks his computer off the floor and sits back down.

"I can assure you that she is not," his wife coos into his ear, her hands on his shoulders. "We had a long chat about that. She was the victim of a character assassination plot. We know how that can ruin your day, don't we, lovey."

She massages his neck and back. She can feel the tension start to dissipate. "In the small world department," she gossips, "did you know that Svetlana's uncle owns Rasputin & Co.? We've never been there, have we?"

"I might check it out," Ivan says, distracted.

Mackenzie looks over his shoulder to see what's captured his attention. It's her web site.

"Should I be flattered?" she asks.

"You're going to get hacked," he says. "It's only a matter of time."

"You're wrong," she swaggers. "There's a back door now so we can clean up loose ends. But after the IPO we squeeze Crazy Glue into the locks, and even our guys can't get back inside again—ever."

Pride goeth before the fall.

41. VICTORIA

IT IS T-MINUS TWENTY AND VICTORIA is a wreck. The grand opening is only one day away—her mother's arrival less than that. She is thankful that the building super is helping out. The GC's foreman has a very accurate watch. Tim is walking in just as all the workmen are clearing out at five o'clock on the dot. Why is Victoria surprised that the cute basement boy is wonderful and efficient? In just one stroll through the rooms, all the errant dangling wires simply disappear and every cam has a red LED aglow. On the other hand, it's still a little awkward seeing him since she cried on his shoulder. In his defense, he was a total prince that night—just *tea and sympathy*—no wandering hands—so he is without sin.

But awkward doesn't do justice to how Tim and the head maid are getting along. Victoria has to bite her tongue not to laugh when they pass by each other. Tim surprises again. He has the moves of a ballet dancer. Just as Fifi tries to pinch a tight bun through his baggy jeans, he executes a jeté that lands him safely away.

Tim leads Victoria into the machine room—a butler's pantry in a previous life—and shows her the bank of monitors that cover every inch of public space in *Miss Lavinia's House of Mirth*, as he refers to the place.

"Don't let my mother hear you say that," Victoria says.

"Mum's the word," Tim replies.

Crash!

He points to the screen of the crime. The guilty maid looks into the camera. The arousal of culpability colors her face.

"This has to end," Victoria bemoans. "I can't stand it."

"A plague of butterfingers?" Tim asks.

"A means to an end," she replies. "That's the lookout with the BDSM crowd."

"The sadist can always punish the masochist by doing nothing," he points out.

"But we've run out of wineglasses—and canes," she replies.

Tim thinks for a moment. Then he grins.

"You need to make the punishment fit the crime," he says.

"We've punished," she explains. "Oh how we've punished. Feefs and I can't raise our arms over our shoulders anymore. We're both swatted out."

Tim shakes his head rejecting that notion.

"I'll be right back," he says.

After he hurries away, Victoria stands and stares at the images from all the spy cams arrayed before her. There is a grim fascination while snooping on all these gurls—covertly watching their every move. Is voyeurism a power trip? Or is it the banking of secrets? She zooms in closer to study each one—deciding that there are no secrets here after all. Over the last few days, Victoria has been paying attention. The maids have become more and more extroverted as more and more cameras have gone online. And tomorrow there will be thousands of paying customers watching them—hopefully. Maybe this wasn't such a bad idea after all.

Victoria pours herself a whisky and begins yet another walk-through before the final one with her mother. At the thought of that dreaded event, she tosses the contents of her glass down in one gulp—to the sound of cracking dishes and shattering glass in distant rooms. That is what is most upsetting. Her staff is out of control. Her mother will smell that just as surely as a parent can sniff out dissipating tobacco smoke in the loo. Worse—her shame will be heightened and manifest when the staff miraculously tows the line after just one raised maternal eyebrow. All her work of the last two months will be tossed into the crapper with that dismissive look, which will begin as a simple scold at the maids but conclude as a devastating disappointment by the time it gets around to her—the look that ultimately evolves into *Must I do everything?*

Her reverie is broken at the sound of another goblet breaking. She rushes to the dining room and is disheartened by what she sees. One of the maids has created a pyramid of brandy snifters while another is staggering around bearing a silver tray holding an antique lead crystal decanter with even older port in it. What makes the situation more dire is that the gurl is running blind because she's got not one but two pairs of panties pulled down over her head—directoire bloomers, to be exact.

Victoria is in a panic. "Please," she pleads. "Stop where you are."

But that entreaty only seems to make the gurl bob and weave all the more. The decanter of Miss Lavinia's port slides back and forth across the tray approaching the rim as if it were a loose nuke in a James Bond movie.

Victoria desperately tries a different approach—going cross schoolmarm.

"Constance," she chastises. "Behave yourself this very moment."

This is to no effect. The gurl careens off the sideboard and is on her way to certain disaster when a *deus ex machina* named Tim walks back into the room. Once Victoria gets over the Halloween Indian headdress that he's now wearing, she can't get over the determined look in his eyes.

With one swooping gesture, Tim pulls the knickers off the maid's head. Then with two hands he steadies the silver platter.

"Behave yourself," he says coldly—eye to eye.

"I can't help myself, sir," the maid says defiantly. "Even if I might be punished for it."

Tim keeps one hand on the tray. With the other he reaches into the train behind his neck and plucks a turkey feather from the headdress. He twirls it in front of her eyes, which are growing bigger and rounder by the moment.

"Ticklish?" Tim asks.

There is no answer. The blood drains from her face as the maid hands the silver tray over to him and runs from the room screaming, "Miss, protect me. He's a monster."

Tim smiles in achievement as Victoria watches the fleeing gurl with wonderment. He twirls the turkey feather in front of her eyes and says, "Your Excalibur, my lady."

"My hero," she says and kisses him on the cheek.

Tim looks at her with bemusement. Then he takes her face in his hands and pulls her to him and kisses her on the lips. This surprises her for the brief moment before shock turns into want.

42.
SVETLANA

THE HOLLYWOOD POWDER keg is doing espresso shots like they are Stoli. She is hosting the last working group of The Shiny Penny Foundation before the benefit. To be honest, the real sponsor—the one picking up the tab—is her uncle Dmitri—but who's counting. They are convened upstairs in the only quiet room at Rasputin & Co. As far as Svetlana is concerned, a meeting preplanning your funeral would be more exciting than this. She is at the dead end of a long table. Mackenzie Greenbriar is facing her at the head, and on either side are two rows of wealthy white girls who only confirm the reason why everyone hates white people. It's worse than that. These ladies are all married to filthy rich men. They want for nothing. If they think of something—anything—they just have to snap their fingers and there it is. But on what do they waste their finger snaps? Thirty-thousand-dollar sofas and seventy-thousand-dollar window treatments. They are so lacking in sophistication that Svetlana figures there isn't a bidet in the bunch, and they must average five houses a head. If she had access to so much money she would certainly do something with it—buy something fun—like a movie studio, but not these safe, conventional ladies—these Botoxed beauties.

When the head of the flower committee begins her presentation, Svetlana can't bear it a minute longer. She removes herself without ceremony and transplants her butt downstairs to a barstool off the lobby in Zhivago's—a cross between the Ice Palace from the movie and the Hall of Mirrors at Versailles. Here she drinks vodka like it's coffee and admires her many reflections. She's wearing a breast-flattering peasant blouse, a long skirt, and high boots. A bright Uzbeki scarf is tied around her head at a rakish angle—no babushka here. Svetlana toasts herself in the mirror. Her gypsy look totally rocks.

It's a bright, sunny afternoon. The door is open to the street. She cannot miss the blur of a yellow Lamborghini as it screeches to a stop just past her sight lines. She has seen this car before. She would never forget or confuse it. She grooms her eyebrows with her thumbs. She pulls the blouse lower down off her shoulders—studies her reflection in the mirror. She pulls it back up, deciding that the girls look better under wraps—Potentiality vs. Actuality—Svetlana has read her Aristotle.

She sits back on the stool with her boots on the footrest, then rejects that. She scrunches her ass forward and crosses her legs together—in tight parallel. Yes. She confirms the position in the mirror. It's uncomfortable, but who cares about that. She looks both hot and fucking demure at the same time. It's perfect. She looks up again . . .

He is just steps inside the door and already he is staring at her. Frozen—but not for long. Steadily her tractor beam draws him in—closer and closer. Before either of them blinks he is standing just feet away—looking—analyzing. She is immediately moved by his presence. Her skin tingles. There is less oxygen in the room. Her heart races to keep up. She should have trained for this moment at altitude. His eyes are all-seeing. In real life they aren't beady or ferret-like at all. This is not Ivan Greenbriar, celebrity. This is *the man*—a raw, natural power source. Svetlana immediately realizes that she has entered a bullshit-free zone. She scraps her old plan.

Without taking his eyes off her, he points at her drink and the bartender nods knowingly, pouring him the same. They clink glasses. She is amused as he tries to hide the searing fire as it pours down his throat.

He shrugs it off and says, "It was you."

"Perhaps," she replies. "Perhaps."

43. TIM

THERE ARE ONLY TWO SOURCES of illumination in the basement apartment. Ambient street light leaks in under the small curtain hanging over the window in the well next to the sidewalk, interrupted into a flicker by the feet marching by it. There is also the large LED display of his clock that creates a slightly greenish hue to one side of the room. Regardless of both, the darkness wins out, which is just fine with both of them. We are at the feeling phase of the evening—the looking phase died with the bottle of wine.

Tim notes that it is 03:00 when she comes back for more. Her assaults have been consistently on the hour. He leans back into the onslaught, feeling her satin baby-doll smooth and cool against his naked back. He opens up his arms and legs, allowing hers to reengage—entangling yet again in a different configuration, beginning a new process though heading toward the same result—but who's complaining. He rolls over to face her in the shadows and kisses her. She arches her back and presses into him, but her legs are coyly locked together.

"Tease," he says and kisses her harder—clutching her shoulders, trying to use his knee like a crowbar.

She matches him kiss for kiss, besting him with a more aggressively probing tongue. Her fingers pinch his tender nipples in a way that borders on unpleasant—if there were such a thing as below sublime when rolling around naked with a divine lover.

He kisses her neck and cups her ass cheeks, pulling her tightly against him—patiently working to spring the mechanism and part her legs. He is rewarded with a bite on his neck. Then she bends up and licks one of his nostrils, which is thoroughly disgusting. But before he can complain she flips him over and pins him to the futon. She's got a strong hold. He is immobilized. She licks the other nostril—doubly disgusting. He struggles. Her grip on his wrists tightens. She moves up the futon and clamps his head with her knees. He is locked down. He can't move his head.

A car in the street makes a U-turn. Its headlights flood the room. He is shocked at what he sees—just inches from his face—a huge bouncing erect penis.

"No," he tries to shout, but his voice is strangled.

He looks up past the huge threatening boner just as the car makes another turn. The headlamps focus squarely on the maid's face—stark—severe—Mephistopheles in drag. The spotlights brighten—intensify. All shades and shadows fade out. It is a blinding light. All he can see is her thick eye makeup—her lipstick—and her . . .

"Wake up. Wake up."

Tim is shaken until his eyes open with a jolt.

Victoria is looking down at him. She's wearing a Saint Andrews (Scotland) rugby shirt, and she's a girl—he can tell, he checks—no Adam's apple.

"You're beautiful," Tim says stupidly.

She touches his forehead with an almost maternal concern. She looks into his eye. "Are you all right?" she asks.

"I'm fine."

"What was that?"

"Post-traumatic stress disorder," he explains.

"Afghanistan?" she asks.

"Fifi," he replies.

He looks around—disoriented until he remembers that he is in what Victoria calls the *lounge*. There is an open pizza box on the coffee table with a single slice left next to six or seven Whatley's beer cans—along with a dull roar coming from the flat screen on the wall.

"What's that noise?" he asks.

"It's either Arsenal or Manchester United," she replies. "I can't tell them apart—but it makes for the perfect palate cleanser after a long day of petticoats and suspender belts."

She plops down next to him on the sofa. They both lie back for a moment—hands behind their heads—watching boys in shorts run up and down the field alternating between kicking the ball and kicking each other.

"Does it come in a pre-traumatic version?" she asks.

"I'm not sure," he replies.

"I'm definitely up for a dose of that," she notes.

"It's just opening night jitters," he reassures her. "Don't worry. You're ready."

She shakes two or three Whatley's cans to find one that's still loaded.

"You haven't met my mother," she says as she drains it.

"She is GG, right?" Tim asks.

"GG?" Victoria says, taking umbrage.

She bops him over the head with a sofa pillow.

"Hey," he complains. "Why'd you do that?"

"You deserved it," she says. "Of course she's genetically a girl. She's my mother."

"Just asking." Tim shrugs. "I've only seen pictures of her on the web site, and those wigs could go on anyone."

"I don't think you are the innocent that you pretend to be," she says as she shakes more empties, looking for another swallow of beer. "Where did you learn about GGs?"

"I hacked your chat room," he explains. "I wanted to see how secure you are."

"Well?" she asks, exhibiting a little concern in the tone of her voice.

"I've seen worse," he replies. "It's not a festering sewer . . . *per se*."

"Good for us," she says, popping open a full beer can she finds on a distant table. "What do you mean, *per se*?"

"Give us a taste."

"How terribly Brit of you," she says as she hands him the beer can.

"Cheers," he toasts as he takes a mini chug before handing it back to her.

"Cheers," she replies before she kills it.

"Does your site have some kind of virtual dress code or something?" he asks.

"What do you mean?"

"Everyone kept asking me what I was wearing," he replies. "Fortunately I resisted the urge to make something up because, as everyone knows, it's against the law to tell an untruth on the Internet."

Victoria cannot stifle a snicker.

"I was also able to resist the urge to subscribe to *Miss Victoria's Monthly Mandatory Milking Email*," Tim adds—not in any braggy way at all—so he is understandably surprised when she tries to whack him again.

He grabs her wrist mid-swing. The pillow falls to the floor. When she struggles, he throws a quarter nelson and locks her down entirely.

"Is that a wrestling move?" she asks.

"Yes," he says. "All-state in high school. One hundred and thirty-two pounds."

"If you pin me does that mean that we are going steady?" she asks—batting her eyelashes.

44.
MACKENZIE

THE SPECIAL BENEFIT FOR The Shiny Penny Foundation is in—to say *full* might be stretching it—but it's definitely in swing. A small group of people in formal wear is enjoying the cocktail hour in the massive hangar in the shadow of the spectacular sailboat destined to capture the next America's Cup. The men are starched and white. The women are glamorous. But outshining them all, the catamaran is resplendent—its two hulls dazzling with wax and potential speed. The talk is small and muted as the attendees mingle in a tight circle. They all know each other, of course. This event is a classic New York City parochial small town event—all the names pulled from the same iPad mailing list.

The hostesses of the evening are standing off to the side—split into two groups. One side is looking anxiously at the poor turnout, while the other is working on their advanced degree—a Master's in Toxicology.

"I just love Mackenzie," Eeyore brays. "But this was an awfully big gamble for her first time out."

"How disappointed she must feel," White Fang agrees.

"On a positive note," Camille points out, "it looks like everyone can have their own table."

"Meow," Pippi Longstocking, in the other camp, caterwauls with a scratching paw.

But it is true. Everyone can have their own—with leftovers. There are fifty of them on the other side of the hangar with lavish place settings—four glasses each—white wine (*poisson*), red wine (*viande*), flutes (*Champagne*) and water (*l'eau*)—silverware glinting in descendant order from each plate—and enough floral displays to dress Arlington National Cemetery on November 11.

"Where is everyone?" the Boss Lady Emeritus frets—not begrudging her lost status in the least. She is much more concerned—selflessly—with the success of the evening—as anyone who really knows her would testify to under oath.

"And where is our feckless leader?" White Fang asks before self-correcting. "Oops. I meant fearless."

Mackenzie is in fact outside juggling chainsaws. There is no cell service in the hangar, and she has to talk to her chief engineer in Iceland.

"I have never seen anything like it," he reports. "It is the mother of all hack attacks."

"Has anyone breeched the firewall?" she asks.

"They're bouncing off like Ping-Pong balls," her techie replies, unable to conceal the pride in his voice.

"Good," she exhales in relief.

"But not forever," he adds. "When can we finally lock the back door?"

"Soon," she says. "Got to go."

She hangs up as Pollyanna and Becky Thatcher walk up to her.

"Hey, Mackenzie," Becky says.

"Hey," Mackenzie says.

"Hey," Pollyanna says.

The girls look awkward for a minute until Becky ventures,

"We don't know how to say this, and we don't want to upset you, but—"

Mackenzie holds up a hand to interrupt.

"You don't know how to say what?" she asks.

The girls look unsettled.

"I've got an app for that," Mackenzie says.

She squints at her phone and swipes through two screens and thumbs on an icon.

"This is magic," she says while the app is loading. "It translates."

She holds the phone up to the girl's face and nods.

"We don't know how to say this—" Becky starts over.

"We can't help but revel in your potential embarrassment—" the mechanical voice on the phone responds.

Becky loses her nerve, so Pollyanna picks up the baton. "We're all wearing one-offs," she says.

"And you're wearing off-the-rack," the iPhone translates.

"Talk to me," Mackenzie says, unable to couch the threat and menace in her voice. She is tired. Her feet hurt in these new heels. She has felt stupid in every off-the-shoulder dress she has ever worn. Her start-up is under fire, and she doesn't want to be here anymore.

"There's this bet," Polly starts.

"Kind of an office pool," Becky continues. "You buy a box."

"For what time I go down in flames?" Mackenzie asks. "Or when I burst into tears?"

"Oh no," the girls protest.

"Nothing that mean-spirited," Becky explains.

"Or bitchy," Polly agrees.

"Just how many ladies show up wearing your dress tonight." Becky grins.

"Good clean fun," Polly says gleefully. She cannot resist a giggle.

They smile in tandem until Becky looks at the small smattering of a crowd inside the hangar and concludes, "I guess you won't have to worry about any duplication tonight."

Mackenzie turns to look and shudders. All the chickens are coming home to roost. The board of directors is marching straight at her—Boss Lady Emeritus at the top of the order and poised to be one mean mother pecker.

"I know you must be disappointed, dear," she patronizes. "But it's all for a good cause, and even if we don't have them here physically in body, we have their checks in the cash box fiscally in spirit."

"Actually," Mackenzie stammers, "the major donor of the night was bringing a big check with him."

White Fang is shocked—shocked!

"Are you telling us that your real or imagined anonymous benefactor is a deadbeat?"

"No," Mackenzie protests.

The Boss Lady Emeritus is looking concerned.

"Is there something you want to tell us?" she asks with the caring face of the Grand Inquisitor.

Mackenzie is on the verge of panic when she hears the familiar roar of a twelve-cylinder Lamborghini five-litre engine. She finds it strangely relaxing—and full of surprises. For when the obscenely expensive Italian sports car roars to a stop in front of the ladies and her husband climbs out of the driver's side and opens the passenger door for the beautiful spectacular Russian movie star, the Boss Lady Emeritus spontaneously hugs Mackenzie close to her bosom and whispers into her ear, "You poor dear."

"Must be the seven-month itch," White Fang says fatalistically.

"Check your prenup," Becky adds, trying to be supportive.

45.
MARY MARGARET

MARY MARGARET IS SITTING in a limo stuck in traffic on the Belt Parkway with her nose pressed into a copy of the *Daily News*, working a puzzle, trying to be invisible. But her boss won't have any of it. Tonight he's Chatty Cathy.

"You're too smart for that. You should be doing something hard, like the crossword in *The Guardian*," he says. "But the Jumble?"

"I like the Jumble," she replies, although to be truthful she has no real commitment to the Jumble. But Woody is right about one thing. She is smart—so smart in fact that she finds doing puzzles—all puzzles—as challenging and as interesting as flossing her teeth—but she's cranky. She doesn't want to be either dressed up or in Brooklyn tonight. She'd rather be home in her pj's and—yes—flossing her teeth.

"Nice dress," he says.

"Thank you," she replies. "It's a company dress."

"We made that?" he asks.

"No," she answers. "You paid for it. The company always pays for my clothes when I have to go to places I really really don't want to go to. Like tonight."

"We should do couture," Woody muses. "Can we buy some house or other?"

"You want a line?" she says. "Here's a line. You're going crazy. Have you been eating lead paint off the walls of your antiquey farmhouse?"

"It's a great business model," he replies. "The less material, the higher the price point."

He flicks at the high hem of her dress—she slaps his hand away.

"You want to add fashion to the portfolio?" she asks incredulously—not an act—but sincerely. "What are you going to rename the enterprise—*Smelters, Nukes 'n' Things*?"

"What did you pay for that dress—five—ten thousand dollars?" he asks.

"I have to get back to you on that," she answers.

"That's what you always say," he responds, "and you never do."

"I was going to email you the receipt tonight," she says. "But you dragged me to Brooklyn."

"That's a fallacy," he complains. "If you weren't in Brooklyn tonight, you wouldn't be in that dress. Oh, I like that idea—naked and dressed."

He makes animal noises as his hand lands on her thigh. She pushes it away.

"You're worse than a teenager at a drive-in," she complains.

"Good idea," Woody bubbles with delight. "Oh, driver . . ."

"What is wrong with you?" Mary Margaret asks with an edge in her voice.

"I need something to do with my hands," Woody explains sheepishly. "Maybe I should take up smoking."

"Why are we here?" she demands.

"You didn't have to come," he says.

"Oh yes, I did," she says.

"Why?"

"Because you did."

"That's silly," Woody dismisses. "I'm a grown-up going to a charity benefit. What could possibly go wrong?"

"First of all," Mary Margaret replies, "no."

"No, what?"

"No, you're not a grown-up," she points out. "And why are you starting a war with Ivan Greenbriar?"

"You're wrong there," Woody says. "I'm not starting a war with Ivan Greenbriar. Oh, by the way, I bought a bunch of magazines."

"I know," she says. "I signed the check. You couldn't go with something more cutting edge, like buggy whips?"

"I'm going to be on the cover of *Fortune* next month," he adds.

"Nice," she says. "Waving a red cape at the Raging Hard-On."

"I am merely supporting his wife in her important work," Woody sniffs.

Mary Margaret throws down the newspaper. A victory grin rainbows across her face. She turns to Woody. "I own you, lumberman," she crows with delight. "You don't know what she's selling, do you?"

"She's got a great start-up that I would take over tomorrow if I could," Woody says. "But I'm watching my pennies because I'm saving up to buy Japan."

"That's not what I meant, and you know it," she says. "What is tonight's benefit benefitting?"

"It's a noble effort to improve a major overlooked segment of society," he stammers.

"You've got nothing," she condemns him.

"I will not be cross-examined," he protests.

"Why are we here?" she demands so forcefully that she can see him deflate in front of her eyes.

He toys with her hemline in an innocent, reflective way for a moment.

"Ivan takes it all so seriously," Woody explains. "He doesn't see the fun in all his money. It makes me want to short sheet his bed or something."

"Finally," Mary Margaret exhales. "We're moving. Let that be a lesson to you. The truth will set you free."

The limo turns south onto Flatbush Avenue.

"He's such an asshole," Woody says. "Pardon my French."

"Amen, brother," she agrees. "Now I might enjoy the evening."

They pull up in front of the brightly lit festive hangar at Floyd Bennett Field and park among the throng of limousines and luxury cars already in attendance. Tippy-toed on the edge of an open door, Woody is fumbling with the tie-down on the roof rack.

"Hand me your knife, Mugs," he says.

She flips up her short dress—he is ready for that—preset to take in the view of her garter belt as she retrieves a short dagger from the sheath that's always strapped to her thigh. When she hands it to him, she can't help but notice his focal point.

"You need a girlfriend," she says.

"You think?" he replies as he cuts the cord.

46. TIM

TIM NO LONGER FEELS the same dread when he punches the PH button in the elevator, validating the old adage that familiarity breeds—at least in this case—familiarity. He also now has a handle on the old man's routine. Knowing that his Saturday night bath takes place on Tuesdays gives Tim the opportunity to anticipate and circumvent the weekly flood that soaks the Persian carpets in 11B. Each visit is pretty much the same—step by step. It borders on ritual. Tim rings the buzzer. He can hear the familiar squeak of the wheelchair approaching, then the crash.

"Go away," Mr. Pavlenko shouts through the door.

Then Tim knocks patiently. He can hear the chair strain as the old man pushes against the arms to raise himself up to the peephole.

"Go away," he repeats.

This is when Tim reaches into his pocket and holds a chess piece—today it is a black rook—up to the peephole. There is a barely audible grunt from inside and then the *Dance of the Seven Veils* as Mr. Pavlenko opens the many locks. As Tim enters the apartment, the old Russian is already halfway down the hall, rolling away in his chair like one of Zhukov's tanks. The kitchen is very modest. The most recent update is a massive East German microwave that has dials—and probably vacuum tubes.

Mr. Pavlenko parks himself next to the metal kitchen table. It's white with chipped blue enamel around the edges. He turns his grizzled face to Tim. He's got a military flattop haircut—and he's clean-shaved—every four or five days or so. He is pretty much gray all over, which at his age is a healthy step up from yellow. Dressed in a red velour running suit with a white stripe down the sides, he's got a chest full of medals that look like something he won at a carnival tossing rings onto milk bottles. He slides a collapsed cardboard box across the table. On the top is a faded red star and some Cyrillic characters.

As Tim sets up the chessboard, Mr. Pavlenko drops spoons into glasses and fills them with tea from a samovar on the table. Tim holds up two fists. Mr. Pavlenko taps on one. When Tim opens it to reveal a black pawn, Mr. Pavlenko says without inflection or expression, "You will lose."

The next fifteen minutes are filled with silence as they play chess with great concentration. After his third glass of tea, Tim doesn't play badly for a moment. He does something nasty with a bishop in order to jam up Mr. Pavlenko. This gives him time for a bathroom break as the old guard stares at the board in disbelief.

The layout is a little weird for a big-city penthouse apartment. There is no powder room off the foyer. You have to go into the bedroom off the living room. Then there's the question of the décor. The living room is furnished with mid-century chairs and sofas that are so outdated that they are fashionable again. But what's even more strange is that half of the penthouse is just missing. Tim has been on the roof many times. He's paced it off. It's simply not there. On the other hand, nothing warms a hearth and home like a floor-to-ceiling portrait of Stalin—and it's the real deal—oil on canvas. Tim checked it out. You can get the same one on eBay for ten grand.

He goes into the bathroom and turns off the hot and cold faucets pouring into the tub. Plenty of time to spare. There are inches left to go. He does a quick calculation in his head, weighing Mr. Pavlenko's estimated body mass against the displacement of water. Just to be safe, he drains a little so that it won't slop over. As he stands at the toilet waiting to relax, he opens the medicine cabinet to check out what the old man is dying of. Curiouser and curiouser. Nothing in there but jars of potassium iodide tablets—130 mg—not even a toothbrush.

When Tim returns to the game, he is looking at a different board than he left. He is used to this. He knows that Mr. Pavlenko doesn't cheat—he just forgets when he has last moved. The longer you stay away from the table, the more moves he makes. Tim has observed this from a distance. This time, alas, his extraneous moves have left Mr. Pavlenko in a dire position—he would be mated in three if he were playing with a monkey. It's so bad that the only way that Tim could save the old man from certain ruin would be to trip over his shoelaces and knock the board off the table. He sits down and stares at the pieces, trying to come up with a new way to lose. He is a good chess player but maybe not that good. Finally he has an inspiration. He picks up his surviving knight.

"Ahem," Mr. Pavlenko clears his throat. "I believe it's my move."

He castles—to his opponent's displeasure. Mate in one.

Tim studies the board in desperation. Mr. Pavlenko looks upon it with equal intensity.

After a few minutes, he confides, "I am a prisoner in my own home."

"Really?" Tim responds in surprise. "Who is doing that to you?"

Mr. Pavlenko looks from side to side, then, leaning over, he whispers into Tim's ear, "It's the building superintendent. He wants to break in."

In the past this delusional shuffling of reality would have

inspired Tim to an uncontrollable fit of the giggles, but he has since developed an enhanced capacity for discipline, thanks to just one afternoon with Maid Fifi.

"But he seems so nice and professional," he replies.

Mr. Pavlenko shakes his head ponderously from side to side. His eyes are foreboding. They zoom into Tim's. "CIA," he explains.

"Me?—I mean, he is?" Tim stammers.

Mr. Pavlenko nods solemnly. He eyes drift back to the chessboard.

"Sorry, my friend," he says. "Checkmate."

He moves Tim's queen and knocks over his own king.

"Was good game. You are a quick learner."

47.
IVAN

THERE IS A FRESH BREEZE blowing up from Rockaway Inlet. The smell of the sea intermingles with the heady aroma of brandy in his snifter. Ivan is in a fine mood. He is taking a stroll on the tarmac. It is stuffy inside the hangar. Granted, it is a small crowd—but all his people came. A third of the tables are because of him. He is not surprised. While he worked the phones, his wife conjured with her hens instead. Ultimately they got an anonymous benefactor—more like an anonymous no-show with no check. Being a gentleman, Ivan won't throw that in her face—tonight. He will be supportive in her moment of disappointment. He will be a rock—steadfast—he will be oh-so amusing to lighten the mood. That's one of Ivan's strengths. Whenever someone close to him goes down in flames, he has a deep reservoir of droll wit. One might say it's self-effacing, but that would finesse a certain ambiguity in the target of his sarcasm. It's a gift.

His phone vibrates.

mystery paper u bought has a face value but no fingerprints, his favorite insider trader texts.

Ivan replies. *don't know*, the trader answers. *rumor has it WS is buying land of rising sun.*

can he do that?

u tell me

Ivan puts his phone to sleep and sweeps the horizon one last time before succumbing to social niceties and obligation. It is a beautiful evening. Even a raging hard-on makes the time to appreciate one this sublime. Jamaica Bay is reflecting the rosy sunset in the west behind him. Halyards rat-a-tat-tat against the masts of sailboats tied up in Dead Horse Bay. Then there are the large dark shadows of party boats returning to Sheepshead Bay after a long, boozy day of fishing—crossing the wakes of a steady green stream of running lights passing into Marine Park. He can see the red brakes of the nightly traffic jam on the bridge above the channel—typical—and the long line of limos and black cars streaming down Flatbush Avenue and turning into Floyd Bennett Field—atypical. If he were still on his phone he'd be texting *WTF?*

The parking lot is suddenly full. The drivers are now pulling up onto the runway—no emergency landings tonight—gridlock. Refocusing, Ivan tosses the brandy into the bushes. He does not hear the glass shatter. He is looking ahead—catching glimpses of Woody Steele in a tuxedo striding in and out of pools of light carrying under his arm what looks to be—yes, it is—a big check. A huge check, really. It could be a surfboard built for two. Ivan jogs around to a back door in order to be standing next to his wife when the next act unfolds.

"Ye of little faith," Mackenzie chastises him.

He is disheartened to see that her eyes are flashing—she looks vibrant, striking, hot.

The vibe of the room has flip-flopped—feet in the air, it's walking on its hands—Party Time. The decibels are ratcheting up. Who knew before there was a dance band here tonight? The hangar fills up fast. There is a flood of humanity—Times Square on Barren Island in outfits both formal and forlorn. Woody is ubiquitous—here—there—everywhere. His teeth must be plugged into a power source hidden in his tux. It's a blinding klieg-light smile. But wait—who's that standing next to him? It can't be—but it is—the New Zealander skipper that Ivan fired so recently—and he brought his whole bloody Kiwi crew with him, and the Aussies are here, too.

Ivan turns to his wife for an explanation, but he can't get her attention. She is dreamily gazing at the Big Check leaning against the catamaran.

He clears his throat.

Her face goes rigid when she turns to him.

"I got that on my own," she snaps. Then softening, she adds, "Isn't that Tom Hasbrook over there?"

And of course it is Tom Hasbrook, enjoying a glass of white wine in a group of the last eight covers of *Fortune* magazine—all prematurely undone by unnatural market forces and Ivan's perverse parlor game. But he survives the toxic death ray from that corner. His head is only spinning now because it is bouncing from one pocket of animosity to the next. It seems that every box on the org chart—from CEO and CFO right on down to floor sweeper and head of the mailroom—that he has ever downsized, laid off, furloughed, or fired—is in this room—tonight. All of them.

"Why are you doing this to me?" he accuses his wife.

"Don't be jealous," Mackenzie snaps. "For this one night, it's not about you. It's about the children."

The noise level kicks up two clicks past *Deafening* as the sailors find the booze.

"Excuse me, sweetie," his wife coos. "I have to go introduce myself to our not-so-anonymous benefactor."

Ivan glowers and decides he needs a drink. The bar is a madhouse. He turns to look for a waiter, but what he finds is a recurring nightmare, but in the light of day.

"Hello, Ivey," wives Numbers One, Two, and Three say in unison.

They look so alike that *Vanity Fair* magazine refers to them as the *Greenbriar Triplets*. They are even wearing identical outfits tonight.

"What are you doing here?" Ivan asks, hoping that his voice doesn't sound as venom-rich as his soul feels at the moment.

"We're here for the children," Number Three says.

"We were invited," Number Two says.

"By Woody," Number One says.

"I did not know you were acquainted," Ivan says in the most neutral voice he can muster at the moment.

"Oh, I knew him long before our divorce," Number One replies.

"Me too," Number Two says.

Number Three bites on a knuckle and asks, "Have you ever been to Virgin Gorda, Ivey?"

Group giggle fit.

48.
SVETLANA

WHEN THE RUSSIAN BEAUTY finally takes center stage, her timing is perfect, the party is peaking. The chatter is at its brightest, the lights their most dazzling, and the collective alcoholic buzz still nascent—they are hours away from crying in their beers. Wearing the vermilion gown she red-carpeted in St. Petersburg, she looks spectacular—and she knows it. Tight in the waist—and strapless—off the shoulder—off the collarbone—off everything else except her nipples—*please God.* So stylishly proud—bordering on arrogant—it even has a bustle—haughty couture. The designer was making a statement—which fell on deaf ears, so they let her keep the dress.

Svetlana throws herself into the thick of it, diving into the deep end. All the faces are a blur, as usually happens when she is looking so fabulous. She does recognize Mackenzie standing apart, next to a triptych of recycled bodies with shiny new faces.

"The preexisting conditions," Mackenzie whispers in her ear as they exchange air kisses, introducing the other Mrs. Greenbriars.

Svetlana drifts into a cluster of financial guys. She can tell who they are because their looks are calculating, not lustful—doing the bottom line on leaving a marriage—a cost-benefit analysis of fantasy sex. Their wives are the only ones in the place who don't bother to judge her. They are looking at their husbands, not at her—watching for fixed and dilated eyes or drool—dreaming of Independence Day—the holy of holies, a structured settlement—that can't come soon enough. But where is Ivan?—her future savior—a one-way ticket back to Hollywood—a Vronsky to her Anna.

Yuck. She does catch sight of the other one—her least favorite human on earth this year. He seems to have brought a lot of his lumberjack friends along with him. Poor Mackenzie. Her chic Brooklyn soirée just got moved to the wrong part of Brooklyn. Even worse—much worse—Svetlana is acutely aware that she is not the center of attention. She needs to regroup. She removes herself to the periphery. For a few restorative moments she will play the wallflower—*as if*. But it does give perspective—Napoleon looking down on the fields of Waterloo from his place on the hill—Svetlana away from the fray, standing next to the boy of the hour it turns out. It's true; there he is. Little Joyless James, forgotten and ignored in his high chair.

"Yasha," she says, kissing him on each cheek with one repeated. "How are you enjoying your big night?"

Studying her briefly, his eyes burn into hers—through hers—through her . . .

Mackenzie is right, she thinks, melting a little inside. *He is so wise.*

Then the baby dismisses her entirely and stares away blankly. He is not sad. He is not cranky, colicky, or crabby. He is simply bored out of his gourd. You just have to glance at him to see that. Svetlana crouches down next to his high chair—no small feat in heels and that dress. As an acting exercise, she imagines looking out through his jaded world-weary eyes to see what he is seeing. She sees a large room. Full of grown-ups. Everyone is sitting down now. The cocktail hour is over. Dinner is served. The only sound coming out of the banking sector is knives and forks fumbling with rubber chicken. There is no gaiety here. No peals of laughter. That should be happening at least on the Woody side of the hall, where massive amounts of alcohol have been poured into the empty stomachs of sailors and disgruntled ex-employees—a recipe for disaster among manly men—but they have gone pretty much sotto voce also. Maybe crashing Ivan's party was a better wet dream than a reality—or worse, maybe the riffraff are growing up too and don't want to get spills on their rented tuxedos. How low can you go? The dance band is playing a dirge version of "Bridge over Troubled Water" with a bad idea of an alto sax solo.

Beside her in his high chair, the poster child for early onset infantile ennui sighs audibly.

"Don't be that way," Svetlana remonstrates. "We can turn this around."

As if on cue—or perhaps because the bandleader texted a suicide hotline—the combo explodes in an up-tempo version of "Cheek to Cheek" with incredible jazz licks from the violin.

"Oh, Yasha," Svetlana croons with delight. "They're playing our song."

She scoops the baby out of his high chair, plasters his face against hers, and takes off overland into a frantic ballroom dance—but this time Ginger is leading Fred—cheek to cheek. They are making huge swooping turns and passes around the dance floor—and between the tables. At first the diners are startled. But the music is so infectious—damn, that violin can swing—Svetlana is so lithe and elegant and the boy is so fucking bored—it's laughable. Everyone gets caught up in the magic of the moment.

"The kid looks only a little less miserable than you do when you're dancing with me," Svetlana overhears a hedge fund guy's wife say to her husband when she dips close to their table.

The dance band is digging the moment. They're jamming like she's part of the group—scat dancing—call-and-response. After

Svetlana twirls, the violin plays a shuffle riff. When the dancing couple takes a hesitation step, the drum rolls—with rim shots on every dip.

The beautiful Russian actress hasn't felt this light on her feet—or happy—since they did the ballroom scene in her last movie, where Catherine falls in love with Sergei. It was filmed in The Hermitage and has the longest 360-degree tracking shot to date—except that was a waltz and this is a fox-trot.

She is dancing with so much abandon that she loses her way and drifts into the cheap seats. She is unsettled to find herself next to Woody's table. He's sitting with a lady friend. Svetlana applies some fancy footwork to get the hell out of Dodge—with a little glissando help from a complicit violin. She's practically tap dancing as she hugs the toddler wonder even closer to her cheek. Nevertheless, she can hear every word as clear as day.

"That could be you," the lady friend says.

"Except that she hates me," Woody replies. "And the kid's dick is bigger."

Svetlana takes a moment to make a mental note of that one.

49. VICTORIA

VICTORIA IS STRUGGLING with a hypothetical dilemma. What if her mother got Alzheimer's—or Wisenheimer's—or mad cow—or irritating old cow disease—or any other mind-shrinking malady that would make her an even bigger pain in the arse than she is already? And what if she asked her daughter to help put her out of her misery—to assist in ending her life? Here's the moral quandary: How long should Victoria appear to struggle with this complex, emotional minefield, in the news and confounding ethicists, theologians, and academics around the world—or is this more of a question for Miss Manners? Would an afternoon be enough, or would she have to look serious and talk softly about it for days—or weeks—before she pulled the plug?

Lavinia has been a proper Miss Fitch since she got off the plane. Victoria tries to be sympathetic. She knows that despite all her acquired and affected sophistication, her mother is a terrible traveler, especially when it comes to things with wings. On the other hand, the gurls have been on their best behavior—is this to please her or are they intimidated by Lavinia's reputation—who knows? But it isn't all smooth sailing. There's an awkward moment when she first meets the household staff—that would be the grand entrance of the Queen Mother followed by her vapor trail of gin.

"She's tight," one of the gurls stage-whispers way too loud.

"Lipped or assed?" her junior asks.

"Both," Fifi says definitively. "And drunk as a skunk." She should know. She has worked in the Knightsbridge townhouse—*Junior Year A Broad.*

In the lounge, Lavinia daintily drops into one of the club chairs and pulls off her gloves, finger by finger. Holding one in each hand like a banana peel at a royal banquet, she looks confused or disdainful until one of the maids hurries to her with a silver dish. Lavinia drops the gloves and settles back into the overstuffed chair. She surveys the room. With a barely perceptible nod, Victoria is relieved to see that she approves—as much as she seems to approve of anything that she didn't conceive of and execute herself.

"Tea time," Victoria informs the junior maid, hoping that her mother cannot hear the uncertainty in her voice.

"Yes, Madam," the gurl replies and hurries to the butler's pantry.

The tea ceremony has been prepared long in advance. Her mother is very discriminating about her tea. The blend she prefers—which Victoria thinks tastes like boiled mulch—is only available at one location in all of New York City, which is why she spent two hours on the L train to pick it up at The Tea Wanker in Williamsburg—ever the dutiful, seething, resentful daughter.

She's holding a cane when the maid brings in the tea service on a large, ornate tray. But that's just for show or to cover her ass if any more china crashes to the floor. After she presses a palm against the teapot to make sure that it's hot, she points with the cane to the spot on the coffee table where the maid puts it down.

"That will be all," she says to the gurl. "Should I be mother, Mother?"

No answer.

Victoria shrugs that off and pours out two cuppas. She sets one down next to her mum and sits down across from her, compulsively stirring her own, desperately wishing it contained a dram or two. She takes a sip—yes indeed, mulch. Her mother sits there without moving—stone-faced.

Gawd, I hate that look, Victoria thinks.

She knows that look only too well. She got that look when she failed Latin in the lower school, and she got the same look when she got a single—not a double—first in university. This seems to be the only look she gets from her mother.

"Nice flight?" Victoria asks, trying to break the ice—and not a plate over her head.

No answer. Victoria sips her compost tea. The silence is excruciating.

"It should be a big day tomorrow," she tries again. "Everyone online is excited that you will be in charge of the ribbon cutting. Are you excited?"

No answer.

"We have thirty-five hundred RSVPs and project that by the time we're live we will have over six thousand unique streams."

Nothing.

"That should make it a huge payday," Victoria says. "You should be happy. Uncle Sid should be happy."

The maids are hovering around the door—eavesdropping. She stands and walks toward them, saddened to see notes of understanding and sympathy in their eyes. She closes the door and goes back to her mother.

"What do you want from me?" she demands.

No answer—just a cold, damning stare in return.

Victoria refuses to allow her mother to see her cry. "See you at the launch," she says, biting her quivering lip. "Break a leg."

50. WOODY

WOODY NODS AS THE ORGANIZER of the event, Mackenzie Greenbriar, stops by his table and whispers in his ear. After the plates are cleared he will present the Big Check and make a short speech. He notices that her husband is out of the room while they talk. She thanks him again—flatly—and hurries off to more important committee business. The chairman of the board and his chief operating officer go back to watching the stunning Russian beauty and the diminutive sourpuss pirouette in the shadow of the massive catamaran on the other side of the hangar.

"She can't stay away from you," Mary Margaret says.

"She hates me," Woody replies.

"Why would that be?" she asks.

"I have no idea," he answers.

"Maybe it's because every meeting with you ends up in mortifying humiliation," she suggests.

"Perhaps you're right," he concedes. "Here they come again."

"It must be kismet," she says.

"A bad penny," he corrects her.

"She *is* pretty hot," Mugs points out.

"She is that," Woody agrees.

"You could try the blue pill again," she suggests.

"And watch my little friend turn back into the Bent Monster." He shudders.

"There must be someone you can go to for that," she replies.

"A dick orthodontist?" he asks.

"Just the ticket," she replies.

As they dance back into range, Woody is fascinated by the humorless little tyke—he's so familiar—where has he seen that face before? That's it. It's the grumpy old man face that he sees on all his fellow billionaires of a certain age whenever they are out and about with their barely legal arm candy—waiting for the slights. *Excuse me, miss, does your father*—or worse—*granddaddy want another bottle of Chateau Lafite-Rothschild?* Meanwhile the venture capitalist turned roué is in the men's room taking his own blue pill.

When Svetlana gets close, she flashes Woody a venomous glare. That lights a fuse. She is spectacular—that hair—those eyes—that gown—the slit—the leg—the stockings—the lace—the garter . . . Woody—ever the ladies' man despite recent setbacks—is out of his seat and on his feet. All the men join him—standing and clapping. The bankers follow suit. The photographers are quickly drawn to the spot like sharks to blood. That turns the spotlight on the movie star, who clearly responds in kind. The timbre of the dance shifts. Caught up by the moment and finally back on center stage, Svetlana is clearly trying to modulate this fox-trot into a tango—how creepy is that? Woody grins and sits down when he sees the committee on the dais sending desperate hand signals to the conductor, who brings it all to a screeching halt with the power of his baton—*cha cha cha*.

All the men who are still on their feet explode in applause, hoots, and whistles. Svetlana, with Joyless James tucked safely under her arm, bows and blows kisses. The adulation continues on. The baby remains unimpressed, but the actress is gracious enough to honor her costar. With her hands under his armpits she lifts him over her head and shows him off to the audience, which appreciates him with appropriate admiration. To close out the set she brings him down to face level and kisses him in the style of her people.

After the kiss on his right cheek he still looks grumpy. On the second kiss he appears as if he is interested in something for the first time in his life. He balls his fists and raises them up, so, when Svetlana applies the final kiss, he is ready to grab the top of her gown and pull it down with all his strength. He succeeds. Her spectacular breasts burst free and clear into the open air with what people at tables nearby will swear afterward is an audible pop.

Svetlana screams. The flashbulbs erupt. A dozen hands catch the airborne infant, who is beaming and clapping his little fat baby hands with delight.

"Those two seem to pique his interest," Woody says to Mugs, and laughs so hard that he pees himself. "Uh-oh."

Svetlana is quickly surrounded by a sympathetic band of wives—or is it a buffer zone to protect their husbands? Either way, she quickly brings the runaways back into the shelter.

It is not going so well for Woody. In a panic he watches the pee patch spread on his trousers. This has never happened before. He did his exercises religiously. After the surgery he was as dry as the Mohave Desert. His nurses were impressed. This is the first accident he's had since he was two years old. But this time around, in just a few short moments, he is to stand and deliver—emphasis on stand. Nowhere to run. Nowhere to hide. Everyone will see his embarrassment. This isn't supposed to happen to him. Humiliation is for other people. What to do? What to do?

The excitement on the floor abates. The attendees retake their seats. Gleeful James, still giddy with baby delight, is returned to his high chair. Svetlana is trying to disappear off the face of the earth. Mackenzie is tapping her wineglass for attention. And the stain is spreading across Woody's pants like an animation showing the Nazi occupation of Europe in 1941. He waves desperately at

Svetlana. He can tell that she sees him, but she ignores his invitation.

"Help me get her over here," he hisses to Mary Margaret.

She joins him in beckoning to the actress. Being invited by another woman seems to do the trick. Untrusting, she tentatively approaches their table. Mary Margaret smiles reassuringly, pointing to Woody.

"What?" Svetlana says.

Woody gestures. He wants to whisper something. She hesitates. She looks around the room. Everyone seems preoccupied with whatever they are announcing from the dais.

She bends over to listen to him barely breathe the words into her ear. "I liked them in Japan," he says. "I love them here. You've got a beautiful set of jugs."

She can't believe what she hears. She looks to a sister for a sanity check. Mary Margaret nods solemnly. Woody just grins.

Svetlana bolts upright. The spotlight is refocused. The photogs sprint back to the scene of the next crime, arriving just in time to capture the sequence of events as the statuesque actress grabs—alas the waiters have cleared the table and all the good stuff is gone—a full glass of red wine and dumps it into Woody's lap.

"Swine," she snorts as she storms off.

Woody—far from looking chastised—jumps up on his chair and holds his arms high in victory as if he just got a perfect ten on the floor exercise at the Olympics—showing off his red badge of courage that is blossoming all over his crotch. After a brief moment for digestion, the room explodes with a deafening ovation—including foot stomping—there must be Europeans present.

At the same time, back in his high chair, James has started to give off a beastly smell, but he is still having a high old time—smiling and clapping his fat little baby hands—another miracle cure.

51.
TIM

AN INSANE FRENZY HAS INFECTED Apartment 6A. The building super wishes he could simply slink away, but Tim doesn't possess Harry Potter's Cloak of Invisibility, and every time he gets close enough to the front door to feel the knob in his hand, he hears Victoria's bel canto above the din with a voice so penetrating that he would probably hear it in his basement warren. She is running him ragged.

The place is wall-to-wall with people. Fifi and her crew are flaunting their home field advantage, but the London maids just off the plane have even more attitude—Rule Britannia and all that. There's also a paddling of Mistresses—like a pride of lions—that Victoria rented from *Deidre's House of Pain*—so far east on Delancey Street that it's practically in the river. They're all wearing formal gowns with long sleeves to cover their tattoos. Miss Lavinia's ladies don't do ink.

Tim is on his hands and knees—getting kicked in the head, fingers stepped on—doing last-minute wiring. Victoria wants a monitor in the large foyer where the event begins. She wants to be able to have a cam's-eye view as the action unfolds. Tim wants to stop the bleeding as he takes a layer of skin off his knuckles while stripping wire.

"Grrr," he growls.

"Ten minutes," she says, looking down at him under a table.

He plugs in the cord and the screen lights up, mirroring the mayhem in the antechamber. He watches Victoria say "Ten minutes" to Fifi.

Then the hometown gurls call out as they genteelly clap their white-gloved hands. "Quiet please. Quiet please."

"They think it's bloody Wimbledon," the senior parlour maid from across the pond says. "Show them how it's done, Sarah."

"As you wish, Mary," Sarah replies as she turns to the madding crowd and lets out an *Oi* so profound and powerful that everything made of metal on the sixth floor chimes in—including the fillings in their teeth.

The sympathetic vibrations ring on long after Sarah is quiet. Tim is pretty sure it's a C major chord. That's what the slots pay out to in Vegas. He recognizes it.

He is fine-tuning the monitor where he can watch the brief run-through. The ribbon is stretched out across the foyer. The maids are lined up on either side with the Mistresses distributed evenly in front. Fifi is in charge of the large pair of scissors on a pink pillow with lavender fringe. Victoria picks them up and continues the pantomime.

"Then Mummy will say something upper crusty for the Yanks," she explains. "Snip snip—hooray—toasts all around. Then it's off to your individual chambers for special maid time. The scenarios are in your information packets. Any questions?"

Nothing. They are all trained professionals.

After one last look at the floorset, Victoria lights the fuse. "Pour the wine," she says to the gurls.

Champagne corks pop like a naval salvo.

"Sips, ladies," Victoria cautions. "Make it last."

She takes the first flute poured and positions it next to the cam.

"How's that?" she asks.

Tim looks at the monitor. The elegant crystal brilliantly frames the scene—classy bubbles drifting up with aristocratic patience.

"Lovely," he says.

"Right or left?" she asks.

"It's perfect," he says.

"Then go get my mother," she says.

"Me?" Tim asks in a panic. "Why me?"

"Everyone else is working." Victoria dismisses him with flicks of her wrist. "Go. Go. Shoo." Then she is gone.

Tim pulls himself up and staggers forward—*Dread Man Walking*. How did he get himself into this situation? On the other hand, it's not like he's meeting his girlfriend's parents—it's worse. He googled Miss Lavinia. You don't want to know.

He discreetly taps on the door to the lounge and gets tongue-tied—what's he supposed to call her? He doesn't know Victoria's last name. Hi Victoria's mom? Miss Lavinia? Mistress?—I don't think so.

Tim cracks the door and sticks his head in. "They're ready for you, ma'am,"—a diplomatic compromise. "Ma'am?"

He walks into the room and she looks at him with such a cold contemptuous stare that his blood runs cold. He is forced to look away. She is a Gorgon—except in a huge wig, no snakes.

Victoria's voice penetrates the lounge. "Two minutes," it announces.

"Madam," Tim croaks, "will you allow me to escort you?"

He sidles up to her avoiding direct eye contact until she is right there and he has no choice. He shivers again—but not for so long this time. Tim is a gentle soul at heart—intimidated by waitresses in finer restaurants. But he can be brave. Sucking it up, he comes around for a second pass, getting up close and personal with Miss Lavinia, *dominatrix extraordinaire*. She has an international reputation—a universal following—and, this evening—definitely a glassy fish-eye thing going on. He crouches down on his haunches in front of her chair. She is looking in his direction but not at him. Her skin is reflecting the cool hue from her huge puffy royal blue blouse with the big bow—or not. It might be oxygen starvation instead.

Tim has picked up all his first aid techniques from watching Saturday morning cartoon shows. So he waves his fingers in front of her eyes—*nyuk nyuk nyuk*—to see if there is a response. Mouth-to-mouth is next on the list, but, as he contemplates those blue lips, he hesitates. This is the first dead person he's run into in real life who isn't in a box.

Tim can't resist the urge—he has never touched a corpse before, even in a box. He stands up, bends over, and with a straight finger—and sound effects—he pokes her. *Boink*.

Strange, he doesn't feel anything—that is until—horror—Miss Lavinia starts to fall out of the chair. Tim lunges and catches her. He struggles to his feet with her body in his arms. The house lights come up as the door flies open.

"Curtain's going up," Victoria announces.

"Maybe not exactly," Tim grunts, struggling under the weight.

"Don't tell me she's dead drunk," she gasps.

"You'd be half right," he replies.

Victoria closes the door and hurries over to the macabre dancing couple.

"Put her down," she orders.

Losing control to forces of momentum, Tim unceremoniously drops her back into the club chair.

"Sorry, ma'am," he apologizes.

"Was that addressed to me or her?" she asks.

"Um . . ." Tim struggles. "Both."

"You don't need to apologize to her," Victoria says, holding a thumb to the side of her mother's neck. "My God, she *is* dead."

Tim is totally at sea, floundering and foundering for the right words of comfort.

"I'm sorry," is the best he can come up with, "for your loss."

"Time is all we are losing now," Victoria snaps. "Help me get this blouse off."

It is a spectacular puffy blouse—overdesigned—overengineered—and over the top. They are both struggling to unbutton its many buttons—hundreds—while the corpse is no help at all—falling this way and that—dead weight.

The crowd next door starts counting down: Ten—Nine—Eight—

Finally the blouse is open. Victoria pulls it off too fast and the body falls to the floor. Tim rushes to catch her.

"We can clean that up later," Victoria says, pointing to a different spot on the rug. "Stand there and arms up."

She pulls off his Columbia sweatshirt and pulls on the royal blue puffy blouse.

"What are you doing?" he asks.

"Don't talk. Don't think," she snaps. "Just button."

As he obeys, Victoria ties the big bow with a flourish.

"Stand up straight," she demands, brushing out the wrinkles.

"Three—two—one," they chant next door.

"Not bad," Victoria says. "Let's go."

On the way out the door, she grabs her mother's wig off the floor.

"Don't forget this."

52.
SCANLON

IT'S PIZZA NIGHT IN BAY RIDGE, and although Sergeant Scanlon is on a very strict diet since he got shot in the gut, he will put up with a little discomfort to sit down to dinner and eat with his family. A little discomfort?—he knows for a fact that the members of his surgical team are buying boxes in an office pool predicting the day his spleen comes out for good. They have been calling his gallbladder the *sad sac of woe* since he first rolled into the ER. Dinner?—as far as Scanlon can tell, this is the fourth pizza night this week, and it's only Thursday. His stomach flips as he stares into the open box at the thing—big and round—surrounded by a scabby crust—lying in a pool of oily secretions—tomato stained like a crime scene—or worse.

"Dee-lish," Sergeant Scanlon says as he scoops up a slice and force-feeds himself, gnashing and mashing it down his throat—gag reflex in full repulsive mode, the tomato paste is cloying—the doughy crust is vapid, undercooked pabulum—and the cheese? Scanlon is convinced that pizza cheese is no food product. He believes that pizza cheese is never ingested, digested, or passed along by the human body. Pizza cheese only bonds to itself—doubling in size exponentially—growing larger and larger until it is ultimately rejected like a transplanted organ, along with great pain and loss of blood.

"I don't know how you can eat that crap," Bitzi says as she pops a radish into her mouth.

Scanlon might dislike his stepdaughter, but he lusts after the plate in front of her—not crude for a change but crudités—along with two huge carrots. Children get to write the rules these days. He quickly realizes that he was indiscreet. His roving eyes gave away his hand.

"You know you want it . . ." Bitzi leers at him, waving a carrot wantonly—then stroking it lasciviously, then opening her lips in a big O—sliding the carrot in and out while coordinating the movement of her tongue against the inside of her cheek.

(| (| (|

She pulls the carrot out of her mouth and whispers the end of the sentence so softly that her mother can't hear it, ". . . up your ass."

On the other hand, Bitzi probably could have shouted it out while pulling her stepfather's pants down to go carrot friendly on his ass and her mother would still remain blithely ignorant. Her face has been glued to her phone since Pizza Night Tuesday. But she is about to break her silence.

"Oh," his wife says, texting frantically—she's got the hands of a forty-something but the thumbs of a teenager. "I have to go to Philadelphia."

"Because?" Scanlon asks.

It's hard for him to look away from his stepdaughter, who is nailing him with her patented *I-can't-believe-what-a-sap-you-are* look.

"My sister is at her wits' end," his wife replies.

"Glad to know she's got those back," her husband says.

Stepdaughter clearly likes that crack but barely shows it.

"Go ahead and make jokes," his wife snaps, looking up from her phone for the first time in forty-eight hours—her face ignited with righteous indignation. "Barry is on a ventilator in the ICU."

"I thought Barry died six months ago," Scanlon says. "Didn't you go to the funeral? I think you did. It took five days to bury him, didn't it?"

She looks back at her phone and swipes around.

"It's Larry who's dying," she clarifies.

"Oh, that sister," Scanlon says, happy that everything has gotten sorted out.

"I don't like your tone, mister," his wife says and storms out of the dining room.

"Mister?" Scanlon thinks aloud. "Was it something I said?"

His stepdaughter bats her eyes at him and says with a breathy voice, "Alone at last."

"Yikes," he says and starts to clear the table.

"I will be in my room," Bitzi says. "Stay out."

"Not to worry," Scanlon replies.

After he rinses the plates and puts them in the dishwasher—and puts the pizza boxes outside for the crows—he wipes down the table and wanders into the den. He can hear his wife in the bedroom next door, packing—and singing.

Her name was Lola, she was a showgirl with yellow feathers in her hair and a dress cut down to there

Scanlon opens his personal laptop and logs on to www.coldtrail.com. He is still waiting for a department-issued computer to work at home. But in the meantime, to avoid any hassles from any IAD asshole with his by-the-book bullshit, whenever he does work at home, Scanlon is using this really cool anonymous proxy web site that *oldJim* told him about—just to keep his slate clean.

His heart is pounding as he logs in as *lilSue*, but he relaxes immediately once he sees that *oldJim* is in the lobby. He resists the urge to say "hey." Instead he repeatedly right-clicks on *oldJim* in the list.

Idle for 00:00:02 (hh:mm:ss)
Idle for 00:00:18 (hh:mm:ss)
Idle for 00:00:07 (hh:mm:ss)

Idle for 00:00:15 (hh:mm:ss)
Idle for 00:00:04 (hh:mm:ss)

Sergeant Scanlon of the NYPD is crushed—mad—angry—and above all jealous. It is obvious that *oldJim* is in a private chat with someone else—maybe even a younger girl—with more experience. Scanlon realizes too late that he should have sprung for the white panties with the seven days of the week embroidered on the crotch—*purrrrrrrrr*.

"Bastard," he fumes, but not for long because almost immediately after that the SOB sends him a private message.

oldJim: r u hiding from me hunni?
lilSue: dont want to bother. U R SOOOO BUSY!!!
oldJim: talk to me
lilSue: ur 2 busy
oldJim: SUSAN

Idle for 00:02:04 (hh:mm:ss)

lilSue: IW2CM2S
oldJim: wtf
lilSue: i want to cry myself to sleep
oldJim: Y?
lilSue: my mother is cheating on my real life daddy

53.
MACKENZIE

IN HER MIND, MACKENZIE KNOWS that it wasn't his fault. But in her heart of hearts, she blames her husband for everything that's gone wrong tonight. She is being totally unreasonable, and she knows it. But this is how she feels—and she won't drive home with him either. The thought of spending another minute crammed beside him in that silly Italian penis car just makes her angry, so she hitches a ride back to Manhattan with the other Mrs. Greenbriars—stretch limousine—open bar—all courtesy of Woody Steele, philanthropist, adventurer, all around good guy . . .

"And hung," Number Two shrieks with delight.

"Behave yourself," Number One chastises. "Not in front of your younger sister."

"I want to know," Mackenzie pleads.

They are on their second pitcher of margaritas as they drive along the lower bay.

"Ain't gonna happen," Number Three says. "Our lipsh are sheeled."

The three ladies zipper their mouths before chanting in unison, "What happens on Virgin Gorda stays on Virgin Gorda."

Second group giggle fit of the night.

By the time they roll onto the Brooklyn Bridge, Mackenzie is feeling no pain—and no awkwardness in the company of her predecessors—sisterhood. She offers a toast, "The prenup."

"Oh please," the exes groan as one, and they're off to the races—spinning tales of woe and treachery—the duplicity of men—of lawyers, and husbands.

It's all very harrowing and amazing that they have survived emotionally let alone as well-heeled—Jimmy Choos, by the look of it. Mackenzie takes it all in with a bemused twinkle in her eye. She's not worried. She wrote the contract this time around. It's good. You can take it to the bank—and she will.

They drop her off on West End Avenue. She shakes her head as the limo zooms off with a trail of hooting and hollering—rude comments about her Lord and Master's manhood as well as a bawdy song—swapping out Barnacle Bill the Sailor with Steel Woody the Lumberjack. But her opinion of her husband has definitely ticked up a few notches on the scale. For one thing, he's showing a greatly improved taste in women these days.

There are two domestics smoking cigarettes away from the front door to her building. She's never seen them here before. On the other hand, they look more like they are going to a fancy dress ball than to work here. Another first—she runs into an old guy in a wheelchair waiting for the elevator. He's wearing a bathrobe over striped pajamas—staring straight ahead at nothing.

Bing.

The doors open. Another maid—this one carrying a wig in his left hand, limps out on a broken high heel. Mackenzie thinks he's got a sour puss on. Her opinion is confirmed by the way he storms off.

"CIA," the old man says.

"Excuse me?" Mackenzie asks, turning to face him. She is taken aback by his ferocious look.

"He's with the CIA," he repeats. "They've been spying on me since 1958."

Bing.

The other elevator opens. The old man rolls himself into it and deftly spins the chair around—spry.

Mackenzie starts to follow. He brandishes his cane.

"Private," he hisses as the doors close.

Curious little man, she thinks, once she's in her apartment peeling off her fancy schmansy grown-up party dress and trading it for an XXL Wharton sweatshirt and a pair of granny panties. She slops some jug Chianti into a jelly glass and crashes in front of her computer—the place where everyone she knows relaxes when they are alone. She wakes it up. Her overflowing in-box is stuffed with an equal measure of commiseration and thinly veiled *schadenfreude*—how boring. She reads an incomprehensible and billable message from her lawyers and a strategy plan from her broker. There is nothing from Ivan. She didn't expect anything.

"It's playtime," she says out loud as she refills her jelly glass.

She logs into www.coldtrail.com through the back door. She won't be able to enjoy this guilty pleasure much longer. Next week, just before the IPO, they're going to brick it up like Tut's tomb. But for now, the back door is still wide open for those in the know.

Mackenzie launches the console and instantly she's got a bird's-eye view of what tens of thousands of members are viewing tonight—just point and click on a thumbnail—and OMG what those two are doing certainly can't be legal in most states. The secret destinations of those who crave anonymity break down into a small number of categories: porn, kiddie porn, porn, terrorist bomb recipes, insider trading, drug marketplaces, and porn.

"Note to self," she says after observing what's trending. "Don't take that long holiday weekend in Mogadishu."

She pulls up the metric diagnosticator and clicks on the spikers. But there's nothing at the moment that piques her prurient interest.

Washington scandals with pictures—*Real or imagined,* she wonders.

Embarrassing movie star bikini disasters—*Retouched to look worse.*

Famous UK dominatrix is coming to America.

Double-click on that one.

Mackenzie has to squint at the screen to make out what's going on. Some careless person has placed a champagne flute directly in front of the camera lens. All she can make out is a woman in a huge bouffant hairdo surrounded by a crowd of maids—a lot of black and white surrounding an explosion of cobalt blue.

54.
IVAN

THERE IS NO DOUBT IN Ivan's mind that everything that has gone wrong tonight—this week—this year—even in the times before they even met—is and was his current wife's doing. He doesn't understand the motivation, but he knows the guilty party. He is further incensed when Mackenzie cuckolds him in a New Age kind of way, climbing into a black limo with his ex-wives—Girl Power. Up until now he has been looking forward to being alone with his lovely bride on the long drive home—locking her in the deep freeze—frostbite time. But she stole that away from him too. Now he is just angry. The only good news? He can leave now.

His phone buzzes in his breast pocket. He pulls it out without being rude. He is the only person sitting on the dais by this point. It is an IM from his favorite insider trader.

"re: tranche that ~~we~~ you stole from steelex," he texts.

"tell me," Ivan replies impatiently.

"in hostile takeover u just bought usys at 4x par from yourself," the trader texts back. "congrats."

And Ivan thought he was angry before. To make it a Hollywood movie, Woody's infectious laughter fills the hangar as if on cue. Ivan looks contemptuously at the impromptu gathering of disgruntled—what should he call them—alumni? Whatever. They're all drunk as skunks. He is glad that he can just walk away—her people, her fault. He stands up and slides his phone in a pocket. He's watching Woody mumbling some rude crack—probably about him—which is confirmed by backslapping and snorting hilarity. *Just go*, he says to himself.

Cough, cough.

He turns and faces a mousy woman in a sad chartreuse strapless gown that is unflattering to her breasts—not that they are pulling their own weight.

"The party's over, Mr. Greenbriar," the mousy woman bristles. "Please take your guests with you when you go"—*segue*—her people, his fault.

"They're not my guests," he snaps.

"In all my years," she says, shaking her head in disbelief—or is it disapproval? Her lips definitely look tsk-able—they've got those fine vertical lines radiating from them. "I have never seen a bar cleaned out before—every drop—even the Retsina. That's hardcore. At least they didn't start singing."

Cue the drunken sailors who burst into song with gusto.

He's a lumberjack and that's okay,

He woods all night and he steals all day.

"Mr. Greenbriar," the mousy woman insists, her lips pursed so tightly that it looks like she could turn her face inside out if she just swallowed.

"Excuse me," Ivan says unceremoniously, pushing her to the side. "I'm busy."

Not the character assassination that he intended, but in fact he is busy all of a sudden. Out of the corner of his eye he notices that his motley ex-crew is now surrounding his sailboat. He strides over to them wearing the same seven-league boots that he pulls on whenever he confronts crises around the world—global wildcat strikes, natural disasters, or a coup d'état that will ultimately nationalize one of his industries—*el Americano feo*—at least this is the badass that he imagines he would have been if he had ever actually done any of those things.

Nevertheless, the Great Unwashed do part as he approaches. Some look surly when they recognize who he is. Some laugh at him. When he gets close he sees that Woody is on his back underneath the catamaran looking up her skirt.

Woody sees him too and waves at him. Then he does this irritating, youthful move where he kicks his legs up over his head and in one fluid motion he leaps up onto his feet—filling the hangar with his teeth—teeth everywhere and a 10,000-watt klieg-light smile—hand extended.

Ivan knows he has no options here. He grips and grins—shaking the hand. Being rude in front of all these manly men—personal enemies or not—would be out of the question. What he doesn't realize is that the paparazzi are still around. Who knew? As dozens of flashes explode, Ivan is painfully aware that next to Woody's exuberance, he will look like the guy wearing new sneakers with a deep tread who just stepped in something.

Woody continues to stage-manage the photo shoot. Ivan is so overwhelmed that he complies with every direction like a lump of clay in a Gumby movie. The last thing he remembers is standing next to Woody—side by side—admiring the catamaran in frame.

"I've got to get me one of these," Woody says. "Wait a minute—I did—Dutch treat."

The camera flashes explode. Ivan is blinded.

"See you on the water," someone whispers in his ear.

55. VICTORIA

SHE'S BACK IN BED IN THE BASEMENT. At this rate, Victoria might get comfortable sleeping in the basement—or not. It is very subterranean. She's thinking about that a lot, along with a lot of other things—it is the middle of the night. On the other hand, the boy is sleeping quite comfortably it seems, making blissful happy-boy breathing sounds while he's at it. He is very sweet. This is the third or fourth time they have shared a bed, and he has never forced himself on her. Not once. The late-night reverie leads Victoria to wonder what's wrong with her and why hasn't he? It's not like she ever said *NO* and that he did or didn't respect that—and thereby her. She hasn't been presented with the opportunity to say *NO*. Maybe ultimately she'll have to say *Come on in, the water's fine*. But is that a good idea? They have a professional relationship. Of course that never held her mother back. That thought sends shivers coursing through Victoria's body and her eyes are drawn to what they have been carefully avoiding for that last five minutes and the five minutes before that.

The boy doesn't possess a wig form—why would he? So while they were undressing him, along with the kissing and moderately tasteful pawing, the best they could do was to stand his bicycle helmet on end and put the wig to bed there for the night. They positioned it poorly—drink was involved. As a result, Mummy's wig is between the bed and the tiny window that shows all the ankles walking by on the sidewalk. But there is plenty of light coming in through that small window—enough to backlight the wig and make it feel like Mummy is in the room and watching her.

Victoria is looking into the dark side of the moon and feeling damned. She has been trying to grieve, she really has. Perhaps she will have tears tomorrow at the funeral home when she writes the check. Only morticians have a stronger arm than Uncle Sid. That thought makes her squeeze the boy tighter and closer for comfort.

"I like that," he says dreamily in his sleep.

Victoria hangs onto him like he's the last thing floating after the ship sank. There are two things that she knows for sure. 1) Her mother hid every pound—it's either buried somewhere or stuffed into a biscuit tin somewhere else. 2) All Victoria will inherit is debt—Uncle Sid's debt—and Uncle Sid doesn't recognize bankruptcy courts. On a positive note, if Uncle Sid is her father after all, maybe he will have a soft spot for her and let her pay off the loan by working upstairs in his flagship brothel in Mayfair—that place is so posh that it has hand sanitizers mounted by the door in every room.

Oouph. The boy rolls over and elbows her in the stomach. It *is* a twin bed.

"Thank you," she says, kissing him on the shoulder for snapping her out of a late-night gloom-and-doom fest.

After all, the house did have a very strong evening when all is said and done. They signed up over two thousand new members. She hasn't crunched all the numbers yet, but the by-room analytics show up-trending throughout the night, with a feedback star score averaging 4 to 4 1/2. The only fly in the ointment was the opening—especially the ribbon cutting. The live chat was buzzing with negative commentary over that along with some hostility and rudeness—Welcome to the Internet—but that is to be expected. Miss Lavinia is the brand, and when you hide the brand behind a glass of bubbles—even if it is Veuve Clicquot—you're going to have to pay the Piper-Heidsieck.

On the other hand, Victoria is comfortable with the 17.5% rate increase she plans to roll out next month. Between the focus groups and the questionnaires returned by the super users, she is confident that the loss due to attrition will be less than 5%—that is if she can resolve the brand crisis. Rebranding is not an option at the moment. What to do?

Thinking back, she is amazed that she did what she did do. It was all gut instinct, driven by panic, of course. But she pulled it off. The brand was accepted so successfully that it was criticized as the brand—but that was more a lack of preparation than brand failure. With no makeup and blue jeans instead of a pencil skirt, Victoria had no choice but to push the champagne flute in front of the camera lens. But that was for public consumption. On her side of the wineglass the resemblance was uncanny. There is not a doubt in her mind that—with the help of the maids—she can turn the imposter from the brand's lesbian tomboy sister into her identical twin—there is just one complication: how to get the boy to sign on the dotted line.

Hmmm, Victoria considers the quandary—while rolling him onto his side at the briefest mini-snort that might be a precursor of snoring to come.

She could seduce him with the classic trifecta of feminine wiles, guile, and the power of the pussy. That thought gives her a momentary thrill as she rubs her hands against his firm musculature, but she quickly questions the idea. How would that be any different from working upstairs at Uncle Sid's?

She sighs. Suddenly she feels weary. Maybe she will sleep after all. But she is pleased that as far as saving the brand goes, she is moving the ball down the field. This is good—except for the fact that the brand is her mother and her mother is dead.

Victoria's eyes open wide. All she can see is her mother's backlit head. She realizes that throughout her life that is all that she has ever seen every time they discussed anything important—unseen and unknowable—just a voice and hair. Victoria can feel the first tear—the first that she can ever remember—others follow. She does not know how to do this, but she thinks that she might be crying.

No. She might be sobbing. Apparently one doesn't need to be trained or take classes to be able to this. Tears are flowing down her cheeks. Her heart is aching. But not for losing a mother—she is mourning the fact that she never had one.

56. SVETLANA

THIS IS NOT THE FIRST TIME that she has crashed a Red Carpet. On those earlier occasions she was just starting out—the other side of her career. Since then Svetlana has lost track of how many Red Carpets she has trod—forty-seven exactly. But it was a lot easier in the day. Dress designers would pitch her. Stylists would comp her. The photogs loved her. She was a rising star—an actor of importance—a boldface name—a future collector of statuettes. But then she stepped into the steaming turd pile of *Richard III* (Act V, Scene IV) *My kingdom for a horse*, and now she's sleeping on a Jennifer convertible sofa in her cousins' co-op on Ocean Parkway next to the expressway in Brooklyn. There was a misunderstanding with the cousins in Brighton Beach, and they kind of threw her out. Fortunately the Brighton Beach cousins haven't spoken to the Ocean Parkway cousins for over ten years, so Svetlana is welcomed into their home with open arms—for the moment.

They help her with her dress too. She gets the idea from a fruit basket that Ivan Greenbriar sends her. It has to be from Ivan. The unsigned card reads *The enemy of my enemy is my friend.*

The fruit basket is covered with form-fitting plastic to guarantee freshness—ugly but practical—and oh-so Ocean Parkway. This dress—calling it a gown is a stretch—will eclipse anything that J-Lo, Maria, Bey, Cee, or Dee has ever worn half naked to the Oscars.

Svetlana picks up two rolls of clear shrink-wrap at a restaurant supply company on Kings Highway. The girl cousins hold them horizontal as she pirouettes her naked body around and around until the layers are thick enough to blur her rude body bits—tits and pussy—but only just those. Then the boy cousins are brought in to hit her with hair dryers until the wrap shrinks so tight she can barely breathe—nothing compared to the corsets she had to endure in *Catherine the Great,* however. She can take it. Then it's off to the premiere of *Roto-Robber VIII: This Time It's Mechanical* and hopefully the best performance of her career.

She takes the F train and transfers to the R train at 34th Street. To be inconspicuous in her cling-film splendor, she's wearing a full-length sable coat that she recently lifted from the checkroom of Rasputin & Co. She approaches the theater cautiously. Fortunately, as expected before any premier, there is a traffic jam of limousines. She does a duck down crab walk behind those bad boys—looking for an empty. She finds one near the front of the line. Maintaining her low profile, she cracks the door and slips in, scoots across the seat and opens the opposing door before the driver is any the wiser. When she places her six-inch stiletto down onto the asphalt, she is feeling good. When she sees who is in the queue for the Red Carpet in front of her, she is feeling even better. It's the BBC talent pool—average age eighty-seven. All of a sudden, she is the hot young babe—thank you, Jesus.

Once she slips off the sable and hands it to a stranger—sorry, Uncle Dmitri—the paparazzi cry out. "Svetlana. Svetlana. Who are you wearing?"

"Ai Weiwei," she lies with a beaming, photogenic smile.

Instantly there are cameras everywhere—people everywhere—all around her. Svetlana is back—and she likes it. Being naked doesn't hurt.

"Svetlana, where have you been hiding?"

"In your dreams."

They all laugh at that.

"Svetlana, what is your next project?"

"I certainly hope it's not Anastasia," she replies coyly. "I'm so bad at amnesia these days. I can never remember my lines."

They all laugh at that.

"Svetlana, are you still seeing Woody Steele?"

"We have never been an item," she insists.

"Well, he's certainly seen plenty of you."

They all laugh at that.

"That was just a screen test," she says defensively.

"So it's true. He's casting you in a movie?"

"I didn't say that," she says, frowning prettily. "No studio wants me. I'm tainted."

"So he's buying you a studio?"

"I didn't say that," she says with a smile that would blot out the sun with its brightness.

The press goes wild.

So Svetlana opens with a gambit. Why should anyone be surprised? Chess runs in her family. Two of her uncles are grandmasters in Russia.

Mate in three, and Ivan buys her a movie studio in two.

57.
MARY MARGARET

ALONE AT LAST. FINALLY she can spend some quality time with the love of her life, and there is no better place to spend quality time—lots of it—than on the Long Island Expressway. In this case the object of her desire is a 1956 Coupe de Ville. The Caddy is fire engine red with a white interior, and it's mint. The engine purrs like a large African cat having an orgasm. She is so happy to be finally getting away and on her own. Is there ever a more beautiful sight than the one in the rearview mirror?

Too soon for her taste, she pulls into the parking lot of a diner on the Southampton bypass. The other half of this illicit assignation is grinning as he opens the car door for her.

"So much for under the radar," he says.

"I'm prepared for that," Mary Margaret replies as she pulls a scarf over her head. "I've got a hijab."

He laughs.

"I wasn't talking about you," he explains. "I was referring to this glorious machine that you are driving. You might as well lead a brass marching band down Montauk Highway."

He is the Chief Financial Officer of The Greenbriar Group

LLC and he cannot keep his hands off Mary Margaret's car. He is dressed *Hampton Casual*, which translates to about $100 per wrinkle.

"Nice shorts," she says. "They must have set you back."

"I'm leasing," he explains.

"Who can afford to buy local around here?" she agrees.

"Our bosses," he says. "Let's get out of the spotlight—I mean sun."

They sit in a dark corner booth, the farthest away from the windows. It is a tryst, for sure, but they are not hiding from husbands and wives—the Securities and Exchange Commission is more likely. But the scheme makes sense. If either one of them traded shares in their own companies today they would be on trial a week from tomorrow.

She orders the *Happy Waitress*, an open grilled-cheese sandwich with a tomato slice and bacon. He orders the *Going Postal*, bangers and mash—and two coffees. Once they are alone they take out their mobiles and conspicuously turn them off, placing them side by side next to the napkin holder, where they can both keep an eye on them for the duration. Their relationship is not based on trust.

"I jotted down some subjects for small talk," he flirts, patting his pockets.

"Me too," she says.

"But all I can find is this string of ticker symbols," he replies as he unfolds a handwritten sheet from a yellow legal pad.

"Me too." She sighs, pulling out a wad of cocktail napkins.

The exchange is made. They smooth the lists down against the table and pull out ballpoint pens. Click. Click. Starting at the top, they alternate reading down the respective lists—call-and-response. Ticker symbol—winning transaction. It's all NYSE and NASDAQ.

"Sell," she says. "EPA smells a rat."

"Buy," he says. "Rare earths: no. Gold: si."

"Buy," she says. "Last living member of class action suit croaked."

"Really?"

"Tuesday."

"Short," he says. "Pedophile CEO is a shutterbug."

"Short," she says. "GMO has HOMO gene."

"Estrogen?"

"You bet."

"Short," he says. "It was all a big lie from the get-go."

The waitress shows up with the coffee and the lists disappear as swiftly as betting slips during a police raid at a bookie.

"I don't exactly know how you can do it," he says as he pours sugar into his coffee. "But if I were you, I would figure out a way to short MOSCX. I sure am."

"Man of Steele Cosmetix?" Mary Margaret asks, her jaw dropping incredulously. "It's printing money."

"Maybe not tomorrow," he says taking a sip. "And why would anyone want to buy Woody Steele's Bodywash anyway?"

"He's a hunk and he's hung," she replies defensively. "What have you heard?"

"Just a little birdie," he says coyly, taking another swallow of coffee. "Macho sells only as long as it's mucho."

Mary Margaret is quick. With a flick of her thumb she spins his spoon around before he sets the coffee mug down. She has created a lever. Thank you, Mr. Archimedes. When the mug triggers the fulcrum it goes airborne and lands on his expensive shorts.

"Shit," he explodes.

"Looks like it to me," she agrees. "Cold water."

He hurries to the men's room without another word. She grabs his mobile and turns it on. When it asks for a password, she types in *$TUDMU44IN.*

"In your dreams," she says aloud as the phone immediately goes to email.

Her eyes go round with shock and dismay as she scrolls through his *Recents* while counting out seconds in her head—ten

Mississippi—eleven Mississippi. After a minute she turns off the phone, wipes her prints off it and puts it back next to the napkins.

Still counting out Mississippis, she reaches under her dress between her legs and touches the dagger. Next to that is her burner. She pulls it out of its holster and dials with two thumbs as fast as a twelve-year-old.

"Don't talk, just listen," she bark-whispers into the disposable cell phone. "Someone broke into the quack's office and stole your medical records. They're shopping them around."

Time's up.

58. TIM

IF GENGHIS KHAN OR ATTILA the Hun hadn't been in the right place at the right time to take a shot at world domination—if they had been just ordinary people but with the same DNA—they would have ended up as the head of a co-op board. That's what Tim sincerely believes. He has just spent ten minutes with his boss, Sylvia, the President of 501 West End Avenue LLP—and *capo di tutti i capi*—as well as the head of the local Hadassah chapter. His heart is pounding. His blue work shirt is soaked, and it's not because he's done anything wrong. She is just that scary.

Bad news from the elevator inspector—cab number two doesn't make the grade. He shuts it down for new cables. The tenants are hopping mad. An assessment for $8,200 is unwelcome, but forcing them to take the stairs has them apoplectic. She locks herself in a small room with the lawyer. After two hours and three readings of the bylaws and articles, he agrees to everything and anything that she asks for. Sylvia makes an executive decision, liberating the exclusive penthouse elevator—égalité fraternité—it's Bastille Day at the co-op.

The recabling should take about three weeks, or so they're

told. At this moment the doors to number two are wide open. The cab is halfway between L and B, exposing its works like a pediment. The huge gear in the center is a cogged testament to mechanical marvels of a distant age. The technician from City Shafts is leaning against it, fastidiously eating his lunch. He doesn't want to get any more grease on his coveralls.

Tim is next door in cab number one. He's got a Snake Eyes spanner bit in his cordless drill to back out the tamperproof screws that hold the panel in place. He loves taking stuff apart. His eyes go wide with wonderment as the inner wiring of the elevator's brain comes into view. He can tell that at least this part has been updated in the last twenty years. The logic board looks like it's from this century.

"What am I looking for?" he asks.

"Jumpers," the tech answers, his mouth full of meatball hero.

Tim looks around until he sees a row of blue plugs that correspond to each floor.

"Needle-nose?" he asks.

"Can't lend tools," the other replies. "Company policy."

Tim remembers that his Swiss Army knife has a pair of tweezers in a slot next to the corkscrew. Up until now he always thought that was really dumb—perhaps even girlie—he's happy for them now. He pulls out one of the plugs, a tiny plastic U with copper guts, and walks it next door to show City Shafts.

"That's it," the tech says. "Ninety degrees and two pins to the right."

Tim goes to work. Despite the fact that he is painstakingly careful, one of the plugs gets away. The slippery plastic bit shoots out of the tweezers and up in the air. His heart is in his mouth as he looks for it on his hands and knees. He doesn't breathe until it is recovered and slides safely into the jumper.

"You can't get those anymore," City Shafts says, looking down in the open doorway. "Be careful."

Tim steps into the lobby to catch his breath and cool off.

"I'm taking lunch," the tech says as he balls up the deli bag and tosses it down the elevator shaft. "Back in an hour."

By the time Tim slides the last plug into the last breaker, his hands are shaking so much that he has trouble fitting the drill bit into the Snake Eyes. When he finally remounts the panel, there is a waiting line of tenants—4B, 5A, and 8A. He goes to the starter's station and throws the breaker. Cab number one springs to life. The fluorescent lights flutter and sputter. The doors close and open. The tenants applaud. Tim takes a bow, and when he stands up again he is watching the doors close on a group of happy people. It gives him a moment of satisfaction to watch the numbers ascend as the ornate bronze arrow transits the arc on the wall overhead.

His mind is suddenly multitasking as he slides the tweezers back into his Swiss Army knife while working through today's punch list. Next up: replacing the ballast in the light over the mailboxes. He turns to go in that direction—still focused on the knife—and walks into a wall—not a wall per se—but a wall of a person—a wall wearing size fifteen basketball shoes who is so centered that Tim bounces off him like he hit, well, a wall—landing on his ass.

The giant is a gentleman and offers him a hand up. Once on his feet, Tim can truly appreciate the scale of this human. He's got to be close to seven feet tall, and he's thick too. He is also a basketball fan—how appropriate—in this case the Brooklyn Nets. He is wearing every conceivable piece of merchandise that you can buy at the team store. The black, droopy game shorts contrast sharply with his skin. He's so white that Tim can't determine whether he's an albino or if he is just so big that when they made him they ran out of pigmentation.

"Thanks," Tim says.

"De nada," the giant replies and pushes the Up button.

Tim has a very bad feeling about this guy.

"Can I help you?" he asks.

"6A," the giant replies.

"Did they phone upstairs?" Tim asks.

"No need," the giant replies. "Friend of the family."

"Really?" Tim says, starting to feel afraid but not sure for whom.

"Really," the giant replies. "They know me. I am a business associate of their uncle." He pushes the Up button again.

Tim looks up at the sundial arrow on the wall above as it moves from right to left. The elevator will be here any moment.

"You should go out to the front desk to be announced," Tim says, hoping that the quavers in his voice don't translate to fear.

"I'm just delivering these," the giant says, holding up a tiny bouquet of white carnations—so small that they practically disappear in his huge left paw. They cost five bucks at the corner Korean deli on Broadway.

"I can take those up for you," Tim says with a courage that he would never believe he had.

"I am supposed to deliver them to Miss Lavinia," the giant says with unvarnished threat and menace. "Personally. Hand to hand."

"I can't let you do that," Tim hears himself say. He hears it but doesn't believe it. Never before would he say something like that to someone like this. But nevertheless it comes out. Perhaps he has been turned into a ventriloquist's dummy by some magical force of nature.

The next thing he knows he is off his feet. Slammed against the wall. Legs dangling. No need to breathe anymore because the massive mitt is going to choke him to death. Tunnel vision turns monochromatic as all the oxygen leaves his brain. He cannot hear the dismissive words that escape the murderer's maw, although he can see the cold contempt in his eyes. But not for long, as gray slowly descends down upon his field of vision.

But God sends him a *Ding*. He can hear that. *Ding* and he is dropped to the floor. Thank you, God. He rolls over onto his side—gasping for air. He slowly regains focus. The giant is standing in front of the elevator, filling the frame. He is so big. Tim is finally on his feet, but all he can see is the giant's expansive back. He staggers toward the elevator in a quixotic attempt to protect Victoria. He tries to throw himself onto the giant's shoulders. To bite his neck? He is desperate. But he has no wind. No legs. No strength. The doors open. Tim makes his move. Only to be knocked down to the floor again as the giant turns and runs away—over him—like a scared rabbit.

Dazed, Tim lifts himself up to his knees and looks into cab number one as the elevator doors slowly close.

Mr. Pavlenko is sitting in his wheelchair, aiming a Kalashnikov, and shouting, "You kids—stay off my elevator!"

59.
MACKENZIE

IT IS THE WET DREAM OF EVERY male graduate of the Wharton School to ring the opening bell at the New York Stock Exchange. As she reviews the events of this life-changing morning—alone in the back of a stretch limo hired to carry a crowd—what she is wondering first and foremost is: *What is the female equivalent of a wet dream?* The question seems apt to her at this lonely moment. She thought it would all be so different—her big moment in the sun. They were supposed to be crammed in—her team—too many people packed into that tiny balcony overlooking the trading floor—smiles all around. But it is only her on the day of the IPO—just her—practically alone. The chairman of the NYSE is in Palm Desert at a pro-am golf match. She got a stand-in. Henry Tipkin, barely a VP, some loser from compliance. It was just the two of them barely together on that empty balcony. Ivan couldn't come. He had to see a man about a horse, or so he said. She wishes now that she hadn't blown off her parents. They clean up good. They would have been additional bodies. None of the bodies in the background need to have names. But it was just her and the Hall Monitor when she pushed the big button at 9:30 to open trading for the day. As she sits in the back of the big empty limousine, Mackenzie finally answers the question du jour. The female equivalent of a wet dream is tears.

The car drops her off at the corporate headquarters, a highfalutin name for a modest suite of offices in a rather dumpy building in the shadow of Google—but only when the sun is northeast. The empty offices are even more depressing—kind of like a catering hall when the wedding party just died in a car accident on the way to the reception. It's all open concept, of course. No offices or conference rooms for this generation—just a big bull pen festooned with crepe paper streamers and a hundred helium balloons stinking with ColdTrail logos, buckets of ice and Champagne, trays and trays of yummy snacks of the fatted-goose variety, and pies from Million $ Pizza on Spring Street—truffle and goat cheese specials. But no bodies. Not even one body. Just Mackenzie. Everyone is in Husavik, closing the back door—or trying to. Something's gone wrong. She can smell it.

She grabs a bottle of bubbles and goes to her standing workstation. She hits the space bar to wake up her computer and opens the wine—*pop*—and even though she knows from past experience that drinking Champagne from a bottle is one of the least satisfying pleasures on earth, she takes a big hit until it shoots out her nose. Told you so.

"Fuck this shit," she says as she drags Nancy's stool across the floor. Nancy has a stool at her standing workstation. She got a note from her doctor. "Cunt."

Mackenzie takes another snort and snorts uncomfortably. At this point she'd take it by vein if she could. She clicks the Iceland-shaped icon on the desktop. The video conferencing screen opens at once. She can tell immediately that things are going badly because Hans is speaking in German and no one on his team can speak anything but emoji. She pulls on a Bluetooth headphone.

"Hans," she says. "Sprechen Sie Englisch bitte."

After a double or a triple take—Mackenzie loses count—Hans faces the cam.

"Hellooo," he says. "Congratulations on your auspicious day. I see that we are now trading"—Hans looks away from the cam for a second—"at eighty-seven."

"What?" Mackenzie replies in shock. The initial offering price was $32.

She launches the market-tracking software that Ivan installed on her computer just in case he happened to be around—thanks for that, dickwad—but Hans is right. ColdTrail LLC is now selling for $88 a share. She taps numbers into the calculator on her phone. Her eyes bug out of her head when she sees the result. She's looking at a ten-figure number. The genius who worked up the valuation for the underwriter is probably looking for a new job right now, but Mackenzie doesn't care much about his problems. Barbie just fucked Ken with a strap-on. She's having a great day. This is the best of all possible worlds.

"Talk to me, Hans," she says before she looks back up to the screen, and when she finally does it's, "Oh, Elnur. Hello."

"Whazzup?" her team's favorite Azerbaijani screams into the camera. "Rich lady in the hood."

"What's going on?" she asks as she takes another hit of Cristal—bad idea to do that on cam. It's called *enabling*.

The Caspian C++ Coder—the Brilliant Bad Boy from Baku—waves a bottle of Jack Daniel's back at her with a shit-eating grin.

"Here's to you, pretty woman," he toasts as he guzzles what looks like half of it.

"Please put Hans back on," Mackenzie requests.

But Elnur can't hear her. He is beat-boxing the lead-in to the Roy Orbison song of the same name. He's *Dancin' with the Czars*.

Mackenzie can't bear it a moment longer. She puts her computer to sleep and her mind on autopilot.

"I'm too rich for this shit." She sighs and walks away.

Many questions come to mind:

Do I feel different? is numero uno. But that always is, isn't it? When she joined a church or lost her virginity. Or the first time she got stoned or drunk.

How will this change me? But this is a perennial also—the constant concern that something—anything—will trigger her inner assholedness and she will be revealed to the world as the bitch that she knows that she has always been destined—given the opportunity and means—to become, a truly horrible human.

What about Ivan? That's the gorilla in the handbag. Compared to today's windfall, the prenup pales. On the other hand, the IPO was his—their—baby. What does she owe him? The *Love Honor and Obey* thing is turning into a *three strikes and you're out* situation. Little hope on that front, and she'd rather eat glass than go to couple's counseling. She should have taken that acting class her freshman year so that she would know how to act like she gave a shit. Or better yet, maybe he's cheating. That would be great. It would fix everything.

And finally: *Now that I'm worth one point twelve billion—at least on paper—why I am riding the No. 1 train—and standing?*

As she gets off the subway at West 86th Street, Mackenzie looks around at her fellow straphangers and feels good about one thing. Perhaps change for the worse is not inevitable. But that is pretty much the only upbeat she can dance to at the moment. For now, as she shuffles off to her pied-à-terre, she feels like the loneliest billionaire on West End Avenue.

60.
SCANLON

PERHAPS IT IS TRUE THAT YOU can't go home again, but Scanlon feels that didn't always seem to be the case. He has lost count of how many times he's walked through these doors—in reality, he wasn't counting. While a station house is not a home, nevertheless, there has always been a comforting familiarity about this place: the puke green walls, the din, the gimpy chairs, the wobbly desks with sticking drawers, the broken-down everything else that has the letters *NYPD* written, stenciled, or pasted on it. Not to forget the creeps—wearing either handcuffs or badges. But that was then. Now he feels a little more distant every time he comes back to the precinct. What has changed? Why do his brother officers seem ever more remote? Are they jealous because they aren't walking around with bits of lead in their guts and pinching wounds? Or are they feeling sorry for him—and his little friend? Do they know that Willy hasn't made his wife say "Ouch" and mean it since the incident? If so, who told them? Is it the guy who's doing her? Or are they just tired of him because he is too sad to play the game? Is he on the job or off the job these days? Who can say?

Suck it up, Sergeant, he says to himself as he puts on his cop face and pulls open the door, bracing for the usual onslaught of lowlife scum and victimized citizens.

He is disappointed to be embraced instead by an upbeat vibe—the sort of mood that permeates the house in the presence of celebrity—some actor doing *research* or a rock star starting his stint of community service. His only comfort is that it won't be his ride along. But he cringes when he catches sight of his CO. He's hard to miss with his preternaturally white teeth—Captain Dentine. All the uniforms agree that in a cave you'd be able to read the *Daily News* by his smile. Scanlon is even more discouraged to see that his captain is gesturing to him.

"Exciting developments in the war against the perverts," he says to Scanlon. "The cavalry has arrived."

The cavalry in this case being James Hathaway, recently of the San Diego Police Department—aka *LittleDebbie669*—who was so successful at nailing kiddie predators that he had his own reality TV show for a while. It ran three seasons. Scanlon knows exactly who he is: a policeman wearing mirrored sunglasses indoors—on this coast, seriously?

"Group hug," his captain commands, draping his arms over the shoulders of his crack preteen Judas goats for a photo op.

The briefing room is packed with reporters and TV cameras. It's sweeps week and you know that *Eyewitless News* is going to lead with whatever sex story that they can repackage as a public service announcement. Sex is good. Inappropriate sex is better. Keeping your kiddies safe from the one thing that they really want to do is best—especially if you can watch it happening to the neighbors' children on the television. It can't be just a coincidence that during sweeps week there is a spike in advertising for hand lotion and Kleenex.

"Ladies and gentlemen," the captain speechifies, pulling his prized honey trappers even closer. "The parents of the greatest city in the world can sleep a little more securely tonight, knowing that the long arm of the law is wearing white cotton panties to protect their most precious gifts from a fate worse than . . ."

He pauses—jammed up.

"Lost innocence," LittleDebbie669 chimes in.

"Exactly." Captain Dentine beams.

Lost innocence? Scanlon can only think of his stepdaughter. If her innocence is lost, it must be hiding under the pile of thongs, marijuana cigarettes, and used condoms beside her bed.

"Sergeant Scanlon, how are you feeling?" one of the reporters shouts out. "On the mend?"

"No questions," the captain snaps.

"Little Debbie," another asks. "What does the 669 stand for?"

SDPD whips the mirrored shades off his face for that one.

"Spit roasting." He grins. "My older gentlemen are very fond of spit roasting."

The captain looks at his lieutenant and draws a finger across his throat.

"Thank you, ladies and gentlemen," he says. "That's strictly off the record."

"I'm sure you two heartbreakers want to share trade secrets," the captain says. "But before that slumber party gets going—Sergeant Scanlon, a word."

A word? Scanlon thinks. *I've got a word—retirement—I should have said it to the commissioner when he visited me in the ICU.*

His captain closes the door to his office.

"Are you okay?" he asks.

"I'm fine," Scanlon replies.

"I'm glad to hear that. Honestly," his captain says and flashes a smile so bright that Scanlon wishes he had Little Debbie's sunglasses. "Sit."

They sit.

"I don't want you to get the wrong idea about Little Debbie," his captain says.

"I welcome the help," he replies. "So many perverts, so little time."

"Ain't that the truth," the captain says and takes a pregnant pause. "Here's another . . ." Shifting gears. "Your numbers are way down, Patrick."

Oh, we're on that page of the handbook where we are on a first-name basis. Can I call you Jackass?

"I'm being reassigned," Scanlon explodes gleefully.

"Oh no," Captain Dentine says, shaking his head. "You're way too good at what you do. You are a resource."

Scanlon deflates into his chair.

"We've all been worrying about you," Cap says. "We figured that the hunt was getting stale—that you needed to go to the next level—a small dose of professional rivalry to snap you out of it. Make it fun again."

Sergeant Scanlon feels like he's one hundred years old as he slogs from his captain's office on the way to his workstation in the dark corner of the squad room, except now there are two computers with a low divider between them. Little Debbie is already going to town. Sunglasses on. Earbuds in. Fingers flying over the keyboard. Scanlon collapses into the chair next door.

"Are we having fun yet?" he asks.

"You bet," Little Debbie says too loudly over whatever music he is listening to.

The sides of his computer and monitor are covered with SpongeBob stickers.

Once again, Sergeant Scanlon does what he does best. He sucks it up and goes back to work.

lilSue: hi Daddy

Idle for 00:00:40 (hh:mm:ss)

lilSue: hello oldJim [poke]

Idle for 00:01:32 (hh:mm:ss)

oldJim:	hi hunnie
lilSue:	where were you?
oldJim:	chatting
lilSue:	with who?
oldJim:	another girl. mayB u know her
lilSue:	what's her name?
oldJim:	little debbie
lilSue:	oh no. stay away from her
oldJim:	Y
lilSue:	she's a slut
oldJim:	good 2 know. thank U

61.
WOODY

WHEN HE HAS TO GET AWAY, he goes beyond the ends of the earth. He calls it Woody's Hole, and the place has fallen off the earth—literally. It took a ton of stock to gain enough influence in the company, but he made it happen. As a result, on Google Maps there is this blurred area—just over ten thousand acres—about a two-hour helicopter ride east of Missoula, Montana.

The accommodations are basic—well below the American Plan—a yurt no less. But not one of those New Agey—*ain't we cool, roughing it with WiFi*—yurts made of teak, Kevlar, and mohair. Woody assembled this structure personally, felling and hewing the lumber, as well as taking down the elk and caribou. He cured the skins right here by the lake where the yurt now stands. The lake remains pristine—the cliff face behind it majestic—Woody's Butte, he calls it. He has never brought anyone else here, ever. The helicopter puts him down in the next valley. It takes him two to three portages to move in, depending on how much beer he brings.

As he watches the morning light hit the distant snowcapped mountains, he can feel the tension start to leave his body; the knots in his neck start to untangle; the vise around his head starts to back off its giant screw. He strips off all his clothing and dives into the lake to make it official. Down down down he swims in water that is so crystal clear it seems that he can reach out and touch the rocks sixty feet away on the bottom. The water is cold. He is naked. He swims until he forgets where he is.

Later, catching his breath as he dries off in the warming sun, he feels a little tickle in the back of his brain. He freezes, all senses attuned . . . nothing. He crosses his arms back and forth across his chest—deep breathing—turning his lungs into bellows. He raises his arms high over his head, stretching on tiptoes. He takes a deep breath and holds it . . . *Click*. There it goes again, but this time he knows what it is. That's the sound that the mirror in a single-lens reflex camera makes when the shutter is released—even the digital ones. He pulls on a pair of shorts and ties on his climbing shoes, just in case.

About a hundred yards to the west of camp he starts looking around. There's a depressed area here. Only in late July does it truly dry out. The rest of the time it's pretty boggy. It takes Woody about ten minutes to find what he's searching for, but, once he spots it, the imprint of a heel is there as clear as day. *Small boot,* he notes. From then on it's pretty easy to backtrack. He hears the horses before he sees them. They're standing patiently in a makeshift corral in a dead-end ravine and out of sight. The palomino looks like the brains of the outfit. The gray is there to carry the luggage.

Woody rubs the golden mane. "Where's your rider, boy?" he asks.

The reason for their contentment is on the ground before them—two canvas buckets—one is oats, the other water. Beside them are a couple of large saddle bags. He flips them open. Nothing remarkable, just the kit you'd pack for a couple of days on the trail. That is except for the large manila envelope containing an 8x10 of—*how did he ever guess?*—himself. He feels ambivalent about the box of Remington soft-point rifle cartridges. Out here they could mean anything. But bullets are like mice in the pantry. It's never only the ones you can see.

Woody's next plan is based on the assumption that if whoever is tracking him wanted to kill him, he would be dead already. He jogs back to camp. At the base of the cliff he shouts out, "Want to play? Catch me if you can."

With that he takes off up the rock face like a lizard with a hot foot. He knows this climb like the back of his hand. His feet land on proper purchases like they're the footprints painted on the floor of a ballroom dance studio. He doesn't pause. He doesn't think. He just climbs.

He only slows down as he approaches the top. About forty feet down from the ridgeline there's a place he calls Woody's Step. He named it after Hillary's on Everest. Actually, it's more a leap of faith than anything else. At this point of the climb, if you continue straight up, you encounter this deceptive grip just steps from the top. The limestone is discolored in such a way here that it looks like the perfect crack in the stone for a finger lock or a fist jam where it's wider, or if you prefer something even easier after the tiring climb, there's a pope's nose immediately to the left—except that it's all a lie. There's nothing there at all—just smoke and mirrors—a big mountain practical joke. Woody still doesn't remember how he survived that first climb. In the recurring nightmares he doesn't. On the other hand, if you take the leap of faith around a blind turn at Woody's Step, the climbing is so easy it's like riding an escalator the rest of the way up.

Once he reaches the top he stays low. He belly crawls over to the spot that anyone who is unfamiliar with his rock will aim for. He hooks his toes into a solid fissure and squeezes a limestone Quasimodo with his thighs. He braces himself and waits.

Woody can tell by listening that the climber is agile and capable. He is scaling an unfamiliar rock face with confidence, and, more telling, he is not rushing. But nevertheless he makes steady progress. Woody is impressed that he arrives and passes the leap of faith as quickly as he does. At this point while counting grips, Woody is a coiled spring. He's betting that the climber goes for the pope's nose just to be on the safe side.

Lucky for the climber, he guesses right. As the climber grabs at the optical delusion, Woody pounces over the ridgeline and, reaching over, steel-traps the climber's wrist with one hand. It is touch and go for a moment. The climber is wearing desert camouflage. As he swings back and forth his cover blows off.

"Oh my gosh." Woody giggles. "You're a girl."

She is in fact a girl, which is a good thing, because Woody would have probably dropped a larger man by this point.

"And you're hot," he says. "Oops. Inappropriate speech, but that GI Jane thing you've got going on is smoking."

She responds to that with a soldier's blank, stoic stare.

He swings her back and forth a few times to remind her of certain realities.

"You should bear in mind, my dear," he adds, "that I am twice as old and half as fit as you are."

Her poker face shows a few cracks.

"This might be a good time to begin serious negotiations," he suggests. "Before I begin to lose my grip."

She nods.

"I'll take that camera," he says.

The girl must have been Special Forces or a gymnast. Her upper-body strength is so powerful that she practically levitates, successfully pulling the camera off her shoulder to hand him the strap.

"Thank you," Woody says.

He leaves her dangling as he looks at the image in the camera back—the sad lament of his recently shrunken head.

"That water be cold," he says with a little hesitation on his grip for effect. "But you didn't get my face in frame. That's why you had to come back."

She nods her head yes.

"Is there anything else?" Woody asks, serious.

The girl shakes her head no.

"All right then," he says.

Woody spins the camera strap around his head and slings the camera far out over the lake where it sinks in one hundred-plus feet of water.

"On three," he tells the girl. "One—two—three."

He whips her up onto the high ground like a rag doll. She collapses. He gives her a moment.

"Time's up," he says, sooner than later. "I want a beer."

He pulls her to her feet. Her face is white.

"Say hey to Mr. Greenbriar for me," he says. "I sure hope you're pulling hazardous duty pay." Then he takes her firmly by the shoulders and bores into her eyes. "And don't ever come around here again."

62. IVAN

"DO YOU KNOW WHO I AM?" the Raging Hard-On in the expensive sports car demands.

"I'm sorry, sir," the guard in the nondescript uniform explains. "You're not on the list."

Ivan doesn't bother pulling the Lamborghini over, but he does take it out of gear. He grabs his phone off the passenger seat. His two thumbs tap-dance over it. He hits Send and tosses the phone back onto the leather seat. He looks up at the guard.

"You won't get a reference," he says.

"You're not on the list," the guard repeats.

They glower at each other for the three minutes it takes the Senior VP for Sucking Up to hustle out to them.

"Good morning," he gushes. "Good morning, Mr. Greenbriar, and welcome to Kentile Studios."

Ivan likes obsequiousness so much that he'll pay extra for it—if the brownnoser comes from a good family and a superior school—so much the better.

"Can I drive onto my lot now?" Ivan snarls.

"Of course. Of course," Brownie says. "O'Brien, what's wrong with you?"

"He's not on the list," O'Brien replies.

The gates slowly open. Ivan pops the clutch and zooms through, nearly driving over the toes of both men. He is mildly amused as he watches Brownie sprint after him—but just mildly. He parks diagonally across three handicapped spaces and checks a few stock quotes on his phone while waiting for Brownie to catch up. When he does, sweat is streaming down his face.

"It's good exercise, Brownie," he says.

"Who?" the other man asks—panting.

"Never mind," Ivan dismisses. "Where are we going?"

"Through this door we can slip in the back, as you requested, Mr. Greenbriar," Brownie says. "Or we could go in the front. That would be much more appropriate—the grand entrance."

Ivan drapes an arm over the shoulder of the cowering sycophantic suit.

"A word to the wise, Brownie," he cautions, not without a threatening tone in his voice. "Generally, what I request is what I want."

"I understand that, sir," the studio executive replies. "But the boys and girls will be so disappointed if they can't welcome you properly."

"Heartbreak is an actor's toolbox," Ivan says as he pulls away. "And you should rethink your antiperspirant strategies."

"Thank you, sir," Brownies says as he holds the door.

They walk into the dark half of a massive soundstage. A football field away there are bright lights and people in motion. He whispers in Ivan's ear as they approach.

"Miss Petracova is here as a personal favor to the director," he explains. "They are old friends. She thinks we're screen-testing wannabes. She is the off-camera voice of the Empress Alexandra Feodorovna. Would you like headphones?"

"I'm good." Ivan waves him off as he settles into the canvas director's chair labeled *MOGUL.*

"If you want anything, just raise your pinkie," Brownie says as he darts off to sweat another detail. That seems to be what he does best—sweat.

Ivan is glad to be alone and sitting in the dark. It gives him a chance to catch up with things—and appreciate his brilliance—it has all happened so fast. Not only was he able to buy the studio for a song, but he has structured the deal in such a way that he doesn't have to sign anything. He sold the film catalog to Turner Movie Classics and paid the balance with the studio's own debt, which he is spinning off into a wholly disowned subsidiary that will go into Chapter 11 two weeks from tomorrow—he's got the docket in his pocket.

What happened next is just gravy—symbiotic gravy. *Talent Search USA*, a reality show on a nosebleed cable station—not to be confused with other cable staples: *Talent America*, *Talent R USA*, or *Up With Talent for Jesus*—has rented out the studio to discover the next great American bullfighter and tape it. Obviously they don't read their email or anything else. At the same time, Kentile Studios, which, based on the opening weekend of *Catherine the Great,* has bet the farm—and is about to lose it by going Russian—is currently in the throes of casting for a remake of *Anastasia.* They have to go forward. They're too broke to pay the lawyers to fight the contracts.

In a classic *chocolate collides with peanut butter* epiphany, the two losers join forces to embrace victory. At this moment Ivan is watching the resulting magic unfold before his eyes. There's a mini set built on the soundstage, dressed with a modest suggestion of Czarist opulence—a few chairs on a Persian rug and an ornate table. Next to the stage there are bleachers. Ivan figures that there are fifty bodies on either side. He can't see their faces, but he can feel the vibe—consumable. The banner over their heads reads: *Talent Search USA: Acting like it's Real.*

Ivan watches two or three auditions—pretty fresh young ingénues in bright gowns of crinoline and taffeta running lines with Svetlana in a frumpy chenille rehearsal skirt. He drifts back to his phone and eases a highly leveraged equity that he hadn't been paying close enough attention to. Good thing he woke up. He could have lost millions.

Whew, he thinks. *I must be losing my grip.*

When he looks back to the stage, she is looking directly at him. Svetlana plays the next audition eye-locked—unblinking. At the end she whips open her hand fan and disappears. Ivan is shocked by the impact of that gesture.

He raises his pinkie and all hell breaks loose—confetti, balloons, a trumpet fanfare. All the pretty fresh young things surround Svetlana—kisses all around—and a sash—and a tiara.

"Ladies and gentlemen," the PA system explodes, "introducing the next Anastasia for the ages—Svetlana Petracova."

Applause. Applause. Applause.

Ivan takes a phone moment. He texts his broker: SHORT KENTILE.

But then she is standing before him, so he stands. She hugs him tight.

"You dear sweet wonderful man," Svetlana says.

Breasts. He sighs.

63.
VICTORIA

CHORES ARE CHORES—even the most onerous are just work. *Suck it up and carry on, Victoria,* she says to herself. That cinches it. Things must be bad indeed. She never refers to herself in the third person. On the other hand, she has every right to feel sorry for herself. Victoria has spent the entire morning with an unctuous man with a fake, simpering smile—no, it might have been sincere—it is so hard to judge the sincerity of a simper. On top of which she is carrying a heavy load in her arms. The thought of schlepping it up five flights of stairs makes her ragey and wanting to cry at the same time.

She is accompanied by Ethel, the ugly duckling—or more like the Plain Jane—of the household—especially when all the other maids are preening their best Belle Époque plumage. Ethel has a fetish for the drab maid uniforms that are worn by housekeeping at mid-range motels. She is wearing a dark gray raincoat and a light gray scarf over her set helmet hair. She just made a run to the greengrocer while Victoria was signing legal documents and checks. She is carrying two shopping bags of vegetables, which have more presence and character than she does. She makes your mousiest maiden aunt look like Cleopatra.

They stop off in the mailroom before beginning the ascent to the summit. Victoria puts her burden down on the table with the Tiffany lamp and mines her mailbox for bills with an unwelcomed success. After flipping through them, her mind clicking like an adding machine, she drops the stack of invoices into the shopping bag with the kale and a groan.

"Off we go into the wild blue yonder," she says as she grabs the bronze urn and heads to the stairs.

The women are delightfully surprised by the next change of events—at least Victoria is—Ethel is stoic in all things; it's hard to tell what she is thinking even when surrounded by a crowd with infectious smiles. Across the lobby the atmosphere is festive. The elevator is running.

"Maybe the old man died," one of the tenants muses wishfully.

"*Dasvidaniya*," another salutes.

Victoria and Ethel wait in line as the elevator comes and goes. A smattering of applause acknowledges every time the door opens and closes. When it's their turn to step in, a massive side of beef blocks the way.

"Welcome to New York, Victoria," the giant says.

"Get out of our way," she insists.

"Where's your mother?" he demands.

"She's around," Victoria says as she covers the engraved bits on the urn with her thumbs.

"Sid wants to talk with her," the giant says.

"I'll tell her," she replies.

"Will you?" he wonders. "Sid doesn't think you respect him anymore."

"Why would he feel that way?" she asks.

"Because you owe him so much money," he says.

"Technically," Victoria starts, "I don't owe him anything. It's all a big misunderstanding . . . forgery is involved . . ."

"Tell it to the Marines," the big guy says as he pushes the ladies out of the way and commandeers the elevator. "I've got a personal message from Sid to your mum."

After the doors close, Victoria asks the maid, "Who's working the door?"

"Fifi," Ethel replies.

"Good," Victoria says. "The Great White Hope doesn't stand much of a chance with our Fifi."

The air is shattered by a high-pitched shriek.

"VIX!"

Victoria knows that voice, but before she turns to acknowledge it she has a task for the maid. "Put the bags down and take her for a walk in the park."

She watches Ethel leave the building hugging the urn close to her chest like a cherished infant. As she turns to face the music, Victoria is unprepared and off-balance when the wave hits and she is engulfed in a massive tidal hug. She staggers around trying to maintain her balance—sided but not blind—she knows exactly who her assailant is—her BFF from B-school—Mackenzie Greenbriar, née Alden. They rock side to side as the breath is squeezed out of her—then—poof! She's dropped like a pregnant mistress.

"I'm still mad at you," Mackenzie says.

"What did I do?" Victoria asks.

"You didn't come to my wedding," Mackenzie sniffs.

Victoria sniffs. "You've been drinking," she says.

"Not enough," Mackenzie replies. "Don't change the subject. What do you have to say for yourself?"

"Two things," Victoria says. "One: you eloped; and two: your groom was a dick."

Mackenzie looks cross for a moment, then erupts in laughter. Hugging her friend again, she gushes, "I have missed you so much."

Ding.

The elevator door opens and the giant walks out.

"She wasn't up there," he says.

"I told you that," Victoria replies as if to a petulant child.

"Where is she?" he asks.

"She was just here," Victoria says. "She's gone for a walk in the park."

"Sid really wants to talk to her," he repeats.

"I'll tell her," she replies.

"Oh my God," Mackenzie says as the giant walks away. "Is the circus in town?"

"That was no circus," Victoria deadpans. "That was my life."

"You really do live in this building?" Mackenzie says incredulously.

"I really do live in this building," Victoria replies.

"What time is it?" Mackenzie asks.

"Ten to noon," Victoria answers.

"It seems that I'm rich all of a sudden," Mackenzie notes. "Want to go up to my place and drink the good stuff?"

"Sounds like a business plan," Victoria says.

64.
TIM

ABOVE ALL THINGS HE IS FRUSTRATED—not just sexually. God knows he certainly is that—all this half-naked platonic sleeping together is exacerbating the situation, and he can't exactly do that for release when she's in bed with him, now can he? She is unlike any girl he's ever met, and he's pretty confident about the girl part of the equation. They might have a chaste relationship, but they do sleep close enough that Tim knows for sure that she's missing a major piece of platonic hardware.

At the moment, he is in the butler's pantry sitting on a stool with his laptop balanced on his knees. There are even more switches and routers than before, and cable is hanging all over the place. It's hard to move without getting caught up in a tangle. Fifi is just outside, repeatedly crashing a vacuum cleaner into the door—making guttural noises. Tim figures she's trying to sound French. Having some breathing space now that the elevator is running, he is logged on to the web site as a *Chat-Admin* trying to make himself useful. He especially enjoys watching the traffic behind the scenes.

66.67.1.22 <dress_me_up_buttercup> has joined (14:15:29)
104.32.4.33 <ur_little_pony_girl> has joined (14:18:09)
72.186.16.151 <sissy_hubby> has left (14:22:14)
72.186.16.151 <MistressXtreme> has joined (14:22:15)
111.123.92.12 <want_2B_eaten_4_dessert> has joined (14:35:27)
117.43.33.32 <HelloClitty> has left (14:36:33)

Which is not to say that the running dialogue isn't fun also.

bikini_babe: hi E/everyone
PeepingTom: what are you wearing babe?
bikini_babe: a hot neon orange number
PeepingTom: im guessing 69
HeadMistress: is that supposed to be clever?
PeepingTom: its a reciprocating number
candy2cane: that IS clever HeadMistress. may I private?
FatherOTool: does anyone need to confess?
HeadMistress: no dear you always come and go without saying goodbye
FatherOTool: does anyone want a reason to need to confess? pvt me
PeepingTom: so babe, what are you wearing?
bikini_babe: A BIKINI MORON
PeepingTom: you don't need to shout
bikini_babe: you are so stupid
PeepingTom: smart enough to make you my b1tch

This is Tim's cue to swoop in and restore order.

Chat-Admin: play nice bois and gurls
princess_peach: im wearing a tiara. a satin gown with puffy sleeves and 2 pettis
sissi4Domme: are you alone?
princess_peach: yes

sissi4Domme: want to play
princess_peach: cant im cleaning Bowsers toilet
pedicured: anyone into footworship?
DrScholl: I am
JohnQPublic: is it true that Miss Lavinia is dead?

That last post hits Tim upside the head like a two-by-four.

sissi4Domme: its all over the internet
bikini_babe: i just googled. it's a hoax
candy2cane: Madame Choking Hazard is spreading falsehoods
pedicured: she's bitter since bedbugs shut down her dungeon
JohnQPublic: *www.2true2lie.com* says she was cremated 4 days ago

Tim's brain is six degrees of separation away from boiling. He is frantically cycling through the room cams looking for Victoria.

HeadMistress: when was she last in the chat room?
FatherOTool: its been months
wankadoodledoo: her live milking sessions have been old streams too
JohnQPublic: i think she died

Tim opens the locks and rips the door open, surprising Fifi.

"Where is your Mistress?" he barks in a voice that makes it clear that he won't put up with any bad behavior right now.

"I don't know, sir," Fifi answers. "She took her mother shopping for a new outfit and she hasn't come back."

Tim doesn't bother with a room-to-room search, and there's no point leaving the apartment. She could be anywhere. When you're out and about with your dead mother, the world is your oyster.

He locks himself back in the machine room. He goes back online.

JohnQPublic: her real name was Gladys Boodleneck
pedicured: where are you reading that JQP?
JohnQPublic: *www.2dayindead.com*
HeadMistress: then it must be true

Tim doesn't know what to do. He only knows that he has to do something. In desperation he quits out as *Chat-Admin* and launches the *DefCon4* protocol from the *SysOps Utility Toolbox*.

"Log on:" it queries.

"Miss_Lavinia," he types in.

"Password:" it prompts.

Tim scratches his head over that for a minute and then takes a wild stab at it.

"abc123," he types in.

Tim is a little taken aback as the old chat room screen folds in on itself and then opens up like a blossoming flower. The background is now lavender with a luxurious Laura Ashley border of primroses. *Welcome Miss Lavinia* it reads across the top in a banner.

princess_peach: welcome indeed Miss Lavinia (curtsy)
sissi4Domme: gr8 2 see u Mistress [courtsie]
pedicured: hello Miss. we've missed you soooooo much

Once again Tim goes with his gut.

Miss_Lavinia: The reports of my death have been greatly exaggerated.

65.
SCANLON

IT'S FAMILY GAME NIGHT—the first ever for this family. He and his odious stepdaughter are sitting in the rarely occupied living room taking a break from playing Pictionary while the lady of the house is in the kitchen.

"What have we done to deserve this?" Scanlon sighs.

"She must be between boyfriends," Bitzi answers with a smirk.

"Or watched Dr. Pill or one of those other cockamamie afternoon self-help TV shows," he says.

"Yeah, Detective," she replies. "Mom spends her afternoons watching girl shows on the TV. How did you ever break the case?"

Scanlon's wife enters with a huge bowl of popcorn. Bitzi rolls her eyes.

"What a treat," Scanlon says as he digs in.

It's so salty that his mouth immediately self-pickles.

Is she trying to kill me? he wonders.

"No s'mores?" Bitzi protests.

"S'mores are a treat," her mother points out, "or a sinful indulgence—depending on how old you are."

"And how stoned," Bitzi whispers to her stepfather as her mother fusses with the easel.

She hands Scanlon a marker. The Pictionary word is *Mr. Peanut*. He turns over the egg timer and starts drawing a peanut . . . the top hat . . . the monocle . . . At the same time, he can't help but notice that his wife is surreptitiously casting glances at her phone—almost wistfully. Just as the sand runs out and he gives a cane to the diminutive gent, Bitzi shouts out an answer.

"Your dick," she offers to solve the puzzle. "It looks so gay."

Mom doesn't bat an eye. She's not paying attention.

Scanlon wishes he could have a few minutes alone with his phone too. Actually, it's his second mobile device—a burner that he bought on Canal Street. It's totally against department policy, but he's using it to text oldJim. Not often, just enough to check in when he's feeling isolated and friendless. He has quickly become desperate for any encouragement.

The next Pictionary word is *sonic boom*. Scanlon hasn't played this game long enough to find that curious. But it is challenging. He uses up half his allotted minute thinking about it. When he does begin to draw, it is rushed. First he swoops two arcs. These represent the shock waves created by a supersonic passage. Then, at the point where they meet in the cleavage, he draws a crude rocket plane—his version of an X-15—but it is so sloppy that it is unrecognizable. It could be a hot dog, or a turd, or a . . . ?

"I know. I know," Bitzi screams out, waving her arms. "It's *up your ass*!"

"Behave yourselves," Scanlon's wife chastises them both with great irritation. She picks up her mobile.

"What did I do?" Scanlon asks.

"You provoked her with your crude, dirty doodling," she says, swiping the phone to make sure it's still connected.

Bitzi grins at him like the cat that swallowed a Canary Island.

Her mother looks up from her phone with a serious face.

"You decide what you want, okay?" she says in a voice that

is flirting with hysteria. "If you want to be part of a real family, we have to work at it—goddamn it." She's on the verge of tears.

"It's working for me," Bitzi says. "Right now I'm hating tonight a lot more than that man you married."

"That's a positive attitude, sweetheart," she says, kissing her daughter on the forehead. "Thank you for that."

Scanlon has no idea what to say to that so he picks another card. The Pictionary word is *sphincter*.

"You doctored them, didn't you?" he accuses his stepdaughter.

"Moi?" she replies, batting her eyelashes—the paragon of innocence.

He can hear his wife's phone vibrate despite her best efforts to mute it with her fist.

"Bathroom break," he declares.

"I need to pee," she agrees and makes a beeline for the downstairs powder room.

Scanlon goes upstairs to the master. He opens the safe where he keeps his service revolver and grabs the burner. He locks himself in the bathroom and sits on a closed toilet seat.

"Watching the game?" he texts.

OldJim is teaching lilSue all about baseball. Scanlon loves talking baseball. His wife hates the game—too slow. His stepdaughter once accused him of using baseballs as anal beads.

"Hello darlin," oldJim texts back. "Wearing white panties for Daddy?"

"White panties and my favorite top. #2," lilSue texts.

"I love you in white panties."

"I love Derek Jeter."

"We could use him tonight sweetie. 7-2 in the 6th."

"But whatshisname is pitching tonight."

"Not tonight."

"Y not?"

"Tommy John surgery."

That Scanlon did not know that—perhaps because it's family

game night and he's not allowed to watch the game. He wonders how long he can stay in the bathroom. He wishes he could have a beer. But just hanging out with oldJim is special. It relaxes him. Sure he has to do the sexy talk business every now and then. But he doesn't mind. It's worth putting up with a little hanky-panky if they end up talking Yankee baseball.

"I think we should go to a game together," oldJim suggests.

"I don't think that's a very good idea," Scanlon replies.

66.
WOODY

IT'S JUST LIKE OLD TIMES. He's up before the sun, drinking bad coffee out of a cardboard cup in a room full of manly men. He likes them, and not only because they all hate Ivan Greenbriar. He is comfortable in their company—a company of men. There is no idle chatter. They are taciturn—suiting up—putting on body armor—the new high-tech miracle weave. It's so bleeding edge that it doesn't have a name yet and so thin that it's like a second skin. You can't see it under a guy's street clothes.

Today is the first time he sees the boat he bought—up close and personal. Despite the immense size, he is not blown away. He likes boats well enough. The 12-Metres, for example—that's a pretty classy class of a sailboat—proving once again that Ivan's got no taste. What Woody is looking at now is more like something out of a dark dystopian comic book—two slender, black hulls and a matching vertical wing—the preferred watercraft for *The Evil Destructor*. Nobody but a supervillain would call it elegant. It's like the first time you saw a box kite. *That thing can fly? Yeah, right!*

Not that Woody has had much truck with the white shoe set. Early on, when he got wealthy enough to hobnob, he discovered that yacht clubs had an asshole quotient that was way too rich for his blood.

Today, they spot him at one of the pedestals, figuring that it will be something to hold on to when things get bumpy. They've all taken the sailor's Hippocratic oath: *First don't kill the owner*.

"Just do whatever he does," the New Zealander explains, pointing to the man facing him.

"Aye-aye, Skip." Woody salutes.

"Only backward," the grinder grins.

Woody stands at his station as the boat ghosts past the Rockaway Inlet. Looking into dawn nullifies any metropolis behind it. He is outward-bound. The angry traffic and car horns and the variety of sirens in all flavors just aren't here. The creaking of the vessel as it moves through the water and the water itself against the hulls—that is your only universe. It is a stealth ship. From the beach the only thing the surfcasters can see are the running lights.

The breeze quickly freshens as dawn turns to day. They sail to the southeast on a broad reach. The foils are retracted—at least one hull in the water at all times, just like a regular sailboat. Once they pass the Ambrose Light, however, all bets are off. The wind is steady at fourteen knots. It's time to kick it into overdrive.

"Ready for a little fun?" the Kiwi shouts.

As he works the bicycle-pedal winch with his fellow grinder, Woody gets a taste of what he's in for. It will be hard to get out of bed tomorrow—if his lungs don't explode first. But then the magic happens. When they fall off the wind just a tiny bit, the hydrofoils below the hulls bite and lift the massive boat out of the water, and then it feels as if the afterburners are lit and the rocket takes off.

"Wow," Woody gushes.

"Too right," the grinder agrees.

It's a recipe for euphoria—a mix of mind-blowing speed and power along with body-crushing physical exertion. Woody loves it. After two or three more tacks he becomes one with his boat.

"Little friend off starboard beam," his mate announces.

Woody looks up from his winch to see that a vintage PT boat has pulled up alongside.

"Beautiful," he says.

"Glad you like," Skip shouts forward. "You bought her for us. Thank you."

"Our sparring partner." The grinder grins.

He smiles a lot. He's a happy guy. He must like his job.

Hell, Woody thinks. *I want his job.*

The Packard engines growl. Skip drops his arm, the motorized torpedo boat kicks up a rooster tail, and it's disco fever on the water. How would you describe what happens next? A paso doble? To Woody, from his vantage point, it looks more like a border collie herding. Every time the PT boat tries to get past, the sailboat turns it—getting in the way—windward is best—or failing that—nipping at its ankles.

They parry and thrust for two hours. Despite its mechanical advantage, the PT boat never succeeds in getting past the sailboat. They only break off when commercial traffic starts to fill the channel.

They give Woody the helm on the homeward leg.

"You are probably wondering why we don't practice race starts," the New Zealander says.

"Am I?" Woody replies—concentrating—with his hands full of a lot of boat.

"When it comes to that son of a bitch," the skipper explains with a quiet intensity, "we are only in the race-stopping business."

Woody looks him in the eye and believes every word he says.

67. SVETLANA

THEY WILL BE SHOOTING the ball scene where Anastasia, nervous about her pending interview with the Dowager Empress Marie Feodorovna, dances with General Bounine and quickly forgets about everything that has gone before—like living in a root cellar—and having to save up the roots for special occasions like birthdays and Orthodox Easter. But tonight, Anastasia is in a gown for the first time in what seems to be a lifetime—and waltzing. She is fourteen again. She feels like her feet will leave the dance floor and she will fly.

The cinematographer knows how to pull this off. It's a tracking boom shot that he has spent two weeks setting up. While her dancing slippers remain on the parquet floor, he will create the illusion that she and the general are soaring over all the other dancers.

"Back in my very own trailer." Svetlana beams as she spins in her ball gown waiting to be called for the scene. It must weigh sixty pounds—and she can't breathe. But she can see herself in the mirror, and it's worth it. She looks spectacular.

There is a tap at the door.

"May I come in?" her white knight asks.

"Of course, kind sir," she replies, twirling again to fill her petticoats. "You are always welcome here."

He takes each of her hands in his, raises and opens her arms, and leaning back so he can take her all in, he admires what he sees. "Beautiful and beyond," he says.

Ivan then takes her in his arms and dances two or three steps—enough to tell Svetlana that he is not a dancer. That turns into an embrace and perhaps a few feels. She can't tell. Her corset and all the other foundations that she is tightly laced into are so formidable that she will consider wearing them to a war zone the next time she does a USO tour. She can't feel a thing.

But is that true? she wonders while Ivan continues to do whatever he is doing down there. *Do I feel nothing? Am I devoid of empathy? Am I a sociopath?*

Svetlana is certainly aware of her reputation—that if she has a heart at all it is made of flint, ice, or steel—that she is a man-eater—using them and spitting them out. She has seen the crude cartoons on the Internet of her vagina and the sharp teeth growing out of its labia—with an overbite no less. In her defense, she has had many long-term relationships—boyfriends—and that one girl to make her publicist happy. A few of them even left under their own steam. The others were simply steamed. It's not her fault they couldn't take no for an answer. Bad behavior is out of her control. She's not their mommy.

Has she ever fallen herself? Well, she really liked some of them, but it all seemed so terribly one-sided. By the looks of it—those being the young Adonises half-conscious on her bed with their eyes rolled back in their heads—she must be a really good lover. But in reality she has never had One—an Oh My God—the biggest O—the whole point of the exercise. On the other hand, she thinks that the whole thing is terribly overrated and probably self-delusional. She's convinced that most women lie to themselves about their orgasms in the

same way that people who move to Columbus, Ohio, try to convince their friends that it was a good idea. Which is not to say that she is uncomfortable with lovemaking. First of all, it's a natural acting exercise. Secondly, there's a cyclical rhythm to things. Of course, for obvious reasons, she needs to follow her partner's cue to know when to wrap things up, but that tends to be kind of obvious.

Like now. Her white knight has stepped away and is adjusting something. So all is well again in the valley—as long as he didn't do anything to mess with her costume.

After a quick inspection, she says, "Well done, Ivan."

He appears sheepish, which is an incongruous look for a true motherfucker.

There is a knock on the trailer door.

"They are ready for you, Svetlana."

From here on it's magic. She slips away to the soundstage—into a sea of beauty—beautiful girls in beautiful gowns—bright eyes—bright teeth—diamonds and emeralds—over-the-top ornate, opulent, and sumptuous Russian beauty—fit for a Czar. The sea parts to embrace Svetlana—the most beautiful of all the beautiful girls—the Belarus of the Ball.

"Roll music."

It is a waltz, of course. There is nothing to quicken a girl's heartbeat faster than a 3/4 time signature. The choreography is sublime. Her dancing partner, General Bounine's body double, is superb. She gladly hands her body into his capable arms—trusting and eager to take flight. But she is professional throughout. Without looking, her trained eye is constantly aware of each and every working camera—especially the boom.

She is pleased that they are doing long takes. She is enjoying dancing so much that she doesn't want to stop. When the curious little man in the shoulder-length powdered wig and the brocade waistcoat pounds his scepter three times into the dance floor, her face is flushed and her heart is racing.

"Gentlemen, take your partner for the Mazurka," he calls out.

Svetlana is ready to go airborne. She loves the Mazurka. The music starts. It hits all her buttons and checks all the boxes. She is in the music. She is Anastasia. She releases the hand brake. She throws herself into the moment. All she feels is the Mazurka and a lover's embrace—and her feet leave the floor—taking her higher and higher . . .

Then the music stops. There is an angry sound of binding, grinding metal against metal. Then the angry shouts of assistant directors—and everybody else, including the gaffers.

"Cut! Cut!"

Svetlana's reflex is to look at the boom. Needless to say, she is shocked to see a huge red flag—USSR flavored—waving high above the set—the real deal—hammer and sickle included.

As the boom comes down, security quickly surrounds the old coot who has handcuffed his wheelchair to the camera boom.

Svetlana walks up to him.

"Don't do it, Lanie," the old coot says. "We are a proud people. Nicholas was the murderer."

"Grandfather?" Svetlana asks. "What are you doing here?"

68.
MACKENZIE

IT'S JUST LIKE OLD TIMES. She and Victoria are in plaid—Stewart and MacDonald—flannel nightshirts curled up on her grandfather's worn Chesterfield sofa. The leather is parchment thin in some places and duct-taped in others. They are drinking hot cocoa. They could both be back in school except that they don't have a familiar pain in the pits of their stomachs over the paper they're not writing or the test that they are unprepared for. Tim is fixing something or other on Mackenzie's desktop in an alcove off the living room. They both watch him as he rattles the keys with a quiet intensity.

"He's cute," Mackenzie says.

"He is that," Victoria agrees.

"How long have you two been . . . ?" Mackenzie asks, making a rude coital gesture with her index finger.

"We haven't," Victoria protests. "He's sweet."

Mackenzie takes a moment to get a closer look at a distance. "Give him a chance, Vix," she says. "I think you might be pleasantly surprised."

"I think you might be right," Victoria replies. "But who can risk losing a good techie?"

"Point taken," Mackenzie agrees.

They sit and stare, cradling the mugs in their hands.

Tim looks up. His eyes bounce back and forth between them. He looks perplexed.

"What?" he asks.

"We enjoy working," Mackenzie says.

"We can watch it all day," Victoria chimes in.

Tim adds the rimshot.

"But seriously, ladies and germs," he begins, "you've got one buggy machine here. If you intend to keep using it, I would recommend a hazmat suit."

"Can't be true," Mackenzie insists. "I would know."

She moves to the computer, with Victoria closely behind her.

"Then you are familiar with *Scan4Satan*," he says as he slides a memory stick into the USB port.

"Of course," she replies.

When it pops up, Tim double-clicks on the devil-head icon. The screen goes black. A thermometer dripping with blood appears. It shows slow progress, until halfway home it stalls out. Thousands of bats fill the screen. Then a beastly medieval Lucifer face zooms up big. He looks like a goat in a cardinal's mitre. He stares directly into your eyes—knowingly—for a brief moment before he lets loose a sinister and otherworldly cackle that makes everyone's skin crawl with mounting anxiety.

"You've got something," Tim says as he whips the plug out of the wall outlet. "Something bad."

"But that's not possible," Mackenzie protests. "I'm a professional."

"With lousy support it seems," he says dismissively. "I need another machine."

"There's my laptop," she replies.

"Cooties," Tim says, making a cross with his fingers to ward off viruses and vampires.

He points to a notebook computer under a stack of newspapers—the *Financial Times* of London. "What's that?"

"My husband's," Mackenzie explains. "But you won't be able to use that. It's encrypted."

"Oh, please." Tim rolls his eyes and picks it up. "Let's take a tour."

He puts the thin computer on the coffee table and plops down on the Chesterfield between them. After opening the notebook, he pulls another flash drive out of his jeans pocket and sticks it in the side. As he powers up, Tim holds down the Control and Alt keys as well as three others.

"D Minor," he says just before the computer plays an audio prompt that sounds like a cross between Bach and the A train.

"This is technically illegal but only on the federal level," he explains. "Home Sweet Homeland Security."

After it boots, the screen is broken up into a series of windows of scrolling gobbledygook. Mackenzie is mystified. She turns to her friend.

"Don't look at me," Victoria says. "You're the professional."

They both face Tim. He is transfixed—surfing a cyberwave.

"Uh-oh," he says.

"We don't like *uh-oh*," Mackenzie replies. "What's going on?"

"Incoming," Tim explains. "An army of bots is pinging like crazy, trying to set up a peer-to-peer."

"Where is the attack originating from?" Mackenzie asks.

Tim reads off an IP address.

"Shit," Mackenzie curses. "That's—"

"ColdTrail.com," Tim confirms. "You are so fucked."

"But how?" she wonders. "We closed the back door."

"Almost," he corrects. "Somebody put a piece of black tape on the latch so that it won't lock."

"Can you close the door again?" Mackenzie wonders hopefully.

"After the horse has bolted?" Tim pooh-poohs.

"I don't think I like your young man after all," she sniffs to Victoria.

"Hold on to your socks," he warns. "You've got company."

"Who's there?" she asks.

"It might be easier to list who isn't," Tim muses as he launches another utility and scrolls through a long array. "The NSA never wipes their shoes. Their muddy footprints are all over the place. We've also got the Fibbies, China dolls, Bulgarians—can't have a secure web site without the Bulgarians moving in. Smell the kimchi? That's you-know-who . . . and hello Vladdy."

Mackenzie's mind is racing like a sports car that can go from $1.12 billion to zero in under eight seconds. The blood drains out of her face. Her friend looks concerned.

"Are you okay?" Victoria asks.

The notebook rings out a deep and resonate gong tone.

"Since you're out of the privacy business, Mrs. Greenbriar," Tim wonders. "Do you want to read your husband's email?"

"Certainly not," Mackenzie tsks. "That is so beneath me."

"Oh really?" Victoria asks, unfolding the supermarket tabloid as a reminder.

The headline: CATHERINE THE GREAT MEET IVAN THE TERRIBLE

The photo: Svetlana and Ivan together and looking anything but apart.

Mackenzie is speechless, but her eye wanders down to the computer screen. Her expression does not change. But color does return to her face. Soon it is a raging inferno.

"Motherfucker," she spits out as she grabs the laptop computer and hurls it across the room. It smashes against the ornamental fireplace.

Mackenzie goes ballistic. She staggers around the apartment like a woman possessed, cursing in five languages. She overturns furniture. She smashes an antique porcelain poodle into a Ming vase. She rips the flat-screen off the wall and throws it out the window without opening the window. She only stops when Victoria and Tim jump her and pin her to the floor.

"Sweetie," Victoria coos soothingly into her ear. "Honey, what's wrong?"

"That son of a bitch shorted ME," Mackenzie seethes.

"He didn't?" Victoria replies in disbelief.

"He did," Tim confirms.

"That's awful," Victoria commiserates. "But stop breaking your stuff."

Mackenzie looks at her friend in disbelief. *You think?*

"I haven't touched any of MY stuff," she says. "Will you get off me now. Please."

69.
MARY MARGARET

SHE LIKES THAT WHEN SHE TOOTS her horn, the metal gate rattles then rises up so that she can drive her car directly into the warehouse. Not that parking a mint Coupe de Ville on the street after dark in Paterson, NJ, would ever present a problem, but she appreciates the convenience.

Mary Margaret is dotting her I's and crossing her T's—more due diligence—in preparation for the upcoming shareholders' meeting. While this massive facility may be owned by SteeleX International, for this month at least it is entirely under the auspices of the independent auditors—RSVP LLC—or is it someone else? Accounting firms are getting shut down so fast these days that it's hard to keep track. On the other hand, Maurice always seems to be running the second shift, whatever company name is on the invoice.

"Mary Margaret." He welcomes her with a hearty handshake. "How good to see you. Can you believe it's been another year? Let me get you a bad cup of coffee."

He spirits her up the industrial metal stairs to the office hanging in the rafters and pours her a truly horrid cup of coffee.

"Please, sir," she says in her best Oliver Twist, holding out the mug, and he rewards her with a top-up of Jim Beam.

As she sips the hot drink—trying to separate the good bourbon from the bad coffee with her tongue—they look down at the floor. There must be at least fifty worker bees down there.

"Eighty-five," Maurice corrects her.

They are plying up and down the long rows of tables sorting and counting through boxes and boxes and stacks of paper—so much paper.

"It seems like a lot more than last year," Mary Margaret notes.

"A lot more," Maurice says. "You're in play. That's a fact."

"But why?" she wonders.

"I've been in this game a long time," he replies. "It's never a why. It's always a who."

Mary Margaret is hypnotized by the moving tide of paper ballots—there's a lot of collating going on. She is perhaps watching the last Olde Tyme proxy fight in Wall Street history. Every other major company in the world has their shareholders vote online—but not Woody.

"I don't trust clicks," he explained when she finally held his feet to the fire on the subject. "You should be able to hold your vote in your hand."

Her phone goes *heehaw heehaw*. That's the ringtone she's programmed in to alert her that Woody is being a jackass.

"Excuse me," she says to Maurice. "I have to take this."

She stands in a far corner of the office like she's taking a Time Out and whispers into the phone.

"What are you buying now?" she demands.

"Who, me?" Woody answers, sounding all innocent.

"Yes, you," Mary Margaret hisses.

"Uh . . ." He hesitates. "Maybe a movie studio. I didn't really look closely at the paperwork."

"Tear it up," she orders. "You can't afford it. Every dime you have is tied up in yen."

"It's a sweetheart deal," he insists.

"Fuck your sweetheart," she replies. "And fuck you."

They are silent for an uncomfortable interval.

"Why are we fighting?" he finally asks.

"I'm jealous," she admits honestly.

"That's ridiculous," he snorts. "Of what?"

"Of her," she says.

"But you've never been jealous of a *her* before—ever," he says.

"This time it's different," she says.

"How so?"

"Because this time you like her," Mary Margaret replies. "But I can't talk right now. I'm too busy trying to save your company."

She turns off her phone.

"I have to go now," she tells Maurice.

"Are you okay?" he asks.

"I have to go," she repeats.

"Give me a minute," he says. "We'll organize a convoy to get you out of town."

"Thanks but no thanks," she says as she starts to run down the stairs.

"Wait," Maurice says following behind her. "You shouldn't be alone in this neighborhood."

She doesn't see. She doesn't hear. All she knows is that she is sitting in her car—leaning on the horn—until the gate opens—and then she is driving—alone—driving through an empty abandoned cityscape—boarded up storefronts—burned-out row houses—the urban night terror of lost suburban soccer moms. But she does not notice. She is the only car on the street—until she's not.

She snaps out of her trance when she realizes that she is boxed in—a beat-up Jeep Cherokee on one side and a late-model Escalade on the other. She puts her foot to the floor, but they speed up also. She downshifts. They match her every move. Mary Margaret feels a glimmer of hope when she sees the on-ramp to I-80 in the distance. But while she is planning her next feint, a canary yellow

Dodge Charger with a single white passenger door panel skids to a stop in front of her. She has to slam on the brakes to not drive into it. She throws the car into reverse but has to abort when two Harleys pop up in her rearview mirror. The large men who climb off are wearing gang colors—*Haitian Hoboes*.

Mary Margaret puts her head down on the steering wheel and waits. She doesn't bother to look up at the series of rough faces that peer in the window at her—at the teardrop tattoos on their faces or the gold teeth. Now that she has stopped driving, she is suddenly weary. She doesn't feel like she can move. But when there is a discreet tap on the window she does look up—and, when she recognizes a familiar face, she smiles and rolls down the window.

"Bon aswè, Emanuel," she says in Creole.

"Alo, bèl dam," the gang leader greets her.

"I was hoping to run into you," she replies.

"Or a tree—the way you were driving." He grins.

Mary Margaret laughs.

"I have a job for you," she says.

70. TIM

Miss_Lavinia: Don't private without permission classEslut.
maid4training: Hello Miss Lavinia, Maam [curtsie]
Miss_Lavinia: Hello maid4training and welcome
Miss_Lavinia: *Purchase maid training videos here*
edina: pulling down patsy's knickers
patsy: oh edie
Miss_Lavinia: Get a room gurls!

They are sitting at the kitchen table in the family quarters. Victoria is dictating. Tim is typing into her laptop. Fifi is making beans on toast.

"New apron, Fifi?" Tim asks.

The maid nods.

"It looks smashing," he compliments her.

"OMG," Victoria says.

Miss_Lavinia: OMG

"Cancel that," she explains. "I was talking real time. I was shocked. Shocked! Fifi is blushing. I've never seen that before. Someone has a new admirer."

bovine_beauty: Hello Miss Lavinia
Miss_Lavinia: Welcome bovine
bovine_beauty: we missed you at the last on-line milking seminar
Miss_Lavinia: *Sign up for the free milking email here*
HardKnows: hi lavinia babe
Miss_Lavinia: Excuse me! Manners HK!
bovine_beauty: i been a member for 10 yrs and you never missed a seminar
bovine_beauty: EVER
HardKnows: the cowgurl is right
JohnQPublic: so the rumor is true. she died.
Miss_Lavinia: I can assure you that I am most certainly not dead.
prissy_sissy: how do we know that you are really you?
toilet_slave: U cud B N E bodE
sis2sissy: you haven't been on cam like 4 ever
JohnQPublic: i smell a rat ladies
bovine_beauty: prove it on cam
JustSid: show us your face
NylonStalking: show us your legs
HardKnows: show us your panties
JohnQPublic: cowgurl is right again. show us ur not dead on videochat

Tim looks up at the wrong time and gets a significant look from Victoria. He knows exactly what that's all about.

"OMG," he says.

Fortunately he is saved by the bell. His phone goes off in his back pocket. It is a text from his boss.

"Elevator NOW," it reads.

"Got to go," Tim explains. "Mr. Pavlenko."

"I hate old people as much as the next girl," Victoria admits. "But how can he keep it up? I hear they turned his water and power off last week."

"Yes, we did," Tim confesses. "But that's just water off a duck's back. The old guy was at Stalingrad."

"Well, don't be long, you handsome man," Victoria flirts and blows him a kiss. "There's a little something I need for you to do for me when you get back."

Tim is actually relieved to be climbing stairs. The tenants he passes don't seem to share his enthusiasm. Their stoicism is indirectly proportional to the floor they live on. He takes two steps at a time. But as he gets closer to the penthouse he starts dreading what he is going to encounter up there. In his mind he has decided that Mr. Pavlenko has suffered a stroke—or a heart attack—and he is lying on the floor in the hall with his head halfway into the elevator and the doors keep opening and closing—on his head—crunch—opening and closing—crunch—opening and closing—crunch . . .

Tim is frantic crazy as he gets near. Mountain goat crazy. He takes three steps at a time. When he lets himself into the penthouse elevator lobby with the fireman's key on his massive building superintendent's ring on a chain, he can hear the crunching cycle of the elevator doors. You can imagine his relief when he sees that what is jamming up the works is a metal chair with vinyl upholstery from Mr. Pavlenko's kitchenette set. He pulls it out from between the doors. The chair is so bent out of shape from constant abuse that it won't stand up on its own. The elevator, however, goes on its way without a peep, to the delight of everyone in the building down below.

The door to the penthouse—along with its seven dead bolts and Fox Police Lock—is wide open. Tim pulls a chess piece out of his work shirt pocket—a white pawn—today's safe passage talisman—and walks into the penthouse apartment.

"Mr. Pavlenko?" he announces his presence to both the tenant and his AK-47.

There seems to be nobody home. How can this be? It's not like the grumpy crowd downstairs cursing the elevator wouldn't notice if the troublemaker walked—make that rolled—through the front door.

He searches every room—the kitchen, the living room with the creepy bigger-than-life-sized portrait of Joseph Stalin, the bedroom, the bathroom—nobody's home. Tim scratches his head. Maybe Mr. Pavlenko is hiding in a secret place. There must be one. Tim knows this. The accessible rooms in the penthouse represent a fraction of the apartment's overall footprint.

Case closed? It's not like he's in a big hurry to rejoin Victoria. He knows where that's going. Already he's beginning to itch all over. He knows about grow back. When he was on the JV swim team in college, he shaved his entire body—everything. After the season, when the hair crop started coming up again, he wanted to tear his skin off.

In a final moment of OCD he goes back into the kitchen to check that Mr. Pavlenko did not leave the stove on. He did not. But he did leave the pantry door open—a door that Tim had not previously seen. He enters the pantry and notices another door—a hidden door—no longer hidden now because it is ajar—Oh Alice. Tim goes in through the looking glass.

"Hello," he says as his discovers some of the uncharted territory.

It is a series of storerooms stacked floor to ceiling with provisions—fifty-five-gallon drums of potable water, skids of military-spec biscuits and hard tack, rolls of compressed peanut butter sheets, fifty-pound bags of rice, emergency everything you can think of: kits, generators, desalinization stills, boxes of classical literature—leaning heavily toward Gorky—Tim can just make out the Cyrillic characters.

He wanders further into the warren—past the stacks of WWII K-Rations and CCCP hand grenades from the Afghanistan war. Now he can see the old man. He is sitting in his wheelchair with a propane tank in his lap. There is enough propane in this room to blown the top eight floors off the building. Propane is heavier than air. It is the ultimate trickle-down economic expansion—boom.

Tim touches him on the shoulder.

"Are you all right, Mr. Pavlenko?" he asks.

The old man wakes up. He looks disoriented.

"The generator on the terrace is out of gas," he finally explains.

Then when he recognizes Tim, he adds, "It was a mistake to disrespect us."

He stops and thinks further.

"But it wasn't all your fault," he says. "Yeltsin was a clown."

71.
SVETLANA

SHE NESTLES INTO THE CUSHY seat like a mother hen lowering her buns down onto her precious egglings. Still over the moon that she is back in pictures, Svetlana is cherishing every moment—even the long hours she must spend in the makeup trailer. She used to complain about that a lot. Hell, she used to complain about everything a lot. But she's learned her lesson. As God is her witness, she'll never complain about anything again.

What movie is that line from? she wonders.

It is ten after six in the morning. She is on time—professionally so. She was here twenty minutes ago. That's what time she was called for. Where is everyone else? How will she ever be able to thank the crew when she gets all her awards if the friggin' crew doesn't bother to show up? And her nail polish is chipped. Fuck all. It wouldn't be chipped if it was gel, but Reinhold Wassisname, the overly involved and historically anal director, wouldn't have any of it. In 1918 it was nail polish, he insists. So let's just chip away at her soul for authenticity.

"Hello," Svetlana cries out into the morning. "Star of the movie—dying on the vine—in here."

She can't believe that lame incantation works so effectively, but the door squeaks and groans as a troll enters the trailer. Svetlana doesn't feel that she is doing any disservice to trolls by that appellation—although technically he is large for a troll—and he is a troll with a bad old-man dye job. Trolls tend to prefer turquoise blue or lime green. This particular troll has gone with jet black—hair, mustache, and goatee. It all matches his beret, and can you believe it?—he's wearing a monocle. He's very fastidious. He's wearing plus four plaid knickerbockers and there is a gold watch chain draped across his camel hair waistcoat.

"Guten Morgen," the troll says and clicks his heels.

"Who are you?" she demands.

"I am the unit director for this sequence," he replies. "Wilhelm von Worms—like the diet plan."

"This is unacceptable," Svetlana sniffs. "I must talk to Reinhold."

"I'm not so bad," the troll replies. "Mein freunds call me Billy Wildest."

He starts to giggle—rising in volume and chromatically. He has a four octave range. Svetlana is repulsed.

"Give me a phone," she insists. "I'm calling Mr. Greenbriar."

"Alas, Fräulein, that is of no moment," the troll explains with an unctuous look. "As of last night, he no longer owns the studio."

"I don't have to stand for this," she says as she gets out of the chair.

"While we wait for your makeup artist," he continues. "Why don't we go over the script changes?"

There is something in his demeanor that keeps her protests on the back burner, and when she sees the ream of paper he's holding, the trooper in her just groans over the work at hand.

"All right then," the troll begins. "Scene thirty-seven: in the basement. All the Romanovs have been shot—dead—but you survived because you are under Olga, Maria, and especially Alexei, who, being a hemophiliac, bleeds all over you like the

Trevi Fountain, so you are covered in blood when you have to crawl on your belly through the snakes—"

"What? Like rubber snakes?" she asks.

"Live snakes," he explains. "You know Reinhold. Verisimilitude."

"I don't do snakes," Svetlana insists. "It's in my contract."

"Was," the troll points out. "That contract is null and void."

"I can't believe this," she frets. Her brief moment of happiness seems to be crashing down.

"Not to worry, Leibling," he reassures her. "That is a very short sequence. The snakes are quickly scared away when Czar Nicholas and Czarina Alexandra and all the kiddies are transmogrified into the undead and begin to walk the earth as zombies. Snakes are finger food to zombies, as you well know."

"What?" Svetlana cannot believe her ears.

It doesn't help when the troll turns himself into a zombie troll. He Frankenstein-staggers his way up to her chair, arms outstretched—flailing—until his hands are around her neck.

"Human flesh," he growls.

She screams out. She is terrified. She thinks she is going to be murdered—until she sees a familiar glint in his eye—and then that grin that he can never totally suppress. Now that she knows who he is, she herself is transfigured—into a shrew—not the Shakespearean Kate—but the natural kind—the most vicious mammal on earth by weight. She is out of her chair and on him and they go down. As she pins his neck to the floor with her knee, she smears handfuls of cold cream through his hair. Her hands turn black as his hair reverts to its natural strawberry blond. Through it all Woody is laughing in a sweet and infectious way that only makes her more angry.

"You son of a bitch," she says as she slaps him across the face.

"You bastard," she says as she pummels his chest with her fists.

"You motherfucker," she says as she aims her foot fast and furious between his legs.

Woody sees that one coming and performs what can only be described as a horizontal jeté—world-class—he should play the

Bolshoi. Once on his feet, he offers her a hand. She begrudgingly lets him help her up.

"Think about it," he points out as he wipes the grease and makeup off with a towel. "Nothing that has happened to you was my fault."

Svetlana doesn't look like she is in the mood to be mollified.

"I'm not saying that they are not beautiful," he explains. "Because they are. They're spectacular. It's just that you keep flashing them at me. It wasn't my doing."

He wins a swift punch to the stomach with that one.

"Just saying," he gasps as he tries to get his wind back.

Svetlana is spent. She just wants him to go away. She wants to lie down and hug her favorite pillow. Did he see that in her eyes? Is he human after all?

She looks up into his face. It is a gentle face. He takes her hands in his.

"I'm sorry," he says with a sincerity that she believes in completely. "I'm sorry that you were embarrassed and hurt."

He looks really good—even half-baked by the streaking makeup smears. He squeezes her hands.

Svetlana prepares herself to start acting. She doesn't know what her role is yet, but figures it's a safe bet to close her eyes and stand up on tippy toes and offer lips, tits, and pussy—why the hell not—this one's richer than the last one—and he's not even married.

Then the earth moves.

Well—not exactly the earth—it is the trailer that lurches forward. They are tossed off their feet into a pile on the floor.

"Are you kidding me?" Svetlana shouts out.

"This is not part of the plan," Woody says.

He rushes to the outside door. It is jammed shut—locked. At the same time, through the side window over the makeup stations, they watch the studio gate pass by. The trailer gains speed as it careens toward the expressway.

72.
SCANLON

ANY CONNECTION IS DRIFTING ever farther off as if his tether failed during a space walk. He has been away for only a few days, but the precinct house seems to be even more unfamiliar. He isn't imagining things. Upstairs not only the vibe has changed. For one thing, Scanlon's desk has been shoved into the corner—his chair turned turtle, like in a café after hours. Someone stole his mouse. The guy from San Diego has spread his wings—and spread out. Cute plush animals cover every available surface—a lot of pink and pastels—make way for the unicorns. Next to the *Safety First* admonitions and the illustrated *Mirandizing for Dummies* placard on the wall, he has taped up posters of too-cute-for-school boy bands along with one of a very young Justin Bieber—jailbait.

When Scanlon walks in, the man from San Diego is lost to the world. Little Debbie is deep in chat. His fingers float over the keyboard like Van Cliburn playing Rachmaninoff. He looks a little out of place sitting in a prepubescent girl wonderland wearing his freshly minted NYPD uniform. But perhaps the saddle shoes help to ground him.

"I love what you've done with the place," Scanlon says as he rights his chair.

"You don't think it's a little too much?" Little Debbie says without looking up, his fingers clicking away. "It helps get me in the mood."

"Captain Dentine is okay with this?" Scanlon asks.

"What?" Little Debbie replies on autopilot, lost in his screen.

Before Scanlon can repeat the question, Little Debbie leaps to his feet and waves his arms over his head while gyrating his hips.

"Victory dance," he gloats.

"I suppose congratulations are in order," Scanlon says awkwardly.

He's starting to feel that Little Debbie is giving the entrapment business a bad name.

Little Debbie pantomimes casting a rod and reeling in a fish.

"Got him hooked," he says gleefully. "Hooked on the Debbie girl."

Scanlon tries to sneak a peek at the screen. He need not bother. Little Debbie is in a bragging mood.

"It's oldJim," he crows. "I've been working on him for days. A tough nut to crack. Very old school. Cautious. But I won him over when I got panties with the days of the week embroidered on them. White cotton of course. I said old school. But I knew I owned him once I flashed *Tuesday.*"

"Now he wants me to come to his apartment," Little Debbie continues to chatter like a, well—like a schoolgirl. "It's somewhere on the Upper West Side. I almost got the address today. I'm sure I'll have it tomorrow. I'm going to tell him about my new training bra. I hope that doesn't give him a heart attack. I'll offer to model it for him in person. Of course we have to clear it with the DA's office because it's the standard drill to lure them to our sting. We have a special location—you know that, of course—I'm talking to a past master. But if we can nail him in his own home it saves the department a ton of overtime."

Scanlon is dismayed. He likes oldJim. He'll have to warn him. But he can't do it here. He'll have to do it at home so it won't be traced.

"You're lilSue, right?" Little Debbie burbles. "He's talked about you."

"What did he say?" Scanlon wonders.

"Very cool," Little Debbie says.

Scanlon feels a warm rush of pride.

"As in unhot," Little Debbie explains. "He only chats with you when there are no sluts online. He thinks that you are going to grow up to be a frigid bitch."

"He thought I was hot enough to send a dick pic," Scanlon says defensively.

"Just the one?" Little Debbie asks.

He double-clicks on a desktop icon and opens a slide show. Scanlon is disappointed—and jealous. The dick pic oldJim sent him is almost like something out of the medical examiner's office—just a dick. Little Debbie has a portfolio that you'd shop around to dick modeling agencies: coy flashes between crossed legs, full frontal with face, at the lake, at the beach, poses with vegetables, with a ruler. There is one close-up that particularly stings. Centered over oldJim's dick is a new tattoo—a rainbow with a name—LittleDebbie669.

Scanlon feels his knees wobble and grabs the back of his chair to keep his footing. Little Debbie doesn't say anything. The desk sergeant approaches them.

"Hey, Pat," he says. "How's it going?"

"Same old. Same old," Scanlon replies.

"How's the wound?"

"On the mend."

"They want you in Room 301," the sergeant says.

"IAD?" Scanlon asks.

"The last time I looked," the sergeant answers as he walks back to his desk.

On the one hand, Scanlon is glad that his conversation with Little Debbie is brought to a swift conclusion. On the other, an interview with Internal Affairs is never the palate cleanser that one has in mind. In Scanlon's case it can only be one thing—unauthorized use of non-departmental equipment. As he trudges up to the third floor, his body gets heavier with every step and dread. He does not know how they know, but they know that he has been talking with oldJim behind their backs, and they hate anything that happens behind their backs. He is disappointed further when he opens the door to Room 301. Sitting behind the desk is Ed Cottingham, an old friend.

"Patrick," he says. "How's it going?"

"Same old. Same old," Scanlon replies.

"How's the wound?"

"On the mend."

"Good."

Cottingham shuffles papers for what to Scanlon seems to be an eternity.

"Since when are you IAD?" he finally gets up the nerve to ask.

"Since I needed to borrow an office," Cottingham replies. "Here we go."

He pulls a photo out of the stack and slides it across the table. "We think that this is the bad guy who shot you."

Scanlon studies the enlargement. It is a grainy black and white surveillance shot of a blurry guy in a ski mask who is running from left to right.

"Look familiar?" Cottingham inquires. "He's still a bad guy. I think he's in the market for things that glow in the dark and go bump in the night."

"Dirty bomb?"

"Exactimento."

"Got any lube?" Scanlon asks.

Cottingham goes through the desk drawers. "Jack?"

"Yes, please," Scanlon replies.

Fuck the doctors. The whisky is warm as it goes down. It burns like hell when it hits bottom. But that's okay.

"Do you remember my theory about the flat bomb?" Cottingham asks.

"That the Russians got around a delivery system by building huge atomic bombs in apartments that they bought in US cities." Scanlon chuckles. "How could I forget that?"

"I know they're real," Cottingham says as he fervently points at the blurry man in the photo. "He knows it too."

"So sweep him up," Scanlon says, pulling the stopper out of the whisky bottle again.

Cottingham looks dejected.

"I was reassigned," he explains. "I was told that my theory is an urban legend. I was told that I could chase down your shooter only after I cleaned all the alligators out of the NYC sewer system."

Special Anti-terrorism Agent Cottingham holds up Exhibit A.

"That's the guy. Check it out," he says. "Just saying."

73.
IVAN

THE NEW YORK MARKETS have closed, but all the screens are still fired up in his office. On one he's watching his catamaran clocking over forty-four knots off Sandy Hook in a speed trial. Another is showing the pathetic Dutch boat—the one Woody bought to spite him—grrr. Ivan doesn't have to bother with spies to see what they're up to. His motley ex-crew posts videos of their race prep on YouTube—if you can call it race prep. Would you believe it? There's beer on board—kegs lashed to both port and starboard hulls so that they can tap a new brewski irrespective of the tack they're on. Ivan might be white shoe Miami as opposed to white shoe Newport, but he knows that that is just wrong. On the third screen is the streaming feed of the run-up to the annual SteeleX International shareholders' meeting at the Javits Center. Ivan is highly leveraged and very interested in the outcome. He's driving down tomorrow morning to savor the proxy fight firsthand.

There's a lot on his plate at the moment, and from the sounds coming out of the kitchen some of it will soon be supper. His wife has joined him in Bedford Hills—go figure. That doubles the number of billionaires in residence—at least for tonight. Will she want him to fuck her? Does he want her to? That might depend on how dinner comes out. He will certainly be a white knight in the future when her company's market valuation crashes and he bails her out. She'll thank him for that. A lesser woman would fault her husband for betting against her efforts. But Mackenzie is sophisticated enough—thank you, Wharton—to see his actions for what they are—a hedge. In the past he might have worried about this, but not tonight. Tonight she is a perfect wife.

"Cocktail, darling?" she asks.

She is standing in the doorway to his office holding a silver tray—mixed spirits for him, a white wine for her—totally appropriate. She is a vision of divine wifeliness. Her dress is elegant and perfect for where it isn't. The high thigh slit reveals a garter strap and the wide lacy band of a pricey stocking top—classy not trashy. It's clear that she's made the effort. She bends over so that he can retrieve the martini glass—that's a décolletage that he would never sell short.

"Close down your day," she tells him. "Then meet me out on the terrace for some quality us-time."

He takes a sip as she watches him.

"Yummy," he says toasting her.

After she's gone, he puts the cocktail down. It's her recipe—a concoction she's proud of. It doesn't taste very good—maybe it's the aquavit. Ivan was never a fan of aquavit. But it seems to be growing on him. This is the third or fourth that she has mixed for him over the last week, and he has finished every one.

Ivan sits back and sips the mystery cocktail and watches the screens. He flips to the international markets, but they are nothing more than dancing lines and stampeding numbers. He cannot focus. When he hears his wife singing softly in another room, he knows that is where he wants to be.

Ivan tosses back the drink and wanders into the kitchen. He stands in the door and watches her. She is peeling a potato in such a way that it makes him fall in love with her all over again. He walks up behind her and puts his arms around her.

"You know what I'd like?" he asks her.

"What would you like?" she purrs.

"I'd like for you to pick out the girliest romantic comedy we have in our DVD collection."

He kisses her on the neck.

"And then I'd like to slip it in and cuddle with you all night."

"I'd like that too," his Stepford wife replies.

She spins in his arms and kisses him on the mouth.

Ivan melts.

"Oh no," she says with a start. "I'm burning the rolls."

She rushes to the smaller wall oven and extricates a smoky baking sheet. She opens a window.

The small TV set hanging under the cabinets is tuned to the local news with the sound muted. It's all flashing lights and fire trucks.

"What's going on?" Ivan asks as he turns up the sound.

"There's a huge warehouse fire in Paterson, New Jersey," Mackenzie explains as she fans a dishtowel to clear the air. "I-80 is a mess."

74. VICTORIA

SHE HAS JUST FINISHED DOING her mother's face and is now fussing with her hair. The face is easy. During her lifetime it went unchanged for forty years—never out of style—neo–Dusty Springfield revival. Victoria knows every inch of that face. Today it just happens to be on Tim. She steps back and takes it in one more time. It's uncanny how much he looks like the late great.

They are in the Queen for a Day Room where "Miracles Happen." Tim is fumbling with the clasps of her mother's Guia La Bruna bra, but she's confident that he'll sort it out. Victoria is looking through drawers in the chest of breast forms—size B to J cup—those are in the deep drawers at the bottom—lift with your knees lest you hurt your back. She goes with a pair of quality silicone Ds—but no nipples—out of respect to the dead.

"Yikes," Tim says after she slides them into place. "That's a backache waiting to happen."

"That's just the half of it," Victoria replies as she goes through the wardrobe looking for the perfect blouse.

"Stay off your soapbox," Tim says. "You need me more than I need this. Help me please, this side is pinching."

As she adjusts his bra straps, she checks out his blue jeans and basketball shoes.

"It will have to be top and bottom tomorrow for the webcast," she reminds him.

"I know," he mumbles, readjusting the left strap.

"That means your legs," she adds.

"I know," he complains petulantly, like a boy who doesn't want to try on a pair of pants for *Back to School*.

"How's this?" Victoria asks as she waves a yellow blouse on a hanger to show off its aerodynamic properties.

"That sure is yellow," Tim says. "How many canaries died to satisfy one woman's vanity?"

"You're talking about my mother," she scolds. "Hold up your arms."

He does and she slips a lacy camisole over his head.

"You'll do your legs tonight?" she reminds him again.

"Jeez," Tim complains. "Like there's going to be a tomorrow after Uncle Sid sees through this charade and calls his goons on us."

"Arms straight out," she commands so that she can pull on the blouse.

His arms get tired as she works on the zillion tiny buttons in the back.

"How much longer?" he whines.

"Behave yourself," she admonishes. "Okay. Now turn around."

There's a reason why it's called a bow blouse. There is as much fabric in the bow as in the rest of the garment combined. Victoria ties it into a massive knot that dwarfs the otherwise voluminous poufy blouse.

"Stand there and don't move," she orders.

She grabs a framed picture off the wall. It is a photograph of her mother in the same outfit. She holds it next to Tim's head. They both look into the mirror—comparing Tim to the portrait. They could be twins—idents.

"Holy crap," he says. "You were right. Crazy, but accurate."

"Fait accompli," Victoria crows, basking in the glory of raising her dead. "If I do I say myself."

"One small problem, Einstein," Tim counters. "They know—sorry—knew each other. The minute I open my mouth, all bets are off."

"Not to worry, pretty lady," she coos. "Nobody can mimic the Mater better than I can. *You call that a proper curtsy, girl.*"

"So I'll sit on your lap like a ventriloquist's dummy?" he asks.

"Silly boy," she replies. "I'll be off camera. He'll think you're doing all the talking."

"I can't lip-sync to a song that I don't know," he points out.

Victoria smiles knowingly at that. She goes to a closet and returns with a wild hat—a fascinator—with a huge upsweep and a lot of danglers. She pins it on to the wig and drapes the billowing veil down over Tim's face.

"Rule Britannia," she exalts. "Nobody does cross-dressing better than we do. Even natural born women go out in drag. We even wear hats in the shower."

The egg timer sitting next to the mascara goes *Ding*. Places everyone.

"On cam your lips will be a blur," she reassures him as they walk into the lounge.

Tim wakes up the computer and adjusts the cam so that only what they want in frame is in frame. He sits back in the settee. There are two windows on the screen: the big one where Uncle Sid will appear, and a small one to the left displaying "Miss Lavinia."

"You're going to be great," Victoria reassures him.

"Nice knowing you," Tim replies.

The computer beeps. The larger window fills with noise, then comes into focus—a large towheaded man—with fierce eyes and many extant teeth.

"That's him," Victoria whispers.

The thug looks into the camera like that is where he is going to see the chat.

"Sidney," Victoria enunciates with great clarity.

"Lavinia?" he asks, still not sure where to look.

"I am here, Sidney," she responds. "And I understand why you are upset."

"Do you?" the towhead asks sarcastically.

"I know that Victoria is late," Victoria continues to impersonate her mum. "But you know how young people are these days. Not like we were."

"Fuck all," Sid curses. "You know that money is shite between us. What I want to know is . . ."

The webcam scans his body as he stands up. He is wearing a Manchester United sweatshirt, but he is naked below that—except for the turquoise tutu—and the suspender belt and the fishnet stockings—and, oh yes—the plastic chastity device that is locked around his shrunken dick. There is a tiny padlock catching the light as it flits back and forth at the top of the cage.

". . .where did you hide the fucking key?"

Victoria and Tim look at each other in disbelief and wonder.

What do we do now? Tim mouths.

Victoria shrugs her shoulders, but her grin turns evil.

"How dare you take that tone with me," she chastises the screen.

"I'm sorry," Uncle Sid replies.

"Sorry, what?" she demands.

"Sorry, Mistress," he relents.

"That's better, you pathetic wanker." She winks at Tim. "Show me your flogger."

After some fumbling, the screen is filled with a wide leather paddle covered with pyramid-shaped metal studs inset in a pattern.

"Owie," Tim commiserates aloud before he catches himself.

"Ten of the best," Victoria demands.

Whack.

The body on screen visibly shudders.

"One," the submissive Sid counts out. "Thank you, Mistress."

75.
WOODY

THEY ARE SITTING IN A VERY comfortable sofa in the makeup trailer watching traffic inch along the Brooklyn-Queens Expressway, high over the Gowanus Canal. Neither has a phone. Hers is in her dressing room, his somewhere else. He hates the thing. They had tried to get the attention of other motorists to call for help. They waved out the window and held up signs they had improvised. *HELP! CALL 911.* But everyone in a car on the BQE this morning is either talking on the phone, texting, or playing *Catch the Carrot* on their smartphones, so these desperate pleas for assistance go totally unnoticed.

"So who is it?" Woody asks.

"Who is what?" Svetlana replies.

"Who wants to snatch you so badly that they would go to this much trouble?" he explains.

"Me?" she says. "I'm assuming that they're kidnapping you."

"Nah," he says. "It can't be me. Nobody knows I'm here. It has to be you."

"Why me?" she asks. "I'm box-office poison trying to make a comeback. What do I have that anyone would want?"

"A spectacular bosom," he points out.

"Thank you for noticing," she says.

"How could I not?" he replies. "You shove them in my face at every opportunity."

They both chuckle familiarly at that, like two old friends who are sharing an inside joke. He looks deeply into her eyes—not for the first time, but on every visit he is more intrigued. What he likes best now is her complete lack of fear.

"I'd just as soon not wait around to find out which one of us they want," Woody says.

"But what if he's cute," Svetlana wonders. "I've read that stalkers have no trouble with commitment."

Once they get to Hamilton Avenue and leave the snarl behind, traffic picks up. The trailer is soon fishtailing again, speeding to its sinister destination.

"It's lovely to sit and chat," he says. "But I think we'd better get to work."

"I think you're right," she concurs. "Where do we start?"

"What would MacGyver do?" he posits.

"My thought exactly," she agrees.

They split up and silently take inventory of their rolling jail cell, looking for that combination of common objects—a toilet paper roll, a jar of peanut butter, and a bobby pin—that they can turn into a Sawzall. It's a very posh studio trailer, but that's all it is. The sofa runs along one wall. There are three makeup chairs along the other, each with a mirror surrounded by all those lightbulbs—strictly Hollywood. At the front end is a hair washing station but also a modest kitchen area with a microwave and a full-sized refrigerator. Woody presses his face against the tiny window over the sink. The angle is bad. He cannot see into the cab of the truck that is towing them, but he can make out the reflection of a propane tank in the chrome. On the other end of the trailer is an enclosed bathroom.

"Can we do anything with these?" Svetlana asks. She has an armload of hair spray cans.

"Brilliant," Woody praises her as she drops them on the sofa. "Give me a hand."

Together they rip the microwave from its mount.

"Got a hammer?" he asks. "Any kind. Claw? Ball-peen?"

She hands him a hair straightening iron. He uses it to smash the glass out of the front of the microwave—not so easy, it's tempered glass. They stack the hair spray inside until they can't squeeze in another can. Then they spin the oven around so that it faces forward. They manhandle the fridge around to cover the microwave, leaving only enough room for a contortionist to reach the control panel. They are in the Midtown Tunnel.

Next they pull the cushions out of the sofa and stuff them inside the WC, practically filling the small toilet. They stand the frame of the sofa up against it.

Woody muscles the door open as wide as he can.

"See if you can slither in there, cutie-pie," he says. "Think like a snake."

She does and she can. Now they are on the FDR Drive.

"Okay in there?" he asks.

"I'm hot," she replies.

"Of course you are," he says. "You're a movie star."

Woody waits until the truck pulls into Central Park—the 79th Street Transverse—before he awkwardly reaches around and starts pushing buttons on the microwave. He hopes he is remembering the sequence correctly. He hopes that they don't kill anybody.

When the appliance beeps in compliance, he hurries to the bathroom and struggles with the door. It's tight—worse than trying to get on a 7 train in Grand Central at rush hour, but he finally squeezes inside.

"Hey," she says.

"Hey," he says.

They are stuffed between the sofa cushions. There is not enough room to blink. They are two twins in utero waiting for Mom to get on with it.

"Cover your ears," he tells her.

"I can't move my arms," she explains.

"Then open your mouth really wide," he says. "Hopefully that might keep your eardrums from rupturing."

"Hopefully," she acknowledges.

In their muffled cocoon they can hear the microwave start up. It is angry. Every metallic crease, crimp, or seam on the cans is arcing and spitting in protest.

It doesn't take long . . .

Boom!

Then the propane tank . . .

BOOM!

The front of the trailer is blown off, and one or another of Newton's laws slams the back half in the opposite direction—through a stone wall and rolling between some trees. They come to a stop in a low, boggy area.

Their ears are ringing so loudly that they can't hear anything. But they are both shouting the same thing.

"Let's get out of here."

As he pulls Svetlana from the mangled wreck, he gets a good look at the driver before he speeds away. But Woody will never be able to ID him in a lineup. He is wearing a ski mask.

76.
TIM

HE IS BACK ON THE THRONE in the Queen for a Day Room, but he is not doing anything regal. He is cutting his toenails. Tim wants to be damn sure that he isn't the one who puts a ladder in the dead woman's stockings. He already has her face on—and the big hair—and the bra with the high-tech falsies. Other than that, he's naked from the waist down. That's why he's sitting on a towel. It's a wonder he's allowed to dress himself at all. He and Victoria had a small fight over it when he laid down the law that he refuses to wear open-toed shoes. It takes Fifi long enough to do his mani—but a pedi? I think not. By the way, his relationship with the maid is greatly improved—thank you for asking.

Tim is short on time. He's got to teach a class in the morning—a bunch of English majors fulfilling their science requirement. It's *Physics for Poets* and he's not prepared. He does have some ideas though. They've gone fission this week, and there's no better way to hook their interest than the good old A-bomb—easy to understand—easy to make—especially if you go with the gun-style ignition system. The only speed bump in the learning curve is *critical mass*—that point of no return that triggers a chain reaction. Tim believes he can explain this one easily.

Critical mass is achieved when you are hosting your entire family for Thanksgiving in a very small New York apartment—every seat, every square foot, is occupied—there's barely room for the turkey. The doorbell rings. It's Aunt Pearl and Cousin Clem. She is a member of People for the Ethical Treatment of Animals. He is NRA. The both have strong opinions. They are both geniuses. Once the door closes you have a small space with too much of a good thing—critical mass.

He works the emery board, getting rid of any burr that might catch and run. He wipes his feet with a hand towel and he's ready for the next course. Today's undies are laid out on the chaise. Miss Lavinia seemed to favor—had favored—peach-colored lingerie. He picks up a pair of panties. They are satin and fully cut, which is a good thing. Putting a thong on a guy is like trying to floss the shark in *Jaws*.

Uh-oh.

Tim panics. The satin panties come with a most unwelcome causal efficacy. He has had no problem wearing the wig or a bra, but once he pulls up the satin panties and they squeeze his firm cheeks, on the other side of this equation there is a most dire—and conspicuous—result. He knows that he must rechannel his thoughts. He skips the dead babies and continues with today's theme, trying to focus his mind's eye on the tragic effects of radiation poisoning; the topical burns from exposure; the long-term tumors and necrosis. That seems to help. He looks down at the panties. The sight lines seem to have receded. Good.

He picks up the garter belt—recently a suspender belt before it got off the plane. He fastens it around his waist with no discernible response from you know where. Good.

In a way, a garter belt is just like a bra, he realizes. *It's only there to hold up things.*

Tim sits down and very carefully rolls the stockings up his legs—cherishing them like pages from a Gutenberg Bible. He fastidiously straightens them. Then he clips the garter straps into the lacy band. So far, so good.

He slips his toes into the size twelve pumps and holds his breath. He has been worried about first steps.

"He who hesitates is lost," he says and takes a leap of faith.

Tim is pleasantly surprised. He walks back and forth a few times. Then he vamps. It is a totally different experience for him. He feels so elegant in the heels—practically stately—definitely tall. He has never worn such dynamic clothes before. Everything is in motion—especially the garters, which are in constant flux, like the struts in a race car.

He starts to take glances of himself in the mirror as he passes by. It's hard to believe that is him. Hell, it's obviously an illusionist's trick. He can't look like this. He's so . . . he's so . . . Oh My God. He has caught sight of the panties. He stops and stares. That tent could house the Ringling Bros. and Barnum & Bailey Circus. It is a life-affirming boner. If he lost control of his dick at this moment it could achieve escape velocity and leave the galaxy it grew up in.

Three discreet knocks on the door and Victoria walks in with the blouse and pencil skirt—freshly pressed—on hangers.

"Oh my God," they say in unison.

They both look down at his panties. They both look up into each other's eyes. Tim has never seen *looking* like this ever before. She is very hot. In the history of man, some things will never be truly known, like: Which side fired the first shot at Lexington in 1775 to so radically alter the future of the world? Which came first, the chicken or the egg? Who made the first move, Tim or Victoria?

We will never know. But it happened. And now they are practically inhaling each other—by touch—kisses—groping—fondling—a lot of tongue. They take a minute to catch their breath. Eyes filled with aching hunger. Then they are back at it. Squeezing. Clawing. Running their hands over every inch of the other's body.

She slides her hand into his panties.

Critical mass.

77.
MACKENZIE

SHE IS SITTING IN THE COZY kitchen of her West End Avenue apartment. The aroma of baking cookies fills the air with a comforting ambiance while dense paperwork in three huge stacks on the table drowns her soul with dread. She tries to digest them in rotation. She has to take it slowly or her eyes will roll back in her head and she will choke on her tongue. She has pushed all the stuff from the lawyers to the side. That makes for lamentable reading. She is an unsustainable charity case, they inform her—a penniless billionaire. If she exercises any stock options before this is all sorted out, she can be charged with wire fraud—wire fraud? Seriously? What if she performed her nefarious deeds via Pony Express? Currently she is trying to make heads or tails out of a little something called the *Forensic Users' Comprehensive Knowledgebase Update*.

"My thoughts exactly," she says as she checks out the acronym on the spine of the report.

This is an independent and very expensive audit of her—ColdTrail.com—network's traffic, health, and well-being in the days leading up to the event—failure or attack—whatever you want to call it. Did some irresponsible teenager simply leave the back door unlocked, or did a gang of cyber crooks—terrorists—China—blow a hole in it? No one seems to know. Mackenzie has her own suspicions—but that reality would be so unconscionable that . . . she prefers to go with known facts. The SOB shorted her. That's bad enough. In fact, that's a Sin with a capital S. It's in the Bible somewhere. *Whom God hath joined together let no man put asunder—or sell his wife short.*

At least she has something to do with her hands. It was hell to quit smoking the first time around. She certainly doesn't want to go back to the coffin nails now. Mackenzie throws a handful of birth control pills into the kitchen mortar and picks up the pestle. She starts grinding slowly and exceedingly fine. At the same time, her face is in the book, plowing through the dry, arcane material like she used to in B-school—foot by foot—one word after another, like a verbal Bataan Death March. She turns the page.

Packet Analytics: A Metrics-Based Composite of Real-Time Throughput.

"Lord have mercy," she groans and throws four tabs of Wellbutrin into the mortar mix.

She read about this one online. It's an antidepressant with great side effects. Not only does it tend to make people—especially men—less able to control their emotions—creating a big weeping baby man (it's called the pseudobulbar affect. She Wiki'd that)—but if that wasn't enough—and it is—there's more: This med will make him also grow tits. Just what the doctor ordered.

There is a familiar knock on the door. Mackenzie dumps the mortar's powdered contents into the empty feminine product container where she has been stashing previous batches.

"It's open," she sings out once she has sealed the lid on tight.

Victoria staggers into the kitchen—stagger is the only way to put it. Mackenzie would usually be concerned by her forlorn appearance, but she is so desperate for some comfort food—especially of the girl friend variety—that she is out of her seat and hugging her tightly.

"Vix," she warbles. "How did you know? I need you so badly right now."

When she finally relaxes her hungry grasp, Victoria asks meekly, "Coffee?"

"Fresh pot," Mackenzie proclaims.

She pours two mugs. There are wire racks of Toll House cookies cooling next to the coffeemaker on the counter.

"Have one," she says. "Fresh baked."

Victoria reaches out a hand and Mackenzie slaps it away.

"Stay away from the ones with M&M's," she explains. "Those are for Ivan. Special Reserve."

Victoria takes a plain chocolate chip and nibbles at it.

"Yummy," she says, sliding into a chair—putting down the mug—putting down the cookie—and staring blankly in front of her.

She is so dazed that Mackenzie finally climbs far enough out of her own ass to notice that there is something wrong with her friend.

"Honey," she asks. "What is it?"

"Sex," Victoria answers flatly.

"What about sex?"

"Had it."

"Okay," Mackenzie replies, trying to figure out what the heck is going on. "Was that a bad thing?"

"It was brilliant," Victoria answers. "Better than brilliant. It was magical."

"That sounds like it was a good thing." Mackenzie smiles weakly. She is confused.

"I think I need a psychiatrist," Victoria continues. "Or a team. Or an entire hospital wing. I was enjoying it as long as I kept my eyes closed," she explains. "But whenever they opened up . . ."

She gets on her feet and gyrates her hips for emphasis.

"Whoop—There she is."

"Whoop—There she is."

"I don't get it," Mackenzie says.

"It's okay," Victoria replies. She shakes her head to clear her thoughts. "I got what I was waiting for, and it was good—it was brilliant—and it's not like this was the first time that I was fucked by my mother."

"Baby, what happened?" Mackenzie demands.

Victoria pops the whole cookie into her mouth and says, "I think it might be a little more complicated than an Oedipus complex."

78. SVETLANA

IT PRETTY MUCH GOES UNSAID. While she is delighted to be alive—especially to be alive and no longer kidnapped—she's just not in the mood to call the police in on this one. At the time when they were kidnapped the police would have been nice to have around, but now, on the other side of the trauma—sitting endlessly in a dingy squad room?—not in the cards. Woody hasn't brought it up so he must be in agreement. They do have to clean him up a little before they go any farther so that a Good Samaritan doesn't call it in and they end up at the precinct anyway. There is a nasty gash on Woody's head. His beret is soaked through with blood—*Le Rouge et Le Noir*. It takes forty dollars of designer water that they buy at *Eau du Monde* to clean up his face. The cashier looks concerned.

"You should see the other guy," Svetlana slides in quickly.

Hardy har hars all around.

Samaritans! Svetlana hates those guys.

Someone drops a tray of dishes. There is a crash. She jumps into Woody's arms.

"I'll call my people," he says.

"There's a place nearby," she replies. "I have a toothbrush there. I so want to brush my teeth."

"Plucky girl," Woody says and kisses her on the lips.

Svetlana likes that.

They walk the eight blocks to her grandfather's building. The doorman recognizes her and waves her in.

"Maybe you can talk some sense into him," he says.

"Who?" Svetlana asks.

The doorman simply rolls his weary eyes. "Who do you think?"

There are a dozen tenants milling around the lobby—drifting back and forth between the mailboxes and the package room. The anxiety vibe is palpable. When she and Woody get to the elevators, the reason becomes clear. The elevator doors on the right are open. The cab is up or down but nowhere in sight. The shaft is empty. There is yellow hazard tape stretched across the opening as well as a safety barrier that reads: *Caution. Men at Work*. There is not a soul in sight.

The elevator doors to the left are also open, but these are blocked by some kind of barricade—seemingly a pile of street trash and construction debris—to make passage impossible. But on closer inspection—maybe it's the window-rattling snores emanating from within—Svetlana determines that the barricade is nothing more than old-man apartment clutter duct-taped to a wheelchair. She leans over the pile of crap.

"Dedushka?" she asks affectionately.

She is answered with a snort.

"Grandfather, may I introduce Woody Steele?" Svetlana says. "Woody, this is my grandfather, Colonel Pavlenko."

Now awake, the old coot reaches up and grabs her by the collar, bending her over, pulling her down—face-to-face.

"Where is Zhukov?" he demands.

"Going up," she informs him and rolls the wheelchair back into the elevator.

"I've been invaded," he mutters. "It was a pincer movement. They came at me from all sides."

As the doors close he curses in Russian while fieldstripping the wheelchair so that by the time they reach the penthouse he rolls himself out free and clear and ready for action.

"You," he barks at Woody. "Follow me."

Woody shrugs his shoulders and grins at Svetlana as he follows the old man. She comes in a distant third—treading carefully. The elevator crew is using the foyer as a staging area. There's a spool of cable—piles of tools—stacks of scrap—even an acetylene cutting torch on wheels. Once inside, the penthouse of 501 West Avenue is clearly on a wartime footing. The open cases of hand grenades are the first giveaway—or perhaps it is all the Kalashnikovs leaning against the wall.

At the same time, the elevator work going on above their heads is deafening. The technicians are obviously taking out all their personal frustrations by attacking anything that is loud and metallic with a sledgehammer. On the floor below, it sounds like an air raid.

By the time Svetlana catches up with the menfolk, they are gathered around a large wall map of a certain city on the Volga. The colonel is gesturing with a long pointer while carrying on a running commentary. Woody appears to listen intently. Whenever the old man waves his magic wand, Woody replies, "Da, da."

Svetlana sidles up behind him and whispers in his ear, "I didn't know you could speak Russian."

"Today I wish I didn't," he says out of the side of his mouth.

"What's going on?" she whispers in his ear, just before she puts her tongue in it.

"Your grandfather thinks he's back at Stalingrad," Woody explains. "But not in a good way."

79.
SCANLON

IN THE DEN, HE SETS DOWN a bottle of vodka and a small glass beside his laptop and starts typing.

lilSue:	hi Daddy
oldJim:	hey darling
lilSue:	im so glad ur here i want to do everything today
oldJim:	sorry sweetie not today
lilSue:	pleez Daddy ANYTHING
oldJim:	no can do hunnie. daddys got a date tomorrow
lilSue:	live for today Daddy
oldJim:	daddys getting a haircut so he looks special for a special girl
lilSue:	NOOO!!! dont tease me

This is what Sergeant Scanlon has been dreading for days. The trap is finally set—officially. The DA must have just signed off on it. Scanlon has to be careful. The department is certainly monitoring oldJim's traffic at this point. If he spills the beans now he'll end up on charges. In all the months they have been chatting, not once has oldJim suggested anything inappropriate—outside of fantasyland, of course—but that's why you go to chat rooms—duh. It's that cheap blonde from San Diego. She's no good. She's out to entrap him.

lilSue: don't tell me its littledebbie
oldJim: how did you guess?
lilSue: i warned you about her Daddy she's no good
oldJim: i remember
lilSue: shes a slut and she says you dont like me
oldJim: she made that up to make you jealous. you know i like you
lilSue: stay away from her
oldJim: I like her 2
lilSue: but shes got a grown up lady disease
oldJim: what?
lilSue: she told me it burns when she tinkles
oldJim: now yur making stuff up
lilSue: no its true
lilSue: and shes got ants

This is just wrong. OldJim is a thoroughly decent citizen. He has been totally supportive during Scanlon's recent rough patch. He certainly knows what's going on in the Yankees' clubhouse. So he likes to talk about white cotton panties—in depth—that's better than white collar crime. It's victimless—as long as Scanlon can get to him first. Otherwise there's a victim for sure, and he doesn't deserve to be incarcerated with the real creeps. There is not a doubt in Scanlon's mind that if the two of them had a heart-to-heart he would see the error of his ways and get back on the straight and narrow—with a copy of *Anne of Green Gables* and a Victoria's Secret catalog for maintenance.

lilSue:	Daddy?
oldJim:	yes darling
lilSue:	can i come too?
oldJim:	tomorrow?
lilSue:	yes
oldJim:	what will you tell your mother?
lilSue:	that I have a playdate with Debbie
lilSue:	she doesnt know my friends
lilSue:	and she drinks
lilSue:	in the morning
lilSue:	say yes pleez. it will be 2X the fun
oldJim:	i dont think thats a very good idea
lilSue:	iv got a sailor suit just like the ones japanese girls wear to school

Scanlon grabs a pencil and writes down old Jim's address in his notebook. When he sees something moving out of the corner of his eye, he closes the laptop with one hand and clamps the other one tightly around his stepdaughter's wrist. He's got Bitzi, and she's got the vodka bottle.

"Good evening, Sergeant," she says with a straight face.

"Can I help you?" he asks.

"I don't think so." She shrugs. "Nothing that I can think of at the moment."

"What do you think your mother will say when she hears about this?" he wonders.

"Well, that's a question of jurisdiction, isn't it, Sergeant?" the fourteen-year-old replies. "First you have to catch her in the County of I'm-Listening-to-a-Word-You're-Saying in the State of Like-I-Give-a-Shit."

"You know I can't let you have this bottle," Scanlon naively explains, like he's from this century or something.

Bitzi totally ignores that. She tries to make a break for it, but it's clearly Aesop's Fable Time. As long as she's got the Smirnoff, he's got her.

"I'm thinking about what Miss Ringwald would say," she throws as an aside.

"Who is Miss Ringwald?" he asks.

"My phys-ed health teacher," she explains. "She records inappropriate touching. It's a fetish of hers. She keeps them all in a loose-leaf notebook in a safe."

"If she were here," Scanlon says, "she would find nothing inappropriate going on."

"But she's not here, is she?" Bitzi replies. "If it's Tuesday, she must be at her fat lesbian man-hating support group."

"You're making that up," he accuses her.

"Can you afford to be wrong?" she flirts, batting her eyes at him.

"That's extortion," he argues.

"Extortion is such an ugly word," she says. "I prefer *let go of my fucking hand.*"

"No," he insists.

"She's got a seventy-four percent conviction rate," she notes.

Scanlon eases his grip only slightly. That's all it takes. Bitzi, like all young girls, is a contortionist. In a fraction of a second she is free and clear and walking away with her prize, grinning in victory.

Scanlon smiles too. He sits back in his chair and waits.

The scream comes sooner than he expected. She must have taken a swig the minute she left the room.

"What the fuck!" Bitzi screams.

She charges back into the den, spitting to either side as she goes.

"You tried to poison me," she accuses. "This is gasoline."

"Not to worry, Sweet Pea," he explains. "It's only cider vinegar."

He chuckles with delight as she dumps the bottle over his head—happy that they are finally bonding.

Score one for the old guy.

80.
MARY MARGARET

AT THE JAVITS CONVENTION CENTER, located on the island of Manhattan between 11th Avenue and New Jersey, they are taking their seats for the pregame show—the first of bookending press conferences. This is one of Woody's brilliant ideas that she particularly hates. The nightly business reports, on the other hand, love it. The before-and-after mug shots of Wall Street high rollers, looking like they have aged ten years in two hours, are always a hit with the plebes.

To her right at the table is Ivan Greenbriar. He's only here because of Woody's second brilliant idea—which Mary Margaret loathes and detests even more than Brilliant Idea Number One. When the *activist investor* became a thing—euphemized from what was previously called a *raider*—Woody decided to give him a seat at the table—*keep your enemies closer* and all that rubbish.

"But no modesty panel," he directed. "During the reading of the balance sheet, point a camera at his willy and see what floats his boat."

Ivan smiles moistly at Mary Margaret as he takes his seat, pulls out his phone, and proceeds to check his mail.

What a dick, she thinks, nodding to her aide.

"They are ready to take your questions, ladies and gentlemen," he announces.

The first question is so predictable that Mary Margaret starts to answer it before it is asked.

"Mr. Steele is our greatest resource, but unfortunately we have to share him with the world," she says. She does not say, "And the bimbo du jour."

Her cool performance deserves an Academy Award or at least an Obie. But inside she is seething. Woody has never missed a shareholders' meeting. The fact that he might have dumped her—not that there was ever any them there—has nothing to do with it. She blames his damaged goods. This would have never happened during his tomcatting days. He might have showed up fifteen minutes late with a smile on his face—but he would have showed up.

In the seat next door, Ivan is answering the next question—cutting and pasting every sports metaphor in the playbook—concluding with ". . . moving the ball down the field."

"You forgot *locked and loaded*," Mary Margaret whispers to him.

Ivan aims his index finger at the reporter who asked the question, cocks his thumb and clicks his tongue.

"Locked and loaded," he declares.

Then, without missing a beat, he is back into his phone.

"Aww," he sighs audibly.

Mary Margaret's curiosity overrides all her filters. She leans over and looks directly at his phone. Someone is sending him pictures of puppies. They're damn cute—she has to admit it—especially the terrier sitting on the blond-haired blue-eyed moppet. He's got a pageboy haircut—the moppet does—and the terrier is balancing on it. They are both staring into the camera lens. They both have the exact same smiles—priceless.

The next question from the floor is about the Paterson warehouse fire.

"While this unexpected and tragic event was catastrophic," she replies, "we are thankful that there was no loss of life. Moreover, the wisdom of our founder—and that would be Mr. Steele again—has imbued our corporate bylaws with mechanisms to deal with unexpected contingencies."

She turns and smiles at Ivan. He is lost in his phone—Puppies 4 Ever.

You have no idea how fucked you are, do you? Mary Margaret thinks as she watches his eyes ping-pong back and forth across the screen with delight.

She is confident because she knows her bylaws. She wrote most of them—Woody was off somewhere being Woody. The relevant one is a corker. If anything should happen to the proxy votes—like a flood or fire or locusts—*all elections to the board and resolutions before the board will be determined by paper ballot marked by shareholders in attendance on-site declared to be a quorum on a pro tem and non-precedentuary basis.* She also knows that Ivan is cheap and small-minded and that he cashed out most of his position in SteeleX International once he mailed in his proxies. A little birdie told her that at a diner in the Hamptons.

"Oh my God." He giggles into his phone.

Mary Margaret is incredulous.

"Will you look at that," he gushes and turns the phone so that she can see the screen.

Someone has sent him a video. The adorable puppy is bouncing all over the cute moppet like a goat. They are rolling around on the grass. The moppet is laughing infectiously. The puppy is licking him all over the face. Tears are streaming down Ivan's face as he watches the magic moment unfold before his twinkling eyes.

"What are we, girlfriends?" Mary Margaret dismisses caustically.

Ivan does not respond. He is lost in his own world—so far at sea that she has to poke him sharply in the ribs to bring him back to shore. He looks up at her in blank confusion.

"It's your question," she hisses at him.

"Please repeat the question," he says.

The reporter stands up.

"Ivan," he begins. "As your infamous feud with Woody enters its second decade, what makes you feel that there's a chance for a different outcome this time around?"

"What do you mean by that?" Ivan bristles.

"I mean that every time you take on Woody Steele, you end up looking like a jerk," the reporter clarifies.

"Like that's so hard," Mary Margaret mutters.

That brings Ivan to his feet.

"Not this time," he bellows.

His new power and confidence suddenly unnerves Mary Margaret.

"I know things," Ivan proclaims. "Woody Steele is not half the man he used to be."

His phone vibrates on the table.

"I've got to take this." He instinctively picks it up and thumbs a button. Mary Margaret can't believe how flaky he is. She is on her feet, looking over his shoulder. They watch together as the heartbreaking events unfold on the tiny screen.

The cute moppet is playing Frisbee with the adorable puppy in the quiet street outside of a suburban split-level. He throws the disk high. The puppy jumps high and catches it in its jaws. He throws it far. The puppy runs fast and far . . .

The SUV comes from out of nowhere.

The moppet is holding his dog in his arms—still—unmoving.

Even coldhearted—ice water in her veins—Mary Margaret can feel a tear debating whether or not to form in one of her eyes.

But there's no question for Ivan. Ivan is wailing like a banshee—crying the tears that Job contained. He is standing there shaking in sorrow—weeping and sobbing—snot cascading down in rivulets along with the ocular gushers.

Mary Margaret is unsure of what she should do. She certainly isn't about to comfort him—hug him—no way.

"Take it outside," she tells him.

He nods and sobs louder. She hands him his paper ballot to wipe his nose. Then she sits down and watches the biggest, weepy baby girlie man of all time leave the building. When the side door finally closes behind him, she grins.

"Any other questions?" she asks.

When the doors in the back open to welcome the shareholders, her smile broadens. There are hundreds of them, and they are mostly women.

In the day, when Mary Margaret instituted an aggressive outreach to hire women, Woody thought it was good PR. Then after that, when Mary Margaret lobbied to pay them with stock, Woody thought it was cost saving. And now the hens have come home to roost.

She stands up and holds open her arms to embrace them all.

"Welcome, ladies," she says. "Want to take over a company?"

Sorry, Woody, she thinks. *Hear me roar.*

81.
WOODY

HE HAS NO IDEA WHEN SHE LAST ATE. He doubts she had any breakfast. They got kidnapped early in the morning. Catering service wasn't even there yet, so she hadn't eaten anything on the set. She must be starving, but you would never know it from the way she carries herself. He really admires her.

While Svetlana cleans up—and brushes her teeth—he is putting together a small repast for the three of them. He assumes it's still three, even though the old man has rolled off somewhere. Woody scavenges everything he can from what looks like the kitchen you'd get after you were downgraded from Siberia. He has boiled four eggs. He found some pickled beets. He's got black bread and good butter. There's also herring. He passes on the blini, which looks like it's left over from May Day. But the vodka will more than make up for that. It's not too early. Woody figures that at this point, they're all on Moscow time.

"Not bad, if I do say so myself," he says, carving roses out of radishes with a paring knife—hopefully a lively garnish will help tart up this otherwise rather bland fare—presentation is everything.

Svetlana floats into the kitchen. She is wearing a huge, raggedy sweatshirt—CCCP MOCKBA 1980—and probably panties. Barefoot with skinny, naked legs and a towel turban—she has washed her hair—she is adorable. No longer a glamorous movie star, she is now better than that—a pretty girl standing in a kitchen. Woody is smitten.

"Yes, please," she says when she sees the vodka bottle.

She pours some into a glass, where it remains for the blink of an eye. She then spoons up some pickled beets as a chaser and makes a face as they go down.

"Love them. Love them," Svetlana effuses, grimacing and slapping the table with her palm. "Just like Granny used to make."

"I saw the jar," Woody replies. "She probably did."

She slices off a piece of the black bread and slathers butter on it.

"I should probably phone the studio," she says.

"Just talk to me," he replies. "I own it."

"For the moment," she points out. "You and Ivan should get married and fight properly. Good bread."

As she eats, Woody dotes on her like a babushka. The eggs and herring seem to take the edge off her hunger—protein good. The vodka seems to blur all her edges—potatoes better. All his edges are easing also. He is happy just watching her chew . . . until a mechanical wail shrieks throughout the apartment.

"What was that?" he asks, jumping out of his seat.

"Pneumatic impact wrench," Svetlana explains as she kills the pickled beets.

"What's he doing in there?" Woody asks. "Rotating his tires?"

"He has to do that every day," she explains, licking her fingertips and pointing to her empty glass. "If you don't vent it, pressure and heat builds up and it could explode."

"What could explode?" he asks.

"It's kind of like a hobby," she replies.

"What could explode?" he repeats.

Svetlana beams with pride. "My dedushka has a bomb—an

atomic one—he built it himself," she explains. "It's been here like forever. I remember playing around it when I was a little girl."

"I-I don't believe it," Woody stammers.

"It's true," she says defensively. "Grandfather is very clever. Uncle Joe gave him a medal."

"Uncle Joe, as in Joseph Stalin?" he asks wide-eyed.

"Who do you think?" She rolls her eyes. "Look around, why don't you?"

Woody does and sees what he did not notice before. The apartment is a museum to the cult of personality, right down to the Stalin dish towels—slightly frayed—and a Stalin commemorative plate collection displayed proudly in the hutch.

"Can I see it?" he asks.

"If you show me yours." Svetlana giggles.

At this point she is hugging the vodka bottle. She got tired of waiting for a top-up.

"Nap time," Woody announces.

"Mmmm," she purrs—all dreamy.

The pneumatic wrench once again breaks the peace. Woody finds it irritating but hardly worthy of phoning in a DEFCON 4. As far as Woody can remember, the only medals Stalin gave out were for sucking up to Stalin. He takes the vodka bottle out of the pretty—now slightly tipsy—girl's hand and puts it on the counter. Then he picks her up in his arms. She is as light as a feather.

"You are my Count Vronsky," she whispers to him.

Woody likes that idea. He will google *Vronsky* the minute he gets home.

"Where's the bed?" he asks.

She scrunches up her nose.

"I have standards," she informs him. "Do you really own the studio?"

"It's only nap time," he reassures her. "And yes, I do."

"In that case," she explains, "there are plenty of beds through the pantry door over there. There's a bomb shelter behind it—but not exactly your regulation bomb shelter. In this case, the intent is to shelter the bomb."

She sighs and sinks deeper into his arms. The warm air of her exhalation laps against Woody's neck—a pretty girl zephyr. His heart is full.

82.
SVETLANA

SHE DOES NOT WAKE UP so much as come out of a coma. She has no idea where she is or how she got here. But she knows that she is safe. She can feel that. Maybe it's the strong arms that are holding her. She tentatively opens her eyes.

"Tough morning," Woody says.

Svetlana nods.

His face is inches from hers. His unblinking gaze is taking her all in: learning her, memorizing her, knowing her—*Zen and the Art of Archery*.

"You were very brave," he tells her, stroking a cheek.

She doesn't feel very brave at the moment. She snuggles in closer to him. He has a powerful body—but not aggressive or threatening—more capable and secure. She wraps her arms around him. She sees that that makes his eyes twinkle. That makes her smile. She closes her eyes.

Minutes or hours later she stretches—raises her head—kisses him on the lips. He kisses her back chastely, like a gentleman. She won't have any of that. She pulls herself out of their embrace and squirms up onto her knees. Bending over, she takes his face between her hands to hold it still so that she can give him a proper kiss. He responds appropriately—less gentle—more man.

"Thanks for noticing," Svetlana acknowledges as she lies back into his arms.

She settles down into his hypnotic breathing pattern—joining in—pulling oxygen directly from his diaphragm. Then their heartbeats fall in sync. She closes her eyes. There are no distractions. No sound. No this or that. No other. No thoughts at all.

Minutes or hours later there is a discordant element—a distraction—a jarring panting noise that is disrupting the sonorous rhythm of their breathing cycle. To Svetlana's dismay she realizes that it's coming from her and—worse—it's prompted by desire. She is suddenly very cross with herself. How did she let things get so far out of control? It is time to reestablish the proper balance of power here. That she knows how to do. There are strategies and techniques for this sort of thing. Rolling on her side, she raises up her head again. This time she makes goo-goo eyes at him as her hand massages his thigh, working its way toward the Promised Land.

But he's not buying. Before Moses can get to the mountaintop, Woody grabs her wrist. He pulls her hand up so that he can kiss her palm. Then using that arm as a lever he rolls her onto her back. He lies down, the entire weight of his body on hers, crushing her breasts with his chest—*yes, please*. Hands clamped around her wrists, he stretches her arms above her head. He flashes a Cheshire cat smile before gifting her with a totally improper kiss.

Svetlana feels embarrassed for whoever is making those totally inappropriate groaning sounds.

But Woody's chain clearly jerks him back to chivalry. He rolls off on the bed beside her.

Hey, where are you going? she thinks.

He nuzzles his face into her neck. His hand casually drops into her lap.

If those panties are in your way . . . just . . . you know . . .

His breathing becomes regular.

She closes her eyes.

Svetlana is in a rowboat. She's taking easy, gentle strokes—a lazy day on the lake—pull—then watch the rings in the water where the blade entered and left.

Pull. Drift. Pull. Drift. Pull and drift. Pull and drift. Pull. Pull. Pull. Pull.

As the stroke increases, so does her pulse. It is exhilarating. She's really rowing now—being part of a machine. Feeling it in every part of her body—her arms—in her heart and lungs—even where her seat rubs against the bench with every stroke.

Beads of perspiration form on her forehead. Stroke. Stroke. Stroke.

A breeze is blowing through her hair—her breeze—made by her stroke. But there is a warm breath in that movement of air—something tropical. She lifts the oars out of the water. Drips streaming off the tips make complicated concentric patterns. She turns in her seat. There is a growing chop on the water. She is heading into a squall.

She throws herself into the task. Pulling harder—faster—more vigorously on the oars—raising the stroke. The first gust catches her unaware. It slides the boat to the side. She takes a strong, deep stroke to correct—and another. She works hard to keep into the wind, which is intensifying. Then the rain comes. It is a cloudburst. She is wet—sitting in a puddle.

Now it is wind and rain—the rain horizontal—the wind coming in all directions. She is losing control of her oars. Gust after gust catches the boat. Deep stroking seems to only make it rotate more and more out of control. She holds on to the gunwales of the boat desperately as she watches the oars drift away.

As the eddy turns into a maelstrom, she loses all perspective. The world is spinning by too fast. Then the bottom drops out from under her. She is dragged down deep into the funnel—water water everywhere.

As the sky above goes missing and the cascading torrent crashes down, she cries out. She screams an incantation that ultimately provides her release. The boat begins to rise—gaining speed as it climbs from the darkness below. It pops through the surface like a cork at the end of a fishing line cast into a tranquil pool in a beautiful grotto.

Svetlana opens her eyes.

"Oh," she says.

Woody's eyes have a dreamy look.

"I lost the oars," she confesses.

"Don't worry," he reassures her. "There's more."

83.
SCANLON

HE DOESN'T CALL THE STATION house to find out when it's going down. He doesn't want to leave any fingerprints—or a footprint—to show that he's been sniffing around. Not that he has to ask. He's been on the job long enough that he could run this one in his sleep. As he walks up West End Avenue, his trained eye catches all the telltale signs of an operation cranking up. He spots the beat-up van that they use as their mobile command center parked down the block. If that isn't conspicuous enough, there's a bunch of uniforms standing around it gossiping. He can even smell the coffee and doughnuts. By the sight of things it's two hours before launch. Out of morbid curiosity he takes a detour to inspect the troops. Scanlon has done enough plainclothes work in his career that he blends in good.

This confidence is borne out when Little Debbie flies around the corner—distracted—sucking on the straw of a Caramel Ribbon Crunch Crème Frappuccino—slamming into him with a chest thump. Little Debbie doesn't pause. He does not apologize. He's texting on his phone. The only reason why he looks up at all is when he is flattered.

"Nice outfit," Scanlon says.

Little Debbie doesn't reply, but he does beam—still no recognition—then he tries to take a selfie with Scanlon, who is way too cagey to get caught in frame.

But he's right. It is an appropriate outfit for this particular sting. Little Debbie is wearing gold lamé hot pants and a *My Little Pony* tank top—bedazzled. If only he didn't have such an ugly man head—yet Scanlon admires anyone who so enthusiastically embraces his work. He can also now appreciate why oldJim prefers Little Debbie to him.

There is no rancor—no sour grapes. There is just a job to do now. He figures he's got thirty minutes to convince oldJim to get into a cold shower with all his clothes on. *Whatever you think—Whatever you think you want—Don't answer the door.*

Scanlon turns his tracks toward 501 West End Avenue. He doesn't debate why he is risking his pension over saving a drifting soul. He just . . . what was that? Out of the corner of his cop's eye he sees nothing—and he knows that it is something.

In the dark your peripheral vision is best. Scanlon knows the drill. You can't tail someone who's invisible—you can't see invisible—but you can see where there is no reflected light. You can see that clearly if you're looking out of the corner of your eye—where you can see what you cannot see best.

Across the street, a shadow obscures in stages a Mister Softee ice cream truck. Scanlon gets a good sideways view. If he were in SoHo, he wouldn't bat an eye. Guys wearing a balaclava and black pajamas are a dime a dozen down in Artsy Fartsy Town . . . but the Upper West Side? The matrons around here have standards.

"Are you kidding me?" he says out loud. "A ninja?"

It wouldn't be his first—well, if Eddie Cottingham is right, maybe it is his first—the same one—what goes around comes around. He can feel his spider sense start to tingle. The dark figure is overly cautious and takes the long way around a line of squad cars. Moving fast, Scanlon is positioned just in time to step out from behind a blue and white—right in his path.

"Remember me?" he says to the startled, masked phantom.

Clearly he does. His eyes register surprise. Scanlon remembers also. Even hidden behind a ski mask, he will never forget these eyes—the eyes of the guy who capped him. They were both focused in tight that night—eye to eye—with the mystical third eye—the barrel of a pistol aimed between Scanlon's . . . Why he lowered the gun and shot him in the nuts is anyone's guess.

The reunion is short-lived. When the sergeant pulls his Smith & Wesson service pistol, the ninja does a backflip worthy of Jackie Chan in the good old days—Hong Kong Kung Fu—and they're off to the races.

He hasn't run like this for over a year. First of all, his doctors wouldn't allow it—then it was all desk duty—not a lot of running in front of a computer. But now Scanlon is not only hotfooting it—he is in pursuit and he feels great. His wounds are barely pinching, and, if anything, the bullets that remain inside of him feel more like *ben wa* balls than anything else—rolling with the flow. It doesn't get any better than this—and if he can take down his personal shooter? Just thinking about it gives Scanlon his own version of a boner—diminutive but legit.

The ninja is now running along Riverside Drive. Scanlon is not only keeping pace, his endorphins have kicked in with such a vengeance that he is convinced that he can run all night—running along with the guy who shot him.

After all, it wasn't so terribly bad. Sure, it hurt—but not for long. They gave him wicked cool drugs in the hospital—and what a doggie bag. He floated for weeks at home on the couch in front of the TV. Up until this point, Scanlon had led a sheltered life. Before he was shot, he didn't know about daytime TV and the dramas that that entailed—*would Sheila ever tell Stuart the truth about Scott and Angela?*—throughout his convalescence, Scanlon cared deeply about these things.

Getting shot in the nuts also made things easier at work. NYPD is very generous when you're shot in the nuts. He didn't have to take the Sergeant's Exam when they promoted him to sergeant—sweet.

Of course, getting shot in the nuts took a terrible toll on his marriage. On the other hand, since he got shot in the nuts he's got this kind of connubial *Get Out of Jail Free* card. No longer does he have to spend all that time and effort to disappoint his wife. He is officially damaged, and that seems to work out just fine for the two of them—soon to be a series of Hallmark greeting cards.

The ninja darts down through a basement door. Scanlon follows with stealth. The ninja might be invisible. But the sergeant was shot in the nuts. His shadow doesn't have a shadow.

84.
MACKENZIE

SO SHE'S NOT A BILLIONAIRE TODAY—in her own right, that is. The market value of her share of the take is hovering around $937 million and still going down. She is hoping that at least the elevator is working. The ups and downs of Wall Street are bad enough. Having to take the stairs is adding insult to injury. It's almost enough to make her move back in with her husband—almost. Speaking of the devil—her phone groans. That's Ivan's ringtone. She taps *Ignore*. The only good news is that the guy heading up the SEC investigation of her IPO is a guy she dated at Wharton. He got really drunk one night, and she knows he doesn't remember a thing that happened. *Uninvited touching is such an ugly word, Commissioner—I prefer blackmail.*

As she enters the lobby, she heaves a sigh of relief. It looks like the elevator is running. Vix and her newly minted boyfriend are waiting for it, along with that maid, who is carrying two shopping bags. Mackenzie is so happy for her old pal. Victoria has found her soul mate. Mackenzie would like a soul mate, but it's too late for her—she's married. Her phone groans. She taps *Ignore*.

"Hi, guys," she says. "Is it running?"

"We think so," they answer in unison without realizing it.

They are so cute. They are even dressed in matching outfits—lime green bow blouses—the bows are huge—with big puffy sleeves—along with charcoal gray pencil skirts, stockings, and nosebleed five-inch pumps. They could be twins—at least sisters—only Tim's big Texas hair implies a *separated at birth* event.

"Looking good," Mackenzie dishes.

"Feeling good," Victoria replies. "We signed up five hundred new members in today's live feed."

"New curves?" Mackenzie asks Tim, patting his derrière. "You used to have such a bony ass."

"Padded panty girdle," Tim explains as fact. No blushing.

Victoria slaps her hand.

"His bony ass is mine," she insists.

"Pardon me for living," Mackenzie sniffs and turns away.

Then she is grabbed roughly from behind.

"I think someone is overreacting," she complains.

Then she feels the knife against her throat.

Then she sees the guy holding a badge and pointing a gun in her general direction.

"NYPD. Drop the knife. Let go of the woman," he demands.

Then she is leaning back on her heels being dragged into the elevator. The knife is so sharp that there is no pain as it nicks her, but she does feel the trickle of hot blood on her throat.

Damn, she thinks. This is her favorite scarf, and it's not like she's a billionaire anymore.

She is surprised at how calm she is. She only hopes that the guy with the knife is thinking logically about things and realizes that if anything happens to her, he's got nothing—zip.

When her unseen captor's knife hand starts to tremble, she tries to calm him. "Chill, dude."

In his firm grip time stands still. She looks out of the elevator with an ambiguous look on her face—it might be desperate. Tim and Victoria hold hands and watch with horrified expressions.

The police guy waves his gun all over the place with nowhere to shoot. Fortunately, it seems to Mackenzie that he doesn't want to pop the hostage.

"Penthouse," her abductor directs.

That request makes sense to Mackenzie. His hands are full. She pushes the PH button and the doors close.

Being alone in a New York City elevator with one other person is always awkward. Small talk is forced—if it exists at all. In this case it seems anything but—more like nerve-racking or harrowing—the trip to the penthouse takes forever.

When the doors finally open, Mackenzie is shocked to see two grown-ups making out like teenagers.

"Get a room," she says.

When that breaks them out of their clinch, she is surprised to recognize the couple. The guy's not looking too much the worse for wear—nothing takes the edge off a man's appearance more than smeared lipstick on his neck.

"Nice hickey, Woody," Mackenzie says as she is dragged farther into the foyer.

Woody does not reply in kind. He has eyes only for the knife at her throat. Without blinking he pushes Svetlana away.

"Go to your grandfather," he says.

When she protests, he bellows, "Now."

Once the girl is inside the apartment—just barely and clearly visible peeking around the open door—Woody starts to test the waters. When he feints a move toward the rifle leaning against the wall behind the welding torch, the ninja puts down another line in the sand—a bright red one across Mackenzie's neck.

"Oh my God," she moans—finally taking the exercise seriously.

Woody is getting pissed off.

"So you want to dance," he snarls.

He moves in closer—circling—a *pas de deux* to die for.

Although his eyes betray a capability, Woody admits, "I have never killed a man before."

Unfortunately, he has also never been to paramilitary training camp in Chechnya or played enough chess. In this dance routine, the ninja has been leading all along. When their clumsy box step brings him close to the open door, he shoves Mackenzie against Woody with sufficient force to knock them both down to the floor. The Russian beauty is surprised and shocked by the immediacy of such physical violence and she is frozen in place. The man in the mask grabs a fistful of Svetlana's hair and drags her inside—slamming the door and throwing all seven dead bolts, including the Fox Police Lock.

"Dammit," Woody curses as he kicks the steel door in frustrated rage.

85.
VICTORIA

SHE IS SHOCKED TO WATCH her friend dragged away like that. The policeman is shouting into his radio as he runs to the stairs. Tim is rather cool and collected. He pushes the elevator call button.

"Not in these shoes," he says.

"What can we do?" Victoria asks, her voice shaking.

"Keep our wits about us," Tim cautions in a reassuring voice—Mother knows best. "There are three of us and only one of him."

He gestures to Fifi, and she hands him a shopping bag. He unwraps one of today's purchases. Removing a large strap-on from its harness—it matches the color of his blouse—he slaps it hard against an open palm like a blackjack bludgeon. The blow echoes with great menace throughout the lobby.

"And we're armed," he adds.

Victoria is impressed. Tim is growing in stature before her eyes—and it isn't just the heels.

By the time they get on the elevator, they are pumped. Each one of them is gripping a weapons-grade dildo like a truncheon—lime green, turquoise, and houndstooth—ready to rumble. They are quiet on the way up—lost in their own thoughts—watching the floor numbers ascend: 9—10—11—PH—*Ding*. They brace themselves. The doors open . . . they peer out into the foyer . . .

The air explodes with a percussive crash as Woody rails against the locked door with a sledgehammer. Mackenzie is dialing her phone—fruitlessly.

Victoria runs up to her and hugs her.

"Thank God," she exhales with relief.

Mackenzie shrugs, looking at her phone.

"Must be a dead zone," she explains.

"Look what the brute did to your scarf," her friend commiserates. "But at least you're safe now."

"He dragged Mrs. Ed in there with him," Mackenzie tells her.

All the while, Woody is doggedly attacking Fort Knox. He's making a heck of a racket and going nowhere fast.

Tim extricates the acetylene torch from the pile of work-site detritus and rolls it over to the door. He pushes Woody's sledge away with a pinkie. "Ain't going to happen."

He pulls a welder's helmet over his head. "This will ruin my hair, I know it," he groans, then clicks the striker and lights the cutting torch. As he color-corrects the flame, he explains, "Locks strong—hinges weak."

"Hey," Woody exclaims in surprise. "You're a dude."

Flipping up the hood, Tim looks him in the eye—man-to-man—and replies, "So are you."

"Feeling good about that." Woody grins. "For a change."

"Stand back, bro," Tim warns and touches flame to metal.

Sparks fly.

"Rosie the Riveter, eat your heart out," Victoria brags.

She has a strong case. In her day, Rosie's bandana and blue work shirt might have been the bee's knees—but oh-so low-rent. Wielding a cutting torch in an outfit from Imbroglio London makes Tim look upmarket—and hot—especially with that skirt—and those legs.

"That's my boyfriend," she gushes.

"So you've said," Mackenzie replies patiently.

The door groans. Tim turns off the torch.

"Feefs," he calls out. "Two flat bars."

She responds quickly, retrieving the tools from the bone pile then scampering over to the door where she presents them with a modest curtsy.

"Hey," Woody says after he zooms in for the close-up. "That's a—"

"Damn good maid—best in New York City," Tim interjects as he hands him one of the priers. "On three."

The manly men throw their backs into it and pop the door out of its frame—seemingly without effort.

"Fudge," Tim curses. "I chipped a nail."

Woody takes charge.

"Follow me," he commands—once more unto the breach—by way of the kitchen pantry.

Mackenzie amazes herself by not only walking the walk—she grabs a Kalashnikov as she passes by the stack—checks the clip—slides it home. She moves forward with a steely look. But why is this a surprise? Victoria knows how much she really loved that scarf.

"Where are we going?" she asks, grabbing the first weapon she can lay her hands on—an iron skillet.

Tim passes on anything else. He's fine with the flat bar.

"Go toward the din," he replies

The din is easy—the going not so much. The floor is covered with all sorts of pointy pokey things, including broken glass. They're not about to kick off their impossibly high heels. They storm into the next room like two ladies-who-lunch faux-running to catch a cab. They manage to get through the large storeroom without breaking an ankle. The wall on the far side is wide open—a massive fire door hanging from wheels rolled up an incline.

"That explains it," Tim comments to himself.

86.
TIM

IT IS SURROUNDED BY A CAGE that takes up most of the room. It is massive, with spikes. It looks like it is made of iron—like something that Jules Verne cooked up for Captain Nemo. But Tim thinks that it must have a lead covering to confound the Geiger counters. However you cut it, the thing is awesome—a beast—and the Beast must be very demanding when it comes to its care and feeding. There are hundreds of cables and dozens of hoses connected to it—and to the tanks mounted along the wall—air compressors, Tim figures. There is a bank of dials with dancing needles. Dozens of belts are humming overhead, delivering mechanical energy to pumps and whatever other machines are powered to feed the Beast. The belts also create a high level of static electricity. The room feels turbocharged. Everyone's scalp is prickling.

In the cage, the ninja is throwing switches and pulling levers with one hand while aiming an Uzi submachine gun with the other. The focus of his attention is on the old man, who has jammed his wheelchair so that the door to the cage cannot be closed and locked.

They are shouting at each other in some language that Tim doesn't recognize. It sounds like they're making it up as they go along—maybe something Slavic-based with a lot of diacritical marks and spitting. Tim is always embarrassed that he can't speak a foreign language. Sure, he can say *bonjour* and *adios*. But if you held a gun to his head he would not be able to say good morning in Chechen, Azerbaijani, or Uzbek.

Svetlana is trying to extricate her grandfather and roll him out. The colonel is not cooperating. He's throwing everything he has into wheeling himself up against the interloper. Woody and Mackenzie are covering Svetlana, aiming their rifles at the ninja, waiting for that moment when he lowers his guard.

Tim is struggling with the logic of this approach. In most hostage situations, you don't want to do anything precipitous to endanger the hostage. In this case, however, he feels that they are being overly concerned, protecting a cranky old son of a bitch while the other guy primes, arms, and prepares to detonate a homemade—Tim estimates uranium 235—atomic bomb.

Therefore, it is understandable that Tim is not concerned that he comes off as callous or cold when he shouts out, "Just shoot him."

Woody and Mackenzie turn to him with questioning looks.

"Shoot him," Tim repeats. "Dead."

Woody and Mackenzie aim their weapons back at the ninja, who is so busy trying to blow up the Upper West Side that he seems hard to distract. But this simple act of self-preservation is clearly out of their comfort zone.

Victoria gets it.

"Shoot him," she calls out.

The old man gets it. He stops fighting his chair.

"Give me a goddamn rifle," he commands.

But the Mexican standoff continues.

"NYPD," Scanlon wheezes as he staggers breathless into the room.

His service automatic is drawn and he is moving it in a sweeping arc all over the place, just like they do in the procedurals on TV.

Woody and Mackenzie reflexively turn to face him with their firearms.

"Drop your weapons," Scanlon demands.

Woody ignores him and returns his attention to the ninja.

Despite the fact that Mackenzie is a successful entrepreneur, she is still a girl with a dominant compliance gene—so she readily obeys. Safety first. She aims the Kalashnikov away from the police sergeant when she drops it, which is why, when the weapon accidentally discharges as it hits the floor, Scanlon is not shot in the nuts—but instead after three ricochets—including one off the Beast—he catches one in the left buttock. How embarrassing.

"Oh my God." Mackenzie cringes. "Sorry."

This is exactly the diversion that the ninja terrorist has been waiting for. He blows through his checklist—all his ducks are in a row—the red button is blinking on and off—bells are ringing—a Klaxon is going *A-OOGAH A-OOGAH.*

He slams down the detonator, then hops around with his arms over his head like he just scored a goal—World's Cup.

"What happened to Allah?" Tim asks Victoria, who shrugs her shoulders.

She looks really scared.

The old man shouts something unintelligible but very loud. Tim has a gut feeling that it is Russian for *Fire in the hole.*

The decibel level amps up. The last thing Tim can hear is Victoria demanding, "Kiss me, you fool."

He does, and she hangs on to him for dear life.

"It's too bad," she says. "I think I love you."

The belts are screaming overhead. All the dials are redlining. The pneumatic hoses are under so much pressure that they are keening. The Beast begins to vibrate. The whole building starts to shake, rattle, and roll.

Just as the Beast seems like it will rip loose from its mounts, all the pneumatics engage at the same time. Tim knows exactly what that has to be—a dozen highly enriched uranium pellets have been shot into the core, which will force a chain reaction.

Only the good die young, he thinks, on a positive note.

The Beast shudders mightily.

Then the Beast shrugs.

Click.

The rest is silence.

87.
IVAN

IF YOU ASKED HIM, he would not be able to tell you the last time he had been in a flower shop. Although he could assure you that he had never lingered inside one for so long by any stretch. In the past, it wasn't about flowers at all. They were arrangements—$200 for a dead employee, $100 for his wife, $500 for a member on the board. But at the florist today he isn't just looking. Today it is an education—as if he had been blind and now he can see. So many colors and textures and smells—yes—today Ivan Greenbriar is finally stopping and smelling the roses.

Along with his newly heightened senses, Ivan discovers *Ikebana*. For over two hours, he and Mr. Yamatoma design one exquisite floral creation after another—enough to guarantee his lovely wife a daily dose of beautiful perfection for over a month. It would be cheaper for him to buy the shop—*lock, stock, and orchids*—and freesia?

"Where have you been all my life?" Ivan whispers to the first sublime stem he ever truly lays eyes on . . . *as if wandering through the gray pall of a planet without freesia could be called living*. Being alive seems to be the theme of the day.

There have been so many recent life-affirming moments that he can't track all of them. But his first encounter with this delicate blossom will never be forgotten. He makes up a special bouquet of them to take to her today to thank her for being . . . her. He can't say that often enough. Ivan is in love with his wife, and it has changed—no—jump-started—his life, as if you could call what went on before *living*. What is wealth but a little number followed by a lot of zeros? Mackenzie is everything to him.

Suddenly Ivan is desperate to gaze upon his bride with loving eyes. He gathers up the swag—the box of chocolates, the adorable light-blue, stuffed bunny rabbit with the goo-goo eyes and long lashes, as well as the fistful of freesia. He starts up West End Avenue on foot—as if his feet are touching the ground. If it were raining he'd be singing and dancing in the rain. But the sun is out, so his enthusiasm translates into a light skip—or maybe not too light—maybe more like an age-denying, gender-inappropriate young schoolgirl skipping.

At least that's how it might appear to a disinterested third party—someone as blasé as—say—a New York City police officer.

"Nice day for it, sir," he says to Ivan.

"Nice day for what?" Ivan asks.

"Nice day for whatever you're doing," the officer replies. "What *are* you doing, sir?"

"I'm walking on air," Ivan answers.

"You do seem a little light in the loafers," the policeman notes.

"I've got a date with an angel," Ivan gushes.

"Nice bunny," the policeman says.

"His name is Evelyn," Ivan explains before the giggles overtake him.

"Nice to meet you, Evelyn," the cop greets the bunny with a shallow bow.

"EE-velyn," Ivan corrects him. "Evelyn, with a long *E*. Not Eh-velyn. He's English, and he's a he." Unfortunately this explanation is followed up with another bout of giggles.

"Might I see some ID, sir?" the officer requests.

Ivan's eyes open wide as if he is waking from a dream. This is the moment when he realizes that he is not being confronted by a lone policeman—but by a squad of them. There must be a dozen uniforms surrounding him—watching with accusatory expressions—and close by there is what looks to be a hooker. He assumes they have arrested her—but he's wrong.

"It's him," the creature in the gold lamé hot pants shrieks, hopping up and down and clapping his hands. "It's him."

"ID, sir," the intervening officer repeats.

Ivan finally realizes that things might be more serious than he first imagined, so he falls back on the old—ever popular—tried-and-true formula—the perennial crowd pleaser: "Are you fucking kidding me?" he snarls. "Do you know who I am?"

"I do," Little Debbie replies. He walks up to Ivan—close to him—squeezing his knees together and biting on a knuckle, he stands up on tippy-toes in his ballet slippers and goes eye to eye.

"Hello, old Jim," he says. "Glad to finally make your acquaintance."

"What the fuck are you talking about?" Ivan flails. "What is *that*—that freak—talking about?" He looks around at the policemen, pointing to his accuser.

Little Debbie is clearly insulted by his flamboyant misuse of a pronoun. He pulls the full-frontal dick pic—with face reveal—out of his short shorts and flashes it in front of Ivan.

"Perhaps this will refresh your memory, old Jim," he says.

"Eew. Gross," Ivan yelps. "Are you saying that's me? That's not me."

"Says you," Little Debbie rebuts, then commands. "Cuff him, boys."

And they do. Not because of anything Little Debbie says or for any probable cause. It's just that in the culture of the day, NYPD handcuffs on principle any asshole who says, *Do you know who I am?*

Little Debbie breaks into his victory dance, strutting around like a mini-Mussolini. But he is soon to be disappointed. All the radios suddenly go crazy—crackling and popping and squawking out reports of a dire situation at 501 West End Avenue.

"Sorry, Debs," one of the cops shouts as they start to run to the scene en masse. "Got some real police work to do."

"This is real," Little Debbie sniffs, stamping his feet petulantly.

"That's my wife's building," Ivan says, the desperation clear in his voice. "Unlock my hands."

Little Debbie rolls his eyes.

"You have a *wife*, Perv?" he asks, making air quotes with his fingers.

Ivan doesn't think. He just smashes his head against the little sissy's skull as hard as he can. It hurts a lot, but it is remarkably satisfying—especially when Little Debbie collapses into a steaming pile of dog shit on the sidewalk.

"Glad I didn't step in that," Ivan says as he runs faster than he has ever run in his life, and with his hands locked behind his back, it's not easy.

But his feet have wings—compliments of Eros—he is in love. The lack of doughnuts doesn't hurt. He quickly catches up to the uniforms and can overhear their conversation.

"Scanlon called it in."

"Scanlon's a cop again?"

"Seems like."

"Got shot again too."

"No way."

"That's a gold shield for sure."

"If he can get himself shot two more times, he'll make commissioner."

88.
THE BEAST ET AL.

THE ERSTWHILE WANNABE terrorist is in custody. The not-so-little French girl who tackled him is keeping an eye on him—like he's going anywhere. Scanlon is so pissed at the guy who had shot him in the nuts that he cuffs his right wrist to his left ankle.

He loves the determined look on her face as she aims the perp's own Uzi right between his eyes. The sergeant gently guides her hand down so that the machine gun is pointed between the ninja's legs.

"That's better," Scanlon says. "Give him something to think about."

The French girl is really cute. Maybe he'll have to take her in for questioning. Why the hell not? He's feeling better about everything these days.

Svetlana is frustrated. She rattles the door to the cage. It won't budge.

"Dedushka," she demands. "Open up. Let me in."

"Just a few more minutes," the old man replies. "It works. I know it will work."

He has opened up a panel in the side of the bomb and he is

soldering something. A cloud of burning flux surrounds his head as it disappears into the Beast.

"Stop it right now," Svetlana pleads. "Don't be crazy."

"Crazy like Sakharov," the old man cackles gleefully.

He screws the panel closed and hits the button.

As if waking from a nap, the Beast picks up where it left off. The belts start screaming—the dials spinning—the pneumatic hoses groan. The Beast begins to toss from side to side.

Then a cough and a wheeze.

Click.

Grandfather rolls his chair over to the other side of the bomb.

"I can fix this," he insists. "I know I can. I will."

Woody watches with a bemused smile. The old man is just like his granddaughter; the over-the-top earnestness; the pride in an outrageous idea doomed to failure. He likes this girl. In the past, he'd never had the time to engage in such entanglements. But today is different. Woody guesses he will not have to go to work tomorrow, or the next day, or the one after that. He can feel Mary Margaret seething from blocks away. He only wishes he was there to see how she steals the company out from under Ivan's nose. Speaking of whom, look what the cat dragged in.

Woody chuckles as he watches his arch nemesis lurch forward trailing a mob of NYPD. *Just step away from the bomb.*

Victoria just cannot keep her eyes off her boyfriend—Boyfriend? That word alone is a shocker—unimaginable just a week ago—but here he is—and so good-looking. She can't believe how well he handles himself. Such poise. Such stature—barely a stumble, and in those heels.

Of course, they must go shopping soon. They can't rely on her dead mum's wardrobe forever. But that will be a challenge in itself, won't it? Her boyfriend is a clotheshorse. He looks good in any rag you drape over his shoulders. That seems a little unfair. Tim will always be the prettier sister—and she the Plain Jane. No surprise there. Dare she even hope for . . . *trouble and strife?*

For Ivan, things are not going as planned. This was supposed to be the best night of their relationship . . . until tomorrow evening, which would be even better . . . until the day after that. Now he can't even take her in his arms. He can't even tie his shoes.

All Ivan wants is to make her happy—to be there for her. He wants to be the best husband ever. He tries to reach out—he can't. His hands are locked together.

He can feel his eyes well up. But he is unclear as to the cause. Is he crying in frustration because he cannot reach out and touch his beloved's cheek? Or are they tears of joy because he is once again in her presence? The only thing he is certain about is that whenever he is bawling he feels wonderful.

As Mackenzie looks at her husband—manacled and weeping—she realizes that the case could be made that she is a castrating bitch. That gives her pause. She takes a moment to think it over. But after looking at it six ways from Sunday, all she can come up with is a question: *Being a castrating bitch is bad because . . . ?*

She does a 360-degree scan, the room is packed with men: police; the old guy in the wheelchair trying to kill a lot of people to prove that he hasn't wasted the last fifty years of his life; the billionaire dickless wonder—yes, it's all over ColdTrail.com; the cop who at this moment is trying to dig a bullet out of his ass with his fingernails; the nerd in the 1950s girlie retro outfit; and then there's Ivan. Mackenzie realizes that it could be a lot worse—and she's done all the heavy lifting already.

She guides her husband by the shoulder.

"Let's go home," she says.

"Really, darling?" Ivan replies. His delight and relief are palpable.

"Really," Mackenzie confirms. "You're going to buy me out right now—in cash."

Ivan is crestfallen.

"The company," she clarifies.

"I can do that," he says, beaming in relief.

"Yes, you will," she agrees.

I've got to remember to push his head down when I put him in the back of the Jaguar, she reminds herself.

Meanwhile, Tim doesn't like what he hears. The old man has tried to set it off again, and this time it sounds different. There is a new timbre—a deeper basso to the Beast. The compressors sound more efficient. There are no more spits and rattles or clanks—just the sound of one smooth-running, well-oiled machine. Time to panic.

Tim knows that it's a waste of time to try to get into the cage, a dozen policemen can't. So he looks around to see what's coming out of the cage. He has to hurry. The pneumatics are ratcheting up. He figures he's got seconds before they fire, and then nanoseconds to critical mass.

There it is—he almost missed it—but it is exactly what he is looking for and up to spec for the rest of the Beast. He kicks off his heels and gets down on his hands and knees—to hell with his stockings—and follows the ancient extension cord to its source.

It's a classic old man installation. On the far side of the room there is one outlet with over eighteen cords plugged into a series of adapters—all under a rug to keep it safe.

Just as the Beast is reaching a fever pitch, Tim yanks at the tangle and it powers down—to sleep—perhaps to dream.

"Good night, sweet prince."

89.
THE PISSING MATCH

IT IS A BEAUTIFUL DAY for a boat race: deep blue sky, deep black water, blinding-white puffy fair weather clouds. The wind is blowing from the east-northeast. The committee boat is south of the Romer Shoal Lighthouse, just off Sandy Hook. The course is not optimal. There are bottlenecks and some dodgy shoals. But these catamarans draw only inches of water, and positioning the race so close to Staten Island, Brooklyn, and Sandy Hook will successfully turn the America's Cup into a spectators' sport—much to the chagrin of the New York Yacht Club—*Getch yer hot dogs heeyeh.*

Money to Float IV, Ivan's newest, largest, and ugliest bathtub toy, is anchored just past the committee boat, with a perfect view of the starting line. Mackenzie is sitting in a deck chair on the fantail, drinking a cup of coffee and reading the *Wall Street Journal.* The air above her head is buzzing with helicopters, like bugs on a hot summer day, and the water below is filled gunwale to gunwale with pleasure craft—mostly runabouts and Boston Whalers and skiffs and some gorgeous, antique Chris-Crafts—a mess of deaconly Grady Whites—and countless inflatables zooming this way and that—like bumper cars that think they are water taxis. There are a few sailboats present—but not many. Piloting a sailboat through this traffic is like bringing a knife to a gunfight.

"Ahoy, the ship."

Mackenzie goes to the starboard rail and looks down, waving to Woody, who is darting around the chop in a small racing dinghy.

"Lovely day for it," he announces.

"Spectacular," she agrees.

To stay alongside, Woody is sailing tight figure eights, guiding his boat with the grace and confidence of a gold medalist leading his partner in ice dancing.

"Are you ready to leave that lethally boring stick of a man who you married in a moment of madness and run off with me?" he asks.

"Not today." She smiles. "I have to wash my hair."

She's allowed to flirt. Having survived the end of the world together, they have the casual intimacy of old friends.

"A little birdie told me that you don't have an empire anymore," she points out coyly.

"Don't need one. I've got moves," he brags. "But how are you holding up, Mackenzie? Really."

"I'm fine," she replies, touching the scab on her neck reflexively. "And you? How are they hanging?"

"Like melons, missus," Woody replies. "Like melons."

He has to tack away as the flotilla gets thick around the yacht. The race is about to start. Mackenzie watches him sail away. What he is sailing looks a lot more fun than what Ivan is racing. Of course, her husband could take the pleasure out of that too. She goes back to her paper.

"Hey, Mrs. Greenbriar, can Ivan come out and play?"

Woody has returned.

"We're here to win," Ivan sniffs as he comes on deck through the saloon doors. "Not play."

He still has enough testosterone left to feel competitive. He watches with a critical eye as his boat sails by. The crew maneuvers with precision—each one is a cog in a well-balanced machine—sharply kitted out in black and red uniforms—helmets, and body armor. They salute as the powerful catamaran speeds by.

Ivan has only contempt for the other boat—a feeling that appears to be mutual. Woody's former crew also salutes—but in a different manner and with greater fervor as they pass by, going in the opposite direction. They are a ragtag bunch of sailors. The only uniformity in their appearance is slovenliness. Those that are wearing any top at all favor either Hawaiian shirts or tees touting heavy metal bands. Some are barefoot. Some are wearing flip-flops. One is wearing a sombrero. When they recognize Woody in his tiny dinghy, dwarfed by all the larger vessels around him, they cheer, whistle, hoot, and holler—thumbs-up.

"You must be very proud," Ivan sneers.

"See you at the wake," Woody signs off as he comes about into the wind.

Helm's alee.

"This race is over the minute it starts," Ivan informs his wife.

Moments later it seems that events will bear him out. At the two-minute warning, Ivan's boat enters the starting box on a port tack—as it should for greatest advantage. The opposition is—can you believe it—sailing upwind, away from the starting box.

"Are they simply incompetent, or that drunk?" he asks dismissively.

"Or that angry?" Mackenzie wonders, flipping through *Vogue China*. Wall $treet was boring her.

"We'll be halfway through the first leg before they even start," Ivan estimates. He's looking through binoculars now. "They're coming around. One of them must have sobered up a little."

With seconds to go before the start, Mackenzie segues to *Cosmo*.

"Hey!" He jumps to his feet. "Hey—hey—hey."

Woody's boat is not returning to the starting box with its tail between its legs to make a proper start of it like it should be doing. Instead, it is sailing directly toward Ivan's boat in a fifty million dollar game of chicken.

Ivan's boat has the right-of-way. The crew is shouting, "Starboard tack, starboard tack," like schoolchildren at sailing camp.

"What a bunch of pussies."

Ivan looks over the side. Woody is still there—sailing in circles. He smiles and waves.

His skipper bears off long before any foul, but Ivan's skipper panics and jibes away from the starting line—it's not pretty. The boat veers sharply. The port hull is driven deep into the water. Through his binoculars, it looks like one or two crewmembers are swept over the side. Fortunately, due to the quality of the boat and their professionalism, things are quickly put back to right.

On the downside, since they are all upwind, when Woody's pirates burst into song, Ivan can hear every word of their rude sea chantey.

Alas poor Joe—wouldn't you know
His fair wife's ardor is afading.
Joe knew the joker—his own stockbroker
He caught him inside her—trading.

Ivan is steamed and frustrated as he watches his boat try to get back into the starting box. But the vessel now flying the Jolly Roger has the weather gauge and it can go wherever it wants to. Within minutes—and there is no polite way to put this—Woody's boat is chasing Ivan's boat out of the starting box entirely—going the wrong way. As they pass by Ivan in review, the blackguards form a kick line to serenade their mortal enemy.

The cabin boy—the cabin boy,
He was sure a gross one.
He filled his ass with mustard gas
And condimented the bosun.

"Bravo." Mackenzie applauds, until she feels the frost from her husband's icy stare. "Sorry, darling."

"Don't take it personally," Woody calls up from over the side. "Well, maybe you should."

Ivan looks down at him. He is hanging onto a fender, letting his sails luff.

"But why?" Ivan asks sincerely. "They can't win."

"And you can't either," Woody replies. "Except on a weenie technicality—and that would make you the weenie."

As one boat chases the other toward Raritan Bay, they are almost out of earshot. But the pirates are still in full voice.

So with a hey hey ho ho
It's o'er the briny we go,
But watch your step when you're down below
The deck is covered with seamen.

Looking up at the confusion and hurt on the weenie's face, Woody feels almost sorry for him.

"Let me buy you a drink," he says.

Ivan snorts and turns away.

90.
MARY MARGARET

JUST TWO DAYS AFTER THE Supreme Court opened up the Virgin Valley Wildlife Nature Preserve in Oregon to commercial logging, she is standing on the side of a mountain dressed for success: tall rubber boots, rain gear, hard hat, goggles, and industrial earmuffs.

Big Red walks her to the prepared sequoia. It is a massive, stately creature, just about cut through. There's a small Day-Glo-orange circle spray-painted where the tree is barely holding it all together. He fires up a mini-chainsaw that the boys refer to as *Lumberjack Barbie* and passes it to Mary Margaret.

She guns it two or three times—it sounds like an angry june bug—then touches it to the demarcated spot. Within seconds, thousands of years of history come crashing down safely onto the forest floor.

Her board of directors, which is on hand to witness this renewed tradition, applauds enthusiastically.

She hands the chainsaw back to Big Red.

"Down for the count," she declares.

91.
BOYS

SCANLON AND WOODY ARE SITTING at the bar in a waterfront dive, each with a beer and a bump.

"I still miss him."

"Me too."

"We used to go everywhere together."

"We were joined at the hip."

"It was like he was doing the thinking for the both of us."

"But he never took responsibility for his actions."

"Son of a bitch rat bastard."

"The morning after the night before he always put his head up, looking all innocent, like he's only there to take a piss."

"So sneaky."

"But you better pee in a hurry, or he's sending out the wrong signals all over again."

"But it was never his fault."

"Says him."

"But a day doesn't go by . . ."

"I know."

The two men click their shot glasses.

They toast, "Absent friends."

They drink. The bartender refills them without asking.

They take their shots. They chug their beer. They belch like men. They sigh. They notice the shadow of a huge presence looking down at them. They look up.

Ivan roughly throws his arms around the two of them.

"I love you guys," he blubbers as he embraces them in a manly group hug. "And you like me too? Right?"

The Three Musketeers study themselves in the mirror behind the bar for a moment.

"Not really," Woody finally replies.

Made in the USA
Columbia, SC
22 October 2017